GOODHOUSE

GOODHOUSE

PEYTON MARSHALL

FARRAR, STRAUS AND GIROUX   NEW YORK

Farrar, Straus and Giroux
18 West 18th Street, New York 10011

Printed in the United States of America
First edition, 2014

Library of Congress Cataloging-in-Publication Data
Marshall, Peyton, 1972–
     Goodhouse / Peyton Marshall. — First edition.
        pages   cm
     ISBN 978-0-374-16562-8 (hardback) — ISBN 978-0-374-71015-6 (e-book)
     1. Boys—Fiction. 2. Eugenics—Fiction. I. Title.

  PS3613.A7756 G66 2014
  813'.6—dc23
                                                              2014008671

Designed by Jonathan D. Lippincott

Farrar, Straus and Giroux books may be purchased for educational, business,
or promotional use. For information on bulk purchases, please contact the
Macmillan Corporate and Premium Sales Department at 1-800-221-7945,
extension 5442, or write to specialmarkets@macmillan.com.

www.fsgbooks.com
www.twitter.com/fsgbooks • www.facebook.com/fsgbooks

10 9 8 7 6 5 4 3 2 1

FOR MY PARENTS

The master's tools will never dismantle the master's house.

—*Audre Lorde*

CONTENTS

THE MASTER'S HOUSE

ONE

The day I committed my first crime I was dressed in civilian clothes—a wool suit and a wide, brightly patterned necktie. Many boys before me had worn these clothes. Goodhouse kept hundreds of donated items at the ready so that its students might feel comfortable going into the world without their uniforms. They wanted us to feel like everybody else, but I'd never seen civilian boys in suits. I flexed against the fabric of my coat. It was too small.

"I'm losing feeling in my hands," I whispered.

"Stand still," said Owen. He was my roommate, a stocky kid with black hair and a birthmark on his right cheek that looked like a cluster of freckles. He'd been out on a number of these and I considered him the expert, though today we would be separated. He was headed somewhere alone. He said it was an interview. "Nothing bad will happen as long as you act right," he said. "Do what you're told and don't make eye contact."

We were in the gymnasium waiting for permission to board buses and spend an afternoon with a host family in town. In principle, these Community Days were meant to prepare us for our eventual integration into society. I was seventeen and I'd never been inside a civilian home—I'd never eaten in a restaurant, never owned anything that didn't first belong to the school. But soon I would graduate. In a year I'd pick one of the professions available to me and I would step into a wider world. I had to be ready.

"I feel like I'm going to be sick," I said. "You think I could stay behind if I puked?"

"I'd report you," Owen said.

I unbuttoned my wool jacket. We all stood at attention, shoulder to shoulder. It was unusually warm for May and the room smelled strongly of sweat and moth repellant. The polished floor was full of colored lines for different games that I'd never played and couldn't name. Originally the gymnasium was part of a series of buildings that made up the Preston School of Industry. It had been founded in Ione, California, in 1894— just under two hundred years ago—and it had been a reformatory for regular boys. The gym was a beautiful remnant. Tall wooden windows lined its longest walls. They were rounded at the top, their uppermost panes of glass splayed like fans.

Over our heads the footsteps of proctors rang on the metal balconies. The proctors left dark silhouettes against the windows as they passed. Only our class leaders actually stood on the floor with us, circulating among us, keeping order. Unlike the proctors, who were forbidden to touch us, class leaders were free to use their fists.

"Just keep your mouth shut," Owen said, "and look really grateful, no matter what they say. And don't touch anything," he said. "They hate that, and it's hard to do when they have candy dishes and little glass elephants, and once, this kid had a plastic box full of ants that he said he was farming."

I stared at Owen. "Farming?" I asked. "For food?"

"Who knows." He shrugged. "It's always a freak show, and they write detailed reports about you afterward, and staff pays a lot of attention to them."

I felt a jolt of nervous energy. I still had nightmares about what had happened at my last school. I took thirty milligrams of monofacine every evening. It was supposed to help me sleep, help me forget.

"And don't talk to the women," Owen said. "Nobody likes that."

"I wasn't going to," I said. I pulled off my jacket and plucked at my shirt, trying to circulate some air. Years ago, a Goodhouse boy named Ephram had attacked a civilian girl on a Community Day. He'd been strangled to death by her father. Even I—a recent transfer to Ione—knew the story. "I'm not going to end up like that Ephram kid," I said.

"Then don't look all sweaty and bug-eyed," Owen said.

More boys were pulling off their jackets. One student a few yards from where we stood actually fainted in the heat. Some boys cheered and one called him a pussy. Proctors shouted at us to stand still.

"You want to know the real reason they strangled that Ephram kid?" Owen whispered, but I could tell his tone was playful.

"Never mind," I said. "Forget it."

"Because he touched their ant farm," he said.

"Shut up," I said, and Owen punched my arm to warn me that our class leaders were passing. We both went silent and still.

Class leaders had special uniforms. They wore the same denim pants we did, but their blue button-down shirts were a darker hue and the school crest on the front pocket was embroidered in gold. Headmaster Tanner called these boys his right hand—the hand of correction. At my last school they had been different, more constrained. Here, it seemed, there were no limits.

We had two leaders for our year. The first was named Creighton. He had ruddy skin, white-blond hair, and white eyebrows like albino caterpillars. He wasn't very tall, but he was thick in the chest. No one had been able to depose him. Our second class leader was Davis, a lanky black kid who always had a sweet expression on his face. Owen had nick-named him Diablo since he was friendly and solicitous, right until he punched you in the gut.

The only way to become a class leader was to beat one of them senseless. But there was always the danger that you would fail and end up like Lowell, who was currently mopping the floor of the gymnasium, running into boys as if he didn't see them. There was a small but important dent in Lowell's fore-head, and he often sang to himself—his voice flat and mean-dering, like he was speaking a different language.

•

I'd been at this school since January, but I'd been in the Good-house system since I was three years old. The first thing they did when you entered the system was change the name you were given at birth. I once believed that I'd recognize my orig-inal name, that I'd know when another boy was called by it—that it would sound some bell inside me, trigger some alarm. The school had called me James after St. James the Greater, an apostle who'd found God around the time he was run through with a sword. They'd said it was a name to grow into.

Goodhouse had come out of an idea—a program meant to map the genetic profile of prison populations. What the researchers had found was this: The worst inmates, the most impulsive, the most violent, the least empathetic, all shared certain biometric markers. But these were prisoners. They cost the state millions of dollars to warehouse every year. And they'd been children once. They had not always been beyond help. It was too late for adults, but young boys were different. They could be molded, instructed, taught. If intervention oc-curred at an early age, they could be salvaged.

And so, for the past four decades in America, genetic test-ing had been mandatory for the family of anyone who committed a violent felony. More and more people were being tested each year. More and more families were brought to the courthouse for a cheek swab—to be released if they were normal, to be registered if they were outside the age limit, to be immediately surrendered if they were positive and male and under the age of six. That had been me.

I understood that I was part of a lucky percentile—the ones who were given a new life, the ones who could be remade from the inside out. And so I'd grown up reading only Goodhouse-approved books, practicing Goodhouse-approved meditations. I'd watched endless instructional videos showing us the lives we could potentially lead—orderly, right-thinking lives. Imagine busy, happy citizens taking great joy in painting houses, cleaning windows, installing water reclamation systems. "The wrong-thinking boy will seek to take advantage of your better self," the videos told us. "Vigilance is the only defense." Goodhouse encouraged us to think of ourselves as two people in one body. One person was fine and ordinary, while the other was filled with bad impulses. "Always question your motives," the school taught us. "Double-check an impulse. Know which boy you are talking to."

Owen said that Goodhouse treated all its students like budding schizophrenics. And though we joked about it, I was sincerely worried that I'd never experienced this duality. I knew myself to be only one person—and how good or how evil this person was, I didn't really know.

·

Overhead, the speakers crackled and Headmaster Robert Tanner walked out onto one of the balconies. He stopped in front of the safety railing and frowned at us. The microphone in his collar activated and I heard the faint suck of his breath. He wore his customary black suit. His skin was prematurely wrinkled, as if his body were sheathed in crumpled brown paper bags. His entourage stood behind him, his secretary and his personal security guard.

Tanner looked grim. His hair was graying at the temples, and it seemed to have worsened overnight.

"Good morning," he said, his voice booming around us. The proctors stopped pacing. The whispering subsided.

"We find ourselves on the threshold of yet another Community Day," he said. "I don't have to remind you that it is a great honor to represent the school—to act as ambassadors, if you will. Please remember that these families are the building blocks of a society that has nurtured you—fed, clothed, and educated you with its tax dollars. You will greet them with humility and gratitude. They are your champions, and I expect every boy here to make us proud. That said"—he cleared his throat, a growling bark that was worse for the amplification— "some of you will be staying behind."

I felt a surge of hope. As curious as I was about regular people, I didn't want to go to their houses and be their guest. I'd been having nightmares all week and I was seeing things again—just little flashes of red out of the corner of my eye, or else I'd glimpse a friend from my old school standing in a group of boys. Then, when I looked again, he'd be gone. Sometimes I smelled phantom smoke, but the worst was the breath on the back of my neck, like someone was standing only an inch behind me, lingering until I was weak with fear, afraid to move, afraid it was the man I'd seen, the one with white hair, the one who'd taken off his mask. Not a mask. A balaclava. That's what the police had called it. The word had been previously unknown to me, but now it stayed in my head. It conjured images of boys with blazing bodies and always—always—this man with his composed, almost bored expression. He was a civilian. He was one of them.

"I have just received word that a delivery of roofing tiles

will arrive this morning. I know you are all eager to see your Founders' Day pavilion finished." Tanner forced a smile that made his paper-bag face look especially crumpled and sour. "It is," he said, "for every one of us, a matter of pride that this important edifice be completed in a timely manner, and so—I regret very much that some of you must stay behind to unload the truck."

The boys around me looked sullen. No one was excited about Founders' Day next month. Goodhouse would be fifty years old on June 15, and Ione was hosting the celebration. But so far, the event was synonymous with longer days and endless work details.

"South Dormitories," Tanner said, "you will return to your rooms and prepare for service. The rest of you, get on the buses."

The South Dormitory boys, who were among the oldest, exploded into protest as they pulled off their neckties and woolen coats. "Quietly," hissed Tanner. "Quietly! Get in your lines. I will not tolerate antics. You there, stand still." He gestured for several proctors to descend, and they jogged down from the balcony. Their steel-toed boots made the metal stair treads hum.

"I will not have chaos," Tanner shouted. "The rest of you, line up." But we were already in our lines, standing shoulder to shoulder with our roommates, organized by distance to our destination.

"Bus 1," a proctor bellowed. The line to our left shuffled forward. Some boys appeared to be holding hands, but I knew they were *palming*—sending messages through sign language, one hand making shapes into the palm of another. It was extremely complex, all but unlearnable unless mastered young. As a transfer I was considered unlucky. New roommates were randomly assigned on the first of every year. Students were always paired with like-standing students, but that was the only guideline. There were no reassignments, no preferences. I had been an unfortunate choice for Owen. I was unable to palm, so I'd condemned him to a semester of silence. He'd tried to teach me the alphabet, and when that was hopeless, he'd taught me *shorts*—gestures that communicated different phrases and commands. There was a lot of profanity in the shorts. I caught on fast.

Creighton and Davis patrolled our lines. "Hands apart," Creighton said. "Can't have you ladies gossiping." I felt a little surge of hatred, which I struggled to master. Class leaders couldn't give demerits, but they were allowed to do whatever else they wanted; they could break your bones or assign you to an overnight work detail. Every class leader in the Goodhouse system was promised a Level 1 job after graduation. They ate the best food; they lived in private rooms; they could drive patrol vehicles within campus limits. At most schools they were appointed by the administration. At Ione, however, you could appoint yourself. All you had to do was step forward and announce that you wanted your chance.

Creighton and Davis had been my welcome there; they'd taken me into the bathroom and knocked me around. It had been a relatively mild beating, just a taste of what was possible. A proctor had stood watch to issue demerits if I fought back. It took everything I had to submit, not to feel cornered on the lawn at night with the building still on fire.

"What are you looking at?" asked Davis. "Eyes to the front." He slapped me on the back of the head.

"Bus 2," a proctor called. Our line shuffled forward. We walked outside and were directed to a yellow school bus with a magnetic Goodhouse logo affixed to its side—a *G* and an *H* intertwined. Underneath the logo was a small, simple line drawing of a swan. This was the symbol on all our delivery trucks, on all of our boxes of food and many of the products we used, on our toothbrushes and on our soap. For the past ten years, Goodhouse had been owned by Swann Industries, a private company that produced pharmaceuticals and—it seemed to me—everything else.

I hurried onto the bus and sat down, eagerly sliding my hand between the fold in the cushions. These buses were used by the public school system and sometimes we found plastic buttons in the seats, found coins or brightly colored candy wrappers. This time, however, the seat was clean. As a boy in the system, I didn't possess anything, and I craved the experience of ownership. I coveted anything with beauty: a fluffy tuft of wheatgrass, a dead ladybug, an autumn leaf struck red or gold. I'd pick them up and fold them into a shirt cuff or a sock, and this always made me feel powerful.

Sometimes I start my story here. I say, Things turned out the way they did because I was too long in the habit of acquisition. But if I want to be truthful, I'll say that my story begins on a freezing night in January of that year. I lay on the icy lawn watching my dormitory burn. There were boys trapped inside, beating on the safety glass of the windows. Little stars of impact bloomed again and again as a spotlight swept lazily over the façade. Men in red balaclavas wandered the yard, checking to make sure that no one got out.

I have only to close my eyes and I'm back there, shivering on the grass, choking on smoke. The fire moans and hisses like a monster. It's still feeding on the building, on the bodies of my friends, and I can do nothing but cower and hope that when the men find me they will use a gun and not their boots and hands.

I'd assumed that it was the end. I never thought there would be more.

TWO

The bus lumbered down the main road, circling the old athletic field, which was currently being tilled and planted with vegetables. In the distance was the partially finished Founders' Day pavilion, its exposed beams and rounded shape giving it the look of a half-eaten turkey carcass. We passed the Proctors' Quarters—that cluster of gardens and homes where most of the staff lived. Some of the houses were older, brought in from Ione itself and positioned there, made into a neighborhood. Every structure had been painted gray with white trim. Red geraniums hung from window boxes, and from afar they looked like gashes in the siding, blood welling and then freezing in place. In one yard laundry dried on a line—empty shirt arms and trouser legs kicked and waved us on.

Nearer the gate, we passed the wooden kennel where Tanner kept his bluetick hounds. They were just for show now. There were better ways to track an escaped boy, but the hounds were a tradition at the Ione Goodhouse. They were supposed to be mascots of sorts—though we didn't have a sports team or anything we needed to rally against except ourselves. Tanner had cut their vocal cords, and as we drove past, the dogs lunged at the fence, their mouths opening and closing in a pantomime of agitation.

Our bus stopped at the main gate, taking its place in the

line of buses waiting to be cleared. At my old school in La Pine, Oregon, the campus had been rural and isolated, not well protected. But since the attack, Goodhouses nationwide had been increasing and standardizing their security. Now, instead of simply having guardhouses and fences, there were concrete barriers at every entrance, iris and facial scans for all staff members, embedded microchips for every student.

We pulled to the front of the line, and several guards scanned the bus, checking their handhelds to verify the passenger list. One guard stepped forward with a round mirror on the end of a long pole. He dipped it under the bus and walked along each side. A moment later another guard deactivated the electromagnetic barrier and waved us through the gate. Almost immediately, we entered open landscape. The summer droughts hadn't yet begun. There were still green patches and lots of jackrabbits moving away from the road, their splayed ears visible above the grass.

In a year I would graduate, and if I kept my status high, I might qualify for a job, a marriage license, an apartment—I might slip into civilian life, with its private spaces and things, so many things. I was waiting for my real life to start, and a student's status level at graduation controlled all his options and freedoms. I'd heard rumors of graduates who lived off the grid, who lived in the drought country, in the Midwestern towns that had been deserted in the middle of the twenty-first century. But the whole point of graduating was to begin something—not to hide, not to remain on the margins. Sometimes this seemed unfair, as if Goodhouse were a game that ended. But I'd had it explained to me like this—you achieved control or you did not. Without a deadline, students would never truly feel the sum of their choices.

I knew we were close to a town when we started passing

billboards. One claimed, *Vacationland is for the whole family!* It featured children holding balloons and ice cream cones. Beyond this billboard was a tent city, a large one. I'd seen smaller ones in Oregon, but this city stretched to the horizon, and I smelled the unpleasant reek of raw sewage. Some of the tents had walls and plastic windows, but most were just open-sided tarps tied to poles. A few men leaned against the fence, staring at the road. They all had beards, which were forbidden at school and which I'd rarely seen.

The bus downshifted as it pushed uphill, and the engine revved. Citizens who had been hunched over cookstoves now stood and watched our ascent. A pack of children surged toward the fence, shouting something. One woman who'd been draping wet laundry over the top of a tent turned to stare at us. I had the impression of disruption, a feeling of drawing unwanted attention.

I glanced at Owen, who just shrugged and picked at the dried yellow paint on his cuticles. Today he was interviewing for a scholarship to the San Francisco College of Art, meeting at the house of an alumnus, someone important—a man who'd endowed a building or two. Owen had been up late last night, unable to sleep, laboring over a commission for a proctor—a canvas of an icy mountain range. He charged a lot of credits for his work, and nobody knew how much money he'd saved. It was a special privilege to have art supplies in our room, and he'd forbidden me to touch them.

And then we were driving through a downtown, not Ione, but some other gold rush–style town with boxy wooden buildings, all painted different colors. Only a few civilians were out on the street, most of them women. One wore a skirt that ended above the knee, and all the boys stared. The ones on the opposite side of the bus stood up to get a better view.

"Sit down," a proctor shouted. "Everyone in his seat."

Proctors stalked the aisles, and I noticed, for the first time, that they had real guns strapped to their sides. At school they wore Lewiston Volts—standard-issue tasers—bright red, the color of caution, of warning. Last week a boy had bitten off a part of his tongue when a proctor had used one to subdue him outside the cafeteria. Today, however, the sight of their guns frightened me more. I grabbed Owen's hand and palmed, "Why?"

He didn't understand, and I didn't know the sign for "weapon."

"Is that normal?" I whispered. "With the pistols?"

"No talking," a proctor said. He pointed his handheld in my direction and scanned the chip in my belly. Then he checked the screen embedded in his device. I knew my picture would show up there to confirm that it was me. I glanced at Owen. He was furious. At the end of the day we shared each other's demerits, and Owen palmed a short that meant *fuck off.* I shut my mouth. I couldn't lose control like that. I couldn't lose control at all.

·

We drove to an upscale gated community called Meadowlands. There were no meadows in sight. Presumably, the development had obliterated its namesake. The bus stopped beside a gatehouse. Two guards stepped forward. Both were overweight and appeared to be stuffed into their brown coats and pants. One took our information into a little booth, and the other collected iris scans from the proctors. This guard was the first civilian I'd seen wearing a suit and tie. We had not been dressed to fit in, after all.

"This is a nice area," the guard said. "We won't tolerate any trouble."

"No, sir," we chorused.

They waved us through—no mirrors, no dogs—and on the

other side was a real neighborhood, a park with a little stone path and two iron benches. Each home seemed gigantic to me, imposing, set on a slight rise at the end of a driveway, surrounded by a yard—a lake of synthetic lawn.

A proctor at the head of the bus called roommates forward and assigned them to various addresses. The bus traveled deeper into the neighborhood, stopping and starting. The seats around me emptied. Owen was dropped off at an enormous estate. I watched him ascend a long, sloping driveway lined with trees. I was taken to a street where the houses were smaller and closer together. "James Goodhouse," a proctor called. "Address 3715." He pointed to a residence with a red front door. A little flagpole jutted from the front of the house. On it was a banner with the picture of a leggy bird carrying a sack in its beak. When I didn't immediately rise, the proctor said, "Don't make me drag you out."

I walked down the aisle, and then I stood on the sidewalk listening to the bus retreat and turn a corner. It had been months since I'd been alone. At Ione, I was contained by the new security protocols, but at my old school I'd been good at sneaking out of the dormitory. I'd spent hours lying on the banks of the Deschutes, listening to the owls hunt, watching searchlights cross the school commons—beautiful beams of light, luminous tunnels, like gods come to earth.

I stepped up to the red door. There was a glass panel at the top and my reflection stared back at me. My skin was a light brown and my eyes were a bright, vivid green—a color that was evident even in the muted quality of the glass. I had grown enormously in the last year. By the time I'd transferred to Ione, I'd hit six feet, and I was grateful. It had bought me a little respect. Now I worked to make my face expressionless. I straightened the collar of my shirt, and then there was no point in putting it off any longer. I knocked and waited.

A teenage girl answered the door. "Yes?" she asked. Her long brown hair was braided into a glossy rope that draped over one shoulder. She was very thin, and a scar rose from the neckline of her sundress like a red, puffed worm. I lowered my gaze. I wasn't sure if I should speak to her. But there was no one else.

"My name is James, ma'am."

"*Ma'am,*" she repeated, then smiled as if I'd said something funny. "No one's ever called me that before. Are you saying my dress is too matronly?" She made a show of looking herself over.

"What? No, ma'am," I stammered. "I would never comment on your clothing."

"But you just did," she said.

I backed away. This was all going wrong.

"I'm kidding," she said. "It's a joke. Can't you tell?"

I didn't know what to do, so I stuck to the script. "My name is James Goodhouse," I said. "I'm here for a Community Day. I'm eager to be a respectful guest in your home. Please let me know if I should remove my shoes."

The girl's smile faltered. Something about my speech sobered her, though I couldn't imagine what, and this heightened my impression of being out of control.

"Aunt Muriel," the girl turned and hollered. "That boy is here."

"Not till Sunday." A woman stepped forward and opened the door wider. She was plump, and her flower-print dress was extremely colorful and slightly blurry, as if it were moving. Her short bangs had been swept to one side and artificially stiffened like the bill of a hat. "You're a day early," she said. "Did they change the date?" She looked into the yard as if checking for additional visitors.

"It's just me," I said.

"For heaven's sake," said the aunt. "Why can't anything work out?"

They led me down a hallway. The girl with the braid followed close behind.

"You're totally going to ruin Cousin Rachel's baby shower," she said. She spoke in a low voice, just loud enough for me to hear. I hurried to put some space between us, but she kept up. "Hey," she said. "My name's Bethany."

·

There was no Goodhouse equivalent for girls. The same markers in women were not predictive of future criminal behavior the way they were in boys and men. And as I entered the house, as I walked into its inner recesses, I felt very aware that I had never, as far as I knew, stood this close to a girl my own age.

Bethany followed me into the living room. A dozen women clustered on couches and chairs. They stared at me, gaping openly, eyes moving from my stiff formal collar to my tie to the shiny gold buttons on my jacket. A pregnant woman was ensconced in a chair with bunches of blue balloons tied to its back. Colorful streamers cut across the white ceiling. The room was oddly familiar. I was sure I'd been in a room like this as a small child. I was sweating through my shirt. The tie seemed to tighten of its own accord. I was supposed to give the speech, and I struggled to keep my eyes open and my voice level. I realized I could skip the part about the shoes. Everyone was wearing them.

"My name is James Goodhouse and I am honored to be a guest in your home. I am happy to be of any assistance. Please do not hesitate to ask. I'm grateful for the opportunity to give back to the people of this community." I made myself look at them. The speech, which had seemed just another bland necessity at school, felt surprisingly humiliating to recite.

"Our tax dollars at work," one woman said. "Wars, roads, and manners."

"Very pretty," said the aunt. "Now, I think I do have a few small tasks that need doing." She led me into the kitchen.

It looked very different from the ones I'd labored in. There were no cameras, no molded plastic workstations. This kitchen was decorated like a living area. A large painting of a cityscape at night hung above an upholstered bench. Food like I had never seen dotted a polished stone countertop—a cake frosted to look like a basket of flowers; fresh fruit sliced and arranged in arcs of color, like a sunset.

Everything seemed preposterously small. Goodhouse staples came in fifty-gallon drums, but here was a jug of milk I could lift with one hand, a mixer the size of a toy, a sink so shallow as to appear useless. And where was the sand tray? At school we scoured our dishes with sand first, but these people didn't seem to have a tray. It wasn't until I saw a stack of plates and a line of mugs that I felt a little calmer. These, at least, were the same size, and it steadied me. I was going to be okay. *These people are like us*, I thought. *It's just a different scale.*

"James?" the aunt said, testing out the name as if she was unsure it would work. I realized I'd been standing there with my mouth open.

"Yes, ma'am," I said. "Please excuse me. Your home is very interesting." I winced. This might sound critical. "Very beautiful," I corrected. But maybe that was worse. She might worry that I would touch or take something.

The woman frowned. "Please follow me," she said. The hem of her dress swayed as she led me through the kitchen door, down a few stairs, and into a large, fenced backyard. It abutted a row of other yards of similar proportions. A maple had been recently felled and the trunk cut into sections like vertebrae in a spinal column. The branches and leaves were missing.

"I'd like you to split logs," the aunt said. "You do that, right?"

"Yes, ma'am."

"Good." She went into the shed and returned carrying an ax. There was a moment of hesitation before she surrendered it. *Weapon*, I thought, and quickly corrected myself. *Tool*. At school we learned our thoughts were powerful. If it was in a mind, it was in a body, and soon it would be in the world for everyone to see.

"Split into eighths," she said. "You know how many that is? Eight pieces?"

I was confused. Did she think I wasn't a native speaker? I did have a slight accent, a touch of rural Oregon. "The whole pile?" I asked.

"Whatever you can do." She hurried into the house, locked the door, and spoke through the open kitchen window. "Stack them next to the shed."

I glanced at the other yards. They were all deserted, but manicured. A red plastic car, only large enough to hold a child, lay on its side, the roof bleached pink by the sun. Ornamental sage grew in clumps along the fence, and I crushed a leaf between my fingers, rubbing its scent on my hands. The maple was newly cut. The wood still had a golden hue and there was no sign of disease, no apparent reason for its removal. I knelt beside the tree and counted back seventeen rings from its outer edge. My finger stopped on a narrow ring. There had been a drought the summer I was born.

I took a section of trunk and made this my chopping base. I rolled it near the shed, then removed the hated jacket and necktie. I stretched my back, reached over my head. Holding the ax in two hands, I imagined this was my house, my yard, my tree. It took several strokes to warm up and find a rhythm. But once I did, I felt relief to be outside, doing something I was good at. I knew when to relax into the swing, when to tense and when to exhale. I knew to go slow, to pace myself. It was like one of the tasks at school where work had no ending, only an endless middle.

I continued for a while, humming under my breath, and then, since nobody seemed to object, I sang a little louder. As I worked, shade ebbed across the yard. I lost track of time, and my mind was finally quiet, my body working, a melody surrounding and protecting me. I knew mostly religious hymns. At my old school I'd sung in the choir, and I missed the music.

I heard the kitchen door open and I went silent. Bethany was walking down the stairs carrying two cups of dark liquid. "Thought you'd be thirsty," she said. Her feet were bare and her toenails were painted an astonishing candy-pink color. I quickly dropped the ax, not wanting to frighten her. "They're drinking Bloody Marys and playing bingo," she said. "Totally moronic. Rachel's lost like two babies, and I bet this one will flush, too. They all go at five months. Aunt says it's God's will and that some children are too pure to be born, but I know it's farm runoff in the water. That's why I drink root beer and nothing else." She seemed to shimmer in the sunlight. Her brown hair had red highlights that had been invisible indoors. "Here." She handed me a cup and I was surprised to feel real glass. *Weapon*, I thought.

"I don't really want kids," she said. "But I do believe in adoption. It's the right thing and a lot of people think it's wrong to adopt out of the country and I definitely agree, since it's racist if you don't want an American baby just because it's too brown or on drugs or whatever. Your voice is beautiful, by the way," she said. "I was listening to you just now."

"I thought I was alone," I said.

"I had my window open"—she shrugged—"so technically, you were."

I didn't know what to say. It had been months since I'd sung in front of anyone, and now the thought of an audience made me surprisingly nervous. I took a sip of the root beer and almost gagged. It didn't taste like food.

"Let's stand in the shade," Bethany said. She grabbed my arm and tugged me toward the shed, then rubbed the spot where she'd gripped me as if trying to erase the contact. Her touch was electric and startling. It made my whole arm tingle. "I read all the literature your school sent," she said. "We're supposed to evaluate your cleanliness, which struck me as bizarre. Wouldn't the school know how clean you were? You're hardly likely to get dirty coming over here. I felt like they were all fake questions." I was so preoccupied with her lightly freckled shoulders and the thick, angry-looking scar on her chest that I didn't immediately realize she'd gone silent.

"Excuse me?" I asked. I pretended to take a sip of the soda, but kept my lips tightly closed. I didn't know where to look or what to say, so I stared at a small jeweled barrette that twinkled above her ear. The crystals were a bright, clear blue.

"Can I tell you a secret?" she asked.

"You probably shouldn't," I said.

"I hacked Auntie's calendar," she said. "I shifted the dates for Community Day so she wouldn't know you were coming."

"Why?" I said. I glanced at the other yards to make sure we were still alone.

"They were going to send me to church while you were here," she said. "Make me help out with the charity suppers, only I'm not allowed to do anything strenuous, so I just fold napkins or sneak into the priest's office and read his letters. He's in love with his neighbor's wife, coveting her and all that.

I read it." She stared right at me, the sort of unflinching look I associated with birds. "Everybody treats me like a glass trinket," she said. "I get so bored. What are you really thinking?"

I shook my head as if I didn't understand. I was only ever thinking about the right thing to say—the thing that would show me in the best light. This wasn't the same as having thoughts.

"Come on," she said. "I know you're thinking something."

"You shouldn't break into other people's offices and read their letters," I said.

She rolled her eyes. "Stop that."

"And also," I said, "it's wrong to share pilfered information."

"Pilfered?" She laughed. "What does that even mean?"

"Stolen," I said. I didn't really think that this was a trap, but I couldn't take a chance. At school, if you failed to speak up against wrong-thinking you were considered no better than an accomplice.

"Cut it out," she said. "We might only have a few minutes and I want to know everything about you. I'm moving to campus soon. I'll be living with my dad. I'm going to be doing lots of programming and coding—very dry, very dull. Do you think we can meet secretly?"

"No," I said.

"Dad wanted to keep me here," she said, "but I made myself *unwelcome*. That's Auntie's word."

"I'm sorry," I said.

"Don't be," she said. "I consider it a personal triumph. I'm very goal-oriented, and getting kicked out of Meadowlands has been objective number one. Now Dad has to *take responsibility or else*. Those are Auntie's words, too."

I nodded, but I didn't quite follow. I was looking at the stone patio and the plentiful trees. I was sure that if I lived in a house like this, I wouldn't want to leave. "You don't like it here?" I asked.

" 'All oppression creates a state of war,' " she said. "That's a quote. And perhaps it's not explicitly in reference to girls entombed in suburban homes. And perhaps you think that I'm a little dramatic, but I won't trivialize my experience."

She frowned, her expression determined and a little mutinous, as if she expected me to challenge her. "I should get back to work," I said. I tried to return the root beer.

"No, no," she said. "I'll shut up. I just talk too much. Tell me what you really think about things."

"Like what?" I asked.

"Tell me the worst thing you've ever done," she said.

I stared at her barrette. The blue crystals were the same color as the lights on the civilian police cars.

"Okay, forget that," she said, seeing the look on my face. "Do you have a pet? I hear they do that—give you animals to take care of."

"At my last school I had a goat."

For some reason this made her giggle. "And?"

"She liked to eat mops. We'd leave them to dry on the back porch and she'd eat the cottony parts. She ate a shirt once, too, but it wasn't mine."

"Sounds like she was a bad influence," said Bethany.

"But a clever thief," I said. "Not that I value that in a friend. Not a friend, but you know, a goat." I wiped sweat off my upper lip. "You make me nervous."

"Dad says nervous people die young." She touched the scar on her chest. "I'm supposed to stay calm."

"Are you sick?" I asked.

"If anyone tries to argue with me, all I have to say is, You're upsetting me, and they have to be quiet. Except lately that hasn't worked," she said. "I think I've overused it. Or else they want me to keel over dead. Do you consider yourself a maniac?"

"No," I said.

"But that's just what a maniac would say." And I must have looked worried, because she started to laugh. "You don't know when I'm joking," she said. She took a step closer. A drop of condensation ran down the side of the root beer glass. It rolled over my finger and she reached out to collect the droplet before it fell.

A surge of laughter rose up from inside the house. Bethany stood so close to me now that I felt the heat radiating off her. My gaze darted to check the kitchen door to make sure no one was watching. My body language was guilty. *Only the appearance of sin is needed*, the school said. *Animals live moment to moment as they follow their desires. You must ask yourself: Am I an animal?*

I stepped back, and an instant later the kitchen door squeaked open. Bethany darted away. "Don't tell," she whispered.

The aunt had brought me a bottle of water, but paused, seeing a glass already in my hand. Her eyes narrowed. "Where is she?" she asked.

"Behind the shed," I answered.

·

I was allowed to come inside and eat a piece of cake. Bethany was sent to her room. She marched upstairs with loud, angry-sounding footsteps.

"Walk, please," called the aunt. I pulled on my jacket and tie, and then the aunt sat me in the living room and began bringing me plates of food. There were little sandwiches with cucumbers and puréed meat, bowls of berries and ice cream, fresh vegetables and white cheese flecked with herbs. The reward for my good behavior was so swift, so delicious, that for a moment the world felt ordered and right. I started smiling and couldn't stop. The food was incredible. I ate everything, and the ladies took notice. "All boys can eat at that age," one said. "Mine were like that."

"He has a hollow leg," another said. "Isn't that right, honey?" She looked so expectant, so resolute, that I nodded. "That's right," she said.

I'd never heard of hollow legs, but a boy at school had a plastic leg that looked like a hockey stick poking out of his pants.

"Wish I'd had a boy," said the aunt. "They're so useful."

"You have a son-in-law," said Rachel. One hand was draped protectively over her belly while the other dipped a carrot stick into a glass of champagne.

"Of course," said the aunt, "a charming young man." She looked around the room, nodding and showing off a too-bright smile. Her stiff bill of hair vibrated slightly.

Balls of crumpled wrapping paper littered the floor. The balloons tied to the chairback had drooped, slackening their strings. "May I read a magazine?" I asked. There were some stacked on the coffee table, all quickpaper editions that looked and felt like old-fashioned paper but held rotating down-loaded content.

The aunt told me to help myself, and I sank into my chair and went through them—page by beautiful page. I'd been told that the availability of real media was one of the biggest perks of Community Day. Regular citizens were able to con-sume media without needing a moral interpretation, and I was eager to read as they did.

I started with a newsmagazine. There were pictures of un-smiling men in elaborate military camouflage. Behind them was an arid landscape. Things burned in the distance, sending plumes of black smoke into a big white sky. Most of the arti-cles were about how the war was being mismanaged and how the subsequent resignation of a certain general was just the sort of move that gave a false sense of progress. I thought I understood the article, but I'd been warned that I'd feel this way. The school said: *People are not aware of their limitations because those limitations prevent awareness.*

There was an editorial page in which people wrote letters debating the newly reinstituted draft. One man felt that his children shouldn't be asked to risk their lives for an unending, unethical war. Another man argued that the reason the war dragged on was that we refused to really commit. "Either we're one nation united or we're just a bunch of people that can't get anything done," the man said. "If we don't implement a draft, we can't purchase the freedoms that people here take for granted." I reread this page and tried to imagine each of these men as my father, one keeping me close and the other proudly sending me away.

I shut the magazine. Sometimes I'd seen parents at the fence, especially at my old school, where the security was light. They would be looking for their children, calling out a name. A proctor would intercept them. We knew better than to approach. Those people were dangerous. Goodhouse had drummed this idea into our heads: Contact with a genetically compromised parent meant certain failure. Our birth records were destroyed for this reason. The fastest way to become a criminal was to go home.

"What do you read in school?" My head snapped up. I found one of the guests, a woman with large, rabbity teeth, sitting beside me. Her name, she told me, was Gayle. While I'd been reading, most of the women had left.

"I read whatever they tell me to," I said.

"But what do you read in your spare time?" Gayle asked.

"We have pamphlets and videos," I said. "Everything has a purpose, of course."

I didn't want her to think I was reading for fun. We'd had

a library at La Pine, but Ione was different. Reading for pleasure wasn't allowed, and I was afraid that hers was a trick
question. I picked up the newsmagazine. "For example, you
have an article about troop withdrawal and the possible out-
comes of different decisions. I guess the magazine wants you
to learn about the difficulty of choices when both appear to
be right-thinking. But for us—we only read about the war so
we can discuss how fortunate we are to be living in a stable
society."

"You must be kidding," Gayle said.

"I don't think so," Rachel said. "They don't know how to
do that." She bit into her carrot stick and looked at me with
such malice, I felt she was imagining that the carrot was my
finger.

Bethany walked out of the kitchen eating a slice of cake
off a paper plate. I hadn't heard her come down the stairs,
and judging from her aunt's annoyed expression, neither had
anyone else. "You said I could come down after the party." She
took huge, mouth-bulging bites and glared at her aunt. "You
said." She wore a long green T-shirt pulled over her sundress.

"You know," Rachel said, "if you weren't taking Uncle
A.J.'s money, then we wouldn't have to let these people into
our home."

"Rachel!" the aunt interjected. "Be polite."

"You think A.J. can work at a sewage treatment plant and
not smell like shit afterward?" Rachel said.

"Enough!" The aunt clapped her hands as if to make a
noise loud enough to cover her embarrassment.

"Ignore her, James," Bethany said. "She's mean to everyone. Can I ask a personal question?"

"No," said the aunt. "You cannot ask him anything of the
sort."

"What do you really think about Ephram Goodhouse?"

she asked. She was perched on a chair arm, licking chocolate off her fingers. "You've heard the story, right?"

I nodded. I felt the cold, creeping fear return, and I realized that I had let myself relax here. I had been bought off with food and magazines.

"Very sad," said Gayle. "The whole affair was utterly tragic."

Rachel snorted in disbelief. "That's not what you said earlier."

"I don't condone vigilante behavior of any sort," said Gayle.

"I want to hear what James thinks," said Bethany. "How often do we get a chance to ask a primary source?"

"I'm not Ephram," I said.

"But you know what I mean," she said.

"That man was protecting his family," said Rachel. "The boy was deranged—and there was a consequence."

"Out of all proportion," Bethany said.

"It had to be out of proportion," said Rachel. She leaned forward, and the balloons jerked and shuddered as the chair moved. She pointed at me. "You're thinking that just because he looks normal and talks like us, we can appeal to some higher nature. It's not there. I get so sick of this thinking. We can't treat these people like we treat each other."

"One boy's crime should not define us all," I said. The words were out before I could stop them.

Rachel bit into another carrot. "You poor, dumb animal," she said. "You really don't understand."

I sat very still. The room seemed to shrink around me.

"I'm sorry, James. It's the hormones." The aunt gave me a tight smile. "She's just not herself."

"Don't apologize to him," Rachel said. "I'm not the only one who thinks this way. Why did you rush to grab that beacon bracelet as soon as he got here?" The aunt wrapped her hand around her wrist, covering whatever she was wearing.

"Because you might only have a few seconds to call for help. Security is waiting out there, waiting for something bad to happen. But do you know why I feel better? Not because they're there. I feel better because that Ephram boy is dead."

I shivered inside my jacket. I didn't know if anything she said was true. It could all be true.

Rachel clutched her belly. "You're lucky my mother is so softhearted. You should all be sent somewhere else, away from us, some island where you can rob and kill each other all you want and leave us alone."

"Shut up," Bethany said. "You hateful cow."

"I am so sorry," the aunt said, and at first I thought she was apologizing to me. But she reached over and touched her friend's arm. "This is so embarrassing, Gayle. They're not usually this bad."

Then Rachel twisted in pain and threw up a nasty, orange-tinted slurry. It dropped to the beige carpet with an awful wet sound.

"Oh my God!" Gayle leapt to her feet.

"I'm fine," Rachel groaned. "I'm fine." Then she vomited again.

As the women hustled Rachel from the room, Bethany stood up, pulling at the end of her T-shirt. "Flush," she said, "there it goes."

THREE

They all left for the hospital. I was told to wait outside for the bus, but in the confusion they'd forgotten to close the front door. I sat on the stoop for ten minutes, then wandered back into the house. I was still shaking. I wasn't getting less angry as time went by—the way I usually did—but the opposite. I stood in the hall and practiced the school's deep-breathing techniques, bending at the waist and letting my arms dangle. I counted—*one, two, three*—then exhaled in a loud burst of breath. But the anger remained like soda bubbles inside me, rising out of nowhere, effervescing, filling me with a directionless urgency.

I tried to practice empathy for myself, for Rachel. *Empathy.* The word that we used so often at Goodhouse. Our greatest aspiration. Could we feel it? the school would ask, as if we were listening for a far-off sound, a small bell ringing in the distance. Could we hear it from where we lived?

I walked back into the living room. There was a stain on Rachel's chair, a smear of dark blood on the yellow upholstery. The vomit had been cleaned up with a dish towel, but I could still smell the sour stench of bile. It might be the end of her child—her normal civilian child—but I felt no empathy, just a dull sense of horror. There was so much wealth here, so much half-eaten food, so many textiles and pictures and brightly tinted paint, that even the stench didn't seem real, like it must be coming from these borrowed clothes, from the regulation haircut—from somewhere inside me.

I began to roam the house, opening closet doors, touching their coats, their things. In a kitchen drawer I found an envelope of fifty-dollar bills. The paper was thick and substantial. A serious, bewigged man was featured on the front. He was green like a goblin. I selected two bills and took them to the bathroom, where I tore them into tiny pieces and flushed them away. But this wasn't enough. I wanted to know what a hundred dollars was worth, so I rooted through the kitchen cabinets looking at the little ornate food boxes, searching for their price tags. I wanted to think about the money in terms of food destroyed—this was something I could understand. But there were no numbers, no indication of value.

I went upstairs. I found Bethany's bedroom at the end of the hallway. Most of her things appeared to be packed, but her desk was still cluttered. It had several small, incomplete electronic devices lying in a heap on its surface—handhelds, perhaps, broken apart. A screwdriver and a soldering iron lay beside them, next to paper blueprints and diagrams of some kind. And there, sitting atop the papers, was one of Bethany's blue barrettes. A few strands of her hair were tangled in its clasp. I picked it up and then I pressed the metal setting between my fingers until the sharp edges gave me a tiny flash of pain. I don't remember putting it in my pocket, but of course I did. It was habit.

•

The bus ride back was relatively raucous. The proctors were preoccupied, clustered at the front, not issuing demerits, even when boys were blatantly talking. I was so relieved to see Owen, to be getting *away*, that I didn't think much about it.

"How'd it go?" I whispered. Owen shrugged. He was peeling paint off his hands. It was green and brown. The yellow from the morning was gone. "Did you get in?" I asked, but I realized that this was unrealistic and things probably didn't move so quickly. "When do you hear?" I'd expected him to have good news—but he was sullen and angry. He glanced at the nearest proctor.

"Come on," I whispered. "He's not paying attention."

But Owen wouldn't risk it. He stared pointedly out the window as we circled through the neighborhood, collecting the rest of the students. Some boys appeared grim or resolved, others electrified. Regardless of what had happened, every dorm would be full of conversation tonight.

The guards waved us through the Meadowlands gate, and the bus accelerated into the countryside. More billboards—advertising laser-therapy clinics, turbocharged vitamins—lined the roadway. Our true velocity was only apparent in the moment we passed the billboard itself, in the astonishing way it flashed and disappeared behind us.

"Do you think any of us could ever live like that?" I whispered. "In that kind of neighborhood? I mean, you'd have to be Level 1. You'd need a different surname."

Owen pressed his forehead to the window glass. The birthmark on his cheek darkened, the way it did when he was irritated.

"Or do you think it's just impossible?" I asked.

Level 1 students could change their last name upon graduation—they could assimilate more fully. Level 2s had to keep the Goodhouse name but could still own property, could still vote. Sometimes Level 3s and 4s weren't told where they were assigned until they shipped out. If you were going to one of the recycling platforms in the Pacific Ocean, the school thought it was better not to know. Too many would try to run.

"Sometimes," I whispered to Owen, "I don't believe in the

afterward. I mean, I know *something* will happen. And I do practice my outlook." We crested a hill. Wind flowed through an open window, filling the bus with a flat hum. "But I can't see it," I whispered. "I can't see becoming one of them."

"Just shut up." Owen turned toward me. His eyes were glassy, as if he were furiously fighting back tears. "Are you really saying anything I need to hear?"

I looked around. "Everyone else is talking," I said.

"I will not have my life fucked up by a second-tier roommate," he said, and then added, "Sorry, but it's true. I've worked too hard to keep my status."

"I have, too," I said.

"Just stay the fuck out of my way," he said.

And then the tent city was rushing past—the chain-link fence and the different-colored tarps and structures. Several bearded men stood by that same fence with their arms above their heads. I thought they were waving at us. I remember being confused because there was a sudden tapping sound, like hail on a metal roof. It took me a moment to understand that the men were throwing rocks. One hit the window just ahead of our own, and the glass fractured into a web of lines. "Stand down." A proctor spoke through the external address system. "Stand down," he said. The sides of the bus were booming now, and then something large hit the windshield. The glass went opaque and the driver lost control. The back end of the bus spun as if it were going in a separate direction from the front. The tires shrieked. I felt a sickening sense of weightlessness as we left the road, then a shudder as we punched through the fence. The bus bounced wildly, like the body might detach from the wheels. I glimpsed flashes of color out the window, tents and tarps going by.

When we came to a stop, I was on the floor underneath several people. I smelled smoke—an oily, acrid stench that gave me a jolt of adrenaline. I couldn't see, couldn't orient myself. "Fire!" I shouted. "It's on fire." I felt tangled in bodies, struggling with the elbows and legs of other panicked people. I looked up and had a moment of vertigo. I realized that the bus was on its side, and with half the windows underfoot it was much darker—smaller somehow, a metal tube.

"Clear the roof," the address system barked. "Clear the roof. This is your last warning. We will open fire." Footsteps sounded overhead, shadows crossed the windows. They would drop a match, I realized. That's how it would happen. I had a general sense of where the back door was located and I began moving toward it, fighting and flailing, but there were too many of us, all crowded together. There was no exit.

"Do you smell that?" I asked the boy beside me. His name was Harper. He had a line of blood oozing from his mouth, darkening his teeth.

"What?" he asked.

"It's the Zeros," I said. "They're going to burn us."

"They would have done it already," Harper said. But his expression was uncertain, and now there was a drumming sound—people banging on the sides of the bus, metal on metal.

"It's gasoline," I said. "I know the smell." It was what they'd used in the dormitory at La Pine. It was why the fire had been so unstoppable. I struggled to stand on one of the seats. I used it to boost myself up to an open window. I was tall enough to get my hands around the edge of the frame.

"You idiot," a proctor shouted. "Stay *in* the bus." Someone pulled at me, trying to drag me down. I kicked him.

This is what the Zeros did. They wanted to purify, to cleanse. They didn't believe in reforming us. We were how the Devil was made flesh, how he crept into the world and did evil. There was a map now, a way to find us, a genetic story. Zeros interpreted the science. They believed that when the world was cleansed of evil, when evil had no more flesh to occupy, only then would the oceans teem once more with life, only then would the weather normalize, the aquifers refill, and the drought break—only then would there be peace.

"Code 15," a proctor called. "Code 15."

I wrapped a hand around the edge of the window frame and heaved myself partway through, just far enough to get my head and one shoulder out. I looked down the long, battered flank of the bus. A crowd had surrounded us, a terrifying sight. They were chanting something I couldn't make out. I struggled to free myself, twisting in the window frame, and then I saw two men rushing toward me. Each of them wore red—one had on a balaclava and the other a bandanna tied at the neck. They were only a few feet away when another student emerged from an intervening window. They seized him, trying to lift him out, even as he fought.

"You fucking killers," I screamed. "Leave him alone."

I heard shots—a cluster of them in quick succession—and then a proctor appeared to my right. He stood on top of the bus, so I was level with his feet. "Inside," he bellowed. He kicked at my shoulder, forcing me down as he passed. I slid to the ground. There was some kind of foam on the floor, filling the damaged cavity. It would be the fire retardant. The foam had a gritty chemical stench, like the substance they used in the school latrines.

"Don't get it in your eyes," a boy beside me said. "Don't touch your face."

The drumming stopped. It happened all at once, no more banging, no more shadows overhead. Little flecks of foam hung suspended in the sunlit air, glowing like bubbles. All of a sudden it was eerily quiet, and we were huddled together—

everyone looking up, waiting. "They're here," someone said. "They've arrived." And I didn't ask who *they* were, just someone bigger, just someone more.

•

An ambulance took away the students with broken bones. The rest of us were deemed well enough to walk. They marched us out through the back door of the bus. Proctors formed a corridor and we traveled between them, arms folded, stepping over debris—a quickpaper comic book, a red plastic spoon. Sleek black-and-white helicopters whirred overhead. Police in riot gear with black vests stood at intervals, and peace drones rumbled past. These drones were large metal boxes on thick rubber wheels. Each one had a telescoping neck and a heavy coat of graffiti. They roamed the tent cities, going where officers couldn't. They had probably converged on the bus moments after the accident, trying to record the identities of the perpetrators.

I walked down the aisle of our new bus. This one was a commuter model with cloth seats and little white shawls to protect the seat backs from dirty hair. Owen waited for me. It was surreal, a revision of our departure from Meadowlands, except now we were all disheveled and bloody and our clothing was torn. "You okay?" Owen whispered. The foam had left oily smears on his jacket.

I nodded. "You?"

"Fine," he said.

My hands shook and I sat on them. There was that terrible feeling that someone was standing behind me, breathing on my neck. I was ready to run or fight; my body was tense and frustrated by inaction. I closed my eyes, but quickly opened them again. Behind my eyelids there were people I didn't want to see or remember. I was unreliable. I was wrong. There was no gasoline. I'd been reliving what had happened at La Pine. It had never stopped, the fire still burned, and the panic used this moment as an opportunity to burrow deeper, to claim me more fully. I had to exert all my willpower not to vibrate out of my seat.

"I hate this part," I said.

"What part?" Owen asked.

Police officers had cordoned off the accident scene with orange tape. All the tent city residents had been moved back a hundred feet or so, and everything near the site was abandoned. Mundane objects lay in the dirt like they had been swept up in a great wind and then dropped—a blanket, a blue jacket, a plastic bottle for filtering water.

Nothing had really happened, I told myself. We were all accounted for, even the boy I'd seen pulled halfway through the window. It was a crime of opportunity and we all knew that the Zeros were out in the world, knew what they thought of us, and yet, still, it felt somehow surprising, as if I were learning it all for the first time.

"Yes," Owen said, out of nowhere. "It's possible."

"What?" I asked.

"I'm answering your question. We can live in a neighborhood like that. Why not? These people aren't better than us. No way."

I leaned back in my seat. "Subversive," I said.

"Fuck the statistics," he said. There was a gleam in his eyes, and his voice rose continually as he spoke. "When I have a career and when civilians pay for my work, I will not sell to Zeros. If they don't like this planet the way it is, they can fuck off—set *themselves* on fire and clear the fucking air."

One of the boys behind us slapped Owen on the shoulder. "Little O," he said. "Tell it."

"Don't call me that," Owen said. But it was just Runt, a

short, ferrety-looking kid who had too many teeth in his mouth. He'd been Owen's roommate a few years back.

"This one here." A proctor with a torn sleeve stopped beside our row and pointed at me. The name on his tag read *McIntyre*. "Two demerits," he said.

"For what?" Owen asked. "For what?"

But the man scanned my chip. "Climbing out the goddamned window," he said. "Disorderly conduct."

"Me?" I said. "I was disorderly? They were going to kill us."

"You want another?" the proctor asked. "I'm in the mood." He had a frayed, slightly manic cast to his features. Owen and I both shut up. The proctor waited a moment to see if we had ourselves under control, and then he moved on.

When he was gone, when there was no chance of being overheard, Owen turned to me and said, "What the fuck is wrong with you?"

But I just looked away. That wasn't a question I could answer.

It felt unbelievable that just a few hours before, I'd stood beside a civilian girl, been close enough to see the faint spray of freckles across her cheeks, the slight curl of her tongue as she spoke, the shape of her body, not stuffed in a uniform but in a dress, tight at the waist. She was another species altogether, more like the birds that migrated overhead. For a moment we'd breathed the same air, felt the same sun and wind. But there was no pleasure in thinking about impossible things. The memory of this afternoon just confused and depressed me now.

Finally, we were cleared to go. We drove past the site of the accident. There were several citizens injured near the fence. I saw a shape under a blanket, but I didn't turn toward it. I knew how images could get caught in your head, could hang there like some obscene piece of art that you couldn't take down. They could press on you. Work on you. I looked at the sky instead, blue, with a few puffs of white cloud. It was empty space—vapor—something unrelated and indifferent to humans. When one of the tent city women started chanting "Murderers, murderers," I tried to send her voice into the sky. Away. Away, I thought. Away.

•

We returned to Goodhouse with a police escort. I felt relief when the campus came in sight. First I saw the fence. Electricity ran between its tall black poles. From a distance the fence looked like a giant comb jutting from the ground. And then I saw the Vargas Administration Building with its huge Romanesque façade, the red brick glowing in the late-afternoon sun like a fairy-tale castle. It was another remnant of the original Preston School of Industry. Built on a rise, visible from over a mile away, Vargas was all ornament, sweeping arched windows and graceful balconies. It had two turrets and a defunct clock tower—a truly odd counterpoint to the more modern, utilitarian architecture that dominated the campus.

Far in the distance, below the castle, I saw the guard towers for the Mule Creek State Prison. This was where California warehoused some of its worst criminals, and the irony of its proximity was not lost on us. It was where our wrong-thinking might take us: into that concrete fortress, that web of razor wire and chain-link fencing—a campus that made even Ione look welcoming.

We drove along the west side of Goodhouse, passing the factory, a dark brick box of a building with a tall smokestack. It was where the school produced the bread and cupcakes that made up a part of Ione's income. Every student worked in some capacity, and I spent my afternoons in the factory's mixing room, moving sacks of flour and sugar. We weren't allowed to eat sugar, only artificial sweeteners—the kind that didn't rot teeth and create dental bills. But sometimes a leaky bag would leave glittering crystals on my clothes. A wet finger could lift them to my tongue, and then the taste was unbelievable: an awakening. At the end of our shift we walked under a blast of air to clean us off, but the taste had been imprinted on me. It remained.

As the bus pulled through the main gate, the silent hounds raced back and forth in their pen. We passed the gray-and-white Proctors' Quarters and the old athletic field, driving into the heart of campus, coming to a stop in front of the main laundry buildings. The other Community Day buses had already returned. A thick line of boys stood outside the laundries, waiting to shed their civilian clothes, gawking at us, palming furiously.

Those with injuries exited first. Several infirmary nurses, all dressed in their tan-colored uniforms with the Goodhouse logo in red, were setting up a table—unpacking a case and a screen. Surprisingly, Tanner himself stood nearby with his entourage and a couple of men, one of whom was tall and skinny, like a stretched shadow. I tried to be patient, but I felt claustrophobic. The bus was a cage, and every little noise made me swivel in my seat.

When it was our turn to exit, I pushed into the aisle, struggling to make the muscles in my arms and legs obey. The crowd felt as if it were compacting around me, a solid wall of flesh. It took all my attention to mimic normal movement, to maintain some composure, and still, I stumbled into the boy in front of me. He elbowed back, almost connecting with my chin. That's when I saw the white-haired man, the one with the rangy body—the man I remembered from that night in La Pine. He seemed to be standing alone behind the nurse's table, wearing the clothes I remembered, the black pants and the tailored shirt. He stood out as a still figure in the busy yard. *Hallucination*, I thought. *Phantom*. And I made myself look away. I wanted to forget. I wanted to get better. Wrong-thinking started in the warping of perception, and I couldn't permit myself to keep reliving the worst moments, reinforcing them. I had to make a choice.

We exited the bus, and a proctor directed us to wait in a long line at Laundry 1. Ahead of us, students were already pulling off their jackets, stripping down to their T-shirts and underwear. A sour smell wafted from the open doors, and proctors were shouting instructions, their broadcast voices interrupting each other and contributing to the confusion they were trying to dispel.

"Pants to the right, jackets to the left."

"To the right," another shouted. "You there, stand for inspection."

"Each item will be placed on the countertop, and you will not be dismissed until the items have been cleared."

The two boys in front of us palmed with speed and dexterity. Their fingers formed shapes I couldn't recognize, and then they both laughed at the same time. Rows of thick red boils dotted the backs of their arms, and above each boil was a number written in a marker directly onto their skin.

I stuck my hand into my jacket pocket—and encountered the prickly metal of Bethany's barrette. For a moment, I just stood there, unsure of what to do as the line advanced. I began to dig at the inner seam of the coat, hoping I could force the barrette into the lining, hoping it would be overlooked in the inspection. But there wasn't time. We were about to go through the laundry room doors. I quickly tossed the barrette away from me and into a clump of dirt to my right. It fell short, landing near the path—a bright, unnatural blue against that brown earth.

I felt Owen watching me and I slowly turned toward him, surprised to see even the smallest hint of indecision. If he reported me, he'd be cleared of our earlier demerits.

"Please," I said.

But he raised his hand in the air. "Proctor!" he shouted. "Proctor to me."

FOUR

Two proctors pulled me out of the line and led me to a basement room underneath the gymnasium. They told me to strip. "It was an accident," I said. "I picked it up to return it. I was going to give it back."

"Strip down," the proctor repeated. I did so, taking everything off, turning slightly away as if I were modest. I wasn't. The band of my boxers hid an infraction more illegal than theft. I'd been taking one of Owen's pens and marking the site where I'd been chipped, months ago, on intake. I now had a semipermanent black scar on the right side of my belly. It wasn't very visible, merely a freckle, but all the same I kept my arm over the mark.

One of the proctors pulled a little plastic bag from his pocket, scanned the code on the front, and tossed it to me. I snatched it out of the air.

"Take your pill," he said. I recognized the round lemon-colored tablet.

"I'm supposed to take it with food," I said. "They were very clear about that."

"Please show your compliance," the proctor said. He sounded almost bored.

I pinched open the bag and quickly took the tablet. "It's down," I said. The man clicked on a pin light and I opened my mouth to show him that I'd swallowed the pill. It was, in fact, stuck in my throat.

"Are you experiencing any unusual dizziness, fatigue, or chills?" I thought of the sickening, weightless feeling of the bus leaving the road. "Are you experiencing any anxiety?" he asked.

I stood before him, shivering and naked. "Seriously?" I said.

He left me in that room for a long time, or maybe it only felt like a long time, because there were no windows, nothing to look at but a concrete floor with a drain in the middle and a lightbulb encased in a metal cage. I didn't want to sit on the ground, so I stood. It was much cooler in here, a relief at first—and then the gooseflesh started to rise and I paced to keep warm.

I tried to cough up the pill, but this only made it lodge deeper in my throat. I needed water. I knelt and peered into the drain, where a dark liquid glinted below the metal grate. My own eye stared back and I jerked away, imagining people under the floor.

At La Pine we didn't have rooms like this. Our headmaster's idea of punishment was to make you weed a field or rewrite an essay until you "said something intelligent." Of course, the Goodhouse schools were supposed to be identical. And maybe they were now, after the attack, but it would have been easier to adjust to Ione, to accept everything, if I hadn't felt like I was living in a distorted memory of home. These boys looked almost like my friends, with their blue uniforms, their short hair and their swagger. I seemed constantly on the verge of recognizing someone or, more precisely, I'd recognize a walk or a gesture—but if I stared, the likeness would disappear. Dr. Beckett, my intake doctor, had promised me that time would dull memory. And so I was taking my evening pill, swallowing the monofacine in anticipation, waiting to forget.

•

The sound of a door opening made me startle and turn.

"Country boy," Creighton called. He exaggerated his vowels, both imitating and distorting my slight Oregon accent. He looked like he'd been in a fight. His eye was purple and he was favoring his right leg. He seemed pissed off, and it gave me some satisfaction.

Davis followed him into the room. He was carrying my shoes and a new, clean uniform. The proctor who'd given me my pill remained in the hallway.

"Sticky fingers," Davis said. He shook his head in mock disappointment. "We were very surprised. One of our model students."

"And you don't have enough hair to wear a barrette," Creighton said. "Or was it for your girl Owen? Now, that is beautiful."

Davis tossed me the clothes, and I quickly pulled them on. My stomach hurt. The pill felt as if it was burning a hole through me.

"I need some dinner," I said. "I'm not supposed to take medicine without food."

Creighton frowned. "Every boy gets dinner," he said. "It's regulation."

"Are you saying you've been mistreated?" Davis asked. "Because that's a serious accusation—something your class leaders want to know."

"Personally," Creighton said, "I'm very committed to the well-being of my fellow students."

"Never mind," I said, stepping into my shoes. "I had enough lunch. Forget it."

"Wait," Creighton said, cocking his head as if he was confused. "So you've eaten already. I don't understand."

"It doesn't matter," I said. But he took a step toward me, and I had to force myself to stand still and let him approach.

"You lied and now you claim it doesn't matter?" Creighton said. I felt his breath on my face.

"Now hold up," said Davis, his voice soothing. "We don't want to rush to judgment." He walked up to me and it was just as Owen described. I looked into his eyes and he had a soft smile there, and then his fist was sunk deep in my belly and I was lying on the floor waiting for air. When it came, I heaved up a white, foamy substance. "Boy hasn't had any dinner," Davis said.

Creighton hobbled closer to peer at me. "Look at that," he said.

But I was looking at Creighton's right leg, the one that bore all his weight. He was like a flamingo, perched, vulnerable—a house on stilts. His red face, still fat with childhood, was balanced at the top. I tried to do a breathing exercise and to think about my status, that thing we all guarded—that pass to a good life. I must have believed in fairness still, because I felt how unfair it was, and this burned in me.

I kicked Creighton as hard as I could in his bad knee, and he crumpled with a howl. He cut the sound short, instinctively swallowing it, though he continued to writhe on the floor. I scrambled to my feet and prepared to face Davis, but he just stood there, hands at his sides, watching me, waiting to see if I was going all the way in an attempt to join their ranks.

"Demerit," called the proctor.

"Shit," I said, realizing the full magnitude of what I'd done. "Shit."

"I'm gonna destroy you," Creighton said. "You're fucking dead." His face purpled with rage. He struggled to stand, but was unable to put any weight on his injured leg. "You're never going to graduate," he said. "You're going to stay right here and be my little bitch."

"Easy," Davis said. He pulled Creighton to his feet and then restrained him. "That's not the plan."

"It is now," Creighton said.

But Davis merely smiled, his expression sweet and satisfied. "No," he said. "We don't have to get our hands dirty with this one."

•

They were gone for hours. When Davis returned, he was alone. I began apologizing the moment he stepped into the room. "I don't know what's wrong with me," I said. "I don't understand what happened." And it was true. I'd been reliving the moment, trying to pinpoint my error—to see what part of myself had given its consent. "I just want to tell you that it won't happen again," I said.

"I know it won't," Davis said.

An infirmary nurse hurried into the room. He was a short and muscular man with a considerable underbite. "This one?" he asked.

Davis nodded. The nurse pulled a metal case from his uniform pocket and began to prepare a syringe.

"What's going on?" I asked. I retreated to the far wall, my hand touching the crumbling cement of the foundation.

"I heard you were trying to get back to your people today," Davis said. "Is that right?" He leaned against the doorframe, watching me.

"What do you mean?" I had no idea what he was talking about.

"I mean, you crawled out a window and waved your arms and said, *Here I am*."

"I was trying to get away," I said.

"Funny how it looks the same," Davis said.

"Bullshit," I said. "You weren't there."

The nurse stepped forward and held out an alcohol swab.

"Right arm," he said. I didn't move. "Please show your compliance."

"Is this for an Intensive?" I pointed to the syringe.

"We don't know that word," the man said. But he did. Everyone knew the school tested drugs on students. To sign up for testing was the fastest way to burn off demerits. The studies were listed as Maintenance Intensives, but of course you had to be careful. You never knew if your fingernails would fall out afterward or if you'd be unable to sleep for a week.

Whatever was in the syringe made me almost instantly sick. It sent an icy shock through my body, up past my shoulder and into my chest. The sensation was so intense that it reminded me of January in Oregon—the way a sudden breeze could leave you breathless, the way thin mountain air could cut through clothing, penetrate lungs and ears and fingers. It was overwhelming, and I almost expected to see the frosty cloud of my own breath.

Two seconds passed and the sensation lessened. Two seconds more and whatever it was had flowed through my heart and into my brain. It was a part of me.

•

Davis cuffed my hands together with a plastic cord. He made me jog behind one of the school's T-4s. These were little white carts that the proctors used to get around campus. They ran on a battery, silent except for the distinctive humming of their engines and the hiss of their rubber wheels on the pavement. They had two rows of white vinyl seats and a sun canopy overhead. It was hard to keep pace with my wrists lashed together. I was off-balance—too tall and uncoordinated. Davis swiveled in his seat to watch my efforts, to relish every stumble. I tried to keep my face free of expression, to deny him this at least.

"It was just a barrette," I said.

"What are you bitching about?" Davis said. "I never had a girl on my Community Day."

We were on the old campus, skimming across the cement walkways, passing the original Preston School stables, the old metalworks, the science building. They were all built of brick, with columns sunk into the façades. It gave them a grand and collegiate appearance, now at odds with their designations as Laundries 1 and 2 and Storeroom 6. We looped near the dormitories—a series of long, squat, cinder-block buildings that the boys called bunkers.

It must have been late at night because the walkways were clear, and the school seemed deserted until we got closer to Vargas, with its huge redbrick façade. A work detail was preparing the long-unused flower beds in front. I smelled the compost. I saw a black, loamy pile of it on a nearby tarp. Bushes and plants were lined up in the road; the large ones had root-balls bound in burlap. Overhead, a cloud of insects clustered with all the frantic energy of electrons circling a nucleus.

The T-4 stopped, and for a moment I thought I was joining the work detail. I felt a surge of relief. I wasn't afraid to stay up all night and dig. I'd done a lot of farm labor in Oregon and I knew I could handle it. Davis walked me toward the crew. The boys looked sullen and slump-shouldered. I recognized some faces from my class, and then I was shocked to see a La Pine boy. At first I thought he was another hallucination, but I blinked and he remained. He was a little kid named Harold. He was maybe twelve years old, and looked pitifully small next to everyone else. He had brown ragged hair and eyes that were too close together, giving him a wild appearance, almost like a feral cat. I nodded to him, but he looked away.

I didn't join the group. Instead, Davis marched me out of range of the floodlights, away from all the others. I began to get nervous. "Where are we going?" I asked.

"Shut up," Davis said.

We passed a T-4 boxer with a boy inside. These were specially modified units, the backseat replaced with a black-painted wooden box that forced a boy to stay in a seated position, his head poking out of a small circular opening, his body encased in what became an oven during the day. It was a common punishment, and the boy inside had badly swollen lips. He tried to say something as we passed, but it sounded more like a grunt. A bottle of water had been set on top of the box, just a few inches from his face.

I looked down at my bound hands. A little dot of blood had crusted to my sleeve at the injection site. "You called me a Zero," I said. "That's a bullshit rumor."

"I like rumors," Davis said. "They always have a little truth in them."

I shook my head. "You haven't been out there," I said. "You don't know what it's like—otherwise you'd never say that."

"I know what it's like," Davis said.

"You should hear the things people say about us," I said.

"Like what?" he asked.

"That we should all be sent to an island somewhere so we can kill each other."

And for some reason this made him laugh. "There's an idea," he said.

We were practically off campus now, fast approaching the fence. It was making me panic. We were headed for the big field that separated the Goodhouse facility from the Mule Creek State Prison. At Goodhouse, our fences were a series of black poles, but the prison was different. It had more old-fashioned barriers, observation towers, and razor wire. The stretch of land dividing the two institutions was called the Exclusion Zone—and it encompassed a wide swath of grass and a small hill covered in some kind of leafy vine.

We approached the fence poles, and the hiss of the electricity was audible. The stench of burnt ozone grew stronger. Our chips should have sounded an alarm by now, and I was suddenly worried that Davis meant to shove me into the current. I stopped. "Whatever you're doing," I said, "you don't have to. I have cash. I can pay you."

"How much?" Davis asked.

"Twenty-seven credits," I said.

It was a tiny amount, and Davis didn't bother to respond. He just walked to the fence and then stepped between two of the poles. The current was off. And this appeared true for several segments.

"You want to run?" he said. "Now's the time."

The Exclusion Zone stretched away from campus—like a dark road disappearing into the distance. I felt the pull of the hills beyond—that fake freedom. But there was nowhere to go, and he knew it. I stepped between the poles. I followed him and he walked me closer to the leafy hill, and then I could see that it wasn't a hill at all but the foundation of some abandoned building. A little path led to a stairwell and a sunken door. "Come on," Davis said.

"No," I said. "I'm not going in there." I slowed and started to back away. The basement door opened, and two men in brown uniforms jogged up the stairs. They had yellow patches on the sleeves of their shirts, something in the shape of an old-fashioned shield.

"I brought you a live one," Davis called, and I realized they were Mule Creek guards, their thick black belts equipped with different sorts of weapons and restraints.

I turned and ran. The two men caught me easily, knocking

me to the ground, using some kind of wooden baton. One of the men put me in a choke hold. He dragged me down the staircase and I clawed at his arm, which seemed as thick as a python. When they tried to open the basement door, I kicked the door closed. The man with his arm around my neck squeezed until I saw spots. The last memory I have is of looking up to see Davis leaning over a rusted metal railing, grinning down at me.

"Welcome," he said, "to the island."

FIVE

At Ione there were rumors about boys who disappeared, boys who were taken somewhere and never came back. We lived in fear of being sent to PCB, the Protective Confinement Block, with its dark, windowless rooms and solitary cells. No one graduated from PCB. There were stories about boys who found human bones in there—boys who'd pulled out loose teeth just to have something to toss and locate in the darkness. But worse, we were afraid of vanishing. Some roommates never showed up at lights-out. They were not listed as being in Confinement, not on a work detail, not transferred. They simply did not return from their day.

The corrections guard released his choke hold on me and I sank to the ground, unsteady and confused. I was briefly in a small room, like a waiting area. Other guards were there, too, and then a man grabbed my shirt and dragged me through a warren of little hallways dotted with doors—each with a hand-painted number on the front. Everything reeked of urine and mildew, and one wall had a green slimy substance growing around a pipe. The walls were a tapestry of graffiti, some of it done with real aerosol paint, but most rendered in marker or chiseled out of the concrete itself. I heard people in the other rooms. One was chanting a song I didn't recognize. Somewhere two people were having a muffled argument.

The guard opened a door marked 25 and pushed me inside.

The lock clicked into place behind me. There were two mattresses in a pile and a closet without a door. Peeling linoleum tiles checkered the floor, and a toilet jutted out of a wall that was partially torn open, revealing the plumbing. The room smelled of mold. I got to my feet. I told myself this wasn't too awful. At least I had my clothes.

Somebody shoved me from behind, and I only had time enough to register a blur of movement before I hit the ground. A foot kicked me twice in the ribs. "Don't get up," the voice said. I rolled over, scooting across the disgusting floor on my back, trying to get as far away as I could. The man who stood there was bigger than I was, taller but not much older. Tattoos covered his arms—a tangle of birds in bright grays and blues. His thick hair was much longer than Goodhouse regulation and he was wearing an orange jumpsuit with the words MULE CREEK CORRECTIONS printed on the front. Here was the embodiment of all our worst impulses, I realized. Here was our wrong-thinking self—personified and unredeemed. We were never supposed to be in the same room with these people.

"Damn," he said. "You must be in some serious trouble. What'd you do?"

"Stole a barrette," I said.

"For real?"

"Accidentally," I said.

"Yeah," he said. "I do a lot of stuff accidentally."

I coughed, tasted bile in my mouth, and spit onto the floor, trying to rid myself of the flavor. The young man was watching, his head cocked to one side. His voice, when he spoke, was a quiet deadpan.

"You're a real hardened motherfucker," he said, and for some reason this made me laugh. "My name's Tuck," he said. I told him I was James, but he wanted to know what my real name was. "The one you were born with," he said.

"Don't know." I shrugged. I got to my feet. "Just a name."

"You should find it out and get that slave name out of your mind. What are you doing with a girl's hair clip, anyway?"

"I was out on a Community Day," I said, "to learn about civilian life."

Tuck circled me, and I turned to keep him in sight. He had a fluid walk and a way of leaning his head back as if he didn't believe what he was seeing. "You must be so screwed up," he finally said. "We talk about how you all are being groomed to be serial killers, all next-door-neighbor-nice and then, *bam*. I heard about one of you who got put in here and he tried to get his cellmate to do breathing exercises, make them both feel all *right-thinking*."

I leaned against the wall, then stepped away, feeling the damp.

"So, how's it working out," Tuck said, "all that brainwashing? You feeling pretty good?"

"I do know a great breathing exercise," I said, and felt a rush of joy. Not since La Pine, I realized, had I been able to speak so freely. It made me like Tuck—and then a sudden fear caused me to check the ceiling. This might be a trick. I instinctively searched for a camera, looking toward the uppermost corners, where they were usually mounted. Tuck followed my gaze.

"There's no surveillance in the rooms themselves," he said. "And we have to get those off." He nodded to the plastic cuff that cinched my wrists together. He told me to try and pull my hands as far apart as they would go. It wasn't far.

He dug through his pockets and produced a lighter. "Hold them out."

I realized he was going to try and melt the plastic wire. "No way," I said.

"Trust me. This is necessary." He clicked the lighter and a

flame appeared atop the plastic cylinder. "You don't want to be caught in here with your hands bound."

"You can't melt it," I said.

"I can weaken it," he said. "And then you can snap it."

I tried to hold still, but the flame burned my wrists and the room filled with the awful reek of smoking hair. I jerked away.

"No," Tuck said. "You really do want this."

"Why? What happens?"

"It's always different," he said. "Usually they turn off the lights and try and flush us out into the main area. Just stick close."

I wanted to press him for answers, but I was having a hard time holding still. We worked on the cuff for several minutes, until I was sweating with pain. The insides of my wrists were starting to bubble. I pulled hard. Then I squatted down and used my knees to push my arms apart, and that seemed to do it. The cuff stretched enough to wiggle one hand out and then the other. I sat on one of the pallets, which was a mistake. It smelled like a dead animal and released a cloud of fleas. Somewhere in another room a boy started yelling. The words were indistinct. I licked the blisters on my wrists and then blew on them. It helped.

"So, what'd you learn," Tuck asked, "about civilian life?"

I shrugged. "I worked. I chopped up this tree, but they acted like I was there to rob them." I thought of the money with a pang. It brought me up short. I *had* robbed them. "What's it really like out there?" I asked. "What's a day like?" But Tuck seemed both amused and mystified by my curiosity. "We just don't get to talk much," I said. "And you have to be careful. People try to get you to say wrong-thinking stuff so they can report you. Not your friends, but, you know."

"You snitch in here," he said, "we kill you."

I tried to explain. "At my old school we had a group. Four

of us. We never reported each other—or actually, we had to a few times a month or else they'd have split us up. But it was always arranged ahead of time—who would get tagged for what—and it was always small stuff. We actually worked out profiles like personal problems. I was supposed to have a problem with swearing." I paused. I hadn't said any of my friends' names out loud since the fire. And I found I didn't really want to conjure them. "Another one of us was supposed to be prone to taking the cafeteria spoons back to his room. Just stupid stuff. Not real wrong-thinking, nothing that got you too many days in the field."

"You have no idea how crazy that sounds," he said. "I hope my brother isn't as screwed up as that." Tuck kicked at some trash on the floor. He seemed to be lost in a memory. "You ever see a little kid who looks like me on campus, you say hello."

"I'll keep an eye out for him," I said, lifting my chin slightly. But the gesture wasn't truly my own. I was imitating Tuck—stealing his mannerisms, adopting the cadence of his speech. I'd felt this before, the ability to impersonate, to become like the people near me—and I wondered if this was what I'd really learned at Goodhouse, the art of appearing to be something I wasn't.

"What time was it when you came in?" Tuck asked.

"Don't know," I said. "After lights-out."

"Which is?"

"Ten."

He stood up and ran his fingers over a piece of molding around the ceiling of the room. He pulled a piece of lathe out from the hole around the toilet. But the wood was brittle and snapped in half, and he threw the pieces away. "Shit," he said. "It's getting to be that time and we've got nothing." He tore several strips of cloth from the mattress covering, revealing the stained cotton pad underneath. "Here." He handed me two pieces of fabric. I watched the way he wrapped the cloth around his wrist and knuckles and I tried to do the same. I stared at the birds on his arms. Some of them had their mouths open as if they were calling to each other. Some of them looked startled. "Just fight hard," he said. "If you get into the lighted area, you'll see the guards. Don't pay any attention, even if they say they'll let you out. They won't. Just swing until you can't. You know, they place bets. If you do well, somebody will probably lose a lot of money," he said. "There's always that."

I persisted in asking questions, but he cut me off. "I don't know any more," he said. "I'll help you if I can, but I won't go out of my way. That's not how it works. What did they train you for, anyway?" he asked. "They do that, right? Give you a job skill."

I gave up trying to wrap the cloth around my wrist and just covered my knuckles. I wasn't a good fighter, and the strips of rag seemed almost laughable. "I sing," I said.

Tuck stared at me. "Everybody sings," he said.

"Yeah, but that was my skill," I said. "What they chose for me." Tuck told me I was useless. "But that was the best part," I said. I blew on my wrists. "Learning to do something useless felt like they let me out," I said. "For a while, anyway."

"That's just how they keep you busy," Tuck said. "Give you a little taste of something you want."

"Maybe," I said. I felt heavy with fatigue. After my initial reaction to the drug, I'd had no other side effects. Still, I knew it must be inside me, metabolizing.

"Sing me something," Tuck said.

"I only know church songs," I said. But Tuck was waiting.

"Go on," he said.

I stood up straight. I closed my eyes, and strangely, the little chapel where we practiced was there, waiting for me on the inside of my eyelids. I could smell sage and cedar and the heavy perfume of lilies on the church altar. At the last Christmas concert I'd sung the opening of Handel's *Messiah*. And now I heard the violins beginning the overture, and our little organ followed and then the harpsichord—an old, worn-out box that had been donated to us, one of its legs broken and propped up by a two-by-four. My throat muscles felt too tight. For a moment the notes were elusive, but then, all at once, the air pushed through me and I relaxed. My voice grew richer and deeper and it felt natural to sing, like I was exhaling a cloud of melody.

> *Comfort ye, comfort ye, my people, saith your God.*
> *Speak ye comfortably to Jerusalem,*
> *and cry unto her, that her warfare is accomplished,*
> *that her iniquity is pardoned.*

I opened my eyes, forgetting they were closed, and I was shocked to see the room anew, in fact to see it at all, to smell the mold and see Tuck's astonished expression.

I went silent then, feeling as if I had invoked some sort of forbidden magic in this place, crossed some line. The entire building was quiet, and I realized I'd sung as if my body itself were a pipe joining the surge of the church organ, pushing to surpass the little orchestra, to reach the back row, where our headmaster sat. I was shaking. I had been there. In the chapel, that dead life was still going on inside me, playing and replaying.

"Jesus," Tuck said. "You're like some kind of fucked-up bird." And then the lights went out and I heard a clicking noise. The locks on our doors had automatically retracted. Deep silence suddenly gave way to a collective roar. Footsteps pounded through the hallway. Tuck pulled me over to the door. He opened it wider and we stood behind the slab. It was so dark I couldn't see, but Tuck seemed to have a grasp of where everything was. He made a low shushing noise, just barely audible, and then I heard someone enter the room with shuffling steps. I tried to breathe quietly, but my heart was hammering. The blackness was like a thick, suffocating soup. I stifled the urge to lash out. Tuck's hand gripped my arm, sensing some change, though I hadn't moved.

"It's clear," a voice said. "Check next door."

There were sounds in the hallway, and the brief illumination of a flashlight beam cut through the crack between the door and the wall. Then we were alone. Tuck pulled me after him. "I got to find my people," he whispered.

It's hard to remember exactly what happened. Down the hall somewhere a boy was howling like a wolf. Someone grabbed me from behind and tore at my shirt. I struggled and fought. The blisters on my wrists burst. I was having little effect on my opponent, or perhaps there was more than one, and then suddenly I fell into another room, just fell through an unseen opening and lay on the floor.

I crawled a little way and stood with my back to a wall. All the ambient noise was conjuring memories of the fire. It was peeling away time, and I felt certain that the hallway was filled with the angry remains of my friends. It felt like I was in two places at once. I was seeing little bursts of orange light out of the corner of my eye. They were phantoms, just like the smell of smoke, just like the repeating chorus of the school choir, chanting:

But he is like a refiner's fire, like a refiner's fire.

And the violins were sawing away and we were all sweating in the little church and then we were on fire, choking, clawing at each other. And there was that breath on the back of my neck: the white-haired man had found me and was going to open the back of my head. He was checking his gun. What was taking him so long?

I was swinging into full panic, my hands digging into the wall, kicking and thrashing. When I felt the touch of a human hand, I turned toward it in fury.

•

This is what happened. On my last night at La Pine, I awoke to the sound of the fire alarm. Our room was already filling with smoke. I shouted at my roommates to follow me, but the hallway was chaotic. All of our training—the orderly fire drills with the marching lines of boys who stood on the green line and counted off—hadn't prepared us for the darkness, for the chaos. We had been hunched over. Walking on all fours, bellowing and pushing—terrifying each other. The flashing red light of the alarm pulsated as it shrieked. There were no adults. Smoke filled the halls, a black, undulating ceiling that sank lower and lower. I was knocked to the ground, crushed for a few panicky seconds, kicked and stepped on. The air felt acidic in my lungs. I thought of that picture of Hell in the chaplain's illustrated Bible: men with dog bodies and donkey tails and fire consuming their hair, maggots erupting from their mouths, a chaotic tangle of maimed and damaged limbs.

Then, somehow, I was up and running, staying close to the wall as I sprinted to the back staircase. I saw Ian. My friend Ian, the one who stole cafeteria spoons. Ian. That was his name.

I grabbed his arm and pulled him after me as we raced for the stairs, pushing against a tangle of boys headed in the opposite direction. I had a secret. I'd been sneaking out. The dormitory was old, and all the wooden windows had been replaced with metal sliders of impact-resistant glass. They opened only four inches to circulate the air. But the janitor's utility closet on the fourth floor was an exception. It had its original double-hung sashes, and I knew the access code—I'd seen a class leader punch it in.

The upper hallways were worse, filled with a more acrid, stinging smoke, with an almost unbearable heat. We crawled to the utility closet and I punched in the numbers. Stumbling over buckets and bottles of cleaning fluid, we managed to raise the window and suck in great gulps of cold January air. I was already regretting my decision to race for the closet. Surely most everyone had made it out the main door. Surely it was not as bad as it seemed moments ago. "I'll take responsibility," I said. "You should turn me in."

"I'll say the closet was already open," Ian said. "Nobody will check."

We expected to see boys flooding the yard below. I expected to see my friends lined up in rows, but instead, the yard was dotted with men in black jackets and red balaclavas. Bodies—proctors, mostly, but some students—lay unmoving on the lawn. It took us a moment to process it all. The snow at the base of the building had melted. Ash floated in the air, little black flecks like crows against a stormy sky.

"I'm not going down there," Ian said.

"We have to," I said. The smoke was getting heavier. It was hard to breathe even with the window open. "Follow me." I told him to put his feet where I did, and then I was on the ledge, trying to dig my fingers into the rotten molding, usually soft enough to find a grip, but tonight, frozen and slippery. Ian kept grabbing for me, and I moved away from him, afraid he'd knock me loose.

"Wait," he said. "You're going too fast."

"Just do what I do," I said.

We crept toward the corner of the building where the decorative edging had been cut to look like stone—and the pattern created a series of handholds and footholds. As we descended, we passed several open windows, one of which was broken, the safety glass bulging in its frame. A single limp and disembodied arm had been wedged through the four-inch opening.

Purifying fire. This is what the Zeros preached. We'd all read Matthew 13—the parable of the weeds. We all knew that the Zeros used this—this single biblical chapter—as the foundation of their doctrine, their justification for the use of fire. In the parable, an enemy has sown weeds among a farmer's wheat, but Jesus tells the farmer to wait. He tells him not to remove the weeds, not to risk damaging the crop. It's only when everything has grown—when everything has been safely harvested—that the weeds must be bundled together and burned. This was, the Zeros said, the word of God. This was his truth.

As I climbed to the ground that night in La Pine, as I struggled to grip the side of the building with my shaking fingers, I felt the blaze intensify. Paint bubbled off the siding and smeared onto my pajamas. My palms burned. I jumped the last ten feet and lay still beside a fallen proctor. Whatever was happening, I knew it was better to blend in and disappear. A dead boy had the best chance, and I assumed that Ian would follow me, do what I did, like he had for the duration of our climb. But as soon as his feet touched the ground, he ran for the woods. I could have shouted for him to stop, but I didn't. I lay there on the grass watching his pajamas flapping, breath issuing from his mouth in clouds of condensation.

Someone shot him from a distance. He fell, and then a man with a red scarf around his neck, a man dressed in the garb of a citizen, stood over him and shot him in the head. Even in the flickering chaos of the flaming building, even through my partially closed eyes, I could see the man's composed, almost bored expression. His thick white hair was slicked back like a helmet. And then this man was walking toward me, feet crunching in the frosty grass. He was humming to himself, a little tune I didn't recognize. He stood there for what felt like a very long time. There were little metallic clicks as if he were checking his gun. It was probably no more than fifteen seconds, but it seemed interminable. I imagined I was dead. *I am grass. I am air*, I thought. But I was glowing with life, waiting for some treacherous limb to twitch, half wanting to stand up and fight. If it had to happen, if I had to be shot, then I wanted it to be done already. I wanted to be on the other side of the experience—away from the dying. *I am empty*, I thought, *I am empty*, and when the proctor beside me groaned, the man fired into him. I was the frost on the lawn. I was the night itself. I was nothing at all.

And so I was simultaneously lying in the grass and fighting my way through the hallways in the Exclusion Zone. There was a breath on the back of my neck, and even when I spilled out into a lighted room, I was blind. I was everywhere and nowhere, dimly aware of guards cheering behind some sort of wire cage. But I was fighting the men in red masks. I was fighting my way back into the burning building, racing up the corner of the dormitory and into the janitor's closet. My friends were all still alive and I could get to them. I was stronger than time, stronger than fact. I would open the walls, splinter the windows. This was a rescue mission, and my terror gave me the strength of two, and any person in my way was just a door to blow open. It was not until several guards pinned my arms and pushed me flat that I saw where I was. I saw the body I was fighting, the one that now lay very still. I saw the blue-inked tattoos, the shaggy hair, and then I saw my mistake.

PART TWO

THE SAFEST
PLACE TO BE

SIX

I don't clearly remember leaving the Exclusion Zone. Several guards subdued me even though I'd stopped fighting; one of them hit me hard on the side of the head. I do remember being carried outside through the night—I remember hearing Davis shout at someone, his voice tense and angry. At one point I opened my eyes and saw Tuck beside me, lying on a stretcher in some kind of triage facility. It was tiled like a shower. Machines loomed above me; a plastic bag dripped saline into my arm.

"They're both stable," a voice said. But when I opened my eyes again, Tuck was gone. A pile of blood-soaked bandages and cut-open clothes had been heaped onto the stretcher. A female nurse—a woman with short red hair and a bright blue stethoscope around her neck—leaned over me.

Time passed in fragmentary images. I faded in and out. Water stains like rust-colored flowers bloomed on the ceiling tiles overhead. The clock above the door had a broken hour hand that twitched as it pointed to the number 6. At one point, Ian sat on the end of my bed. He was still in his pajamas, telling me some story about how he'd covered the doorknobs with Vaseline. He left muddy footprints on the floor, and I worried I wouldn't be able to clean them before they were noticed.

When I finally came to, it was evening. I could smell the faintly salty, meaty stench of cafeteria food. My door was open, and Bethany stood beside me. At first I thought she was another hallucination, but her hand felt warm on my arm. "Wow," she said. "You look like a cobbler. I mean, your face does. Have you had cobbler? I think peach is best, but not made from canned fruit."

"What are you doing here?" I said. "Where am I?" But my mouth felt thick and the words ran together. She was wearing a white lab coat that was much too big for her. The sleeves were rolled and the name Dr. A. J. Cleveland was embroidered on the pocket in blue thread. Underneath the name was the image of a swan. She followed my gaze.

"This belongs to my dad," she said. "You know, they used to paint everything white in hospitals so patients thought the surfaces were clean, which, of course, was a fallacy. Lots of people died of infections." Her hair was loose and curly at the ends. She smelled vaguely of coconut. "Did you know," she continued, "neckties are the most dangerous part of a doctor's outfit? Nobody washes them. They're Petri dishes."

"How is it that you're here?" I said. "How long have I been out?"

"Almost a whole day. But don't worry. It's shift change and Dad's downstairs. He thinks I'm in the labs. I work here now," she said. "Sort of. I just started and I'm not technically supposed to interact with students. I'm more of an information custodian. Dad says he needs somebody he trusts, but I suspect he just wants to keep an eye on me." And then she stopped and pursed her lips. "I think I'm upset," she said. "I talk a lot when I get upset. You look really bad."

"Am I in the infirmary?" I looked around at the whitewashed walls, the little tubes and cords that were attached to my arm. "Where's Tuck?" I asked.

"Who?" she said.

"He was right here," I said. "I saw him."

She shook her head. "It's just us."

There was a snapping sound in the hallway and Bethany looked over her shoulder, freezing like a nervous rabbit. She was quite beautiful, I realized—her features were very delicate, and she wore some kind of pink lip gloss that sparkled.

"You need to leave," I said.

"I want to apologize," she said. "I'm usually a good liar, and I definitely would lie to keep you out of trouble, but I was wearing the matching barrette when they questioned me. I'm so sorry, but I had to warn you. It would be worse if you said you found it on the bus or got it from some boy."

"I would never say that."

"Really?" she said. "Why not? The penalty would be less."

"This is crazy," I said. "I can't be found with you."

"We'll need to be more careful"—she nodded—"in the future."

I searched for a button to summon a nurse. It was better to turn her in than be discovered. "What are you looking for?" she asked. "Don't move around." I tried to sit up. Pain shot through my left elbow and shoulder. I recoiled.

"I'm going to make it up to you," Bethany said. "I feel like it's all my fault." She lifted a handheld out of one of the voluminous pockets on her lab coat. She showed it to me and quickly put it away. Several of the components were different colors, as if they had been spliced together. "I'm not supposed to have one of my own," she said. "But I did have a very dull childhood. I think when you keep children indoors it makes them sneaky. If I ever have kids, which I definitely won't, I'll send them out in the yard as much as possible." She nodded as if to confirm this resolution.

"I don't want to scare you," she said, "or sound too crazy,

but I need you to know—I have planned the most amazing field trip for us. Only we should meet first. Get to know each other."

"We can't meet," I said. "And I don't go on—what did you call them?—*field trips.*"

"The real obstacle is your roommate," she said. "But I know you'll find a way to deal with him."

"That's insane," I said. "Where do you think we are?"

"Tell me you don't like me," she said. "And you never want to see me again."

"I shouldn't like you," I said. "And I shouldn't see you again."

"That's not the same."

I was waking up now, feeling each injury. I was also aware that I had a catheter, and there was a little bag of yellow urine hanging on the edge of my bed. I was wearing a backless robe.

"Believe me," I said. "If I thought it was possible to sneak out, I would."

"It is possible," she said. "I'll tell you a secret." And when I opened my mouth to cut her off, she said, "Just listen. I'm good with machines. It's not like an inflated sense of ability or something. I rebuilt that handheld from a scrap pile. I mean, what kind of idiots leave all their spare parts lying around, right? And I've been testing out commands using the passwords of ex-employees, because somebody never purged them. And I'll tell you another thing—half the people who work here are too lazy to change their default password. They're just typing in their ID number. How stupid is that?" She mistook my look of astonishment for an expression of contempt for Goodhouse security. "I know!" she said. "And Dad is all puffed about how impregnable this place is, and you wouldn't believe what I've been authorizing boys to do. I've been typing in all kinds

of crazy commands. I mean, if they knew." She started to giggle. "I guarantee you won't set off one of their alarms. All you
have to do is get to the south kitchen entrance without being
seen. Easy," she said. "Two a.m., next Sunday night. A week
from today." I just stared at her, unable to speak. "Is that a
yes?" she asked. She sat on the side of the bed and leaned toward me. She was so close I could see the fine hairs on her
cheek.

"If I get caught," I said, "they'll lock me in Confinement.
Do you know what happens to those boys?"

"Chicken," she said.

This shouldn't have bothered me, but it did.

"You don't understand," I said. "I can't. I won't."

"Chicken." She lowered her face to mine and hovered
there, then slowly pressed her lips against my cheek. I went
very still. I could feel a vibration of life inside her, the slight
stick of her lip gloss on my skin. It was all I could do to keep
my hands at my sides. "Chick, chick, chick," she whispered.
"I can make you happy. And happy is the safest place to be."

•

After the fire, I'd hidden inside one of the school vans. I'd
curled up on a bench seat and watched the arrival of the police,
the firemen, and the paramedics. Each man had a hat: a fire
hat, a police hat, a watchman's cap—even the paramedics had
matching baseball caps. I remember thinking that we were beyond hats, that they were some twentieth-century relic, but
when something needed to get done, everyone had a hat. Men
ran past me, their footsteps crunching on the gravel of the
parking lot. They covered the bodies on the lawn with tarps
and blankets. There was some problem with the water, and
firemen were shouting into their handhelds, hurrying in every
direction.

The Zeros were gone, or at least their hats, the red balaclavas, were gone. Later it became clear that many of them had still been on campus, wearing their official Goodhouse uniforms. Blending in, then disappearing, one by one. They'd infiltrated the school—as members of staff, as proctors and technicians. They'd been with us all along.

A policeman found me and a paramedic checked my lungs. They gave me something hot to drink and wrapped me in a thin metallic blanket, like the coatings they put on hot-water pipes. I was evacuated along with the other surviving students, all of whom were much younger and had been housed in a different part of campus. We were taken to the basement of a little church in Bend. Army cots had been set up, and the local police watched over us. They tried to comfort the smaller ones, who hadn't seen much but cried anyway. Bibles were placed strategically around the room, and I remember touching the yellow cover of one and leaving a gray smear of a fingerprint.

People gathered in the parking lot outside the church. The crowd was chanting something, but I couldn't make out the words. At first I could see their feet through the tiny basement windows, but then the church covered those with plywood and they played classical music loud enough to drown out sound.

It took a few days for our La Pine proctors to join us at the church. They all had to pass a security screening. Some had spent a night in jail despite their innocence, and all were angrier than we were, or at least more vocal. In the early-morning hours, when most of the younger boys were asleep, I'd creep into the hallway and listen to the proctors talk. They had lost friends. They knew the names of each Zero, the men who had lived with them, who'd had dinner with their families.

The school interviewed me, as did the police. They wanted to know why I was the only living member of my class. I had to offer them some explanation—but I was afraid to tell the truth—and so it was easier to credit the proctor, the one I'd lain next to on the grass. "We were friends," I said. And I'd felt free to grieve for this fictional connection, to become inconsolable as I described how he had saved me. I couldn't speak of my real friends. Thinking of them was a trap—a cage, a sort of blindness. And even if the school did not fully believe my explanation, they believed in my grief. They believed that, no matter what, I'd been truly punished.

I had no intention of meeting Bethany again. It had been disturbing to see her in the infirmary, to have her here in my world, within the walls. I tried to put her out of my mind, to focus on more important things. I had struck a class leader. I had beaten another boy senseless. There was something wrong with me, some weakness manifesting itself. Seeing Bethany was a reminder that I had to be more careful. She was a threat. Even if she thought she wasn't, I knew better. To imagine any future together was to invite wrong-thinking; it would be the beginning of some larger transgression. I had to forget about her. But I couldn't.

•

On my second day in the infirmary I awoke to an alarm. The overhead lights dimmed and the door to my room slammed closed.

"Campus is now on lockdown." A prerecorded message echoed throughout the building. "Please report to a secure area."

The top of my door had a glass window and I saw someone race past. The message repeated itself, and I rolled out of bed. I yanked the IV from my arm and wobbled over to bang on the door. It was firmly latched. I was trapped.

"Campus is now on lockdown," a woman's voice repeated.

I was looking for a tool, something I could use to beat at

the glass, feeling how bruised and sore my body really was, when a man in a tan nurse's uniform stepped into my room.

"Back in bed," he said. He had to shout to be heard over the alarm. "It's only a drill."

"What's going on?" I asked. We'd never had a drill before.

"Relax." The nurse held up his hands and gestured for me to calm down. The torn IV site had sprayed an arc of blood onto my infirmary gown. I probably looked wild. At least the catheter was gone.

"Boy, they weren't kidding when they said you were jumpy." The nurse smiled at me. "Haven't you ever heard of emergency preparedness?"

I got back in bed, but perched on the side of the mattress. And then, abruptly, the alarm ceased. A little chime sounded an all-clear and the lighting reverted to its normal greenish hue.

"See?" the nurse said. He pressed a thick gauze pad to my wound. "What did I tell you?" His tone was kind, and I glanced quickly at his face, wondering if I had misinterpreted something. His hair was freshly cut to regulation, his uniform a little too large for him—the fabric holding the shape of the pressed seams more than it folded to his contours. He was new.

He used his thumbprint to unlock a drawer. He removed a roll of surgical tape and secured the gauze pad.

"I'll have to put a new port in your forearm," he said.

"Okay," I said. He gestured for me to extend my right arm, and it took me a moment to comply. I was struggling to calm myself. In a place that prized control, to feel out of control was the worst feeling. I just wanted to know what had happened to me. But I couldn't ask directly. "I don't think," I said, and I had to clear my throat to get the words out. "I don't think the drug you gave me had any effect."

"I'm sorry?" he said. He swapped out my IV, opening a new port in my arm. The tiny flash of pain made me want to hit him, an impulse I easily curbed, but still, its intensity was startling.

"It wasn't you," I said. "Another nurse."

"What other nurse?" he said.

"The one who gave me the injection," I said. "For the Intensive."

"What are you talking about?" I waited for him to say that he'd never heard of that word—but he didn't. "When was this?" he asked.

I shrugged. I said, "I'm a little confused about time."

The nurse checked my IV bag to see if perhaps there was a tag on it, some specification. Then he brought out his handheld and tapped at the screen. I wasn't sure what I was hoping for. If the Intensive was in my record, it meant that Creighton and Davis were somehow acting within the confines of the school, which was confusing. But off-record meant it might all be a sham. It meant that maybe that needle had been full of nothing. No *Intensive*, just savagery. It only took a few seconds for the nurse to flip through my file. His eyes scanned text. The dull white glow of the screen reflected in the black of his pupils.

"There's nothing here about testing," the nurse said finally. "I'm going to step back your pain medication. I think you're confused."

"But I do remember somebody," I said.

"Opiates can affect cognition and memory," he said. "That's not unusual. The foggy feeling should clear up very soon. Then you can get up, access the wallscreen." The man peeled off his gloves, preparing to leave. "And when you're up," he said, "you'll need to log in for meditation and reflection." He walked across the room and activated the wallscreen. There was Tanner, speaking in a slow, sonorous voice. "A half hour is required today," the nurse said. "That's all."

In a moment, the nurse would be gone. He'd be replaced at the end of his shift by someone with more experience. "Wait," I said, my mouth dry as I issued the command. "Wait," I said again.

Soon he would not turn around when a boy spoke to him. He would learn, or he would be dismissed. "Do you think—" I started. It was hard to get the words out, to make them as loud as they had to be. "Can you find out where they took me two nights ago?" I asked. "I was led off campus. It's a building in the Exclusion Zone."

"Excuse me?" The nurse shifted his weight, uncomfortable now.

"It should be on my tracking chip for sure. But I need someone to check. I mean, how do they account for what happened to me? My class leaders authorized it. Some proctors know about it, too, the ones that work with my year. So I need your help. After I'm discharged, I won't know who to ask," I said. "Can you get word to a supervisor? Or someone in administration?"

The man flushed. His cheeks reddened. I was witnessing his education. "Now, wait just a minute," he said. "It's not my job to relay messages." And there was the look that all proctors had to some degree or another—resentment, the *job* being made more difficult. "I'm sure there's a protocol for grievances," he said.

"Not for this," I said. "I need your help."

He backed out of the room. "I'll find someone for you to talk to," he said.

But no one ever came.

•

Later that night, I logged my time on the wallscreen and then opened my personal page, typing in my name and password.

Each student had one of these pages. A photo of me, taken on my first day here, was in the top right corner. Beneath the photo was my location and my heartbeat, ticking along, broadcasting from my chip to the screen. Sometimes proctors stopped boys whose heartbeats were elevated, presuming they were up to something—and often they were. More than once I'd seen boys sitting with their personal pages open, breathing deeply, getting coached by a roommate or a friend on how to calm themselves. You were supposed to turn people in if you saw them doing this. They were planning on deception, which was wrong-thinking itself. Owen would have turned them in, but I never did. Seeing roommates together, planning something, reminded me of how lonely I was.

I clicked on my infraction page. I scrolled through the days until I hit Saturday. Immediately I saw my demerits from the bus accident, followed by the charge of theft, and then—a charge of predatory violence without provocation. Creighton was listed as the injured student. This was one of the worst violent infractions you could get. I clicked on the incident, but there were no further notes, only a Disciplinary Committee hearing, scheduled for Friday, June 7, ten days from now. I stared at the screen. In the space of a few hours I had dropped from a high Level 1 to a mid Level 2.

I went back to my page and clicked through the list of medical studies and Maintenance Intensives. These were the best way to work off demerits, but every study was full, with hopelessly long waitlists. I closed the page and looked down at my hands. I had red welts between my knuckles, broken blood vessels from the punches I'd thrown. At La Pine, where fighting was banned, we'd developed a way to fight that didn't leave a mark. It was the sort of thing that happens to an isolated group. It was like the palming here at Ione, just another adaptive language. At La Pine our fights were fought with our legs.

We were like kangaroos, or cartoon kangaroos, anyway, and every part of the body that was covered by clothing was a target. We developed special kicks, and they circulated like a fad through the school, the smaller boys imitating the older ones. Some had talent for it, a natural way of hiding their intentions until their foot was planted in your diaphragm. Just the way some were good at math or reading, some boys could really kick.

But hitting with the hands felt more personal. It felt taboo and strangely animal, almost as if I'd been digging in the dirt. I'd had no choice, I told myself. But I'd done real damage to another person, and perhaps this wouldn't have bothered me if he had been a competitor or a Zero. But it sickened me to think of my hands tearing into Tuck. He'd been motionless when the lights came on. His face had been slack.

No, that wasn't right. I was forcing myself to hold on to the remorse, the revulsion. These were my true feelings, but they flared and dimmed in a strange way. It was as if this memory were a distortion—something I didn't quite believe in, more like a dream than a concrete event. Perhaps I'd reached the limit of my emotional capacity. The school taught us to look for this, for this moment of deadening. But my memories of the Exclusion Zone just felt wrong. They were all duty and detachment. They didn't agitate the busy, anxious part of myself, didn't mix with the me that I knew. The memory of that night felt impersonal. And yet, who else had been there? There was no one else but me.

SEVEN

I was discharged after breakfast and given orders to return for a cortisone shot the following morning, and every morning for the next week. I wanted to stop by the dormitory and talk to Owen, but my clearances instructed me to report immediately to the factory. I ran most of the way there. Everybody had an AJT, or an Allotted Journey Time, after which the computer automatically generated demerits for tardiness. The lower your status, the shorter your AJT, and I was so worried about it, so stressed by the invisible clock, that I arrived at the factory shaking and out of breath, my arm out of its sling.

The smell of baking bread was intense. Several large tractor-trailers were just pulling out from subterranean loading bays, their engines downshifting as the big trucks crept up a steep ramp, carrying our products off campus. The front of the factory was bare. Dust caked the brick surface; lightning bolts of rust threaded through the metal handrails and staircases. All the improvements that the school was doing for the celebration, all the new paint, the resurfacing of the sidewalks—none of that was necessary here.

I took my usual route to the mixing rooms, following the south staircase to the second floor. The first wallscreen I passed stopped me. "James Goodhouse," it said, "please report to your supervisor's office."

That wasn't good. I tried to log on to my personal page, but the screen locked as I typed in my password. "Please report to your supervisor's office," it said. "Allotted Journey Time is still in effect."

"Shit," I said. I ran up the stairs to the offices on the third floor. Another wallscreen told me to wait, but there was no bench, no obvious place to sit, so I just stood there.

Even though the machinery was in a different part of the building, the drone of thousands of moving metal parts made the atmosphere buzz. A series of doors punctuated the wall to my right. All had a red light above them to indicate that I would not be admitted. To my left was a long bank of glass observation windows. They framed the shipping department one floor below. Men in orange jumpsuits and hairnets wheeled big stacks of trays into different areas. It was a shift of convicts, a common occurrence at the factory, where Mule Creek inmates often worked as a step toward their eventual rehabilitation. Now I looked at these men with renewed curiosity and a sense of unreality. A few nights ago, I'd had been among them.

At the end of the hallway, a line of exhibit cases displayed historic packaging for a variety of Goodhouse products. I walked over to examine them. I knew a little of the history. In the beginning, the Ione factory baked a lot of different breads, but only the cupcakes had sold. The public was uncomfortable buying staples from us, but they liked the idea of charity in the form of something harmless and sweet, almost like a Girl Scout cookie. Over time, the cupcakes became Swann Cakes—each wrapper emblazoned with a drawing of a happy swan carrying a picnic basket. The slogan read "Everything is better with chocolate." The Goodhouse logo was shrunk and moved to the back.

"James?" a voice behind me said. A man in the green uniform of a Goodhouse alum walked out of an office. He had large, unnaturally bright teeth. His name was Tim. He scowled at me now. We'd met only a few times before, but I knew that the other students disliked him—almost, it seemed, as much as he disliked us. "I see you're on light duty," he said. He stared pointedly at my arm, the one that was still out of its sling. I tucked it back in. "I'm sure you'll be recovering quickly," he said.

"Yes, sir."

"You make any trouble here and I won't hesitate to confine you," he said. "Got it?"

I nodded. The words *Predatory Violence* appeared at the top of my record now. Staff would be watching more closely.

Tim said he'd forgotten something in his office, and I turned toward the observation windows. An inmate stood in the middle of the room, staring up at me. His stillness caught my attention. Dozens of wheeled carts were on the move; boxes of bread were being prepped for shipment. But this man was like a ghost—arrested and staring. Just as I wondered if the glass was mirrored, if perhaps this was a coincidence, the man raised his arm to point at me. His mouth moved, but the words were lost.

"You ready?" Tim asked. I started at the sound of his voice. He marched me to the suiting-up room and then to the Quality Control area, a narrow, isolated space with two grain storage silos standing in the back. There was a small station where a boy perched on a metal stool in front of a conveyor belt. I'd heard that most of the production equipment had been scavenged from defunct bakeries, and here the machines had mottled exteriors, with numerous patches and replacement parts. A metal box with the words HOT ICING stenciled on the side looked like a long coffin on legs. The whole room was saturated with an earthy confectionery smell.

"You'll do the rest of your shift here," Tim said. He was shouting to be heard over the machinery. "You see an ugly cupcake, you put it on the tray. And don't reach past this point." He gestured to the place where the conveyor belt dove into the cooling tunnel, taking the cupcakes toward packaging. "In this section the machines are over a hundred and eighty years old," he said. "They eat hands, arms, whatever you feed them." He held up his own hand and showed me where he was missing the top of his right index finger. "You're replaceable," he said. "They're not." He asked me if I had any questions.

"Did that happen here?" I pointed to his finger.

"Not everything is better with chocolate," he said. He patted the hulking side of a cooling tube. Then he turned and left.

I watched him go. There were rumors that Tim had given his finger to the Zeros, that they'd captured him and performed some ritual—condensing the demons inside him into a single digit, then removing and burning it. Tim was also famously surly. But I thought I'd be bitter, too, if I'd ended up working here after graduation, treated as less than a proctor, forced to wear a chip and eat with the students. I'd rather go to a recycling platform or one of the shale mines in the Aleutian Islands.

I sat on the stool and inspected cupcakes as they emerged from the hot-icer. I felt increasingly sleepy, and soon all the cupcakes blurred together. Occasionally, I saw one that looked lopsided and I put it on the tray. Chocolate frosting left damp curls on my fingers, and it took all my willpower to clean up with the towel, to refrain from sampling anything. There was a camera aimed at my station. It would flag any suspicious movements; it would notice if I brought a hand to my mouth.

Hours passed and I felt dull and empty. I kept thinking about Tuck, examining and reexamining the memory of beating him, probing it for some feeling, some remorse. I was waiting to recognize myself. The blast of a horn announced a problem down the line and the machinery quieted. The hot-icer hissed and fumed.

"Turn around slowly," a voice said. In a second I was on my feet and pivoting toward the sound. Standing between two metal storage silos was a solitary figure in an orange jumpsuit. He stood with his feet slightly apart, as if he were ready to fight. The words MULE CREEK CORRECTIONS were written across his chest.

"Just stay where you are," the man said. Underneath the white cloud of the hairnet, I saw thick, wavy black hair. There were little pockmarks on his cheeks, something that gave him a mottled, scarred appearance.

"Don't do anything stupid," he said. "Don't try and call anyone."

He studied the camera and I followed his gaze. He couldn't get close to me without being filmed.

"What do you want?" I asked. I slipped my arm out of the sling.

"You're the one who got Tuck," he said. "Isn't that right?"

"How is he?" I asked.

But the man just nodded as if I'd confirmed something. "Showing your face today was incredibly stupid," he said. "Tuck's people are looking for you."

"Can you get him a message?" I asked.

"Are you listening to me?" the man said. "They're going to find you."

"It was an accident," I said. "It was dark."

The man seemed like he was about to say something, but he hesitated, as if reconsidering. "My name is Montero," he said, "and right now, I'm your only friend in Mule Creek. You want protection?"

I looked around. "Do I need it?"

"I'll keep his people off you, but it's got to be in exchange for something."

I frowned. "If Tuck's people knew how to find me," I said, "they'd have done it already."

"They'll figure it out," Montero said. "I did. And now they're motivated." Sweat prickled in my hairline. My jumpsuit felt like a humid plastic bag. "They know where you work," he added.

The hot-icing machine hissed, and the smell of molten sugar and chocolate was thick in the air. I didn't like this man's civilian confidence, the way he stood with his chin jutting forward. I stared at the little metal rungs welded onto the sides of the grain silos. The rungs formed a ladder. There was a catwalk overhead, running between them and extending out of sight. I realized that this was how he must have gotten in. "What do you want?" I asked.

"Here," Montero said. He slid something across the floor. It collided with the toe of my shoe. It appeared to be a shallow white box, no more than an inch and a half in width and a quarter-inch in depth.

"What is it?" I said. "What's inside?"

"It's not a present," Montero said. "It's a print reader."

I recognized it now. Proctors opened doors with their fingerprints. In the newer buildings these devices were built into the handles and push plates, but in the older, retrofitted buildings, print readers like these were surface-mounted.

"Go on," he said, "pick it up."

I lifted my heel and stepped on the box, not hard enough to break it, but enough to threaten. "What is the Exclusion Zone?" I asked.

"Do not fuck with me," Montero said.

"I'm not sure I need your protection," I said. "But if you

want me to listen"—I shifted my weight onto the box—"answer my question."

He glanced at the door. The machinery made some sort of groaning noise, followed by a hydraulic sigh. "That device is worth more than you are," Montero said. "You break it and I'll slit your throat."

I lifted my heel slightly. "What is the Exclusion Zone?" I repeated. "Is it a punishment?"

Montero smiled, but it looked more like a baring of teeth. "It's a job," he said. "That's all. It's money."

"But that doesn't make sense," I said. "Why would they pay you to fight?"

"My turn," Montero said. "Move your foot." I did, and he rattled off instructions on how the box worked, how it could act like a reader but would capture the print of whoever touched its surface. He repeatedly asked me if I understood, but he didn't wait for a response. He was in a hurry.

"I haven't agreed to help you," I reminded him.

"I want you to capture fingerprints," he said. "For sure, I need whoever brought you through the fence. Maybe one of your officers?"

"Class leaders," I corrected.

"Good," he said. "You have two weeks."

"But why do you want a Goodhouse print?" I asked. "It's useless at Mule Creek."

A terrific clanging noise split the air. The warning bell announced that the line was about to resume. "Get me that print," he said. "And then maybe you'll find out."

The machines started up again. I glanced away and—in that moment—Montero seemed to disappear. For the rest of the shift I stayed vigilant, one eye on the production line and another scanning the periphery of my vision. I thought about the man I'd seen on the shipping floor, the man pointing up at me. A few times I was sure there was someone on the catwalk, but whenever I turned to look, I found myself alone. I was also very aware of the print reader, of the way it gleamed on the cement floor—glossy and white, like a little cube of ice. A few days ago I would have reported Montero, handed over this device. But now I wasn't sure what to do. I had to consider my situation. The reader would be worth something, and I suspected that if I'd had anything to bribe Davis with on Saturday, I might not be here at all.

At the end of my shift I took a chance and retrieved it. The moment I folded it into my palm, I felt a surge of joy. This was the kind of equipment that proctors used, the sort of device that characterized the adult and civilian world. And I was holding it in my hand. I possessed it. But even as I pulled at a loose thread on my cuff, even as I slipped the reader into the seam, I knew that this impulse was a bad one—that this would be like the barrette, the sort of infraction that only led to more trouble. I told myself that I would just keep it for a few days—I would keep it and then I'd let it go.

Tim was waiting for me at the end of my shift. He stood just outside the door to the Quality Control room. "James," he said, "everything go all right in there?"

My hand reflexively curled around the cuff of my shirt. I was carrying contraband and I'd just been threatened by a Mule Creek inmate, one who'd appeared and disappeared at will, promising to kill me if I didn't cooperate. "It was fine," I said. "Not a problem, sir."

"An easy assignment," Tim said, "gives you lots of time to reflect."

I nodded, unsure what he meant by this. He was staring at me, looking intently, as if he could sense some transgression. "And did you?" he asked. "Did you reflect?"

"Yes, sir," I said.

His hand rested on his Lewiston Volt, on the red taser strapped to his hip. "You boys," he said. "You memorize the handbook, anticipate the right answer. But none of it," he said, "goes any further."

•

I had ten minutes to get back to my dormitory. I walked quickly, keeping my head down. Every hundred feet or so, I passed a tall metal pole supporting either a bank of lights, a cluster of speakers, or both. Groups of lower-school boys were gathered around each pole—some boys stood on ladders; all had sanding blocks or plastic scrapers. They were chipping away at loose paint, trying to prepare the surface for a new coat.

The sun was setting. The sky was shot through with the sorts of colors that reminded me of Bethany's living room and the dresses that the women wore—pinks, dandelion yellows, and silvery blues. Barn swallows rocketed across the sky, hunting bugs, performing aerial loops. Sometimes they moved independently or in a row like a long, undulating ribbon of birds. They switched from chaos to order and back again, their black silhouettes popping out of the horizon and then disappearing into it.

I passed Vargas with its imposing towers, and then the pavilion, which still had the look of a turkey carcass, the roof now partly lowered into place. Two civilian workers in orange hardhats had the building plans spread over the nose of a T-4. They were deeply engrossed in discussion, oblivious to the work details moving past them—dozens of boys loading small but heavy-looking boxes into the cavernous bay of a tractor-trailer. I approached the residential section—long, squat dormitories built on a grid, row after row. As I walked between the buildings, I felt the warmth radiating from each one. Sun had soaked into the concrete all day, and now, when the temperature dropped, the walls gave off heat as if the buildings themselves were alive.

I rounded the corner, hurrying toward North Dormitory 8, but I slowed at the sight of Creighton and Davis standing on the building's staircase, waiting. A T-4 with two proctors was parked nearby, watching us. There was a bumper sticker on the cart that read I WAS MADE FROM RECYCLED MARITIME PLASTIC!

I walked closer, not slowing my pace. There were no windows at the front of the dormitory, but boys were crowded in the open doorway, watching, anticipating. I acted like I didn't notice, a strategy that became harder when Creighton and Davis stood directly in front of me at the base of the stairs. Creighton's blond eyebrows glowed strangely in the twilight. He still favored his good leg, keeping his weight off the one I'd kicked. Davis was eating a green apple. It had a civilian grocery store sticker on the side, so it must have come from an employee. It was a small detail, but the sticker was a display of power.

"Little bird brought me some news," Davis said.

I took a step forward and tried to pass, but Creighton shoved me back.

"Asshole," I said, and then I clamped my mouth shut. I hadn't meant to speak aloud.

Davis smiled. "This one's getting quite the mouth on him," he said.

"What do you want?" I stood there, staring past them to the front door. I probably had less than a minute on my AJT.

Creighton pinched my face in one of his meaty hands and yanked my head down so that I looked directly at him. "That's better," he said. "We want to look at that pretty face of yours." I assumed he was talking about the bruises, which were, a few days after the fact, especially gruesome. "I'm going to take you all the way to the bottom," he said. "Whenever you fuck up, I'm going to know about it. You understand?"

I nodded.

"So, what happened in there?" Davis asked. He stepped closer, keeping his voice low. "I lost money on you."

"Good," I said.

He lunged, lightning quick, and punched me in the ribs. It was the exact spot that I'd bruised. I staggered backward and bent over slightly, trying to breathe against the pain.

"Arms folded," the proctor said. He sat in the T-4, one foot on the dash. I folded my arms.

"Before you get any big ideas," Davis said, "before you get all talkative, just remember we're happy to put you in a cage and leave you there." His watch beeped. "Look at that." He smiled. "One demerit."

"I'll report you both," I said. I raised my voice. If they wanted privacy, I wasn't going to give it to them. "Whatever that place is, it's not part of the school. It's illegal."

"Take your predatory and consider yourself lucky," Creighton said.

"You can't shut me up," I said, though I wasn't exactly confident. My ribs felt like they were grinding together. I just wanted to crawl into bed. "I'm going to have a lot to say at my hearing."

"You do that," Davis said. "Everybody knows you tell the best stories." And then he slapped me, open-handed, across the cheek. The force of the blow spun me to the side. My ear rang and I tasted blood in my mouth. One of the proctors got out of the T-4 and stood nearby, in case he was needed. "Arms folded," he said.

Davis flexed the hand he'd hit me with. A slight ghosting

of chapped skin decorated his brown knuckles. I assumed he was enjoying himself, but when I glanced up, his expression was thoughtful. "You think *we* did this to you?" He shook his head and gestured between us. "You and me," he said, "we're brothers. We're the same. You did this to yourself."

Owen pushed his way through the crowd in the doorway. I saw him emerge and then jog partway down the stairs. We hadn't seen each other since Community Day. He stopped at the sight of me, momentarily startled by the bruising on my face, by the sight of my arm in a sling.

"Let him inside," he said. "I have to share that demerit."

"Your boy owes us money," Davis said.

"For what?" Owen asked, but he was looking at me. "What did you do?"

"Three hundred credits," Davis said. "That should cover it." The crowd in the doorway murmured. Not many of us had that kind of cash.

"He's not my boy," said Owen.

Davis's watch beeped again. "Oh, look at that," he said. "Another minute late."

"AJT can be such a bitch," Creighton said.

"I'm warning you," said Owen.

"Then pay the fuck up. Now it's four."

"Fine," said Owen. He was, easily, the richest boy in the school. And of course Creighton and Davis knew that. They stood aside to let me run up the stairs.

Most of the other boys stepped back when I entered, giving me space. But Harper stopped me. "You going to let him slap you like a little bitch?" he said.

"Shut up," I said.

"You've got to fight him," Harper said.

"Lead the class," called another boy in the crowd. "Or suck some ass."

The students in the common room were gradually returning to the plastic chairs and benches, all of which were bolted to the wall. For some reason they liked to sit on the backs of the chairs—their feet planted on the seat itself—all in a row, like roosting pigeons.

"Four hundred credits?" Harper said. "I wouldn't spend that on you. I'd take him down instead."

"You would not," said Runt. "No way. Don't say stupid shit." The heels of Runt's shoes had worn through the cuff of his too-long uniform pants, creating dusty, ragged half moons at the back.

"I'd do it for two hundred credits," another boy said, and immediately there was speculation on his chances. But I knew none of them would risk it. This was a Level 1 and 2 dorm. They all had their status to think of.

When I got to our room, I immediately pulled the print reader out of the seam in my shirt and jammed it under my mattress. I collapsed into bed a little too carelessly, and was rewarded with a jolt of pain. My side ached, and I felt disturbed by something. Davis had known exactly where I was injured. This probably meant that he'd read my medical file. And this made me feel hopeless. I closed my eyes and listened to the wheeze of the inadequate air-conditioning system.

Every dormitory in Ione was laid out the same way—a common room at one end, a bathroom, and a series of bedrooms all opening onto a central hallway. Every room had two beds, two built-in desks, and a screen embedded in the wall. Even with all the sameness, the rooms on the south side of the building were significantly more desirable. They got sun during the day, while the north-facing rooms were perpetually dark. Some rooms had peeling floor tiles or water damage, so they could vary, even on the south side. But because of

Owen's credits, we had the nicest room in Dormitory 8. This wasn't saying much, but I did appreciate it. Depending on the time of day, a yellow square of sunlight would fall upon the floor. It always looked to me like a portal, an escape— some shining end. I looked forward to waking in the morning and seeing the square of light. It began to seem alive, like a pet. Of course, sunshine was everywhere outside; it was becoming oppressive as the season got hotter. Yet when it came through the window, it was friendly—a visitor, all spirit and no body.

But mostly our room was superior because Owen was allowed to keep some of his projects on hand. Each student had a trunk for storage, and Owen had painted his like a galaxy, swirled with stars, planets, and comets. Usually it cost thirty-five credits to have Owen paint your trunk, but now that he was working so intently on the Founders' Day mural, he'd stopped most of his commissions. Above his desk hung a large quarter-scale mock-up of the mural. It showed our six founders in a brightly lit classroom, sun streaming through a bank of windows. Young, adoring children sat cross-legged at their feet. Many nights Owen stayed up late with a flash-light, laboring over the canvas, painting in shadows and then removing them.

When Owen returned to our room, he walked directly to his work area and selected a white stick of chalk. He knelt and drew a pale, shaky line down the middle of the room, dividing the floor space between our two beds. "When I am on this side of the line," he said, "you don't see me. You don't talk to me. We're not in the same room."

"I don't think it's working," I said.

"What?" he asked.

"I can still see you." I sat up and looked at him. "And I can hear you. We're having a conversation."

His face flushed red. His brown birthmark looked like a smudge on his cheek. "I just paid your debt," he said.

"I don't owe Davis anything," I said. "And don't pretend you spent that money for me."

Owen went to the wallscreen and brought up his personal page—where my demerits were also displayed, since he owned them now as well. The two AJT citations topped a long list. Owen's heart rate ticked rapidly under his picture. He was probably hoping I would do something really terrible and land in Protective Confinement. That was a good way to lose your roommate.

"You reported me," I said.

"You stole from civilians," he said. "Let's start there. What's wrong with you? Didn't I warn you not to touch anything?" Owen kept scrolling over the demerits, inspecting each one.

"Can you only see half the wallscreen?" I asked. "You know, with the chalk line and all—do you need me to tell you what it says on my half?"

"You were so obvious," he said. "I had to report you, or somebody else would have."

"Yeah," I said. "It would've been a shame to let someone else get all the credit."

"I don't blame you for being mad," Owen said. "But it's your own fault."

Outside, a T-4 whirred past and a proctor shouted for somebody to hurry up. The air conditioner turned the dusty, dry smell of Ione into a musty odor that reminded me of rainy springs and rotting pine duff. Suddenly I saw my personal page flash on the screen. I stood up. "What are you doing?" I asked. "How do you know my password?" But I didn't react fast enough.

Before I could stop him, Owen had scrolled down the page

and registered me for a month of extra work detail. "You're going to make this right," he said.

"Delete those," I said. "You little shit." I crossed the room and tried to erase them myself, but the computer wouldn't allow this. A message appeared in my in-box congratulating me on my successful registration.

Owen backed away, expecting some kind of physical retaliation. "You owe me," he said. He stumbled against one of the beds and then stepped behind it. I was a little taken aback by how genuinely afraid of me he seemed. "Four hundred credits," he said. "And I've spent most of the rest on applications. I'm out of money. I can't go to college as a Level 3. You fucking owe me."

"You handed me to Creighton and Davis."

"I told you not to touch anything," he said. "I told you."

He was on the other side of the room now, as far away as he could get in such a small space. I took a deep breath and tried to control my anger. I realized that I knew his password, too. I'd seen him type it in dozens of times. I'd learned it without even meaning to. In less than two seconds I'd opened his personal page and found his work detail registration. He tried to knock my hand away as I typed in his name, but I was ready for him. I was nearly six inches taller and my reach was longer.

"Stop," he said. "Just stop."

"We'll make it right together," I said. "It'll be a field trip." I was quoting Bethany.

I clicked Accept, and it was somewhat mollifying to watch Owen try to delete his own name.

"You didn't really have empathy for me until now, did you?" I asked. "See, I'm helping you. Roommates have to instruct each other."

"You asshole," he said.

"Work on your outlook," I said.

Owen was still touching the screen, scrolling through various options, trying unsuccessfully to transfer his name elsewhere. He was mouthing a word, not giving it enough breath to say it aloud. It looked like he was saying, *Shit, shit, shit.*

No one from La Pine would have turned me over to our class leaders. No one would have put my name in a work detail. They were my people. They were my family, and I felt them at my back now. I didn't belong here.

"It's the Zeros, right?" Owen said. "You saw them again and now you're breaking down."

"That's not it," I said.

"You leave the school for a few hours and you generate a ton of demerits and two AJT citations? Just like that?"

I didn't know what to say. Something *was* wrong with me. I walked over to my bed and lay down on top of the covers. "You aren't depressed, are you?" He sounded hopeful. "You could report yourself. You might get a doctor to say you weren't mentally sound on Community Day."

"I'm not reporting myself," I said.

"You have to let the Zeros motivate you in a positive way," Owen suggested. He spoke as if this was rehearsed. "I've been thinking about it a lot. I was on that bus, too, right? A lot of us were, and I've been doing double meditation and it's been totally helping."

"Good," I said. "Then you won't mind logging on and doing my meditation, too."

"It's not a bad thing that happened on the bus," he said. "It's just a reminder that we have to be careful with our status. We have to be grateful for what we have. No one was killed, right? It was just the Zeros letting off steam. That's always good—if no one gets hurt. They feel like they made a statement, and we were scared but mostly okay, and now we're more aware of how important our choices are in the next year. It's"—he stuttered—"it's good, really."

"No, Owen," I said. "It's not good."

"You have to handle it," he said.

"I am handling it." I sat up. "Look, something happened to me the other night. What do you know about the Exclusion Zone?"

"It's off campus," he said. "Off-limits."

"Davis took me to some building," I said. "He gave me a drug, too. I don't know if it was just to make me sick or scare me. But there's a basement where all the convicts fight each other." Even as I said the words, they felt false, too fantastic. "And the Mule Creek guards bet money," I said. I saw the disappointment in Owen's expression. He thought I was lying.

"You asshole," he said.

"You've been here longer than I have. You must have heard rumors, some kind of talk."

"I'm trying to help you. And you're deflecting," he said. This was what the school called it when you held other people responsible for your own wrong-thinking.

"This is real," I said. "I promise you."

"Oh, I believe you," he said. "My spectacularly sane roommate who just last week woke up screaming, 'Lie down or I'll kill you.' I believe everything he tells me."

"I didn't say that," I said.

"You don't remember saying that," Owen corrected. He leaned over to his trunk and pulled out a small cardboard box of crackers. He also had a bar of chocolate with the words *Swann Industries* printed in silver-on-blue paper. When he was agitated, he ate like a squirrel—sitting at his desk, taking small bites of cracker and chocolate, clutching his food in two hands. "No, I don't want to know what happened, James," he said. "I'm not your *buddy*," he added, as if the word tasted sour in his mouth. "I'm not going to ask you personal questions. You aren't part of my future, and that's all I care about."

I stared at the ceiling. The overhead light was a long fluorescent bulb in a wire cage. It looked like some sort of mythical glowing wand. I thought of La Pine and the brutal power of the fire itself—the way it had grown out of the windows and doorways in long columns of flame. And then I revised this memory. I saw the flames rising from the palms of my own hands, saw my fingers holding the flare of a match.

"Why didn't you ever ask me what happened at La Pine?" I said. "Aren't you curious?"

This was clearly not what Owen expected to hear, because he glanced up from his tiny chocolate meal.

"Well," he said after a moment, "what happened?"

"You wouldn't believe me," I said.

Owen nodded to himself. "Just being a dick, then."

"You're no better than the rest of us," I said. "If you think some art program is going to make you normal, you're more unbalanced than I am."

"I *am* better than the rest of you," Owen said. "If I don't think so, who will? And if you had any brains, you'd do something with your training."

"What training? I sang in a choir. Tanner and the rest of them couldn't care less about that."

"We can do something that other people can't—not even civilians. Why don't you take advantage of it? You're supposed to be really good. So: write a song to sing at the ceremony. Why do you think they're building the pavilion? They want to showcase us, to show off the really bright ones. Put a good face on Goodhouse. If you had any sense, you'd organize something, make people notice."

"All I do is make people notice," I said.

"Then stop being a fuckup," he said. He paused. "So, did you do it? Did you help burn down your school?"

"No," I said. "Of course not." I turned to the wall and pulled my blanket over my shoulder. I closed my eyes and let the darkness reach out and flatten over me. "Why would anyone think that's even possible?"

EIGHT

That night, just before ten, Tanner appeared again on our wallscreens—this time to give a speech about Founders' Day and how we were preparing to have the "eyes of the nation upon us during this very special time." He'd obviously taken pains with his appearance. The impressions of a comb were still visible in his thin, wet hair, and he'd spread some kind of orangey makeup under his eyes.

I lay in bed. My elbow throbbed. My body was tired but my mind was clenched and alert. I hated that we couldn't turn off the screens during official announcements. The volume was always high, and there was sometimes a delay between rooms, so the sound was discordant, filling the dormitory alternately with words and gibberish.

"I am personally asking you to be on your best behavior," Tanner said, "to let the world see what important work we are doing here. You are part of a great tradition, a promise kept. Let yourselves shine as an example to every nation. I am counting on you. God bless." He kept glancing offscreen as he spoke. I overheard the boys next door calling him a talking turd.

After lights-out, Owen clicked on a flashlight and tinkered with the abstract for the mural. Usually he labored over the faces and expressions of the founders, checking his work against old photographs. But tonight he took orange paint and drew what appeared to be a tiger lolling on the floor of the classroom, tucked in among the children. Its green eyes were like my own.

"I don't think that's strictly accurate," I said, leaning on my good elbow and peering through the flashlit dark.

"Leave me alone," Owen said.

I waited until he was asleep, until his breathing deepened into a snore, and then I reached under the mattress and pulled out the device Montero had given me. It was designed to slip over the front of an actual print reader. It was just a few millimeters wider, and it would be hard to distinguish from the real thing once it was in place. I felt a kind of awe just holding it in my hand, something so small and powerful—contraband under my control. And yet this moment was undercut by worry, a nagging disquiet. I thought I knew why Montero wanted a Goodhouse print. When I'd first arrived at Ione, there'd been a breakout attempt at Mule Creek. I assumed that he wanted a point for some similar reason. If Montero could find me in Quality Control, he could probably find an exit.

I sensed, then, that I should go to someone, that this was bigger than I'd first imagined. But it was too late. There was no way to explain my delay, no way to justify another theft. And besides, I didn't regret it—not really, not enough. I tugged my blanket over my head and pressed my thumb to the screen. The front panel lit up when it was touched. I relished the way this little slip of plastic was mine, the way I felt when I managed to capture my own print and I saw for the first time that green phosphorescent swirl, a shape that belonged to no one else.

The next day I went to talk to Tim about transferring my shift. He sat on the other side of his desk, clearly distracted. He used the stump of his finger to tap on his handheld. I was thinking that the problem was with the Quality Control room. It obviously wasn't secure—too isolated and remote. I explained that I'd be happy to work nights, any shift he wanted, but that I didn't want to go back. He cut me off. "I'm sorry you aren't enjoying yourself, James, but you do realize, that doesn't concern me."

"Yes," I said.

"Yes, sir," he corrected. "Just because I used to be one of you doesn't mean you can disrespect me."

•

I ended up stuffing the print reader into one of the rejected cupcakes, jamming it all the way down so that the chocolate cake closed over the top. The longer I had contraband in my possession, the more likely I was to get caught. I spent several miserable shifts staring over my shoulder, watching the cat-walk overhead, scrutinizing every shadow at the base of the grain silos. And then Tim transferred me back into the mix-ing rooms, with their long sight lines and brightly lit worksta-tions. I was sure I'd be safe there.

I thought things were starting to normalize. Owen and I were falling back into our routine. My elbow healed quickly, and I went every morning to the infirmary for the shot. I didn't see Bethany. And this was a good thing. I'd been thinking about her too much, thinking about Sunday, about meeting her in person. Temptation was overwhelming my judgment. When I walked through the infirmary, I searched for her; I told myself that I was trying to avoid her, but that was a lie, another self-deception. I didn't know what to do. To contemplate the problem was to magnify it, and so I felt relief each time I left the building to rejoin my routine—safe for another day.

And then something surprising happened. Owen got a de-merit. At dinner on Friday, some Level 2 kid shoved him from behind as we waited in the cafeteria line. The shove might have been accidental, but Owen turned and hit him in the face with his empty tray. It wasn't much in the way of a fight, but Creighton was nearby, ready to make something out of it. I was standing beside Owen when it happened, and I watched with openmouthed surprise.

"Good work," I mumbled.

"Shut it," Owen said. His face was a mask of disproportionate fury. He was obviously as shocked as I was. Though, honestly, it was not completely unexpected. When you lost status, you could fall precipitously. Perhaps you were treated differently and so you became different. It was hard to know where it started or where it would end.

It turned out that Owen's demerit was the one that dropped us both into Level 3. The school didn't let the high-status students mix with anyone lower. We were flagged for a dorm transfer.

The next morning—one week after Community Day—we packed our things and trudged in silence to West Dormitory 35. Proctors in a T-4 brought Owen's art supplies. The school still needed him to finish the mural in the pavilion, so nothing was confiscated. The proctor was even apologetic, saying he was a big fan of Owen's work. He helped us carry in a roll of brown butcher paper that Owen used for sketches, and then the man pulled out a picture of his girlfriend. "Her name is Denise," he said, and blushed faintly, his neck pinking above his black collar. "I'd appreciate it," he said, "if you could do a small canvas. I'll bring anything you need. It's for her birthday next month."

This was the sort of flattery that usually fed Owen's ego. But now he just gave the proctor a dull nod and looked around at our shabby, north-facing room. The window glass had a thick layer of dust. There was a scorch mark on the floor, and the wallscreen had what looked like a profusion of cocks and balls scratched into the plastic.

The proctor left, and I said, "Should I clean the window or are you going to upgrade?"

Owen sat on his bunk and stared at the pile of stuff that needed to be put away. I already knew he wouldn't spend the money.

"I don't know what happened," he said.

"I'm just glad it wasn't me," I said.

"You're a fucking idiot," he said. "And now I am, too."

·

On Sunday morning I saw Bethany. She was standing inside one of the glassed-in cubicles where the infirmary's technical staff worked. The recognition sent a little jolt of adrenaline into my chest. She was deep in conversation with a nurse, a man who was leaning over her, laughing at something she'd said. For many days, I'd been preparing for this moment, imagining it, but when she finally did look up—when her gaze skipped in my direction—she didn't stop talking, didn't give any indication that she saw more than a uniform moving toward her, and then away.

She had changed her mind. Of course she had. I pretended to feel relief, but this was another deception. I found myself obsessing over the nurse, the man who had commanded all of her attention. Whenever I lined up for a meal or waited for a clearance, I considered all the things that he didn't do—didn't have to do.

Bethany had promised that regardless of where I went on campus between the hours of 12:45 and 4:15 a.m. that night, my official activity log would list me as inside the dormitory. If I didn't return in time, the program she used to override my chip protocol would expire and the school's computer would sense a discrepancy. The alarm would sound. But if she had changed her mind, if she never initiated the program, the alarm would sound the moment I stepped outside. Then I would have my answer. I would know for sure.

And so, around midnight, when my new dormitory settled into the deeper quiet of true sleep, I crept to the common area and sat on one of the benches. Two long horizontal windows bracketed the room. They'd been placed high in the wall, meant to provide light without a view. Still, part of a crescent moon was visible. As I waited on the bench, I watched the moon slip slowly out of sight. At different intervals I heard boys in the hallway, walking to and from the bathrooms with soft, measured footsteps.

Minutes and hours accumulated on the wallscreen clock, and then it was time. I stood up and stepped to the front door. I told myself it didn't matter either way, and yet I wanted to know. I'm not sure how long I waited there, trying to summon the courage to test my theory—my hand raised, almost touching the front of the door. I was caught in some vortex, pulled forward but held in place, unable to break my training but unwilling to return to my room. My heartbeat accelerated, leaving evidence of wrong-thinking in my file—joining the hundreds of student heartbeats that were currently flowing into the Goodhouse servers. Sometimes I imagined that this was what powered the school, that we ourselves fueled the lights, the Lewistons, the fence. And I was sure that in my own pulse, I heard the stuttering sound of all of us—a hammering consistency, a steady knock like a fist against a wall.

I stood for a long time, connected but alone. Then I returned to the room. Owen sat up the moment I walked past him. "Where were you?" he asked. And then: "Did you have a dream?"

I looked at my narrow bed—at the Goodhouse logo stamped on the thin felt blanket. "Yeah," I finally said, "that was it."

•

On Monday I arrived at the infirmary for my final cortisone shot. I checked in at the appointment desk, touching my hand to its glass surface. The desk scanned my chip and a voice told me where to go. "Please stay in your green-lit area," the voice said.

It was then that I saw someone I recognized, someone I didn't remember until she was in front of me. It was the nurse who'd worked on Tuck, the one who'd helped me after the Exclusion Zone. She had the same bright blue stethoscope draped around her neck, her red hair visible from a distance. "Excuse me," I called, but she was at the end of a hallway, moving out of sight. I hurried past my exam room, followed her around a corner and into a hall jammed with boys reporting to some medical study. They wore white gowns, their thin legs sticking out of the bottom, shoes but no socks. Some were sitting on long benches; others stood in clusters, trying to keep the hallway clear. The boys had obviously been waiting a long time, because the proctors were having difficulty getting them to settle. Several were palming. All were shuffling and restless. A cart full of little paper pill cups, each with a single blue pill, was parked nearby. It looked like a grouping of miniature birds' nests, the homes of paper robins.

I strained to locate the nurse, craning my neck to see over the crowd. Several posters encouraged us to eat right. One featured a talking carrot and the other a jolly cabbage. The sound of rubber soles on polished linoleum was a kind of squeaking, giggling symphony. I looked left and right. I'd been only a few seconds behind her. She was here. I knew it. And then I saw something that made my stomach clench.

A thing isn't real until other people can see it. A person doesn't necessarily exist until you've laid a hand on solid bone and flesh. And so when I saw a man with a head of thick white hair—a man who moved with the lazy fluidity of youth, despite his age—I had to make sure it was not my imagination. The squeaking symphony of shoes on linoleum became a loud buzz. The man was getting closer, or more precisely, I was walking toward him, feeling increasingly certain that the last time we'd met, he'd stood over me with a gun. He'd been silhouetted by fire, wondering whom to shoot. And here he was, wearing the white lab coat of a doctor, talking with some boy, hiding himself in the mundane world of this hallway.

An alarm shrieked, and for a few seconds I thought it was just some internal bell, the natural acceleration of the buzzing sound that was inside me. But it was the result of me stepping out of my allotted area.

"Don't move," a proctor called.

And another said, "Where are you supposed to be?"

They were converging on me, and I was standing in front of the man with white hair. We were the same height. I'd always thought he was taller, but then, I had been lying down, pretending to be dead.

"Can I help you?" The man smiled, and I experienced a moment of sickening recognition. I knew that lopsided smile. I'd seen it on another person's face. I didn't need to glance at his name to know that he was Bethany's father. Up close, I saw the resemblance, the prominent jaw and the luminous blue eyes.

"Are you okay, son?" The doctor checked his handheld and said, "Are you part of this study?"

Several of the proctors were saying my name, saying it was time to go or I would receive another demerit. "James," they said. "James." But none of them knew me. They were just reading my name off their machines. The doctor held up his hand to silence them.

"You," I said.

"Ah." The doctor smiled. "We got a word out of him. I think he'll recover." He told the proctors he'd walk me back to Room 5; then he put a hand on my shoulder, though staff weren't supposed to touch us unnecessarily. I was so close I could see the quiver of a small vein in his forehead. There were deep smile lines around his eyes and mouth. He was a happy man, and this bothered me.

"I know you," I said, which was perhaps not the wisest thing.

"Yes," said the doctor. "I recognize you now." He glanced over his shoulder. "This is very lucky. I've been meaning to speak with you. My daughter seems to feel you've been unfairly accused. She said that barrette was a gift." He said the word *gift* as if we both knew there was no such thing. "I'm afraid she can exaggerate."

I thought about my nights here in the infirmary and how he must have been walking around while I slept.

"You are the James who visited my family?" he asked. "Or do I have you mixed up?"

"I didn't mean to take the barrette," I said. "It was an accident."

"I don't believe in those," said the doctor. We arrived at Room 5 and I stepped through the door, surprised that he followed. "I'll just wait with you," he said, "if you don't mind."

I couldn't stop staring at him, at the way he performed all the ordinary functions of a living being. His eyes blinked; his chest rose and fell with each breath.

"My sister thought you were quite charming." He leaned against the exam table and folded his arms. "And my daughter wouldn't shut up about you. You've given her ideas," he said, looking amused. "Now she thinks you are all very shy and polite."

I read and reread the words stitched in blue cursive across

the pocket of his lab coat—*Dr. A. J. Cleveland*. I realized the silence was stretching on too long. It was my turn to respond. I tried to imagine what a normal person would say in this circumstance. "Did Rachel lose her baby?" I asked.

"Yes," the doctor said, a little taken aback. "Unfortunately."

"Is it really the farm runoff?"

"Has my daughter tried to contact you?" he asked.

"No," I said.

"You'll let me know if she does," he said. "She can be willful. And I'm sure you realize that this is not a good place for a young girl to take risks."

"Why would she contact me?" I asked.

"That's what I said." He smiled. "Who knew that one child could be so much work?"

A nurse came into the room and was startled to find the doctor. "Sir?" he said. "Excuse me. Do I have the right room?"

"Yes, you're fine," the doctor said. He waved at the man, as if dismissing any doubt. It was the gesture of someone in command. He seemed as at ease here as he had prowling the field of bodies with a pistol.

"I was just leaving," he said. "But, James, do let me know if you want to participate in any of the studies we're conducting. I know that officially they're full, but I'll be happy to make an exception for the boy who chopped all that firewood."

He smiled and gave me a friendly little nod, and then he was gone.

NINE

I told the nurse that I felt fine, but he remained unconvinced. I tried to make a fist and take a deep breath, but for the first time in days, I failed. My hands trembled, and I started hiccupping as if my lungs had shrunk. The nurse sent me back to the dormitory to rest. They gave me a light sedative that I didn't swallow. I spit the pill into my hand, then tucked it into a shirt cuff. When I was back at the empty dormitory, I wandered the hallways, glancing through doorless portals that led into various unoccupied rooms. I paced the common area with its molded plastic chairs and long table. I walked through the green-tiled showers and the bathroom, where several stalls had small, low-hanging doors that offered minimal privacy. Then I returned to my own room, where Owen's things were not yet unpacked. He'd done a sketch of the proctor's girlfriend, but when I looked more closely, I saw that she had canine teeth and the pointed nose of a dog. The dorm was so familiar, and yet all the stains and variations of finish were different. I knew where I was, but I was also somewhere new.

Now that the doctor was no longer in front of me, now that he was a phantom again, he grew in strength. *Vengeance belongs to God.* That's what I'd been taught. La Pine had been more religious, more explicitly Christian, with its Bible classes and its daily church services. Our headmaster had seen to this. But Ione was not the same, and I was alarmed at how easily the patterns of religion had fallen away, how quickly my beliefs had proven to be nothing more than habit. The strong dominated the weak. This was what I knew, this was what I observed every day—it was nature. Maybe I wasn't a bad piece of genetic coding; maybe I was an intentional adaptation to a complex ecosystem. Wrong-thinking could ultimately be a civilizing force. Criminals necessitated law, and law enabled communities to cohere and grow. There could be no Bible without the Devil.

I paced the hall and stopped to check the inspection tags on the old fire extinguishers strapped to the wall. One of the units had a funny smell. Maybe a student had pissed on the floor. Boys sometimes urinated on the threshold of one another's room, and some even tossed cups of urine or shit through the open portals. It was a way to send a message. Or maybe the 3 and 4 dormitories were just dirtier. I returned to our room and sat on the bed.

I never thought I'd speak to Bethany again. I wasn't even sure I'd see Dr. Cleveland when I went in for another checkup. The school was big, almost four thousand students. There were people I saw constantly—boys and staff who were familiar even if I didn't know their names—and then there were ones that I'd never seen before. In that way Ione could feel small and then suddenly vast and strange. It had taken me nearly four months to spot Harold, and now, having a different class and work schedule, I saw mostly new people. Creighton and Davis were still everywhere, probably because they moved at will, but it was not unrealistic to imagine that the Clevelands could disappear altogether with only a schedule change.

I felt increasingly agitated at the thought of those smile lines on his face, at the thought of him nearby but out of sight.

I opened my personal page on the wallscreen and clicked on the Maintenance Intensives. All the labs were still full, and I signed off. The screen went dark. My own dim reflection stared out of the black expanse, a featureless other self.

At lunch the next day, I waited with the other Level 3s until the 1s and 2s were finished eating. We stood in front of the cafeteria flagpoles. It was brutally hot, and sweat rolled down the inside of my shirt. It gathered under my arms in damp, spreading rings. I kept staring at the white-coated kitchen workers I glimpsed through the glass-paneled doors. I knew, of course, that these people in white coats were not the doctor, could not be the doctor himself, but they drew my gaze anyway. They made my heart tick faster. There were Zeros on campus. They were here.

I walked through the lunch line, passing buckets of plastic cutlery, spring-loaded tray holders, and giant napkin dispensers that looked like stainless-steel towers, each with a dangling paper flag at the bottom. I held out my tray at all the required stations—the vegetable station, the grain and the protein stations. Most of the windows in the cafeteria were on the second story, which made the ground floor feel subterranean. There was a catwalk up high where proctors paced; their shadows yawned across tables and students.

After I ate, I returned my tray and went to one of the smaller wallscreens in the cafeteria. I scrolled through a list of faculty members, searching under medical staff. A. J. Cleveland wasn't listed as a general practitioner, or even as a specialist. I finally did a general search for his name and found him listed as Director of Student Medicine. I wasn't even sure a student message to a director would be accepted by the system.

"Hurry up," a boy said. He stood behind me waiting to use the screen. So I wrote:

I thought more about our conversation.
I'd like to take you up on your offer.
—James

To my surprise, the message was approved and sent. I stepped
away. My palms were clammy, and I pressed them to the fabric
of my pants. I didn't know what justice looked like, not really. I knew about beatings and demerits, but these were
corrections—Tanner's right hand. I felt that justice had to be
so much more—it had to be like music, beautiful and mathe-
matical.

I closed my eyes. Behind my lids, I saw the late-summer
light cutting through the thin blue water of the Deschutes. I
saw my friends and the way we'd looked at ten and twelve and
fourteen, wading in the shallows, our wet uniforms plastered
to our bodies, the river cold enough to numb our legs. Everything about us had been unwritten and green. I could still
hear the timbre of their voices. I knew the civilian names they
had chosen for their lives after graduation—I knew the shapes
of their hands, the rhythm of their laughter. In my memory
they were safe. I was their stone marker. I was the sole reposi-
tory of their history.

•

There was no reply from the doctor. A day passed and I grew
more anxious. Dormitory 38, which was adjacent to our own,
was abruptly evacuated and sealed. There were rumors that the
students had been transferred to Protective Confinement, that
they'd all been caught making and selling some kind of drug. I
also heard that they'd been quarantined at the infirmary—that
one of them had contracted an illness on Community Day.
There were always rumors on campus. When Goodhouse didn't
supply us with answers, we created our own.

And then on Thursday morning, one day before my Disciplinary Committee hearing, something unusual happened. I reported to the factory for my shift. I was alone in the suiting-up room, pulling on my protective jumpsuit. The room had a wall of metal lockers with the doors removed. They'd obviously come from somewhere else, because the paint didn't fully hide the old graffiti. Clean jumpsuits were heaped in a gigantic wheeled laundry bin, and piles of dirty suits were in a nearly identical bin. One was marked CLEAN and the other DIRTY, but I knew boys switched the signs. Beside the exit to the factory floor was a dish marked SANITIZED EARPLUGS. Someone had spit an especially colorful wad of mucus into the pile of orange foam pellets. The sound of machinery hummed on the other side of the wall. I hastily yanked on a jumpsuit and was just grabbing a hairnet from the "clean" basket when I heard a voice say my name.

For a second I thought it might be the intercom, but then the wallscreen blinked on and Bethany's face was squinting into a camera, on the other side of some digital connection. Little dangling clusters of metallic stars hung from her earlobes. Behind her was a shelf for paper books and a bulbous cactus in a terra-cotta pot.

"There you are," she said. "You stood me up. Care to grovel?"

I was so stunned that I could only stare. "How did you find me?" I stammered.

"And people tell *me* I need to work on my bedside manner." She smiled. "Aren't you going to say hello?"

"Someone could walk in here at any minute," I said. I glanced at the camera.

"Relax," she said. "I've got a proximity program running and a few others." She patted a handheld on the desk. "We'll have plenty of notice. So, this is where you work?" She looked around. "It's nice," she said.

"I hate it," I said.

"Well, yes. I only said it was nice to be polite." She paused. "Your face is better."

"Yeah." I nodded. It was hard to look at her, to see an echo of Dr. Cleveland in her features.

"I've been trying to catch you alone," she said. "I had to be quite the corsair. You know, their wallscreen security is actually pretty good compared to their chip protocol. I think they're more afraid to let you go online than let you wander around unauthorized. That says something." She nodded. "It really does. The brain is more dangerous than the body, don't you agree?"

"The brain is the body," I said.

"God, I want to know everything about you." She leaned forward to adjust her screen, and the lab coat fell open to reveal a tight blue T-shirt. The red, puffed scar on her chest rose out of the low neckline. "And don't worry, I intercepted your message." She winked. "Clever." It took me a moment to realize she was referring to the note I'd sent her father. She thought it had been meant for her. I scrambled to remember the exact wording. "I've been watching your outgoing messages," she said. "I knew you'd figure it out."

"Yeah," I said. "Glad you got it."

Bethany frowned at me. "What were you thinking, by the way? You had a green light last week. I had you cleared to go almost anywhere in the school and you just sat in your dorm room doing God-knows-what."

"Sleeping," I said.

"Which is a total waste of time," she said. "So we need to try again. And I want to remind you that this is likely to be your last chance to meet up with someone of the opposite sex. At least for a while, and also, that I am actually very mature despite the fact that sometimes people think I look younger and sillier than I am. It reflects very poorly on them and has nothing to do with me. Please don't say no—not right away."

And then I succumbed to some curiosity of my own. "Why are you doing this?"

"What do you mean?" she said.

"Why me?" I said. "Why did you pick me? There's a whole school of us."

Bethany frowned. "Because," she said, faltering, "you're convenient."

"No, I'm not," I said. "Not if you have to override wallscreen protocol and all of that. I'm not convenient."

"Okay," she said. "I like you." And she seemed faintly subdued after saying this—these words that I'd wanted to hear, this confirmation that she'd been waiting for me on Sunday—not her but that other girl, the one who was not the daughter, not the extension of *him*.

"I like you," she said again. "And if you keep asking why, I'm going to run out of good answers, because at some point there really isn't a why."

"There's always motive," I said.

"I can accept that you're a cynic, or else you're doing that boy thing where you have to be a little bit macho, and anyway, why are you so determined to prove me wrong?"

"I turned you in to your aunt," I said. "You didn't like that."

"That *was* rather annoying," she said. "But I might have done the same."

Somehow I had wandered close to the screen without realizing it. We were face-to-face now, and I was suddenly filled with a light, expansive feeling that I didn't immediately recognize as pleasure. I'd forgotten myself for just a moment.

"Your aunt handed me an ax," I said. "A real ax. And then she ran back into the house and locked the door. I think I was more upset than she was."

"She actually poured herself a drink afterward," Bethany said. "I thought she was having a hot flash or something."

"And you brought me a real glass," I said. "Didn't they tell you not to do that?"

Bethany smiled. "I'm sorry we armed you so extravagantly. That must have been confusing."

I didn't know what to do with my hands, and I thought, *That's why civilians have so many pockets in their clothes, so they can tuck their hands away, keep them still.* "Look," I said, trying to impose a limit, to prepare her. "I don't want to sound ungrateful, but—it's too much of a risk. And really, what's the point? It's not like this is going anywhere."

For some reason, this made her laugh. "James," she said, "I'm the girl. That's *my* line."

"And my roommate will report me. He'll wake up. He's a light sleeper."

"Wait," she said. "Is that a yes? Did you just say yes?"

"No," I said. "I'm listing the reasons why it's impossible."

"So, it's more of a soft yes." She nodded. "You're worried about keeping up your end of things. I understand."

"No," I said again. "That's not what I'm saying."

"Promise me you'll find a way," she said. "It's important." And her sudden sincerity brought me up short.

"Any particular reason?" I asked. But she didn't answer this. She just hurried to detail the plan, and seeing her so excited, so animated, I kept having to remind myself of who she was—and how little I knew about her.

Bethany suggested that we meet tomorrow night in the school kitchens. It was the only night she could do it. "It might be out of my hands," I said, actually feeling regret. "I have a hearing that day. I don't know where I'll end up."

"You'll end up with me," she said. "I have a feeling."

There was a little beeping sound and Bethany glanced at

the handheld on her desk. "Proctor coming," she said, and by the time the door to the changing room slid open, the wallscreen was blank and I'd stepped through the exit onto the factory floor.

•

It wasn't that I forgot about my Disciplinary Committee hearing, it's just that it seemed pointless to prepare. Owen, on the other hand, was convinced that our future depended on my performance. He was full of advice. "You've got time to practice," he told me. It was Thursday afternoon, just hours since I'd spoken with Bethany in the factory. "Say you don't remember what happened with Creighton. That you blacked out after the bus attack." He frowned, and then waved his hands in the air as if erasing something. "No, you can't say that. That makes you sound crazy. You remember," he said, "but you're really sorry."

"Are you asking me to lie?"

"Be serious," he said. "You're sorry, right?"

"Sorry I didn't hit him harder."

"No," he said. "That's worse. Definitely don't say that. Just be sorry."

And I did feel sorry—sorry for Tuck, and mostly sorry for Owen. I couldn't stop thinking about Dr. Cleveland; I couldn't stop searching for him on the campus. I put myself on several long wait-lists for Maintenance Intensives under his supervision. I was hoping he'd see my name and remember me, remember his promise. I'd stopped taking my monofacine at night. I wanted the nightmares to return. I wanted to see my friends again, to smell the smoke and feel the past coursing through my body, making me tremble. But, ironically, nothing happened—and to complicate matters, Owen and I were starting to talk, to become allies of a sort. It depressed me to feel as if one part of me could be made whole only by destroying another. Understanding had arrived too late. I'd put down roots here without even knowing it, without really meaning to.

"Practice what you're going to say," Owen urged. "I'll tell you if you get the face right."

"I don't need to practice," I said. "I'm not a complete moron."

Owen paused in a meaningful manner that implied he was unconvinced. I studied his earnest expression. "I'm sorry," I said.

"You have to look down," he said. "They hate eye contact."

I apologized again. And this time I meant it.

•

Neither of us liked our new dormitory. As the newest additions, Owen and I got the usual hassle. We showered last, when the hot water was scarce. We picked our bedsheets last, so there were often holes and unappetizing stains. I was learning that 3s and 4s were very different from high-status students. Creighton and Davis regularly left their mark on the faces and bodies of those around us. Some had already had their sterilization procedures. Most didn't bother to finish the logic games that we were supposed to complete each day, the ones that demonstrated proper brain function. I saw their desks lit during class and the problems unsolved as they palmed with each other almost continuously. I sensed there was a deep bond between these boys, but I couldn't pinpoint it. The feeling moved around Owen and me like a stream bending around a rock. At first I thought their avoidance of us was because we'd lost status so quickly—I thought that they were protecting themselves from a dangerous connection. But that wasn't it.

They all seemed to be trading in some currency that we didn't possess.

Some kid named Carter was always crowding me out of doorways or kicking the bathroom stall door whenever he found me there. Carter had black hair with two patches of white above his right ear. They were like the spots on a fawn. His roommate was Ortiz, an ex–class leader who'd been ousted sometime in middle school and retained a frown-shaped scar on his cheek, a souvenir from his final fight. Ortiz never spoke to me, just watched as Carter made it clear that I was breathing his air and cluttering up his sight lines. I sometimes saw them getting hazed by Creighton, who probably didn't appreciate seeing a ghost of his possible future wandering the campus.

There was another emergency-preparedness drill. It happened while I was on a work detail, scrubbing graffiti off some of the ancient metal fire escapes that still laddered the sides of Vargas. Boys had been carving messages into the metal rails for years. None of it was recent—our chips made it impossible now to even approach the building without clearance—but I was struck by how unchanged our defacement was. In the dorm you could see the same rude pictures, the same threats, boys' names written with a Zero symbol carved over the top—that Zero with a slash. I had seen my own name cut into a window ledge in the bathroom, my own name Zeroed.

This time when a drill happened, when the overhead sirens blared and the woman's voice announced that campus had been locked down, we all disregarded it.

"Don't stop working," a proctor called. "We're not done here."

The more drills Goodhouse ran, the more we were prepared to ignore them.

•

That night, after dinner, Owen and I did one of our extra work details. Students from our dormitory and several others were marched out to weed the large soybean field just to the south of the Proctors' Quarters. It was dusk when we hiked out to the field. Dinner had been especially awful, some sort of stew that recycled the corn grits we'd had for breakfast all week. Owen and I were each given a shovel with a hard plastic blade. Our job was to pull weeds from between the soybean shoots and throw them into large compost bags. Creighton and Davis and several younger class leaders were supervising, but they were far away, little specks of darker blue among our light blue uniform shirts. Fortunately, the field was large enough that we could talk without being overheard or reported.

We worked near the fence that surrounded the Proctors' Quarters, and I kept glancing over at the compound. It looked subtly different. The staff houses had been newly painted or perhaps washed—the gray siding and white trim were crisp, free from the pervasive brown dust that coated everything. The coils of razor wire that topped the fence had also been removed. The main road onto campus ran alongside this field. Razor wire would undoubtedly send the wrong message to visitors on Founders' Day.

After an hour of weeding, my back hurt and I had a rash from the thick embroidered Goodhouse logo sewn into my shirt. It was defective in some way, and itchy. Owen had blisters on his palms. His hands were soft. He had been exempt previously from this sort of work. "Can you pull your sleeves down like gloves?" I said.

Owen shrugged. "They can't keep us here much longer," he said. The light was fading. The vivid green of the new soybean shoots had gone gray in the dusk, and the school hadn't yet turned on the overhead floodlights. A woman, a proctor's wife perhaps, walked along the fence nearby, smoking a cigarette. I could see her silhouette, her long swishing skirt. Other boys watched her, too. The wives didn't usually go near the fence. They probably didn't appreciate the way we stared at them, like a pack of hungry animals. I looked away.

A cool wind began to blow as the sun set. Somewhere—in one of the houses—the same song played again and again. The words were almost audible, the tune catchy but a little haunting, too, dipping unexpectedly into a minor key. It would have been peaceful if I hadn't been so tired. I picked up a dandelion green and ate it.

"Don't eat the compost," Owen said.

"It's a dandelion," I said. "It's gourmet."

"Maybe if you're a goat."

I double-checked the location of our class leaders before I answered. "We did it all the time at La Pine," I said.

"You did it with goats?" Owen asked.

"No, asshole," I said. "You can eat clover, too. It's good for you."

The woman pacing along the fence stopped to watch us. We both went back to work. She was maybe a hundred feet away, and when she took a drag off her cigarette, the ember glowed red in the twilight. I could smell the smoke as it floated toward us across the darkening air. Since I'd seen the doctor, I'd been staring at every staff member, wondering if they were who they seemed to be.

"Hey," I said. I cleared my throat. I tried to make my tone casual. "Do you think you'd know if someone was a Zero?"

"Sure," Owen said. "You'd know once they tried to set you on fire."

"Don't be a dick," I said. "It's a real question. What if I told you there were Zeros here at Ione? How would you pick them out?"

"This isn't La Pine," he said. "You're not at some back-water school anymore."

One of the plastic compost bags was too full and it tipped over, sending a cascade of weeds and dirt into the row. I knelt and began stuffing the material back into the bag. "At La Pine," I said, "they lived with us. The proctors who did it." I paused. "They knew us."

"And they'll fry in hell," Owen said. "Forever."

But I didn't believe this. Not as much as I wanted to. "Do you think *you* could kill someone?" I asked. "I mean, if you had to?"

"Are you really asking me that? Come on." Owen looked around again to make sure we weren't being overheard. "This better not be a serious conversation."

In the distance, Creighton and Davis and the other class leaders called for us to line up. A proctor's voice boomed from a nearby speaker: "Work Detail 15, return your tools." Boys were gathering up bags of compost and heading toward the main road, where a number of T-4s had arrived. Their curved, canopied tops looked like pale seashells, the sort of specimens I'd seen only in a book.

"You remember that kid you hit with a tray?" I asked.

"What kid?" Owen said, but there had been only one incident. He knew what I was talking about.

"Why'd you do it?" I hefted two plastic sacks of weeds over my shoulder, holding both bags in one hand. Owen was carrying the shovels, his sleeves pulled over his palms. We made our way toward the road.

"Does everything we do have to have a reason?" he asked. A slight breeze picked up and a layer of dust lifted off the field. It hovered and spun.

"Yes," I said, "it does."

Later that night, after lights-out, I awoke to the sound of

Owen unlocking his trunk. This was nothing new. I heard the rustle of wax paper as he unwrapped graham crackers and little squares of chocolate. I rolled over and tried to concentrate on sleep, but I was so hungry I drooled onto my pillow.

"You awake?" he whispered.

"Yes," I said.

"Check this out," he said. I sat up. Owen pulled the cap off a can of paint thinner. He poured a drop into our empty metal trash can. Then he used some sketch paper to make a cone with a little hole at the top like a chimney. He scraped the tip of a match across the floor and set the paper on fire. The trash can blossomed with flame.

"Holy shit," I said. I scrambled out of bed to get away, thinking maybe he'd completely lost his mind. "Where the hell did that come from?" I couldn't imagine where he'd gotten a match. I stood back and watched as he sandwiched a square of chocolate between two graham crackers. He used a pair of paintbrushes like chopsticks and lowered the food into the flame until the chocolate melted.

"And you gave me shit about stealing a hair clip," I whispered.

Owen shrugged. "Tastes better melted," he said. He made one for me, and I was so hungry it was all I could do to keep from cramming the food into my mouth. The flavor was astonishing, earthy and sweet. I wanted more. He unwrapped another bar of chocolate and set a few crackers in front of him.

"Tomorrow—" Owen began, but I cut him off.

"I got it," I said. "It'll be fine."

The flame in the trash can faltered and died. Owen reached for more paper and began to fashion another cone. He took extra care this time, folding the sheet, feigning absorption in the task. I watched his fingers as they worked.

"You know why I hit him?" he said. "That kid?"

"Why?" I asked.

"I didn't like the way he looked," he said, and for some reason this made him laugh, a slightly high-pitched giggle that I'd never heard before. I stared pointedly, making sure Owen had time to register my surprise. "I'm very aesthetically sensitive," he said, and this made him laugh harder.

"You're sounding a little crazy," I said.

"Come on, admit it," he said. "That kid was ugly."

I shook my head. Owen made another cracker for each of us, and dropped more paper into the trash can. We sat in silence, staring into the flickering orange maw of the fire. The room seemed to disappear; there were no more walls, no limits. Just a portal of light, a shimmering elsewhere.

TEN

After breakfast a proctor drove me to the Vargas Administration Building for my hearing. I'd never ridden in a T-4 at Ione. In this particular model, a piece of Plexiglas separated me from the driver. Sometimes, at La Pine, I'd driven the trucks they'd used in the logging camps, and they'd infused me with this same feeling—a sort of liberty—an appreciation of the wind in my hair, of the sky churning overhead. I tried to stay positive, but as we sped up the hill toward Vargas, all the pleasures of freedom seemed vivid but fleeting.

Trees like tall emerald columns lined the main drive. They were some kind of evergreen, and it bothered me that I didn't know the names of the native plants, as I had in Oregon. Dew frosted the ground and tinged the air with the mineral aroma of wet dirt. As we got closer to the building, it looked more imposing. The clock tower stood at least five stories tall, and a pair of turrets with conical roofs flanked the massive front doors. Vargas cast a long black shadow, and I felt the temperature drop as we drove into the shade.

The proctor circled past the entrance and parked on the side of the building. He walked me to a large wooden door that led into the basement. A little plaque on the wall read ORIGINAL INTAKE DOOR, PRESTON SCHOOL, 1897. "In Vargas, you have to stay behind the yellow lines at all times," the proctor said. "Do you understand?"

I nodded. He told me to wait in what was marked as the old delousing room. It had originally housed a chemical pool. There was a plaque here, too, with a photograph of a mustachioed man pulling a rope tied to a partially submerged boy. I stared at the picture, at the boy in his chemical bath. He was in motion, so his face was a blur—a nothing.

After twenty minutes I was called upstairs to sit on a bench outside the door where the committee met. A proctor sat beside me. I sweated through my shirt even though the hallway was heavily air-conditioned. Across from me, hanging on the wall, were pictures of past students, full-color photographs, the Goodhouse success stories: here was a research scientist, there an engineer.

When I was younger, I'd picked out my name, the one I'd hoped to earn when I graduated. It was to have been James Nash. I liked the way Nash sounded—a little old-fashioned but also generic. Nobody would ask me where I was from or how to spell it.

Finally, the door to the committee room opened. Some boy I didn't recognize was escorted out. "Tell them to go fuck themselves," he shouted. His shirt was ripped partway open and he had a dark stain across his denim pants. Two proctors dragged him down a nearby stairwell. They were touching him. That was bad.

A proctor stepped out of the room and called, "James Goodhouse." I stood and followed him inside, distracted at first by the narrow pathway of yellow lines on the burgundy carpet. The room was dimly lit. Dark wood paneling covered the walls. It smelled like dust and orange polish. A metal chair stood in the middle of the room. It was clearly meant for me, and it faced a long table where the four members of the committee sat waiting.

Each man had a little brass nameplate and a glass of water.

Tanner was perched at the end of the table, looking different up close—plumper, less like a dried-out man sheathed in paper bags. He adjusted his glasses as he scrolled through something on his handheld. To his left sat an older man. His nameplate read MR. MAYHEW. His yellowing hair had been raked directly back. Beside him was Dr. Beckett, my intake psychiatrist. He was a bald man with a very thick black beard, and his mouth looked like a little pink fish caught in a thicket. I tried to make eye contact with him, but he seemed preoccupied. Beside him sat a fat man wearing red cowboy boots and a bolo tie. His nameplate read MR. M. HAWKE. I wondered why anyone would be stupid enough to wear a cord around his neck, but I instinctively quelled that thought.

"Next up," said Tanner, "we have the case of James, number 7783. Everyone should have the file. James, please sit." He gestured to the chair. I sat, and two proctors stood behind me. I lowered my gaze. The feet of the chair were bolted to the floor.

"I'd like to open the discussion by asking if there are any comments from staff." Tanner looked pointedly at Dr. Beckett, but it was Mr. Mayhew who spoke first.

"He's always been very polite in my class," he said.

"I don't believe he's in your class," said Tanner.

"Oh." The man frowned at his handheld. "Which number is this?"

"It's 7783," said Tanner. "James is a recent transfer student charged with theft and predatory violence. On May 25 he stole from his host family, and that evening he attacked a class leader."

"Oh dear," said Mr. Mayhew.

"We have imposed the usual restrictions and penalties, but"—Tanner shrugged as if he were uncertain that those were enough—"I would like to hear the recommendations of the committee."

"I'll go first," said Dr. Beckett. "If I may."

"Of course," said Tanner.

"I've been reviewing my notes on James, and I want to ac-knowledge that there is a history of good behavior here. His record at La Pine was spotless. No behavioral issues. No seri-ous incidents. However"—and here Dr. Beckett winced as if there were a sour taste in his mouth—"La Pine was not a particularly sophisticated school," he said. "This empty page may be a lack of reporting as much as anything else. As we cannot get a clear picture of his past, I suggest the committee limit itself to what we have observed at Ione."

"That's not fair," I said. "That's not how it should work."

Tanner looked up with a bewildered expression. Students spoke only to answer direct questions, and I saw too late that my outburst would merely solidify Dr. Beckett's argument.

"The boy will not interrupt," said Tanner. "He can pre-sent his point of view at the end of this assessment. Under-stood?"

I swallowed hard, trying to get control of myself. "Yes, sir," I said.

"I'm going to suggest that we start with my initial intake notes from February," Dr. Beckett said. "I'll send them to you now." He clicked his handheld and then continued. "As you can see, James was furtive and withdrawn. He exhibited all the classic signs of PTSD—the hypervigilance, the irritability and paranoia."

Committee members scanned their handhelds, presum-ably reading the report. I barely remembered the intake. Driv-ing into Ione had been terrifying. The compound was huge and we'd passed a group of a hundred feral-looking boys working in the cold. I might have said anything to Dr. Beckett, and now this document would define me. In the ensuing silence I became aware of a rhythmic ticking sound. A housefly beat itself against a windowpane, trying to reach the world on the other side. The tap of its conviction filled the hushed room.

"Our general population is not equipped to handle a student with these kinds of issues," Dr. Beckett said, "but I was hoping that James could assimilate with the help of medication."

Tanner checked his watch. "And what is your recommendation?" he asked.

"It's my opinion that these are not just isolated incidents but the beginning of some larger time of acting out. We could increase his medication, but frankly"—and here Dr. Beckett licked his pink fish mouth—"I've seen this before—the displaced anger, the explosive violence. James is not able to master his own experience and will continue to take out feelings of impotence and rage on others."

"You don't even know me," I said. "You can't predict what I'm going to do." I didn't mean to say the words out loud, much less shout them. "I've already been punished," I said. "I've done everything you asked."

Tanner slapped his hand on the tabletop. "If you are unable to control yourself," he said, "you will be restrained. Understood?"

I nodded. Mr. Mayhew gave me a tremulous smile. "Mr. Beckett's conclusion seems a little extreme," he said. "This is probably an adjustment issue. My own children had a hard time when they switched schools."

Dr. Beckett cleared his throat. "When I say it is my *opinion,* I bring two advanced degrees and twenty years of experience to the matter. I understand, Mr. Mayhew, your sentimental feelings in this case, but—frankly—James's story is an old one."

Tanner nodded in agreement. "It's really too bad." He took off his reading glasses and placed them on the table. He glanced at me for the first time. He looked detached and slightly bored. "Prove me wrong," he continued. "I hope you do. But in the meantime, I'm going to recommend a transfer to Protective Confinement."

"What?" I said.

"That doesn't seem proper," Mr. Mayhew said. "The Confinement Block is where we punish boys. What sort of therapy do you have in mind?"

"The block is where we have the resources to provide James with the supervision that he needs," Dr. Beckett said.

Tanner kept glancing at his watch. "Are we all in agreement here?"

"When do I get to say something?" I asked. But they ignored me. I would rot in Confinement. I would never get out.

"I'm going to need more time to review his file," Mr. Mayhew said.

"Returning him to the general population is just the sort of lazy optimism that has made us sloppy in the past," Dr. Beckett said.

Mr. Mayhew frowned, and his voice, when he spoke, was a higher pitch. "Mr. Beckett—" he began.

"Dr. Beckett," the psychiatrist corrected.

"It is not *lazy optimism* to listen to each boy who sits before us and weigh the particulars of his individual case."

But Tanner was standing up and shrugging into a sport coat. He gathered his things, pausing only to ask Mr. M. Hawke what they were serving for lunch. I had to do something or I was going to be locked in a cinder-block room. I was going to disappear.

"Please don't send me to Confinement," I said quietly. "Dr. Beckett is making me seem like a monster. There's no reason why I should be punished more than everyone else. I'm working extra shifts; I'm doing everything you ask. What happened with Creighton was a mistake. It's not part of some larger acting-out. I just had a bad day, is all."

"No," Dr. Beckett said. "Creighton had a bad day. You had a regular day."

"This isn't what you think," I said. "You don't know the truth."

M. Hawke, the man in the red cowboy boots, took a sip of his water and made a loud crunching noise as he chewed the ice. He had yet to speak, but now he turned to Tanner and said, "Sit down. They aren't going to run out of hamburgers. I don't think they're beef anyway."

"They're a by-product," Tanner said.

"Then we definitely don't need to hurry," M. Hawke said.

Dr. Beckett sat back in his chair, his hairy chin tucked close to his neck. Tanner leaned against the table and sighed, still poised to leave.

"We haven't even talked about the incident," M. Hawke said. "I want to know what happened." He nodded at me. "In your own words, tell me why you attacked your class leader."

"Can you look at my record for that night?" I asked. "There should be an electronic log of where I was. If you examine it closely, you'll see that I was off campus. They took me somewhere, some building in the Exclusion Zone. Check my record. It should all be there."

M. Hawke started to type on his handheld, and then he clicked on something that activated a wallscreen to my right. "What do you want to show us?" he asked.

"Keep scrolling," I said. "It was around midnight or so. Maybe later." But as M. Hawke browsed through the records of that evening, I saw that there was no confirmation of my visit to the Exclusion Zone, just a large red *Infraction* written beside *Work detail 4, 1:26 a.m.*

"It was tampered with," I said. "Somebody changed it."

"Yes, that's very likely," said Dr. Beckett, his tone heavy with sarcasm.

"It's the truth," I said.

Mr. Mayhew shifted uncomfortably in his chair.

"I think Protective Confinement is a good idea," Tanner said. "We don't need any loose ends just now. Adjourned?"

"Wait." I stood up and walked to the edge of the yellow line. "Something happened to set me off. Something very serious." I had their attention now. I felt it in the quality of their silence. "I didn't know who to tell and I was afraid no one would believe me."

"Well?" Tanner asked.

I had no other options. "I saw a Zero on campus," I said.

Dr. Beckett shook his head as if he'd misunderstood. "I'm sorry? A Zero?"

"One of the men who lit the fire at La Pine," I said. "I'm absolutely certain."

"That's a serious accusation," Tanner said.

"I realize that."

"And can you identify this man?" The muscles in Tanner's jaw stood out as if he were angry, but his body was very still. For an uncomfortable moment he held my gaze.

"I saw him in the infirmary. His name—" And then I hesitated, thinking of Bethany and what might happen to her. "His name is Dr. Cleveland."

"A.J.?" Dr. Beckett asked, and he looked amused as he turned to M. Hawke. "He's talking about A.J."

M. Hawke gave a little grunt. "And here I thought this meeting was going to be dull."

"It's not a joke," I snapped. "I saw him kill someone." I looked from one incredulous face to another. "If there is even a small chance that I'm telling the truth," I said, "you need to investigate."

"Wait a minute," Dr. Beckett said, scrolling through his handheld. "Didn't you spend your Community Day with A.J.'s family?"

"Yes, but I didn't know it at the time," I said.

"So the theft was an act of retribution?" M. Hawke nodded as if it made sense.

"No," I said. "It's not related. That has nothing to do with it. I didn't even see him at the house."

"And now that you're caught," M. Hawke continued, "you have a story about how the head of this family is really a criminal."

"Please listen to me." I turned to Mr. Mayhew. "They're twisting my words."

"Enough," Tanner said. He sat down heavily, as if resigning himself to a longer meeting. "There's an easy way to put this to rest." And with that he picked up his handheld and called Dr. Cleveland.

•

Nobody spoke as we waited for him to arrive. At one point my heart raced to such an extent that my chip sent a warning to the proctors standing behind my chair.

I looked at Tanner. "You'll help me, right?" I said. "If the doctor tries something, you'll step in?"

"I think we'll leave security to the professionals, James," Tanner said, and M. Hawke chuckled as if this comment were funny. The fly continued to tap at the window. Undaunted by any evidence to the contrary, it was still on its way out into the world.

A knock sounded on the door, and then it slid open. "Here you are," Dr. Cleveland said. "Forgive the delay. I had the wrong floor."

"Not a problem," Tanner said, and he smiled with such

warm familiarity that I knew they must be friends. I felt a queasy, stomach-clenching despair. "I'm sorry to pull you away from your work," Tanner said, "but I felt you should hear this."

"Of course," he said.

"This is James." Tanner gestured toward me. "He has something he wants to say."

Dr. Cleveland turned as if noticing me for the first time. He was wearing a green shirt, and his cheeks were flushed, as if he'd hurried. "Of course," he said. "I know James." He paused. "Go ahead. Don't be shy." He nodded in an encouraging way.

"I saw you at La Pine," I said, but my voice was thin. My mouth felt numb and I couldn't finish my sentence, though I kept forming the words.

"Go on," Dr. Cleveland said. "Take your time." He waved a hand to silence Tanner, who was about to interject. I stood up. That was the problem. I had to stand and face him—this phantom plucked from the cold Oregon night. I met his gaze, and the pantomime of bravery worked. It was a little like the real thing. "You're a Zero," I said. "You shot my friend. I saw you do it."

"A.J.," Tanner said in a low voice, "I thought you might be interested in responding to this accusation yourself."

"And you were right," Dr. Cleveland said, but I couldn't read the emotion in his voice. He turned toward me. "Is there more?" he asked.

"Isn't that enough?" I said.

"It certainly is," said M. Hawke. "Let's not waste another moment on this nonsense."

"Our recommendation stands," Dr. Beckett said.

"That's it?" I said. "He just has to sit there looking friendly and you all break for lunch. Nobody has any questions?" I looked around in disbelief. Mr. Mayhew scratched at his yellow hair and scowled. "This is exactly how the last attack started. People weren't paying attention. This isn't such a crazy thing I'm saying. It's already happened."

"This is a classic misdirection," Dr. Beckett said. "We're just giving him an opportunity and a platform."

"Agreed," Tanner said, but Dr. Cleveland spoke over them, his baritone easily cutting through the sounds of the committee sheathing their handhelds and gathering their things.

"I think James makes an excellent point," he said.

I blinked at him in surprise. "I guess you would know," I said.

"And," he continued, "I don't want to see this boy penalized for telling what he believes to be the truth. It takes a lot of guts to stand there and denounce a faculty member."

"Perhaps, A.J., you aren't acquainted with the particulars of this case," Tanner said, frowning.

"I saw the file. You claim that he suffers from hallucinations," Dr. Cleveland said. "That he is often unable to tell the difference between what is real and what is not."

"So he believes what he's saying," Tanner said. "That's hardly encouraging."

"Confinement is a mistake," Dr. Cleveland said. "He needs expert care and ongoing psychological evaluation."

"This man is lying to you," I said, pointing to the doctor. "Don't take my word for it. Ask your own questions." I was starting to panic. "He's going to kill me. He knows who I am now. And then he's going to come after you."

"Silence," Tanner said. "Will somebody shut him up?"

"Stay behind the yellow line," a proctor said.

"All your security won't mean anything if you don't arrest him," I said, and then I heard the hum of a proctor's Lewiston. It was poised a few inches from my neck. I shut my mouth and went very still.

"A.J., I can't add this to my workload," Dr. Beckett said. They were having a hushed conversation. Dr. Cleveland leaned against the table, nodding sympathetically as he listened to Dr. Beckett's frustrations.

"I'm not asking you to," he said. "I'll take full responsibility."

"I don't even have time to step in for a consultation," Dr. Beckett protested.

"I understand," Dr. Cleveland repeated.

"And," Dr. Beckett said, "we can't have him in the general population unless you can vouch for his continued good behavior."

I strained to hear the committee, but the hum of the Lewiston Volt consumed and flattened the sound of their voices. I heard only the pounding of my pulse and the gulping suck of my lungs. It wasn't until Dr. Cleveland turned toward me that I clearly understood what he was saying.

"I would be happy," he said, "to make James my personal project."

PART THREE

EXPERT CARE

ELEVEN

A proctor escorted me from Vargas to join my class in School-house 1. He followed close behind, and I kept glancing back at him, unnerved by his proximity. I didn't know what Dr. Cleveland had in mind, but the term *personal project* terrified me. I walked faster. I'd made a mistake today, but that was all I knew, and part of the misery, the aftermath, was not understanding the magnitude of my error.

I found Owen lined up on the second floor of the school-house, waiting to enter our remedial literacy class. Proctors were clearing the classroom, making sure that there was no contraband left behind. Two students stood for inspection just outside the door, their arms and legs spread. Everyone in line was focused on them, waiting for something interesting to happen.

"Hey," I said. I took my place beside him and Owen did a double take at the sight of me.

"How did it go?" he whispered.

I couldn't immediately get the words out. "Not great," I said. I was supposed to report to Dr. Cleveland's office early the next morning.

"But you're here," he said. "That's a good sign. Did you explain everything? Like we practiced?"

"Sort of."

"And it worked." He nodded. "They're reevaluating us."

"No, they're not," I said.

"If they didn't chuck you into the PC block, it means they're reevaluating us." And he seemed so happy, so genuinely relieved, that I wished it were true. "I was worried you would screw it up," he said. "I thought you would just start saying crazy shit, talking about Zeros."

"Yeah," I said.

"Good thing I'm here," Owen said, and then he smiled at me. "You have to show them you're important. Did you propose something?" he asked. "For Founder's Day?"

"Not yet," I said.

"Don't wait too long. You have to make the first move."

The line lurched forward. We were about to enter the classroom. Proctors stood on either side of the door. I grabbed Owen's arm. I started to palm something, a jumble of letters and shorts. He needed to know what awaited us—he needed to know the truth. But that was more than I could convey, more than I even knew, and so I just squeezed his hand—a quick compression—an apology in advance.

•

Out on work detail, everything felt more menacing. I spent the evening cleaning drainage ditches, shoveling through rotting muck and the occasional animal carcass. Each time a student raised a hand to scratch his face, each time a proctor adjusted a sleeve, I was alert, crouched and ready, expecting something—but I didn't know what. In the confusion of the morning, I'd nearly forgotten that I was supposed to meet Bethany that night. She would be waiting in the school kitchens, alone. The doctor was untouchable, but his daughter was not. If anything happened to her, Dr. Cleveland would be sorry. He would feel like I felt.

And still this decision wasn't mine to make. I would never get past Owen. A roommate was there to balance you—report you, act as your conscience when you faltered. Owen would function the way he was designed to function. Whether or not he wanted to, tonight he'd be Tanner's right hand.

Work detail went late, past sundown, and I returned to the dormitory muddy and exhausted. Owen sat at his desk, drinking from a carton of chocolate milk. He had a canvas out, a fresh one that he was priming. I pulled off my damp and muddy uniform, balling it up and dropping it onto the floor as I stepped out of my wet shoes.

"Don't throw your shit on the ground," Owen said. "This is my office."

"It's on my side of the line," I said. But I picked up the shirt and stuffed it into our overflowing laundry bin. And then I stared at it—that white canvas cocoon. Nobody had collected our clothes all week, and this gave me an idea.

"You aren't listening," Owen said.

"What?" I turned toward him, unaware that he'd been talking.

"I spoke to Creighton," he said. He shot a quick glance at our open doorway. Boys were rocketing up and down the hallway, happy to be back in the dorm, showering off the mud and stink of the drainage ditch. It was as much privacy as we were going to get. Owen lowered his voice. "He says that there's been a lot of money traded in this dorm, but it's stopped since we transferred."

"So?" I said.

"If it starts again, he wants to know."

"That's not our problem," I said. I slid my wet shoes under my desk.

"He wants a cut," Owen said.

"Don't cave to him," I said. "Stay tight with the proctors, doing portraits and everything. Find the ones that aren't in Creighton's pocket and kiss up to them."

"And where are you going?" he asked. "Don't talk like it's all up to me."

I sat on the edge of my bed. I knew if I lay down and closed my eyes that I would fall asleep, and this seemed incredible to me. Despite everything that had happened today, my body still wanted food and rest. It was like, on some biological level, it couldn't accept what was going on.

"Look," I said, "if anything happens to me, I have twenty-seven credits. They're on a card under the mat in my trunk. It's not much." I shrugged. "But you can have them."

"What are you talking about?" Owen said. "Is something going on?"

"If I disappear and they say I've been transferred, or if they say I'm in the Confinement Block, it's a sign that the school's in trouble. You need to be careful."

"Well, if you disappear, I'm going to go on a spending spree," he said. "Twenty-seven credits. That's quite a legacy. I'll buy a motorcycle for sure. Maybe a handheld. Definitely some hookers."

"Fuck off," I said.

He smiled. "Can I have an advance?"

When Owen left the room to shower, I opened the dirty laundry bin. I pushed past my wet and muddy clothes and found the shirt I'd worn on my last visit to the infirmary. The sedative I'd spit out was still stuck to the inside of the cuff. It had dried into a pebble. I pried it loose and placed it on Owen's sketch tablet. I pulverized it, using the end of a paintbrush. And then I sprinkled the powder into his half-full milk container.

•

Owen was asleep by the time the evening video played on the wallscreen, and by lights-out he was snoring like a motor. I'd been afraid the pill wouldn't work, that it was compromised, but now I was uneasy with how effective it had been. It was supposed to be a mild sedative. I tucked the covers around Owen. Then I lay on my own bed to wait. I was afraid I'd over-sleep, and I did little more than hover at the edge of conscious-ness, awakening every hour to check the time. By a quarter to one, Owen had stopped snoring. I got up and held a finger under his nose to feel his exhalation. He was still alive.

I put on a clean shirt and left the room, holding my shoes in one hand. I listened hard for sounds of wakefulness, but heard only the stutter of the ventilation system, the deep, even breathing of sleep, and the occasional whimper of a dreamer. I crept to the common room and hesitated before the exit. Behind me, the familiar gray hallway was punctuated by even darker door wells, and before me was a foreign place—the shadowy, still landscape of the school at night.

I wasn't convinced that Bethany would be able to do all the things she promised, so again I lingered at the threshold, undecided. In the end, I had to make myself do it—like jump-ing into a cold river. I opened the front door and stepped out-side in a burst of determination. I braced for the howl of an alarm, but I heard only the chime of insects and the hum of the dimmed floodlights overhead. At the far end of a row of dor-mitories, a T-4 with two proctors in the front seat zoomed past. The headlights were a weak yellow color, and they encased the vehicle in a sickly bubble of light. Everything ordinary seemed transformed by the hour, by the knowledge that I had disap-peared from the computer. There were no patterns to police and monitor. This was what it felt like to be free.

I crept past the dormitories, heading north toward the kitchens, where she'd told me to meet her. The fastest way to get there would take me past the Exclusion Zone and near the fence. But that was too open, and there were few places to hide. I couldn't remember if or where there was a work detail scheduled for tonight. So I decided to take the safest route, weaving between the dormitories, then passing Schoolhouse 2, which was a three-story, L-shaped brick structure.

I passed an empty T-4 boxer parked in the middle of the pathway. The dashboard lit up as I approached, thinking I was its owner. The solid black box at the back seemed especially eerie in the dark, like a cut in the night, a nothingness. A large metal latch—a gray hook with a sharp point—kept the box closed. I glanced at the cameras affixed to the corners of the schoolhouse and above every entrance. I could see their red activity lights go on as I passed, which made me tense. It made me wonder what the computers were seeing.

I was distracted—I was looking up when I should have been looking around—and so I walked right past the two proctors. They were standing in a recessed doorway at Schoolhouse 2, hidden in the shadows, maybe thirty feet from my path. It was a stupid mistake.

"Stop!" one of them called. "Who's there?"

At first, all I could think was—run. I took off like a startled animal and sprinted for the far edge of the building. My legs churned underneath me; I was practically tripping over my own motion. I rounded the corner and ran toward the infirmary, which had a number of shady door wells, but this was exactly what the proctors would expect of a fleeing student. I skidded to a stop. I pivoted back toward the edge of the schoolhouse, retracing my steps, going against instinct— just reaching its façade as the proctors shot past. Now I was behind them, trying not to breathe, pressing myself against the side of the building. Questing flashlight beams darted across the exterior of the infirmary, lingering in the shadows and raking the walls.

"I saw something," one of them said.

"Probably a deer," his partner said.

"In a uniform?"

"I didn't see shit," his partner grumbled. I backed up. If they turned around, they would find me. There was nowhere to hide. That was by design, of course. Open spaces, long sight lines—that was all part of security. But then I remembered the T-4. I bent double and hurried over to the little cart. Its dash was still illuminated.

"Don't call it in," the partner said. I slid open the side of the boxer. The stench was awful, and the metal latch made a tapping noise that seemed disproportionately loud. There was a small step inside, a bench seat, and then an even smaller area for my legs. I wedged myself in, or I tried to. I was almost too big. The door didn't fully close behind me, and my right hamstring cramped. I was about to climb out, to look elsewhere, when the overhead floodlights snapped into their high-intensity mode. I closed my eyes, temporarily blinded.

"Come on," the second proctor said. "Think of the paperwork." They were hurrying toward the T-4, their voices growing louder and breathy with exertion. I heard the whine of another vehicle arriving, the rumble of tires on pavement.

"What are you dipshits running the floods for?" someone said. I tried to keep still, tried to think of the pain in my leg as merely a cramp and not a dire emergency. I inhaled slowly through my nose and exhaled through my mouth.

"I saw something," the proctor said.

"Nothing scanned," his partner said. "It had to be an animal."

I heard footsteps and then felt someone lean on the boxer,

redistributing the weight of the vehicle. Sweat dripped into my eyes and I blinked against the sting. The proctors debated what to do. At one point, I looked up and saw a man's face. I saw the black hair inside his nose and his acne-scarred cheeks, dimpled like the rind of an orange. I thought for sure he would glance down and discover me.

"Last night I saw some kind of nutria rat near the factory," the man said. "It was huge. As big as a boy."

"This wasn't a rat," the proctor said, and he must have picked up his handheld, because his partner groaned and swore.

"I have a 260 sighting," the proctor said. "Unidentified, no scan. Heading southeast from Schoolhouse 2. We are three minutes from sighting. Do you have any data to confirm?"

The vehicle rocked slightly as the man with the dimpled skin stepped away. There was a silence, and when I heard voices again, they were distant, as if the men were walking toward the infirmary. I couldn't take it anymore. I tried to slip out, but my legs refused to work properly. I spilled backward onto the ground, expecting to be apprehended and surrounded. But I was alone. All the floodlights were burning at full capacity, already mobbed by thick clouds of orbiting insects. The school was as bright as it was during the day, except the quality of the light was different. It felt garish and harsh. It would be impossible to get near the kitchens now. It would be impossible to get anywhere except back to the dormitories. They were still in darkness. I started toward them, limping as the blood sizzled through my cramped leg. I was just about to slide into the shadows when I heard my name.

"James," Bethany hissed, stepping out from under the eaves of a Level 1 dorm. She stood a few feet away, gesturing for me to stop. She wore black jeans and a dark zippered sweatshirt. Only her sneakers had a flash of color, pale pink stripes on what appeared to be gray suede. Her hair was in a braid, the way she'd worn it the first day I'd met her. "Not that way," she said. "They'll be waiting."

"Holy shit," I said. I was shaky with adrenaline.

"They keep it dark on purpose," she said. "It's a trap." She grabbed my arm and tugged me after her. "This way."

I followed Bethany to the cinder-block commissary, where boys bought and sold supplies. It was a small, windowless building except for the storefront, which was covered with bars and an additional wooden shutter at night. A slim metal door was recessed into the back wall, and I heard the lock disengage as Bethany touched the handle. She pulled me inside and flicked on a small flashlight. The beam darted over stacks of boxes overflowing with towels and toothbrushes—all nicer than the standard issue and very expensive. There were no chairs, so we sat on the floor.

"We'll be safe here," she whispered, "until things quiet down."

"They were standing right next to me," I said. "I thought I was caught."

"You must have been stomping around like an elephant," she said. "What happened? Aren't you all supposed to be masters of duplicity?"

"Who told you that?" I asked.

"Same person who told me you were all sexual maniacs," she said. Briefly, I imagined her father giving her a lecture—a Zero educating his daughter.

"That's not what they tell us," I said.

"Of course not," she said. "That would be bad for morale, and anyway, it's just the same werewolf story they've been telling little girls for centuries. Something to keep us chaste and afraid."

I didn't know what to say to that, though I felt suddenly

very aware of her body. She was warmer than the air around us, and her every movement—the way she sat on her knees, with her hands splayed out on the ground, the slight contraction of her throat as she swallowed—commanded my attention. I tried to shake the feeling. I needed to focus. I'd been confused and disrupted. I was off track. I forced myself to look around, and as my eyes adjusted further, I saw boxes and boxes of Swann Industries chocolate bars, all stacked to the ceiling.

"We think we're so advanced as a species," she was saying, "but really we're all just animals." She crawled nearer, and then, to my astonishment, she sat astride my lap. Her arms wrapped around my neck. I felt like I had several extra gallons of blood in my body.

"Well, aren't you going to kiss me?" she asked. A lock of her hair touched my cheek. I'd never kissed anyone before, and I tried to hold something of myself back, to be that third person watching. I imagined how smug she must feel, how in control, and I dug my hands into the thick puffs of hair above her braid, clenching my fingers until she squeaked in pain.

"What are you doing?" She yanked her head back and squinted at me. All I could think was that I was holding something that the doctor loved. He didn't know it, but I was standing over him. "James," she said, "what's going on?"

"I don't know," I said. And then I rolled her beneath me. I was double her weight. She jammed her feet into the ground, bucking me upward, but only slightly, opening her legs in the process, so that I pinned her more completely.

"I have to tell you something," she croaked. Her braid had unraveled and I smelled her civilian shampoo. I reached for the memory of the fire, for a feeling of righteousness. I wanted to be engulfed by that moment of transgression, I wanted to let it twist me, show me the way.

"When you turned up at Rachel's baby shower," she whispered, her voice shaky and thin, "that was my idea. I made sure you came to our house."

"What do you mean?" I said. I was conscious of her trying to breathe, her chest pushing against mine. "Why would you do that?"

"I saw you on the news after La Pine," she said. "You were talking about what had happened, and it was like you were speaking just to me—like we were alone."

She was talking about the interview I'd given after the fire, the one in which I'd credited the proctor for saving me. "I made all that up," I said. "It's a lie, a story."

She shook her head. "That doesn't matter." She pushed at my shoulders and I lifted my weight off her a little bit. "Before we met," she said, "I was thinking that I should just pick a day, right, a day when I wanted to die rather than waiting to fall face forward into a plate of eggs or in the shower or something awful. And then I met you and I knew we were alike." She paused. "You don't feel it yet," she said, "but I do."

I rolled off her and pressed my palms into my eyes. I was screwing this up—this easy thing.

"How do I know this isn't a setup and your father isn't going to come through that door and arrest me?" I asked.

"You don't," she said, gulping air. "But I'm on your side."

"You don't have any idea what that means."

We heard footsteps on the path outside. The flashlight lay on the ground beside me. I put my palm over the beam, afraid that the click of the switch would be audible. But whoever it was didn't stop. The sound of footsteps traveled past the commissary and away. We waited, still and silent, until it seemed that this person must be truly gone.

"I'm sorry," I whispered to Bethany. I was ashamed of myself. Of all people, I should have known that the child was not the parent. "I'm sorry if I scared you. I don't know what's wrong with me," I said. "I don't know what I'm supposed to do."

I lifted my palm off the beam, and when I found the courage to look at her, I saw that Bethany lay on her back. Her eyes were open very wide and she was struggling to breathe.

•

"What's happening?" I said. "Are you okay?" I crawled over to her, but then I didn't know how to help.

"I should probably have covered this," she wheezed. "But you can't put your weight on me."

"Fuck," I said.

She dug a small metal container out of her pocket, shook a white tablet onto her palm, and then popped it into her mouth. "I think it's okay," she said. But a film of sweat clung to her face, the tendons on her neck stood out, and her left hand kept opening and closing, as if it were grasping for something unseen.

"We need to get help," I said. I started to stand, but she grabbed me.

"No," she said. "Stay."

I sank down beside her. It seemed wrong to just sit and stare, but that was all I could do. I put a hand out to calm her, but then quickly withdrew it. I had lost the right to touch her, and it flashed through my mind that if she died, I would have my revenge on Dr. Cleveland, and that this would be the worst outcome—to get what I'd wanted.

She took another pill and curled on her side. We sat like this for several minutes, until her breathing slowed and deepened. When she finally sat up, there was dirt on her black sweatshirt and grit on her cheek. "So," she said, her voice smooth, her tone a little too casual, "do you want to get dinner?"

I thought I'd misunderstood. "Maybe you should go home," I said, "and rest."

"Don't do that," she said. "Don't you turn into one of those people." She got to her feet and dusted herself off.

I stood, too, but I was looking to see if she was okay. I was so much taller than she was that I took a step back. "Didn't you almost suffocate?" I asked.

"'Almost' means it didn't happen," she said.

"I almost suffocated you," I said. "I'm feeling a little fucked up over the whole thing."

"That's why dinner is a good idea," she said. "It's something we can do together. It will be very normalizing."

"In the middle of the night," I said. "At a Goodhouse?" I pointed to the spot on the floor where she'd just been lying. We'd disturbed the layer of dust on the concrete. "Is that going to happen again?"

"James," she said, and now her voice had the playful, confident lilt that I was accustomed to, "if you can't handle the answer, don't ask the question."

•

I followed her out of the commissary, across the lawn, to the school kitchens. We went to a side door, one used primarily by staff, and stood in the entryway. "I think I've eaten here before," I whispered, trying to hide how shaken I was.

"Then you know how disappointing it is," she said. "But that won't stop us." She pulled a small plastic rectangle out of her back pocket. It was a print reader like the one Montero had given me. I recognized its shape and size even before she summoned a glowing fingerprint to the screen. She opened the door and we stepped into a long hallway. A series of white aprons hung on brass hooks. They looked deflated and ghostly.

"Well, that worked," I said.

"I keep these all over the infirmary," she said, tucking the device back into her pocket. "They fit right on top of the real readers. You can't even tell they're there." In the narrow hallway I accidentally brushed against her, and then folded my arms closer to my body. "The big downside is that they're illegal," she said. "Ten years just for possession, and I have around fifty of them on campus." She smiled at me. "Don't tell."

We stepped into the main kitchen. Huge mixers lined one wall. They were as tall as I was. Large stainless-steel countertops had breakfast ingredients already laid out in sealed plastic containers as big as mop buckets. Overhead, silver-colored pots dangled from wooden pegs. I heard the faint skittering sound of mice, and then I stepped on something soft. I recoiled, immediately shifting my weight and lifting my foot. Two gray mice were stuck to a single glue trap on the floor. One mouse was dead and the other was on his side, legs moving. He was trying to get away.

"Now I know where the meat comes from," I said. But I felt disturbed by the sight—by this creature's hopeless and persistent struggle. Bethany came to stand next to me.

"The kindest thing," she said, "would be to crush its head."

I put out an arm to stop her. "Please don't."

"I'm just saying, if you're going to kill something, you should do it outright, don't you think?" She looked at me. "Isn't that the best way?"

I paused. "Theoretically," I said.

She reached for one of the plastic bins on the prep table, lifted the lid, and pulled out a handful of cornmeal. She knelt beside the mouse, and its legs ran faster, feet searching for traction. "You know, sometimes their hearts just stop out of fear," she said.

"Leave him alone," I said, backing away. She sprinkled cornmeal beside the mouse, and I thought that it would be worse for him—to have the food he'd been seeking but not the freedom to eat it. I turned away and walked into the dimmer recesses of the room. At the end of the prep area, I saw a huge wall-mounted knife case. Fifty knives gleamed in careful array, outlines drawn on the wood behind them. Every one was numbered. The case itself had a glass front and two metal bands, each with their own lock. I tapped the surface with my fingernail. It was plastic. Shatterproof.

"You're not looking to chop his head off, are you?" Bethany asked. She was standing behind me and I turned with a start. For a moment I thought she was referring to her father.

"What?" I asked.

"Looks like you're picking out a knife."

She opened a nearby bin and pulled out a loaf of bread. "Do you love him?" I asked.

"Who?" she asked.

"Your father," I said. She handed me two slices of bread, which I devoured.

"You were supposed to hold those," she said. "And for future reference, when you're on a date with a girl, you don't ask her to discuss her feelings for her father. It's a little bit of a downer."

"A downer," I said. "Right. Are we on a date?"

She led me through a storeroom, and there, on the floor in front of a prep table, was a picnic laid out on a blanket. Two plates, two glasses, a bowl of pasta, and several covered containers.

"I didn't really know what you liked," she said. "I figured anything but stew. I actually don't know how you choke that stuff down."

I looked at the blanket. A flower lay in the center. It was something from outside the school. She had put a lot of effort into this. We stood side by side. From that angle I could glance down her shirt, which I was both doing and attempting to conceal. She wore a lacy blue bra, the edge of which curved over her small breasts. In the darkness, I heard more mice scuffling. Everything felt surreal.

"James," she said, her voice a little softer, "what's the last thing that you did that you were really proud of?"

I shook my head. "Don't know," I said.

"You can't think of one thing?" she asked. "Not even from your childhood?"

I thought maybe I'd been proud of my time in the choir, of the hours we'd spent in practice, in pursuit of some perfection of sound. But I would never say this aloud.

"If you can't think of anything," she said, "then how do you know that your life is worth it?"

"Worth it to me?" I asked. "Or worth it to someone else?"

"To you," she said. "Other people don't matter."

And then she reached up and touched my hair, her fingernails scraping lightly at my scalp, a sensation that was unexpectedly pleasant.

"You have cowlicks," she said. "And those are permanent. You can't laser them away. You know you can change almost everything about a face now, even your skin color, but not a cowlick. It has to stay. Forever."

"Cowlicks," I said, "are the least of my problems."

She hopped up on a nearby countertop, her legs dangling over the side. "I'm too nervous to eat," she said. "Come here." I walked over and stopped at her knees. She spread her legs slightly, then wrapped them around my waist.

"Is this a good idea?" I asked.

"We'll be more careful," she said.

She pulled me down to kiss her, and I resisted, planting my hands on the table. "I don't want anything to happen," I said.

She moved forward, lifted herself up slightly until her lips just grazed mine. "Too late," she said. And this time I was cautious. I was more in control. "You're supposed to open your mouth," she said. "I mean, not right away, but like on the third kiss."

"Third kiss," I repeated.

"Like this," she said. "I'll show you. But you can't do the slobber thing. Girls hate that."

She tasted like mint, as if she'd recently brushed her teeth, and her face was incredibly soft. "Better," she said. "Much better." She made little sighing noises, and I pressed closer until her legs tightened around me.

We never did eat the food. Somehow we ended up crawling onto the chilly stainless-steel countertop, leaving vanishing handprints on its surface. Bethany pushed me away long enough to tug her shirt over her head. Her bra had tiny flowers stitched on top. And then she had unsnapped it. Soon I was aware only of her. Time slowed and stopped. It became an endless drugging now. I felt that being with her, pressing into her, I was somehow closer to being a real person.

•

At some point Bethany took my face between her hands and pulled us apart. "James," she said. It took a moment for my eyes to focus. "James, you there?"

"Think so," I said.

"I only checked you out until four," she said. "I don't mean to make you sound like a library book, but we have to get you back on the shelf soon." I was lying beside her. My brain was so quiet it barely registered these words. I ran a hand over her shoulder, the scar on her chest, the slight mounds of her breasts.

I felt strangely incautious. That was something they didn't tell you. Because, of course, they told us about sex, about the types of women to avoid, about the basics of it all. But for a moment I didn't care about the chip in my belly, or her father, the Zeros, the bleak tomorrow. This was trouble. This was power.

"James," she said again, "focus." And we both sat up, tugging at our clothes.

"You know, they're going to cook our breakfast on this table," I said, and for some reason this struck us both as hilarious. I slid off and started to back away.

"Don't go that far," she said. "We have to say goodbye." And then we were back where we started, on top of the table. I started to press down on her again, but she stopped me.

"Right," I said. "Sorry."

"It's the ticker," she said. "I didn't cook up right when I was a baby."

"Me neither," I said.

"What's wrong with you?" She looked so concerned that I almost laughed. "Oh, right," she said. "But genetic markers aren't really a deformity."

"Aren't they?"

"They're going to learn how to turn certain genes off and on soon. I really think so. It's the next step for epigenetics, and then it won't matter what you're born with. They'll just give you some cellular software and make you like new. Some of the problematic genes, most of the ones you have, scientists can already turn them off, or they think they can. They did some experiment on cows, but there was a problem. The cows lost the will to eat."

I stared at her. "You read my file," I said.

She froze. "I didn't say that."

"If you know what markers I have, then you read my file. Of course you did."

"I meant markers in general," she said. But she wouldn't meet my gaze and I just waited, letting the silence call attention to her lie.

"What happened to me on the night of Community Day?"

"You got in a fight," she said.

"That's what my record says. But you know I'm not guilty." I paused. "Otherwise you wouldn't agree to meet me, right?"

"Well, you're guilty of theft," she said. "And I still met with you. And anyway, it's not really assault if you fight a class leader and win, so why is it assault when you lose?"

"It wasn't class leaders," I said. "It was Mule Creek inmates."

She pushed at my shoulders. "Let me up," she said. I got to my feet. I backed away from the table. She seemed suddenly nervous.

"Look it up," I said. "I was off campus in a building in the Exclusion Zone."

"That's impossible."

"I'll give you a clue," I said. "It's not just a leafy mound they forgot to clear. It's an old basement, and they still use it."

She pulled on her shirt, taking a little longer than necessary to straighten the fabric. She looked perplexed, but also wary, and I was suddenly afraid that this would be like the hearing. My history would discredit me. "There's something else," I said. "I have an appointment with your father tomorrow."

"An appointment? What do you mean?" She looked alarmed. "Get out of it."

"Civilians *get out of* things," I said. "We don't."

"James," she said, "find a way."

"He's a Zero," I said.

"He's a scientist," she said. "It's so much worse."

"This isn't a joke," I said. "I saw him at the La Pine attack. He was there. He killed people."

Bethany shook her head. "Think about what you're saying," she said. "You might think you saw him—"

"Don't." I cut her off. "Don't disbelieve me."

"Look," she said. "I read his email. I read his diary. I'm practically his biographer. I would know."

"You have access to everything?" I asked.

"It's a point of pride," she said.

"Then find out what's going on," I said. We were running out of time, and there was something else I needed to know, something I was almost afraid to ask. "Bethany," I said, "what's my name?"

"I didn't see your last name. I don't think they even keep that information."

"I want the name my parents gave me," I said. "Please."

She fiddled with the metal zipper on her jacket, meshing the teeth together and then pulling them apart. "It's James," she said finally. "The school didn't change it."

"No," I said. "They did. They named me for some death-bed conversion."

"Maybe," she said. "But your name was James at intake. It's definitely rare, but it happens."

I paused, absorbing the information. "It's my real name?" I asked.

I'd been hoping for some revelation, some secret other person—something to hold on to; something bestowed by my family. Instead, I felt cheated, as if the school had taken even this, even my name. I thought of the thousands of Goodhouse boys who had passed through the system over the past fifty years—all of them possessed of a second identity, a true and original self that was beyond the boundaries of what the school could control. And I didn't even have that.

"What else did you read?" I asked.

"You were born in Idaho," she said, "near Porthill, at the northern tip of the state." I waited, hoping for recognition, for some pang of memory, but there was none.

"My race?"

"Your mother was white and your father was mixed."

"Mixed what?" I said. This was an adjective that would apply to almost anyone at Goodhouse. We were, most of us, an assortment of races and ethnicities. Even so, the word had a certain power. "What else did the file say?"

"That's everything," she said. She checked her watch. "We're out of time. When do you want to meet again?"

"I don't know," I said. I kept thinking the words *mixed*, *all mixed*, *very mixed*. I looked at my arm. I was a toasty brown color wherever the sun touched me, but under my shirt I was pale.

"James," she whispered, "did I do the right thing?"

•

I tried to return the way I came, but there was a proctor standing in the shadow of Schoolhouse 2. He was talking into his handheld and saying, "Sure, sure." I waited a minute or so for him to finish, and then I couldn't wait any longer. I took the fastest route back, dashing along the fence that bordered the Exclusion Zone. The floodlights trained on Mule Creek left plenty of light to spill over onto me. I felt overexposed, and my drugged complacency of only a few minutes earlier was gone.

I rounded the corner to the dormitories and saw a T-4 parked a few buildings away, almost directly in front of my own. One of the proctors was asleep in the passenger seat, and the driver was reading a magazine. I stepped back into the shadows, pressing against the nearest wall. I was being careless. It was only luck that had the proctors looking the other way. I didn't know how much time was left on my clock—maybe four minutes, maybe none.

To make things worse, an overnight work detail was returning home. I heard their shuffling march. They were about to pass within a few feet of where I was hiding. I squatted low in the shadows, trying to will myself invisible. *I am a wall*, I thought. *I am nothing*.

The work detail walked single file. Most of the boys were looking at their feet, already nodding into a half-sleep, hands at their sides, still curled slightly in the memory of whatever tool they'd just returned. I knew they were peeling off one by one to their various dormitories. No one looked my way, and I willed them to hurry, feeling increasingly desperate as the line stretched on.

I joined the end of the line, walking behind the last boy. I passed the proctors in the T-4. They were both awake now, supervising the return. And then I was alongside Dormitory 35. I had to squint at the yellow number painted on the door to make sure I had the right one. I walked up the stairs, trying not to sprint.

"Keep the line," a proctor called, and I froze momentarily, thinking he was referring to me. But he was looking at a different boy. I crossed the threshold and quickly removed my shoes. I crept to my room. The clock on the wall showed 4:13:03. I had less than two minutes left. I made sure to change clothes, to give every appearance of routine. Owen was still asleep, making a light wheezing noise with every breath. When I lay on my bed, I was so tired I felt as though I were falling through it, into blackness. Something was happening to me. As I broke the rules I felt less certain that I believed in them. And there was a recklessness in that, a momentum that frightened me. If the school had taken my name, had made it their own, then I could take it back. There was no rule to stop me—no reason not to.

I was James from Idaho. This knowledge reverberated through me. I was James from Porthill. I was James.

TWELVE

I could smell Bethany on my skin at breakfast. It was a faint lemony odor and I kept turning my head to pick up the scent. The cafeteria was serving oatmeal with some kind of protein-substitute sausage. I watched the boys around me shoveling food into their mouths, chewing and swallowing. I thought of the way Bethany had felt underneath me, the way the heat of our bodies had left vanishing shapes on the stainless steel. My brain was disordered from lack of sleep, and Owen was in a particularly bad mood. He'd received a message on his personal page that morning. It had been sent on some sort of letterhead. When I asked him what it was, he'd immediately closed the screen.

When a fight broke out at a nearby table, Owen didn't bother to look up from his tray. Even when one student shoved another to the floor and jammed his fingers into his opponent's eye sockets, Owen was oblivious. Proctors arrived with their Lewistons out, but it was Creighton and Davis who pulled the boys apart. One boy clutched his face, screaming, and the other was struggling, still fighting, so Davis slammed his head into the table to quiet him. Afterward, there was a red puddle on the concrete floor and—in the middle—a white, gleaming fragment of bone, probably part of a tooth. A student arrived to mop up the blood. Two minutes later, all trace of the disturbance had disappeared.

As my appointment with Dr. Cleveland drew closer, I found myself watching the wallscreen clock. In less than a half hour, I would walk to the infirmary. I would have an AJT to compel me. There was no question that I would go. The rest of breakfast passed as if it were some outsize hallucination. Proctors overhead circulated like clouds in front of the sun, filtering and altering the light. The insect thrum of the cafeteria sounds permeated everything. I felt as if I were watching myself from a great distance, watching myself perform all the usual tasks— carrying my plate to the sand tray, waiting for clearance at the exit. And then I walked down the familiar path to the infirmary. I began to take smaller and smaller steps, slowing my pace, but never stopping. *James*, I thought. *I am James*. And the name calmed me. It could not be unlearned. It could not be confiscated.

When I arrived at the infirmary's waiting room, proctors choked the entrance. "James," the computer said, "please report to the basement level. Room 101." I tried to cross to the main hallway, but a proctor stopped me. "You'll have to go around," he said. "This area is closed." Beyond him I glimpsed a man in a military uniform. He looked like one of the men from the magazines I'd read on Community Day. I didn't know what sort of officer he was, but I recognized rank when I saw it—the colorful bars on his jacket, a gold band on his hat. As I watched, another officer in a similar uniform stepped out of a side room. The two men fell into a conversation, each nodding at what the other was saying.

"North hallway to the east staircase," the proctor told me. "Do you understand?"

The system that usually lighted a path in the floor was offline, so he gave me directions.

"Yes, sir," I said. But I was soon lost. The east staircase was locked, and I found myself moving more deeply into the building, where there were fewer students and even fewer staff. I tried to double back, to return to the lobby, but everything was taking too long, and when I found an open staircase, I just descended. My feet scraped lightly on the treads, the sound amplified by silence. *James*, I thought. *I am James*. And then, at the bottom of the stairwell, something caught my attention.

There were two doors. One was obviously an entrance into the basement, but the other was tucked in the far corner under the stairs. The door itself was recessed and narrow, and its access light was blinking yellow. I stopped to examine it. For all students an entrance was either red or green. There was no yellow light. My first thought was that this was a test. I should find the intake nurse and report the malfunction. I walked closer. It looked like some sliding panel was meant to cover the door, but the panel was partially retracted. On impulse I reached for the handle. It opened.

I stepped over a threshold and stood in a small antechamber. It was noticeably hotter in there, and the ceiling was very low. I could touch it with my hand. A heavy, clear plastic curtain blocked my view, but it had been cut into overlapping strips, and these parted and then resealed themselves as I passed. On the other side of the curtain was a long corridor. Numbered doors were set into the wall every ten feet. Each door had an observation window. I stopped at the first one and peered through the glass.

A young boy squatted on the floor, wearing only a pair of underwear. His right wrist was secured by a wall restraint, and he was hunched over as if dozing in a squat. He looked reptilian, his bony spine pressing against his skin. His eyes were closed, but his lips were pulled back, showing clenched teeth. I touched the glass in the window and it went momentarily opaque as the boy's chart was displayed—a series of notes about dosage and duration. His heart rate ticked in the upper right corner, the way it did on our personal pages. As soon as I removed my hand from the glass, it cleared, and I saw the boy was awake and looking at me. His nostrils were flexing as if he were scenting the air. Then his eyes fluttered closed and he curled tight around himself.

Of course, we all knew the Intensives could be dangerous. In the shower I'd seen boys with deep scars on their arms and backs. The idea that I needed to be modified was central to every conception I had of myself. I expected to be altered, medicated—but this was so much more. The banality of my life here, the relentless routine, I realized that it had acted like a camouflage. The closer you stand to a picture, the harder it is to see it with any clarity, and when you are deep inside the pattern, you are truly blind.

A booming noise startled me. Farther down the hall one of the doors vibrated as if it had been hit. I walked closer and peered into the observation window. At first I saw just an empty wall restraint and a smear of blood beneath it. But then I saw someone I recognized. It was Harold, the only other transfer from La Pine. He was backing up to rush the door. He charged forward and hit the slab with stunning force. It boomed like a drum. He was shouting something, too, but I couldn't understand him. His hair was stiff with dried blood, and his too-close-together eyes looked especially feral. He seemed animated by some terrible energy, some hungry rage. On impulse, I reached for the door handle. Inside, the room was very hot, and it stank like a latrine. Harold immediately ran toward me, and I yanked the door closed, so that he collided with it, making a sickening thump.

I found the intercom button and depressed it. "Harold," I said, "it's me, James. Are you okay?" It was a stupid question, and when I looked through the glass, I saw that he had collapsed onto his side. I thought maybe he was unconscious. I called his name a few times, and then I said, "I'm going to open the door now. Just stay where you are." But as soon as I stepped into the room, he was awake and on his feet. He made a high-pitched howling noise like a balloon deflating and then charged past me. The overhead alarm began to clang and shriek as he ran the length of the dim hallway. He kicked his way through the plastic curtain and disappeared.

I didn't know what to do. "Shit," I said. "Shit."

I ran after him. I sped through the door and out into the stairwell, almost colliding with a proctor. We startled each other, and the man scrambled to get away from me, his body in a crouch, as if he were expecting a confrontation.

"Get on the ground," he said. "On the ground, now." But I didn't comply. Somewhere overhead Harold was keening.

"What's wrong with him?" I asked.

The proctor unholstered his Lewiston. "I've got a Code 34." He spoke into the mic at his collar. "Repeat, Code 34."

The alarm cut and a faint voice chattered from the proctor's earphone.

"You think I'm from the Intensive," I said. I took a single step toward him and he jumped back, his Lewiston slashing in front of him, warding me off. "Why are you so afraid?"

"Get on the ground," the man shouted.

"Or what?" I said. His fear empowered me. We were alone—for a few moments, anyway—a man with a name tag and a student with a name. "When the Zeros come they will burn you, too," I said. "They like to kill proctors. Do you know why?"

He backed toward the staircase. The staccato of descending footsteps grew louder. Many footsteps.

"We might belong to the Devil, but you," I said, "are our servants."

The basement door banged open and Dr. Cleveland stood on the threshold. He wore casual civilian clothes, gray pants and a white shirt. He was holding a handful of pistachio nuts, cracking a shell between his fingers. "James," he said, "you seem to have gotten lost."

"Sir." The proctor moved to stand between the doctor and myself, his Lewiston crackling. Between its two contact points, the arc of electricity was a bright, wavering line. "This is a Code 34," the proctor said. "Return to your office."

Dr. Cleveland popped a pistachio into his mouth. "I'll take it from here," he said. "You're dismissed."

"Sir," the man stammered. "Sir, I have to ask you to reconsider."

"You can ask," the doctor said. He motioned for me to follow. Four other proctors came thundering down the stairs, their Lewistons drawn. "Gentlemen." The doctor nodded. They all stopped at the sight of him.

"We've got a code," one man said. He was out of breath. He pointed to me. "This one?"

"This one's not for you," Dr. Cleveland said.

As I turned to follow the doctor, I noticed that the door to the Intensive was gone. Whatever panel concealed it had slid back into place, and now the wall looked like any other— gray and smooth, like polished concrete, like something that it clearly was not.

•

Dr. Cleveland escorted me into his office, and I recognized the room, the bulbous cactus in a terra-cotta pot, the single shelf that held leather-bound books. Bethany had sat at this desk when we'd spoken on the factory wallscreen, and now her father sat in the same creaking wooden chair.

"What is a Code 34?" I asked. My voice sounded thin and choked.

Dr. Cleveland made a little pile of empty pistachio shells on the desktop. "Have a seat," he said. He motioned to an upholstered chair across from him. There was a large photograph of Bethany on his desk. She looked younger, perhaps twelve, and she stood in some kind of park with oversize lollipops jutting from a snowbank. She was buck-toothed and wearing a red-and-white-striped headband and matching party dress. I quickly checked the corners of the room for cameras, but I didn't see any.

"Pistachio?" Dr. Cleveland asked. I shook my head no. "They were a gift, but they're stale, so maybe a regift." He accidentally knocked a few of the shells onto the floor. "Messy, too," he said, and then bent to pick them up.

In the few seconds he ducked out of sight, I reached forward and grabbed a pen off his desk. I disguised the motion by leaning forward as if shifting my weight. I rolled the pen between my thigh and the chair. It was a thick plastic. High quality.

"What's wrong with those boys?" I asked.

"You've created an awkward situation for me, James," he said, straightening up and shelling another pistachio. "Let's start there."

"You're a Zero," I said.

"That didn't use to be a dirty word," he said. "What is it they say? Youth is curiosity minus understanding. It's a cruel trick. To be young."

"You're a killer," I said. "That's all I need to know."

The doctor made a chuffing noise, a dismissive sort of

sound. He stood and walked toward a small gray metal cabinet. The handle must have been keyed, because I heard the lock disengage as he touched it. I wedged my hand under my thigh. He returned with an ornate green glass bottle. He unscrewed the top, then picked a glass off his desk and blew into it to dislodge any dust. "I'd pour you one," he said, "but without a taste of cheap cognac first, you won't be able to appreciate the flavor." He sat back, holding the glass in his hands. "So," he said, "what shall I do with you?"

For a tense moment we just looked at each other.

"Well," he said, "before you stab me with that pen—which is more likely to annoy than incapacitate me—you should hear what I have to say. Surely you can delay the pleasure a little longer?"

"You shot my friend." My voice was gathering strength. "I should kill you," I said. "That's only fair."

"Fair," he repeated. "Now, there's an idea." He leaned forward, and with a flick of his wrist, he pulled a small paper booklet aside to reveal what appeared to be an old-fashioned revolver. He nudged it toward me. "Take it," he said. "It's an antique Smith & Wesson. Belonged to my great-great-grandfather. The safety is on the right side and you have to pull the hammer back."

I stared at the gun. "It's not loaded," I said, though I couldn't be sure. I didn't know anything about guns. "You just want to test me," I said.

"I shot a lot of bottles with that thing as a kid," he said. "A couple of squirrels, too, which I regret. Do you know what those men were doing to the wounded boys?" he asked. "No, of course, they don't tell you anything. I always thought that was a mistake." He poured himself another drink. "They killed some of them outright, but the others we found a few days later in Umatilla County. It wasn't quick." He swirled the glass and sniffed it. "Whatever my flaws," he said, "and I know they are many, I don't act without reason. Your friend had been shot in the stomach. He wasn't going to die quickly."

"You don't know that."

"Actually, I do," he said.

"So, you were doing him a favor," I said.

"I saved you," said the doctor. "I saved your life. Do you think I like to shoot little boys? The Zeros used to be a very different thing. Back in my day they were all about candle-light vigils and community letter writing." He sighed. "They were not radicalized like they are today. I knew the attack was a possibility, but it was by no means a sure thing. I was there to stop them, but you remember," he said. "Could you stop that fire? Could one man stop forty others?"

"You didn't even try," I said. "You could have helped him."

"Your friend was dying," he said.

"It wasn't up to you," I said.

"Do you still want to shoot me?" he asked. "Do you want to orphan my daughter? Condemn yourself to trial and execution? You can, you know. How's that for power? Or you can listen to my side of the story and find it reassuring or unsatisfying—disgusting, perhaps. But no more curiosity without understanding."

I picked the gun up off the desk. It was heavier than I expected. The stock was smooth—some kind of ancient, oiled wood. "Is this the gun you used?" I asked.

"It is," he said.

I stared at its barrel, the blackened shaft and the round, corrugated side of the chamber. I thought of the boys hunched in their cells, wearing only their underwear. "How many people have you killed with this?"

"Not many," said the doctor.

"Why didn't you call the police?" I asked. "Why didn't you

start shooting Zeros? You must know some of them. You could reveal their identities."

He leaned back in his chair, cradling the glass between his hands. "Yes, that would appear to be the right choice," he said. "But if I stay silent, I maintain access to sources of information. The police can nab a few Zeros, they can lock me away, but for all their well-meaning procedure, they will not be able to predict and prevent another attack. And it's coming." The doctor smiled. "So that's one more layer of gray. Your revenge will cost the lives of other boys."

"You're lying," I said. I stood up. "If you really wanted to help us, you wouldn't gamble your life." I pulled the hammer back and squeezed the trigger, meaning to demonstrate the lack of bullets and—to my astonishment—the gun fired with a terrific roar. I felt the recoil in my body, a sudden kick of energy that disappeared into my arm and chest. I staggered backward and nearly tripped over my chair. The scent of ammonia filled the air.

"You missed," the doctor said. He reached for a pistachio.

"Are you out of your mind?" I said. "I could have killed you."

He waved as if to dismiss this possibility. "You weren't even aiming," he said. I heard the sound of running feet in the hallway and then a knock on the door. "Everything's fine," he called.

"Sir, we heard a noise," a proctor said. I just had time to tuck the gun behind me as the door opened. I stood in front of the doctor's desk, wide-eyed and radiating guilt.

"Everything's fine," Dr. Cleveland said. "As you can see."

The proctor sniffed the air. He glanced between us. A long moment passed. "I'll be right outside if you need me," he said.

"If you like," the doctor said. "But I'm working with a patient. I don't want to be interrupted."

The moment that the proctor was gone, I threw the gun into a small metal wastebasket at the foot of the desk. I wanted the thing out of my hand.

"He knew," I said.

"Of course," the doctor said.

"But you don't have any cameras in here, do you?"

"We're alone," he said. "Though I think my 1858 *Gray's Anatomy* has suffered a calamity." He gestured to one of the books on the shelf behind him. It had toppled and had a hole in its spine.

"You don't seem very upset," I said.

"I expect to die by that gun," he said. "I plan to kill myself, you know. When my daughter dies."

I sank into my chair. I was shaking. "What were you thinking?" I asked. There was a sofa pushed against the far wall, and a blanket and pillow were arranged as if someone had slept there. A pair of old-fashioned reading glasses was perched on the arm, and a small sprinkling of crumpled white tissues littered the floor. The doctor's shape was still visible in the indentations of the sofa cushions.

He quietly poured some more cognac into the bell-shaped glass and pushed it toward me. "I changed my mind," he said. "You should try it. Fifteen years in an oak barrel in Limousin. All the way from France." I shook my head, to say I didn't want any. "Go on," he said. "You'll get the injection when you graduate, and then you won't be able to touch this stuff." I took a sip, just enough to wet my lips and feel the burn of the alcohol. It tasted awful, but I took another gulp, and this one slipped down my throat like a bright star.

"You know, there was nothing you could do," he said.

"What?" I said.

"I was there," he said. "Don't blame yourself. You couldn't help them."

"I blame you," I said. But my voice lacked its previous con-viction.

"Hindsight is all damning clarity and revision," he said. "I'm not sure what the purpose of it is. My father told me that I would regret only the things I didn't do. He died racing a boat, if you can believe that." Dr. Cleveland's handheld beeped, and he silenced it.

The warmth of the liquor spread from my throat to my stomach. I pressed my lips to the glass and the cognac numbed them. The recoil of the gun still vibrated inside me.

"I'm not saying I believe your story," I said. "But you can't play both sides. You can't just pretend to be a Zero. Either you're lying or they know you're using them."

"They suspect," the doctor said. "But so what? Ione is the prize."

"What do you mean?"

"Haven't you noticed?" he asked, his tone a little chiding. "We're about to commemorate fifty years of history here—hundreds of visitors, a weekend of celebration. You've seen that monstrosity they're building in the East Field."

"Of course," I said. He was referring to the pavilion.

"To a Zero, it's a target." And I must have looked puzzled, because he said, "You haven't considered this?"

"No."

"Then it's a good thing I'm here." He used his foot to pull the trash can closer. He leaned in to retrieve the gun, and before I could react, he began to break it down. "The older something is, the more work it is to maintain," he said. He shook the bullets out of the cylinder, then handed the metal piece to me, along with a rag.

"You have to cancel the celebration," I said.

"And give the Zeros another victory?" He shook his head no. "It's interesting," he said. He pulled a pipe cleaner from a wooden box, then used it to clean the barrel. "All you boys are working so hard so you can get out and join the larger world. But, you know, it's not a destination. I'll tell you a secret." He looked at me. "You have," he said, "already joined."

I set the cylinder on the desk. The weight of the metal made me uneasy. The chambers where the bullets rested were dark tunnels, perfect holes. I reached over and picked up the picture of Bethany. She had braces on her teeth. She was a child in the image, but the scar was still visible, rising from the top of her dress. "Is she very sick?"

"You like her," he said.

"No," I said. "I was just wondering."

"Your heart rate increases when you lie," the doctor said. He tapped on the screen of his handheld. "You promised to tell me if Beth contacted you." We stared at each other for a moment. "So has she?"

I looked into his eyes, which were her eyes. I willed my heart to slow. I willed my body to believe what I was saying. My hand tightened on the picture frame. "No," I said.

He paused and made a low, speculative sound, as if he was not truly convinced. "James," he said, "I need you to be on your best behavior. No more acting out, no more threatening staff. If you follow the rules, I can help you. We can help each other. Believe it or not, you may have something of value to contribute to this larger world."

I put the picture of his daughter back, then angled it to face him. He was watching to see if I would give anything away with my body language, but I was very good at being a blank, empty space. I thought of the boys in the hot, low-ceilinged rooms.

"What are you doing to those boys in the Intensive?" I said. "I saw your name on their charts."

"My name is also in the book you shot." He gestured to the books on his shelf. "But that doesn't mean I wrote it."

"Are they going to recover?" I asked.

"Yes," he said. "That's what boys do. Even you, James." And then he smiled. "This session went well," he said. "Don't you think?"

THIRTEEN

Everyone in the school did double work group for the next seventy-two hours. There was just over a week until the Founders' Day celebration and the grounds were not ready. The pavilion itself was almost finished, and I spent several days working in its shadow, constructing plywood molds for new concrete pathways and staircases. The slight vinegar smell of fresh paint floated out of an open doorway. Owen labored alongside me, his hands wrapped in paint rags.

Even with the double shifts, there was more work than the students could handle. Tanner had to hire civilian help— professional carpenters, plumbers, and electricians. The school started training groups of temporary proctors, men brought on to assist during the event. I often passed them as I crossed campus, the new hires moving in groups of five or six, an older proctor showing them where everything was located. They stared at us openly, grim-faced and de- termined, trying to square what they knew with what they saw.

I remember those days felt endless, suffocatingly long. I kept imagining the boys tethered to the wall in the infirmary— their gritted teeth and the reptilian flex of their spines. It felt as if the kick of Dr. Cleveland's revolver were still in my body, rattling around, a spark of chaotic energy. Whenever I passed groups of younger students, I looked for Harold, but I didn't see him.

Only thoughts of Bethany supplied some relief. If I closed my eyes, I could summon her under my hands, feel the softness of her skin. It would conjure some deep lust, something vast that tied me to the world. But even that pull was brief—a flash, a synapse firing, and then silence. I spent hours composing a message to her, or rather, a message to her father in the hope that she would intercept it. But when I hit Send, the message was returned: ACCESS DENIED. AUTHORIZATION REQUIRED.

On Wednesday afternoon we were assigned to whitewash the walls of a guest dormitory—to lug in bunk beds and the creepy black mattresses that looked like rubber rafts. A proctor ordered Owen to paint the words WELCOME SALT LAKE CITY! on the door. The room's wallscreen displayed an itinerary and a roster of names that I disregarded until I saw the word *Choirmaster*. I stopped what I was doing and stared.

"You there," a proctor said, "back to work."

"A choir," I said, reading the word off the screen.

"Quiet," Owen hissed.

But the proctor was tolerant. He mistook my surprise for derision, or something that mirrored his own feelings. "Don't worry," he said. "We'll be phasing that kind of thing out of the system. Salt Lake is the last one."

As I worked, I kept glancing over at the screen. I read the names of the twenty boys, the five proctors, the choirmaster. Maybe it was the fatigue, but I couldn't focus on anything else. The smell of paint fumes mixed with the stench of disinfectant, and all I could think was that in another life, at another time, it could have been my name up there—it could have been me.

•

The next morning, at 5 a.m., I awoke to an alarm. Owen pulled his pillow over his head to block out the sound. A woman's voice spoke from the wallscreen. "This is not a drill. The campus is now on lockdown," it said. "Please report to a secure area."

"Get up," I shouted to Owen. "It's for real." I rolled out of bed and pulled on my pants and shoes. I ran to the window, but there was nothing to see, just other faces in other dormitory windows. Boys spilled into the hallway, everybody wondering what to do, pushing into the common room. "Please report to a secure area," the voice repeated.

The wallscreens were jammed. Students with friends in other dormitories were sending messages, trying to get information. At one point we thought Vargas was on fire, but that rumor was quickly contradicted.

"Fuck this," someone said, and he began to kick at the front door. Several students shouted suggestions, telling him to hit it with his heel, to strike near the lockset—but the door was solid. It didn't even vibrate. And then, all at once, the message service went down. The alarm cut out and the wallscreens went dead.

If the alarm was bad, the silence was worse. I felt my hands curling into fists. We were trapped. The fire exit at the back didn't open, though a dozen students were pushing against it. The sight of their efforts was threatening to unhinge me. I forced myself to turn around and walk back to my room.

Owen sat on his bed. He'd drawn a big black question mark on a piece of sketch paper. "What's that for?" I asked.

"I put it in the window," he said, "for the other dorms to see."

I took a deep breath. My fingernails had cut into my palms. "Did anyone write back?" I asked.

"You're not flipping out, are you?" he said. "You better not be."

I grabbed the sign and returned it to the window. "Why'd you take it down?" I asked. "They might know something."

"But they don't have anything to write with," Owen said. He was almost laughing. "It's completely useless."

The administration released us three hours later. Only a few dormitories at a time were allowed in the cafeteria. As soon as we got there, people were palming. I couldn't keep up, and Owen had to translate everything into the most basic symbols. There had been another attack—that's all I could make out. "Where?" I said. He spelled a word several times, but I didn't understand. "Tacoma," a boy behind us whispered. That was the biggest campus in the Northwest.

"Silence," a proctor called. "Hands apart. You will have ten minutes for breakfast. That is, ten minutes, starting now."

Half the time had passed, and still not everyone had made it through the line. Boys ate where they stood. "Is it true?" someone asked. "Was it Tacoma?"

"Who said that?" a proctor called. "Identify him." But nobody competed for the credit, not today.

And then, just as we were taking our dishes to the sand trays, all the wallscreens blazed to life. There was no preamble. Tanner was just suddenly there, speaking.

"I wanted to take a moment to address my students," he said, "to let everyone know that we will be returning to our regular schedule in just a few hours." A muscle in his cheek twitched, and he passed his hand over the spot as if trying to quiet it. "This morning's lockdown," he said, "is a reminder to us all that what we are doing here at Ione is important and necessary work. The true measure of a society is and has always been how it cares for its weakest and most vulnerable citizens. I am honored to be your headmaster, and I hope each and every one of you is proud to have the Goodhouse name," he said. "Now I invite everyone to join me in prayer." He looked down, off camera. "Our Father," he began, "who art in heaven."

"What the fuck?" someone said. "That's it?"

Everyone began talking at once. Tanner's voice was briefly drowned out by the confusion. Someone jammed a dish in the rotor on the sand tray. A loud grinding, shrieking noise filled the room. "Turn it off," a voice thundered. "Shut it down." The proctors closed around us. They tightened like a band.

"Silence!" they called. "Silence!"

"Lead us not into temptation," Tanner said, and then the power flickered and the transmission was lost, but the final phrases, the ones many of us had learned in childhood, continued to play out in our heads, in our own internal voices, the familiar supplication rattling on, whether we wanted to pray or not.

•

By late afternoon, we still didn't have any official news, but the rumors were getting more consistent. There were just over two hundred dead at the Tacoma Goodhouse. Boys who'd never spoken to me were asking what I'd heard. "They won't take us on work detail," someone said, "not today."

But they did. Before dinner we were marched out to the field across from the soybean crop. Founders' Day would bring close to a thousand visitors and half as many cars, and this field would be the parking lot. The school wanted us to put down a layer of gravel. Creighton and Davis distributed wheelbarrows and shovels. Nearby, a large dump truck raised its bed and dropped a mountain of little rocks inside a cloud of dust.

In an adjacent field, another group was landscaping an area that would hold a row of portable toilets. I could see the main gate from where we worked. There were more guards stationed along the fence. Tanner's kennel was nearby, and I watched the brown, dusty dogs streak back and forth, silent but eager, speaking only with their bodies.

Owen and I were each given plastic square-point shovels and assigned to stand at the base of the gravel mountain. We loaded wheelbarrows when they arrived. The shovel was flimsy and it took a lot of strength to bury it in the pile. "It'd be easier to just pick it up with our hands," Owen whispered. The white edge of his left eye had a red, creeping rash, as if he'd broken a blood vessel.

"Quiet," I said, but everybody was talking tonight.

A dump truck idled behind us, waiting for clearance to leave. I saw the driver watching us in the rearview mirror. He wore a gold necklace with a small cross on it, and when we made eye contact, he spit something onto the ground.

"Do you think Creighton and Davis have to do meditation and reflection?" Owen asked.

"How should I know?" I said.

Runt pushed a wheelbarrow up to our station. We hurried to fill it, and then Harper arrived and we filled that wheelbarrow, too.

"Hey, shitheads," Harper said. He was smiling.

"Hey," I said. I looked around for a class leader and didn't see one. We continued to shovel.

"I got your old room," he said. "But I'll sell it back to you."

"Keep it," I said.

"Good price," he offered. "Or are you all going to stay 3 and 4 forever?"

And then, suddenly, Creighton was standing next to me. "Is there gossiping over here, ladies?" he asked. We worked with renewed effort. "You can tell me," he said. "I don't mind."

Harper hurried off, the wheelbarrow wobbling dangerously, its weight at the edge of what he could control. Under Creighton's watch we made sure we were keeping pace, our backs like pistons contracting, moving, and swiveling—turning a patch of scrubby grass into a road. He stood for a moment, then he picked up a shovel himself. We were all wary. With that thing in hand, his reach was longer, and there was a look about him—a certain testiness—that had me eager to stay off his radar.

"So what do you ladies talk about when I'm not around?" he asked. Nobody answered, and this annoyed him. "I asked you a question."

Blake, a Level 4 boy from our new dorm—a quiet, big-shouldered kid—nodded to Owen. "We listen to this little bitch whine," he said.

"Is that right," Creighton said. "What about?" He was trying to conceal how winded he was after just a minute of work. Creighton leaned on his shovel. He looked heavier; a small belly hung over his belt, and he kept his weight on his good leg. We must have been staring at him, because after a moment he snapped, "I didn't say take a break."

A new kid with an empty wheelbarrow ran up and waited for us to fill it. We got back to work, everyone except Owen. "You *are* getting fat," he said.

I elbowed him. "Shut up," I hissed.

"What did you say?" Creighton asked.

"Nothing," I said. "He didn't say anything."

"It's what everyone's thinking," Owen said.

"Is that right?" Creighton looked around, daring any of us to meet his gaze. "Is there anyone else?" No one spoke. The boy with the wheelbarrow backed away. "Looks like you're the only one," he added.

"I promise you, I'm not," Owen said. His hands tightened around the handle of his shovel. Not far from us, the dump truck started its engine. A blast of exhaust rolled from its tail-pipe and pellets of gravel kicked up in its wake. It began to head down the road toward the exit.

"You want to fight me?" Creighton asked. "You want to make it official?"

"No," I said, "he doesn't." I turned to Owen. "Cut it out."

But Owen was fixated on Creighton with a frightening, almost manic intensity. "You," he said, "are a little pig-eyed cunt."

Creighton responded with a low, growling sort of chuckle. Nobody was even pretending to work now.

I glanced at Owen's face and I recognized then, in my roommate's expression, a kind of reckless desperation. He wanted a fight and he didn't care if he won. I said the only thing that came to mind. "Think about the college," I whispered. "You'll lose your chance. You're going to hear any day." But this only seemed to sharpen his determination, and now all the boys nearby were leaning on their shovels, murmuring to each other. I shifted my weight, getting ready to restrain Owen. I was so focused on him, on what I feared was about to happen, that the siren, when I heard it, didn't immediately make sense. It was the escape alarm—not the throbbing sound of lockdown, not the alarm we'd heard all morning, but just one high, sustained note. A proctor ran past us, down the main road. "Stop the truck!" he was yelling. "Stop the truck!"

•

The dump truck, the one that had idled behind us just moments ago, passed the guardhouse and was now making its way down the civilian road that bordered the school. Guards raced after it, waving for it to stop. The driver accelerated. We were too far away to hear anything, but I could see the men shouting commands. A few guards emerged from the guardhouse with long-barreled guns, and then the driver lost control of the truck—it veered to the right, careening off the roadway, punching through the black, comblike fence, picking up speed and colliding with Tanner's wooden kennel. One side of the structure exploded into timbers. The truck tilted then and rolled onto its side, wheels still turning. Hounds sped in all directions. The scene was just far enough away that it appeared unreal, a disaster in miniature.

Creighton dropped his shovel and started to run toward the gate.

"What's going on?" I asked. But nobody answered. We were all migrating toward the scene, inching forward as if drawn to it.

"I think it's one of us," Owen said.

I heard gunfire then, several sharp, percussive cracks that pierced the sound of the alarm. Proctors swarmed the wrecked dump truck. They dragged a body out of the cab, and we saw another on the ground, thrown during the accident. Nobody rushed to help them. Instead, the proctors focused on the truck itself, investigating it like ants on a slice of apple.

"Line up," a proctor shouted. "Line up. Hands behind your backs."

"What about the dogs?" someone said. They were dispersing onto campus.

"Who is it?" someone else asked. We fell into a line, two by two.

"Shirts off," a proctor called. "Shirts off."

We fumbled with our clothes, but kept glancing over at the scene of the accident. There was an ominous cloud of smoke issuing from the engine, and the proctors were backing away from the wreck. I heard the name Ortiz percolating around me. I threw my shirt onto the ground, adding it to the growing pile.

A boy nearby whispered, "Are you sure?"

"Clasp your elbows," a proctor called. We put our hands behind our backs. Several T-4s raced down the street toward the accident. One of them had a stretcher. Another T-4 with a large fire extinguisher shot past. The late-afternoon sun was hot on my shoulders. I could smell our perspiration. They'd clustered us together in a horseshoe shape. The boys on the adjacent field were in the same formation and their class leaders were telling them to strip down.

"We got one here," Davis called. Creighton marched a boy into the center of the horseshoe and threw him on the ground.

"Don't get up," Creighton said. There was a dark stain on the front of the boy's shirt, a brown smear that could have been mud, but Creighton stepped forward and ripped open the shirt, revealing a deep oozing cut on the boy's belly. He had stuffed it with pieces of bloody rag. I heard the collective suck of air as we saw the wound. He'd dug out his chip, or tried to. I was suddenly afraid they'd see the mark on my stomach, the black dot I'd maintained until it had become almost a tattoo.

"You stupid shit," Davis said. "Where's your roommate?"

The boy just looked at him, resolutely silent. We knew his roommate must be one of the boys in the truck.

"All right," Davis said, and then kicked him in the face. There was a nasty crunching sound, and the boy clutched his nose, moaning. His legs pulled inward in a tight, protective curl.

Davis leaned over and patted the boy's hair. "Where's your roommate?" he asked gently. When the boy didn't answer, he hit him again in the face, then waved to a nearby proctor. "Box this one," he said.

"You," Creighton said, pointing to Owen, the bright light of revelation in his eyes. "You were helping them."

"No." Owen shook his head.

"That's what all the chatter was about," he said.

"I had no idea," Owen said. "I swear."

"You were distracting me," Creighton shouted over Owen's protestations. "Yes, you were."

The proctors dragged the semiconscious boy into the cavity of an open boxer. They stuffed him inside, and his head flopped forward as if he'd passed out. I wondered how long they would leave him in there.

"Box this one, too." Davis nodded at Owen. They opened the other boxer, and I saw that someone had clawed the wood on the interior.

"You're making a mistake," Owen said. "I'm a Level 1 student. You can't do this."

A proctor stepped forward. "Get in," he said.

"No," Owen said. "I had nothing to do with this."

"Get in." The proctor reached for his Lewiston. The boys around us stood wide-eyed, shifting from foot to foot—some straining to see what was happening with the capsized dump truck, some staring at the arrival of Ione police cars. Two dogs dug in the soybean field. Creighton and Davis were huddled, heads together, deep in conversation.

Owen turned toward them. "You can't box me," he said. "I want my chance."

Davis looked up. "What did you say?"

Owen stepped forward, unclasping his hands. "You heard me." The proctors looked to Davis.

"Step back and I'll forget you said that," Davis said, but Owen had a fixed, ecstatic look on his face.

"All the rest of you shitbirds lie facedown on the ground," barked Creighton. "I want every nose in the dirt."

We lay on the ground. I heard the boy in the boxer moaning. I dug my hands into the soil and prayed like I hadn't prayed in months. Owen began to hop from foot to foot in what appeared to be a parody of a boxing stance. I'd never seen him fight, but this told me everything I needed to know.

"I got this," Creighton said to Davis. He wasn't as fast as Davis, but he had meaty, oversize hands that didn't seem to mind running into bone and cartilage. He didn't take pleasure in his job the way Davis did. He just wanted to get it over with.

All the boys in the horseshoe were watching. Nobody had their face in the dirt. Everything that happened here would be reviewed—discussed and analyzed in every common room for weeks. People liked to talk big about what they would do, how they would take leadership. Some stories were legend. Years ago a student had actually stapled some kind of metal grid onto the bottom of his tennis shoes. He'd used his feet to pulverize his opponent's face. Another had made a knife out of a defunct handheld, melting the plastic. That was before they got strict on what kinds of plastic they let us use on campus. These were the more fantastic fights, but I suspected that the biggest asset was really luck. You needed your best day to couple with someone else's bad day. And our class leaders were having a bad day. I tried to send Owen a telepathic message. The knee, I thought, go for his right knee.

Owen was fast. Much faster than I would have suspected. He was able to dodge Creighton's first swing. And I watched as it gave him a dangerous confidence. Owen barely ducked the next punch, and then, when he tried to launch an attack of his own, he mistimed it. Creighton stepped in and easily took the blow in his ribs. He seemed not to even feel it, and then he was past Owen's defenses, up close, where he wanted to be. His big hands had their pick of targets. He hit Owen hard in the neck, just above the collarbone. Owen gave a high-pitched yip and staggered backward.

I hated this kind of fighting—hands tearing and reaching. I thought of Tuck, of the way I had treated his body like a door to be opened. I'd tried to dig through him, to excavate some memory. Every sound that Owen made scratched some raw internal place; it galvanized something inside me, some inner unwillingness to be a witness, to do nothing more than silently sanction.

Owen went down, skidding on gravel. It was just in front of me, and I could hear Creighton mumbling in concentration. He kicked Owen in the crotch, which made him shriek and brought a sympathetic intake of breath from everyone else. Owen writhed and clawed at the ground.

"Anyone else?" Davis asked.

Harper started to rise, but he looked shaky and uncertain as he gained his feet. His roommate Runt was beside him, tugging on his pant leg, calling him an idiot. "Harper," Davis said, "you think you got it? You think you have what it takes to step up, every day? To bust every little asshole with ambition?" Davis grabbed a handful of gravel, knelt beside Owen, and then stuffed it into Owen's mouth. "You ready to work that hard?" he asked.

Harper just stood there. Owen began bucking and choking, trying to spit gravel. My body tensed. I was on my toes and elbows. And then Davis leaned onto Owen, clamping his hand against his mouth. Owen's eyes began to flutter. The cords on his neck stood out as he tried to suck air through his nose.

"He's choking," I shouted.

Harper lay back down. I looked to the proctors, but they were busy. A sleek helicopter wheeled overhead, its rotors slicing the air. Civilian police vehicles encircled the gate, red and blue lights spinning.

"You made your point," I said to Davis. "Let him go."

"Don't get up," Davis said. He looked at me with a steady, bored expression. He took his other hand and pinched Owen's nose closed. "That's it," he added. It was a tone of soft encouragement, the way you would talk to a child learning to walk. "There you go."

And then my body acted of its own accord. The itch that had been inside me all day, the news of Tacoma, the feeling that the air was pressing too close, the dust irritating my skin. The itch overtook me and I swung my foot into Davis, knocking him off Owen in one fluid, explosive movement. It was a kick I'd learned at La Pine, something we'd practiced for fun. It was too fancy a move to use in a real fight. It broadcast too easily. But Davis wasn't expecting it, and it had a lot of power. He was knocked sprawling onto the ground.

My next move was to kick out Creighton's knee. He was kneeling beside Owen and I had a perfect shot. We were both getting to our feet, but he was just a second too slow. I slammed my heel into his kneecap. I heard the crunch of collapsing tendons and cartilage. Or maybe what I heard was the sound of shifting gravel underneath my feet. The chatter of a hundred tiny pebbles. Creighton howled. It took no effort at all to right myself, to reach for Owen, to roll him on his side. One of the boys in the circle came forward to pull the gravel out of his mouth. Owen started to heave and vomit.

Davis made a guttural grunt, something to help him regain his breath. I turned just in time to leap out of his way.

"It's always the roommate," he said. He exhaled sharply to flex his diaphragm. Sweat stung my eyes. As Davis closed the distance between us, I used a basic kick to stop his forward momentum. Any boy at La Pine would have been able to sidestep it, and I was shocked to feel it connect completely. Davis staggered back, his legs shaking, a flash of fear in his eyes. The boys on the ground were calling out advice now, sensing possibility. I couldn't hear individual words, just a rising hiss as if the gravel itself were speaking.

Davis was more experienced and he was stronger; still, it took a moment for him to realize what was going on, to realize that this wasn't just a haphazard flail. I was speaking a different language. I knew what I was doing, and my calm flustered him, more than anything else.

He stepped forward again and I spun to his side, kicking him in the kidneys, which catapulted him forward and made him scramble to stay upright. I kept on him, but didn't get another shot. His arms were too fast and he swung for me, so that leaping back, I was off-balance.

The boys around us were yelling now. Some were standing up. I didn't know where Creighton was. My world had shrunk into this tiny circle. I don't even know how long we fought. It may have been only a minute, but it seemed longer. I didn't go for obvious targets. I knew he'd protect his groin and his face, and he must have had something in his hand, because when it passed over my shoulder, it left a deep cut that soaked my arm with blood. I barely felt it, or rather, it felt like fire and I pulled at the sensation, using it to fuel me, to add power to everything I did.

His face was lit by rage, and the wilder he became, the more calculating and dispassionate I was. But then the fight changed and I was no longer in control. Davis seemed to be everywhere at once. I struck out with my hands, and he knocked me to the ground, where the bigger, stronger boy always won. I struggled to rise, to roll out of his range. I had a fresh cut across my back. I don't know what would have happened next, but two proctors tackled us. "No," I shouted. I was gasping for breath. "I called it. I can beat him. It's my right."

"Shut him up," someone said. I recognized Tanner's voice. He stepped into the circle, wearing his usual black suit. His hair was unkempt, and two of his personal bodyguards stood very close to him, expecting trouble. A proctor twisted my

arm behind my back and then eased when I stopped struggling.

"Get them out of here," Tanner shouted. "Line up and
march. I want every dormitory on lockdown."

Tanner glanced at the gate. A small crowd had gathered.
"Jesus," he said, "that's all we need." He turned to the boxer.
"And what the hell is this? You want to see this on the news?
Get him out of here, too."

Lots of boys reached for their shirts, tugging them on as
they lined up. Owen had a swelling bruise on his forehead,
and his bottom lip was split, but he seemed otherwise okay.
The proctor released me and pushed me toward the others.

"Why are these boys still here?" Tanner asked. "Leave the
shirts. March." And we double-timed it back to the dormitory.
The places where Davis had cut me burned, but I was aware
of another feeling, too. I'd never been outside without a shirt,
not once that I remembered, and now there was the soft, cooling sensation of air lifting the sweat off me. It seemed strange
that I should experience this for the first time at the age of
seventeen—the hot sun overhead, the relief of evaporation as
my body was allowed to function as intended, with no uniform to trap the heat. I must have laughed, or made some
sound, because the boy just ahead of me in line turned around
with an anxious expression on his face. I reached to feel my
chest, the space where the embroidered Goodhouse logo always thickened the front of my shirt. Instead of the chafe of
fabric, I felt only the gentle press of my own skin.

FOURTEEN

The dormitory was quiet when we returned. A nurse came to our room. He brought his med kit and used a tube of skin adhesive to seal the wounds on my arm and my back. He cleaned Owen up, gave him an inhaler to combat the swelling in his throat. The nurse worked silently as a proctor stood in our doorway. The disinfectant they smeared on my arm stained the skin orange, a color that looked even more inhuman beside the bright white bandage. I pulled on a fresh shirt, but I didn't button it. The air conditioner strained and wheezed.

The nurse left, pulling off his gloves, asking the proctor if there was anyone else. They exited through the common room, and the proctor shouted down the hallway that he was locking the main door.

I stared at Owen. "Are you okay?" I said, and then: "What the fuck were you thinking?"

"Doesn't matter," he mumbled. "We're dead, you know."

I did know. You didn't halfway beat your class leaders. And while I was grateful that Owen was breathing, and that I didn't have to endure some immediate consequence, I knew it was just a deferral.

"They'll do it at night," Owen said. "They'll wait until after the celebration and then we'll get a work detail. And that will be it."

"Davis won't wait that long," I said.

Owen stood and dumped the contents of the trash can onto the floor. He knelt and dragged his trunk out from under his bed, then lifted the lid and withdrew a package of crackers, a bar of chocolate, and a can of paint thinner.

"You couldn't beat him," I said. "What did you think would happen?"

He shrugged. He grabbed the piece of paper with the question mark drawn on it. He tore it into strips and folded it into a cone. "Did you know," he said, "that the College of Art has separate rooms for everything, like a room for painting and a room for sculpting, and you can order all your supplies and they just deliver them. You don't have to leave the workshop, not ever."

I lay on my bed and then rolled on my side so I wasn't putting pressure on the wound in my back. "Sounds like campus," I said.

"They'll even bring your meals," he said, "right to the room."

"Why would you want that?" I asked.

"So you don't have to stop working," he said. "So you're never interrupted."

I heard shuffling noises in the hallway. Boys were leaving their rooms, quietly congregating just outside our door. Owen uncorked the accelerant and squirted a few drops onto the paper. "Go ahead and report me," he said. He glanced at the crowd in the doorway and lit the match. Fire erupted from the open mouth of the can, leaping upward, appearing as if by magic. I heard the boys suck in their breath, a collective astonishment. Nobody was going to report us. There was a new feeling moving through the dormitory.

"You want double chocolate?" Owen asked me.

"Triple," I said.

A soft knock sounded on the wall, and I looked up to see

Blake standing at the threshold, having forced his way through the crowd. He was holding a fire extinguisher.

"Authorize me," he said. I looked at Owen. Neither of us made a move to punch in the code that would allow him access to our room. "I've got something for you," Blake said. "We haven't been able to drink it since you arrived. We thought you were snitches."

"We are," Owen said, but this statement was somewhat undermined by his illegal toasting of a chocolate cracker over a blazing trash can.

"Put the can under the air return," Blake said. "You'll get less smoke." To my surprise, he pulled the top off the fire extinguisher. He lifted out a mesh sack and handed it to the boy beside him. Then Blake poured an amber liquid into the sawed-off bottom of a plastic water bottle. He swirled it, picked something out with his finger, and then drank the whole thing. The boys in the doorway cheered.

"Twenty credits a shot," Blake said. "I got both of you."

I glanced at Owen, but he was studiously ignoring everybody.

Blake poured another glass. "Apple mash," he said. "The fucking best."

I got up and typed in the general authorization code on the wallscreen. I let them all in. There was a feeling that life was somehow suspended. What they were doing was much more illegal than what we were doing, and suddenly it all made sense—how clannish the dorm had seemed, how hostile. The light over the door turned green, and a small whoop went up, a restrained sort of cheer, as they jostled inside, sitting on the floor, the desk chair, any available surface.

I walked back to my bed, and boys leaned out of the way to let me pass.

"The cup," they chanted. "Give him the cup." People were

bargaining with Blake, promising credits. Somebody passed me the crinkly bottom half of a water bottle. I had to be careful not to squeeze the flimsy plastic too hard and spill the contents. It was half full of a liquid that smelled acidic and slightly putrid.

"Just toss it back," the boy on the floor beside me said. "Don't taste it."

It was nothing like the cognac I'd had earlier. It felt like I'd taken a fiery sip from the trash can itself. I tried not to gag.

"Pass it," the boys chanted. "Pass it." And someone snatched the cup away, refilled it, and pushed it on toward Owen. He took a sip, gagged, and choked out much of the liquor.

"Another one," the boys said. "Give him another one." But Owen couldn't do it. His throat was raw. He passed me the cup. The second sip was smoother. I could even taste the sweet tang of apple underneath the alcohol.

Owen handed out the remaining graham crackers, toasting one for whoever wanted it. I sat on my bed, watching the boys celebrate, buying shots for each other. They were talking over one another and laughing. I was seeing them as if for the first time.

But then the rush of merriment was like a spent fuel. They were missing two of their own. Ortiz was dead, and we assumed that Carter was, too. We didn't know whom the other bodies belonged to, not yet. We drank a toast to the missing. One boy was particularly distraught. He had dense curly hair that made him look like he was wearing a hat. I didn't recognize him or know his name. "To Ortiz," he said.

And the boys echoed: "To Ortiz." Several were silent, staring at a fixed point in the air as if trying to concentrate.

"He was amazing," Blake said. "He jacked that truck. Oh my God, and when they hit the hound house. Boom. Dogs everywhere."

"That's style," someone said.

When the evening video played, the whole dorm was still packed into our little room. In preparation for Founders' Day, our wallscreens were showing interviews with various class leaders.

"Give us some news," someone called.

"Where's fucking Tanner?" another boy said. "They can't lock us down and not tell us anything."

"That just means it's bad," Blake said. "Really fucking bad."

Creighton and Davis appeared together on the screen, sitting side by side, both wearing their uniforms but looking somehow very clean, and a little younger, too.

"I think the most important thing," Creighton said, "was learning *how* to learn. How to solve problems and become self-sufficient." Davis said something about giving back to the community, and then I couldn't hear, because the boys in the room were yelling so loudly.

It was a strange interview. Creighton and Davis seemed robotic and foreign. Not themselves. It was who they wanted to be. And that was nobody we knew. Someone threw the plastic cup at the screen and said, "Suck my dick." Several others elaborated on this idea. Every few minutes there was a toast to Ortiz or Carter.

"The fucking best," they said.

"To Tacoma," someone said, and we toasted them, too, all the brothers we'd never met.

When the lights went out, Owen lit another fire. Blake covered our window so the flicker wouldn't draw attention, and then he told us about the ghost of a boy who'd been killed in Vargas in the first days of Goodhouse, when the main building was still being renovated. The boy was allegedly found stabbed to death in the delousing pool, and now that the pool had been covered over, you could hear him scratching from the other side of the floor, trying to dig his way out.

"The dead just want to let you know they're there," Blake said.

"No," said Owen. "They want what you have. No matter what it is."

After everybody left, I lay in bed savoring the dizzy rush of too much apple mash and the contentment that came from feeling momentarily safe. There seemed to be less of a barrier between myself and the world. This was how I'd felt pressing against Bethany, and it was a relief to feel it again, to know that I could. Somewhere down the hallway, a sob was quickly muffled. Last night the Tacoma boys hadn't known that they'd had their last meal, their last shower. I wondered if Carter's ghost would return to the dormitory tonight. I wondered if even now it was in the common room, in the hallway—because of course I believed in ghosts. I'd seen them. But more than that, it was impossible to think that there could really be an ending, a full stop.

Blake had predictably sworn us to secrecy about the apple mash, but it had been a gesture only. We were not going to be around long, and it was entirely possible that as boys who'd challenged and failed, we'd drop another status level. I thought of the doctor's words, his assertion that he could help me if I stayed out of trouble. But I was beyond that now, beyond help.

I began to hum the song that I'd heard the night we'd worked late in the soybean field—the melody with a bright, catchy chorus that slipped, unexpectedly, into a minor key. I let the sound calm me, infect me with its beauty, with its swaying refrain, but even this was complicated. My voice was not my own—my affinity for music was a gift from the school, a useless gift, now a redundancy to be phased out. I'd been taught to love something that had no future.

I didn't realize Owen was awake until I went silent and he told me to keep going. "I like that song," he said.

So I kept humming. I started to make up words—nonsense phrases that grew increasingly incoherent as I drifted closer to sleep. Owen sucked on his inhaler, and then, just as I was fading, I felt a sudden pressure on the mattress as he lay down beside me, facing away, back-to-back. I was suddenly awake.

"What's wrong?" I said.

"I got a letter from the College of Art," he whispered.

"And?" I said.

He was quiet for a long time, but I felt the tension in his muscles and heard the uncomfortable rasp of his breath. "That man who interviewed me," he said, "on our Community Day—I don't know that he was real."

"What do you mean?" I said. "Of course he was real."

"I had to do things," Owen said. "At his house." From the thin, reticent tenor of his voice I knew that he was trying not to give life to a memory.

"What things?" I said.

"Not related to art," Owen said. I began to roll over and sit up. "Don't," he said. "Don't move." I lay back down. "I don't want you to say anything."

"Okay," I said.

"Not even that," he said.

There was barely enough room for the two of us on the mattress, but I made myself lie still. After a while I felt him relax into sleep, only to startle awake when he couldn't draw an easy breath. I wondered if it would be like Owen said—we'd get work detail one night and then we'd be outnumbered.

"Still awake?" I whispered.

I heard him suck on the inhaler. Eventually, he got up and returned to his own bed.

"Thank you," he said. "For today. Whatever happens, I won't forget."

.

The next morning, we stuffed a bunch of drawing paper into the trash can to hide the scorch marks. Owen and I checked and rechecked our personal pages, but there were no penalties posted yet—just silence—and this was even more worrisome.

Blake came by our room to collect some of the trash from the night before. Someone had left two reeking sacks of apple mash, and there were bits of charred paper stuck to the linoleum. Blake looked hungover. His eyes were watering, and every time he bent over to collect something, he stood up with a groan.

"They'll do room searches today," he said, "so make sure to flush everything. Wipe the floors, too." They looked dirtier than they should've been.

We had an escort to breakfast, and for the rest of the day they didn't let us travel independently. We moved in small groups of about twenty, accompanied by six proctors. Owen was taken to work on the mural and I ate alone. I felt other students watching me, palming at my approach. By now everyone had heard about the breakout and the fight. I didn't have any visible bruises or lacerations, something that would be unremarkable at La Pine but was considered extraordinary given what had happened on the field yesterday. I tried to move as if I couldn't feel the wound adhesive puckering the skin of my back.

I had a history class later that morning. It was to be my last one, though I didn't know it at the time. The teacher never arrived, so we watched a video documentary of the United States Revolutionary War. It was called *Johnny Tremain*. It looked old—a copy of a copy—and the beginning had corrupted data, so I never did figure out if it was real or just a story. Afterward, there was still a half hour to fill and we sat quietly at our desks. The classroom had a protected podium where a teacher usually stood to lecture or run the media. It had half-walls made of Plexiglas and a desk with a light strip that usually threw ominous shadows across the teacher's face. But today it just lit the emptiness—and so we all sat in the dim room, staring at a glowing tower.

Outside, I watched a group of proctors leading students across campus. They made a loose perimeter around the boys, each man clutching a handheld. The men were looking at the sky. The proctors who'd taken us to breakfast had been like that, too. And then I knew, whatever had happened yesterday, whatever they weren't telling us, the attack had come from above. I stared up at the thin white ribbons of cloud, at the ring of deeper blue at the edge of the horizon. It was vast and ungoverned. With the fence in the distance and the guard-houses, too, the sky suddenly made me feel like I was in a box—a box without a lid.

At noon I was escorted to the factory with the other 3s and 4s. Gravel was still mounded in the fields. A bulldozer—a yellow, square-bodied thing with a long, clawed trunk—tore at the remnants of the hound house. Another truck with a wide loader was on hand to lift the debris and place it in a Dumpster. I kept looking over my shoulder for Davis, for anyone in a class leader uniform. They were conspicuously absent.

When I got to the factory, I was told to report to my supervisor's office. The rest of the group descended the stairs to the suiting-up room, but I trudged to the third floor. I could see Tim's office at the end of the hallway, but to get there I had to pass the large windows that overlooked the distribution center where the Mule Creek inmates worked. I saw them in their jumpsuits, stacking boxes and loading pallets. I ducked below the edge of the window and shuffled forward, hunched over, too tall to really pull it off, but still trying to stay as low as I could.

"What are you doing?" Tim said. He stood in the doorway to his office.

"Nothing," I said. I had my back to the window. "I dropped something."

He glanced at the floor. "Well, pick it up."

"I thought I lost a button." I ran my hand over my shirt. "Guess not."

Tim just watched me, his gaze narrowing as if trying to discern my true purpose. "You got a medical classification," he said. "You're out of the mixing rooms today. Go suit up and relieve Quality Control."

I shook my head. "That's a mistake," I said. "I feel fine. I can lift the bags."

"I'm not asking a favor," Tim said. He walked over to me, standing so close that I could smell the sour, musty odor of his unwashed uniform. When he spoke again, his voice was low but commanding. "Or do you want to test me?"

"No, sir."

"Then you will," he said, "report immediately to your work assignment."

"Yes, sir," I said.

Tim held a bottle in his damaged hand, some civilian drink with a colorful label. He lifted it to take a sip. I was waiting for him to step back, but he stayed where he was, enjoying my discomfort.

"I might not be able to read your file," he said, "but I don't need to. You're all the same." He nodded. "Consistently disobedient."

"Sorry, sir," I said.

"Tell me," he said, "what do you want to do when you graduate?" But his mocking tone let me know that the question was rhetorical. I lowered my gaze, stared at my shoes. "Do you want to work here?" he asked. "Maybe you want my job? Would you like that?" He lifted the bottle and made a show of inspecting the label. "Or do you think it's not important enough," he said, "that *I'm* not important?"

"I just want to work," I said. I was hoping that this was the right answer, the proper amount of submission.

"Work is a privilege," he said. "You forget that. Year after year we have the same boys forgetting the same things. Can you imagine how frustrating that is?"

I nodded, and Tim put the bottle on the windowsill, setting it down a little more heavily than was necessary. The sound made me jump. "No, I don't think so," he said. "I really don't think you can imagine."

•

I reported to the suiting-up room and was disappointed to find it crowded with a different shift—dozens of boys peeling off their coveralls and hairnets. I passed the wallscreen where I'd talked with Bethany and wondered if she could see me now, some electronic pulse on a screen.

I grabbed a set of coveralls from the CLEAN bin. I had just pulled them on when a lanky kid with brown hair swatted me on the back, right across my wound. I spun to confront him, but he gave me a big grin and said, "That's cojones, man." It took me a moment to realize he was referring to the fight.

"Or stupid," his friend mumbled.

"That's cojones," the kid repeated. "But I wouldn't want to be you."

I trudged over to Quality Control. Once I was on the factory floor, the intensity of sound dulled thought. I tapped the previous boy on the shoulder, replacing him, sitting on the tall metal stool and watching the chocolate carpet creep past. White ribbons of frosting spooled out so that the whole thing looked vaguely like a divided roadway, white lines on dark asphalt.

I positioned myself so that I could see more of the room, specifically the ladder in the corner. At one point, I felt a prickling at the back of my neck and the hair on my arms stood up as if there were lightning in the air. I whipped around, searching for movement. Nobody was there. I told myself I was overreacting, but still, I removed my earplugs. Several hours into my shift, after a batch had run and the conveyor belt was empty, I got up to pace. It was only luck that I happened to glance at the exit door. A long iron pipe was wedged through the loop of the handle and jammed behind a similar pipe that ran close to the wall.

I pulled on the pipe, but it didn't move. I swiveled to face the room. It was empty. I stared into the shadows around the grain silos. A loud horn signaled that the line was about to resume. And that's when I saw Montero. He was standing beside the tray where I'd put the rejected cupcakes, eating one, chewing thoughtfully as he watched me.

"You missed your deadline," he said.

"What do you mean?" I asked. I noticed that the main camera—the one that monitored and recorded the Quality Control environment—had been disabled. Montero had stuck something to the lens. It looked like a metal cone. I pointed toward it. "That's a mistake," I said. "They'll send a proctor."

"Let them," he said. "This won't take long."

"They'll lock down the factory," I said.

"Not before we send you a message," he said. He reached over and I thought he was going to pick up another cupcake, but he lifted a knife instead—a compact, improvised-looking blade that fit easily in his hand. "Or should we give you one more day?"

"Who's we?" I said.

Montero nodded over my shoulder. A man stood just a few feet behind me. He was gigantic—easily six and a half feet tall—the right size and shape to force that pipe into place. I began to edge away. He didn't look like anyone I'd ever seen. Black tattoos covered his cheeks and forehead—some kind of swirling pattern that sprawled onto his neck, disappearing into the collar of his too-small Mule Creek jumpsuit.

"I have your reader," I said, "but not on me. It's in my room, in the mattress. I didn't know I'd be working here today."

"He's lying," the giant said.

"Look," I said, glancing between the two of them. "It's not that easy to move stuff around campus." I was just stalling, saying anything. This was my own fault, and I was furious with myself. I should have reported Montero, but I'd been too eager to possess something, to have contraband in my pocket. I'd been greedy, and now it would cost me.

"I think we need to do some clarification," the giant said. He started toward me. "We need to talk to James in a way that he can understand."

"Great," I said. I nearly tripped over the stool where I'd sat these past few hours. It was old—the paint was scratched and one of the legs had a serious dent—but it was made of a thick, sturdy metal. I reached down and picked it up, holding it in front of me like a shield.

"Stay back," I said. "I'm warning you."

But they were both converging now. I turned and threw the stool into the works of the cooling tube.

Montero lunged, but he wasn't fast enough to grab it. The legs were sucked in, and then suddenly the stool wrenched upward as if it had caught in an internal gear. There was a

massive booming sound and I heard the ping of metal strik-
ing the wall behind me. The giant screamed, staggered to one
side, his hand on his shoulder, a piece of metal lodged in the
meat of his arm. The line stopped. Smoke puffed from the machinery. Cupcakes continued to churn out of the hot-icer, cas-
cading onto the floor, until the belt shuddered and snapped
and flung them everywhere. There was an eerie groaning noise
somewhere deep along the line. We all were momentarily
stunned by the extent of the damage.

"You stupid fuck," Montero said.

"You better run," I said. Someone was already banging
on the jammed exit door, trying to open it. "Cupcake?" I
offered.

The camera swiveled overhead, or it tried to. It had been
damaged by a projectile when the cooling tube ruptured.
Whoever was at the door shouted, "Open this right now."

"Get me out of here," I shouted back. "It's jammed."

The giant grabbed the front of my shirt. He threw me
onto the ground. The wound on my back reopened. "Don't
touch me," I said. I tried to scramble away from him, but I
slipped on the greasy floor. His touch had infected me with a
kind of toxic animosity. It lit me up inside, made me stupid
with fury.

I was braced for a fight, but it didn't come. The pounding
on the door was replaced by a sawing sound, and—at this—the
two prisoners scrambled up the side of the grain silo. I ran to
the door. The pipe had loosened, but by the time I yanked it out,
I was alone in the room. The doors surged open. A half-dozen
proctors streamed in. "They're up there," I said. "I know their
names. Well, I know one of them. They're ten seconds ahead
of you."

But the proctors were more interested in getting me on my
knees. Tim stormed into the room. "No, no, no," he said,

looking at the mess on the floor. "Oh, hell no. I want this one boxed. I want him cooked. I want a big fat bow on him."

"Tattoos on his face," I said. "Real recognizable."

"Someone's been this way," a proctor called from the grain silo ladder. "Hatch is open."

"I told you," I said. "They're just ahead of you."

Tim pointed to me. "Why is he still here?"

"They're Mule Creek inmates," I said. "You have to find them."

"Oh, I'm sorry," Tim said with exaggerated solicitude. "Did I cut you off? Were you giving an order?"

Three proctors dragged me out of the factory and put me in the boxer, securing and locking the lid into place. They congregated a few feet away, speaking in quiet, serious voices that I couldn't quite hear. I ran my hand over the interior of the box and felt where the wood had been gouged. These marks were left by the people who'd sat there before me, and I thought of them as chaotic hieroglyphs—some relic of a long-vanished tribe.

One of the proctors drove me to Box Hill and parked. There was a little guardhouse with a canvas awning and a refrigerator. It was just like I'd heard. There was a single chair and the proctor sat in it, eating out of the fridge, watching a wallscreen just inside the door. An old, bulbous air conditioner had been mounted on one wall. It whirred and spit. Water dripped from the condenser coils and left dark, rusty streaks on the surface below.

When the man leaned forward and adjusted the volume on the wallscreen, I heard voices—men and women talking together—then a rumble, like an audience laughing. My knees were jammed into my armpits, and when I tried to shift my weight, I couldn't. There wasn't any room. Very soon the afternoon heat was unbearable. The reeking, ovenlike box exhaled baking air through the hole around my neck. There was a thin lip of aluminum around the edge of the opening, and now I understood why. As I grew dizzy and my head got heavier, I struggled to keep away from the burning metal. I began pushing at the walls of the box, digging at the wood, trying to straighten my legs, to get just another inch. My shoulders strained against the lid, which seemed to press back. It felt bad to struggle and then worse to be still. Sweat ran down my face. It stung my eyes and I couldn't wipe it away. I wondered why tears didn't burn like this. I wondered what made them so different.

•

After sundown, the proctor drove me to Protective Confine-ment. It was far from the main campus. I'd never actually seen the building, just the narrow road that was the turnoff. There was a guard station there, and a man nodded as he waved us through. My lips were cracked and chapped. The uneven mo-tion of the boxer made my head snap back and forth. When-ever my throat struck the edge of the box, I coughed and gagged.

We traversed what must have been, at one point, a civilian neighborhood. The houses had been removed and the land repurposed, but there were still sidewalks and concrete stairs—remnants of a different time. In one of the fields there was a partial chimney and firebox still intact, the brick black-ened as if the house around it had burned.

And then I saw the Confinement Block. It had been built over several of these cleared lots, and even though it was two stories tall, it looked squat—somehow compressed—as if the building had been pushed into itself. An enormous pile of dirt sat nearby. I'd heard that boys had to move it from one side of the yard to the next and, depending on the punishment—they were given shovels or spoons.

The T-4 lurched to a stop, and the proctor said, "Okay, kid. Try not to fall out." He stood and unlatched the side of the box. I slid to the ground. My tongue was swollen, and I had a hard time getting my legs to do anything but twitch. I couldn't tell if I'd pissed myself or just absorbed the smell of the box, but either way, it was enough to make the man choke.

"Did they catch them?" I said.

"Catch who?" the proctor asked. "Can you get to your feet?"

"The Mule Creek inmates," I said. "Did you stop them?"

"Not me," he said. He looked worried, as if I wasn't making sense. A Confinement proctor stepped out of the doorway and walked toward us. This proctor had a neck that seemed on the verge of being swallowed by two deltoid muscles. It appeared compressed, like the building itself. He didn't wear a formal uniform, just a pair of khaki shorts and a navy-colored T-shirt—but he moved with authority. His black, thick-soled boots were recently polished. From where I was crouched, I could smell the inky tang of the leather.

The proctor typed something on his handheld. "Factory kid," he mumbled. "Jammed a stool into the gears."

The Confinement proctor frowned as if I were mud on his boot. "Hope it was worth it," he said, and yanked me to my feet. I staggered after him, weaving—trying to keep pace. As we neared the thick metal doors, I took a last deep breath of summer air, a last look at the shadowy sky.

The doors opened automatically at our approach, and I followed the proctor into a hallway with a guard station at one end. Lowell, the boy with the dent in his forehead, was sweeping the floor. I watched as he shuffled toward us, dragging the broom behind him. One of his eyelids drooped as if it were melting off. He opened his mouth as I passed and made a sudden groaning sound—a sound that made me flinch. "Easy," the proctor said. "Watch it."

The air inside the Confinement Block was humid but chilly, like a cave. The walls were poured concrete, and the grain of the wooden molds used in their construction had etched the surface so that the whole building appeared to be built from petrified wood—some dead gray forest. The guard station had a single proctor watching a number of monitor screens that lit the wall behind him, displaying a maze of passageways. Somewhere overhead I heard a noise—a booming, insistent thrum.

"This way," the proctor in front of me said.

He marched me down a hallway punctuated with narrow doors, many of which were open, revealing rows of identical cells. The rooms were small, like the ones I'd glimpsed in the basement of the infirmary, only here the concrete walls visibly retained the damp. Dim greenish light flickered overhead. A large metal drain cover was embedded in the floor. A tuft of fur undulated under the perforated brass. It was a rat, disappearing down the pipe.

I realized that I was about to be trapped behind one of these doors, forgotten, left to rot from the inside out. I'd heard rumors that men visited your cell here at night—not every night, but some. It was too dark to see their faces, to know if they were proctors or students. They were just devils reaching for you, reaching and finding. I imagined my parents far away somewhere, in Idaho. I liked to believe that if they knew I was in trouble, they'd come for me—if they were out of jail, if they were still alive.

The proctor stopped at the end of the corridor and told me to strip down. "You're home," he said, and nodded toward an open door. The room inside was three feet wide and six feet long. A coffin. It had a shit-smeared hole in the center of the floor and no windows. "Take everything off," he said. But I just stood there staring, and then I began to back away.

"No," I said.

The proctor seemed more weary than angry. "Come on, kid," he said. "This is it. Strip down." Footsteps sounded in the hall. More proctors.

"Wait," I said. "What is this supposed to teach me?"

This made the proctor laugh. But I was sincere. All the calming exercises, all the reaching for compassion—it seemed distant now—but it had been a pillar of my education.

"Don't worry," he said. "There isn't going to be a test afterward."

"How long are you going to leave me in there?" The proctor nodded to a man behind me. "I need some water first," I said. Someone grabbed my collar and yanked at my shirt. The wound on my back had bled and scabbed, drying to the fabric like a second skin. The pain of its removal was so intense, so unexpected, that I lunged at the proctors, just kicking and swinging, ineffectual against so many.

They stuffed me in the little room and the door rammed closed. The darkness was total. I'd lost a shoe in the fight, but I still had my pants. I stood on one foot. I leaned against the wall, but the surface was powdery and wet. I took off the shoe and stood on it with both feet. Maybe an hour passed. I heard rats in the sewage hole. I breathed through my mouth, wondering when I would get used to the smell. The temperature dropped. Night was here. I felt time opening before me, a yawning rictus of misery.

For the first few hours it seemed impossible that anyone could survive in this room. But then I began to understand how it might happen. A person would change, adapt. The room would alter them. It was already happening. I already knew which corner was the driest. I stood beside the door where the air was better and a small beam of greenish light made it possible for me to see my hand. The process was so simple, so natural—and more than anything I'd felt at Ione, it terrified me. It filled me with an angry resolve, a determination not to change—no matter what circumstance, no matter what room.

FIFTEEN

I'm not sure how much time passed, but I was conscious of the temperature falling and then rising again. When someone slid a bowl of watery broth through a tiny panel in the door, I knew I'd survived my first night. I'd slept in fits, ten minutes at a time, and I felt the pain of this in my muscles. After I'd licked the bowl dry, I placed it neatly beside the door. No one came to collect it.

I must have dozed, because I awoke to the sound of footsteps. Someone stopped outside my cell and waited there. I grabbed my shoe and used the toe to scoop out a clump of shit from the hole in the floor. I wasn't going quietly.

But then I recognized Dr. Cleveland's voice.

"What the hell is going on?" he said. "Open this door immediately."

"Sir," a proctor said, "our directive says to keep him here."

I pounded on the wall. "I'm inside," I shouted. "Get me out."

"This is my patient," the doctor said. "He is in my care. I gave explicit instructions for this boy to be remanded to the infirmary in case of any trouble. Whose idea was this?"

"What instructions?" the proctor said. He sounded a little frantic. "Sir, nothing was posted."

The lock retracted and the door opened. I dropped the shoe

and blinked at the light, momentarily blinded. My pupils contracted and my eyes watered. Dr. Cleveland wore a windbreaker and civilian pants, but he held one of his white lab coats in his hand. He pointed to me. "Explain this," he said.

One of the proctors held aloft the glowing square of his handheld, showing the proctor beside him the screen. "I swear there was nothing posted when he arrived," the man said.

"What you saw or failed to see is not my problem," Dr. Cleveland said. "And if my patient suffers any residual trauma, I will hold you personally responsible."

The doctor tossed me the white lab coat. It flew through the air like a ghost, the sleeves lifting from the body of the jacket— empty, handless, grasping arms. I caught it and slipped it on, hugging the sides shut. I followed him out, walking barefoot through the gritty hallways. We passed the guard station, where two Confinement proctors stood muttering to each other. The front doors opened automatically into the yard. It was early evening and the fresh air, the slight breeze, felt incredible on the sunburned skin of my face. I realized I'd been in there for nearly a full day.

A T-4 idled out front, waiting. The doctor and I sat side by side on the front bench seat. He handed me an aluminum bottle full of mineral-enriched water. I consumed it in a single gulp.

"Thank you," I whispered. My hands shook. "Thank you."

"Stop talking," he said.

Dr. Cleveland drove me back to his office. When we got there, he said, "You've bled through the back of my coat. I'll have to patch you up." He took a package of sterilized instruments from the gray cabinet to the right of his desk, but as he approached me, he set the package aside.

"Actually," he said, "you smell like a biohazard." He walked me to a staff shower located off the main hall. I watched as he reached down and authorized my entry with his thumbprint. I kept asking him about the incident at the factory, and finally he told me that no intruders had been found. There was no one named Montero in the facility.

I shrugged. "A nickname," I said. "That's not important. I know his face." But the doctor didn't seem particularly interested in this possibility or in anything that had transpired in the factory.

"Use a lot of soap," he said. "I'll get you some clothes. Towel's over the sink."

The shower was newer than the one in my dorm, and there was no water timer here. When the doctor was gone, I stood openmouthed under the spray, drinking as much as I could. Afterward, I made the temperature as hot as possible. I leaned against the wall, watching steam thicken the air, feeling cocooned in the thrum and echo of water on tile. The heat seemed to be reaching into me, relaxing some inner knot that I was only just aware of. I scrubbed the black dirt from under my nails, scrubbed until my skin was raw. I stayed as long as I dared, and then I shut off the tap. I grabbed a towel and stood in front of the mirror. There was a handprint in the steamed glass. The fingers were small and tapered, the shape of the palm was almost square, and I wondered if it was Bethany's. I lifted my hand to touch it, but when I drew my hand away, I realized my mistake. I'd replaced the mark with my own.

Underneath the light switch, a print reader gave off a faint glow, its green color diffused by the vapor in the air. I remembered what Bethany had said—she had fifty duplicate readers scattered throughout the infirmary. Out of curiosity, I dug my thumbnail under the back edge of the plastic rectangle. It didn't move at first, but when I applied a little more pressure, the front casing popped off, tumbling out and toward me. I caught it just as a knock sounded on the door.

"Are you decent?" Dr. Cleveland said. He didn't wait for my answer, and I barely had time to cover myself, to turn my back toward him, before he stepped into the room. He put a stack of clothes on the sink: a gray button-down shirt and jeans, a pair of plain canvas shoes.

"Put these on," he said. "They're all I could get on short notice." When I didn't immediately follow his orders, he said, "What are you waiting for?"

As Dr. Cleveland stood by, I managed to slip the reader into the pocket of the pants. The clothes were a little loose, but the material was incredibly soft and whispery against my skin—civilian clothes.

"The inmates—the men I saw—they're planning something," I said. "I think they want to escape through the factory."

But Dr. Cleveland only shrugged. "They're criminals," he said. "They lie." He walked me back to his office, where he gave me a cream for my sunburned face. I took off the shirt and he sat me on a little stool, then rubbed anesthetic into the wound on my back.

"I'm going to have to stitch this," he said.

"Did Owen get reassigned?" I asked.

"Who?" he asked. He pulled over a little lamp on wheels, something with an adjustable neck. He turned the beam on.

"My roommate," I said. "It's not his fault. He can't share in this. He can't have this on his record."

"James," Dr. Cleveland said, his voice quiet and serious, "I think you should worry more about yourself." This shut me up. I sat, feeling each stitch—not the pain but the pressure and the tug of progress.

When he was finished, I shrugged into my shirt. The doctor walked over to the gray cabinet and deposited a pair of scissors into what appeared to be a little chrome autoclave. He pulled out the cognac bottle and a single glass, which he filled.

"Do you know what our biggest challenge is here at Goodhouse?" he asked. He stared into the cup, swirling the contents. "It's not data collection. We have lots of data. No—it's an inability to synthesize, to distill." He walked over to his desk. "The computer looks for patterns—it's there to anticipate and prevent. Your file, for example, has been recently flagged."

"For what?" I asked.

"Deviation," he said. "You've been operating outside your pattern."

Something in his tone made me cautious. I didn't know if he was referring to my fight with Davis or the incident at the factory. "I did what I had to do," I said. "That's the truth."

"You promised to stay away from my daughter," he said. "You were going to tell me if she contacted you. And that," he said, "was also the truth." I went very still. He tapped the metal band of a ring against the side of his glass. "You were out with Beth the other night, don't bother to deny it. You let her walk around campus after dark," he continued. "By herself. You encouraged her."

"I didn't," I began.

"She's not interested in you," he said. "She might think she is, but you're just another way of communicating with me."

"Okay," I said. I was stalling. It wasn't clear how much he really knew. But the ropy muscles in his forearms told me that he was gripping the glass tightly.

"My daughter," he said, "has good intentions. I have to believe that. She'll think she's rescuing you. She won't mean to do damage, but she will. And then you will damage her, and that," he said, "is something I can't allow."

"Sir," I said, "I think there's been some sort of misunderstanding."

"Do you know what two points on a graph do?" Dr. Cleveland asked. He set down his glass. "They plot a line, a progression. You are just such a point—a piece of a larger trajectory. She thinks that she can pull you off the line, but she can't."

I looked around the office. The room was full of weapons. On a little table beside the gray cabinet there was some kind of old-fashioned bust. It was a man's head divided into colorful sections, each one numbered and labeled. It looked like a toy. I reached over and picked it up as if I were examining it. The bust was very heavy, and it fit nicely into the palm of my hand.

"You won't survive without my help," Dr. Cleveland continued. And when I didn't react, he just shook his head. "You think I exaggerate," he said. "Okay, James. Tell me, how are you feeling?"

"I won't go back to Confinement," I said. "And you can't return me to the general population. I need to be transferred."

Dr. Cleveland ran his hand over the top of his desk and his computer blinked on. The back of the holographic screen was a shimmering, diaphanous glow. "Have you been having as many nightmares?" he asked. "Incidents of panic? Hypervigilance? Have you noticed any change?"

"No," I said.

"Really?" Dr. Cleveland said, but now that I thought about it, these moments had been less frequent and less intense. "Then I suppose it's a good thing we have an empirical record." He spoke to the computer. "Project to wall."

It was some kind of graph. My name was at the top, above an array of red, blue, and yellow rectangles. "There," he said, "you see. You *are* sleeping better." He scrolled to another graph and then another, faster than I could track. "Your pupils are normal. Your glucose production is down. It's true you're more aggressive, but your years of maintaining a Level 1 are really paying off here. Your control is impressive, and when you decide to forgo that control, your reaction times, your stamina—they are all beyond our expectations."

"What are you talking about?" I said.

"You're responding well to your new medication," he said. "Your history, your abilities—even the attack on La Pine and the way it has altered you on a chemical level—have made you very valuable."

"What medication?" I said.

"Now you have the chance to help thousands of people," he said. "To transform the world you live in. I'm only asking you to choose it for yourself."

"What fucking medication?" I asked. But I thought of the injections I'd received every morning in my arm, just above the elbow. I'd gone in day after day. I'd assumed it was corti-sone, but it could have been anything at all. "Answer my question," I said.

"I need you," the doctor said, "to go back to the Exclusion Zone."

I thought I'd misunderstood. "How do you know about that place?" I said, and then, when he reached into his desk drawer, I said, "If you bring a needle within a foot of me, I will jam it into your eye."

But this only seemed to amuse him. He stood with his head cocked to one side, a very Bethany-like expression. "James," he said, "you really are the perfect patient."

•

I threw the statue at him and missed. Two proctors were through the office door and on top of me in a matter of seconds. "Don't stun him," Dr. Cleveland said. I bucked and kicked. I felt the prick of the needle in my neck, and then a hot, numbing wave unstrung my muscles and liquefied my thoughts.

They carried me to the couch. The cushions seemed un-believably soft, folding around me like warm air. "The sedative feels like more than it is," Dr. Cleveland said. "Just give in to it."

"No," I whispered.

"You need to rest," he said. He sat on the little coffee table next to the couch, his face a few feet from my own. "It won't be as easy as last time. No one's getting a placebo tonight."

"I won't fight," I said.

"You will," he said.

"I'll just sit there," I said. "Watch me." I tried to stand, but could only lift my arm an inch before it became leaden and uncooperative. Fatigue pulled at me. I could hear my pulse in my ears and I felt like I was falling—through the couch, through the floor, into some long tube like a drain.

"Will you give us a minute?" Dr. Cleveland said to the proctors. They stood arrayed behind him, their red Lewistons out.

"Sir," a proctor said, "we need to move him before it wears off."

"Wait outside," he repeated, his tone more commanding. The men left the room but didn't shut the door.

"What does it do?" I asked. "The medication."

"It's remarkable that you're still awake." He clicked on a penlight and shot the beam into my eye. A jolt of pain gave me the strength to swat his hand away.

"Stop that," he said. He held down my arm and tried again to check my pupils, but I shut my eyes against the glare.

"You don't have the right to do this," I said.

He clicked off the light and sat back. "You know why the Zeros kill with fire?" he asked.

"Parable," I said, "of the weeds."

"They think they're doing you a favor," he said, "something that you are too weak and too selfish to do on your own."

I tried to respond, but my mouth felt like a rubber band.

"Without the flames," he said, "you all are condemned to spend eternity with the devils whom you've made flesh."

"That's insane," I whispered.

"They want to better the world," he said. "I might not agree with their methods, but I've got to ask, are your goals as lofty?" He grasped my face, turning it toward his own, pinching my cheeks against my teeth. And I must have whimpered, some animal noise, something I was ashamed of, because his grip lessened. "Go to sleep," he said. "It's a function of your age that you can't see the needs of the many for what they are. You can't feel the urgency, the obligation." His hand slid over my eyes, and the steady warm pressure of his palm consigned me to darkness. "Someday," he whispered, "when you are dead, the work that you do for me tonight will live on inside the people you help, and then they will feel you, even if they don't know your name."

•

I awoke on the ground, my face pressed to the floor, dirt and grit stuck to my cheek. I sat up, sucking in deep lungfuls of air. My hands were bound, tied in front of me with a plastic wire, and I didn't immediately know where I was or what was going on. I looked around the room—at the vandalized walls, at a piece of warped plywood that had been nailed over a window well. Black mold coated a section of the floor and crawled up one wall—little interconnected dots, all part of a pattern. Still, I didn't know what I was seeing. It was always like this—that delay between waking and remembering—a small, bright gap in which I was free of identity and history, and then reality would snap over me like a cage. And this time it felt worse, so much worse, when I realized what was coming.

I got to my feet, and the effort left me unsteady and light-headed. I had to get my hands free, so I paced the room looking for something I could use. I walked over to the panel of plywood. It was warped but still strong and intact, and when

I tried to wedge my fingers between the wood and the wall, it didn't budge.

I knelt beside what was left of an old porcelain toilet. Just a fraction of the original pedestal remained, still bolted in place. I ran the plastic wire over the jagged edge, trying not to stare too hard at the hole that descended into the floor. But I already knew that this wasn't likely to work—that when the door opened tonight, when I was sucked into the darkness, into the chaos of the hallway, justice would be waiting for me. With my hands bound, the other men would dominate me. I would become Tuck, I would be the body on the ground, and that thought made me press the wire harder against the porcelain, file it with all my strength, even though I knew it was hopeless and the wire remained intact even as the friction wore down the ceramic edge. One substance was stronger than the other. It always came down to this.

As I worked, the music I'd sung for Tuck began to creep back into me. It had been a fragment from Handel's *Messiah*, a fragment from our last Christmas performance. I heard the opening bars, then I felt my entrance and tensed as if I were about to sing, about to join that dead chorus. To hear us, to sit in the audience, was to surrender yourself, to be guided and altered. And God, their God, the one I could never quite believe in, he'd felt real when his gospel had been lodged in my throat. His promises, so archaic on the page, had felt, in song, volatile and exciting, a fragment of what was possible.

I stopped filing. I was exhausting myself. Dr. Cleveland was right—my night in Confinement had sapped my strength. Maybe it was better this way. If he wanted me to fight, then disappointing him was meaningful.

And then I heard them—all the people who were being led inside, the opening and closing of doors, the hooting calls, and the muffled sound of talking in the room beside my own.

I stood and faced the door. It was the only new piece of equipment in the room, metal with a gray enamel finish. A few footprints were stamped onto the bottom—tread from civilian shoes. On my first night here the doors had all unlocked at once. Somehow we'd been driven toward the room with the guards, moving as one, as though we were pushed. I was struggling to remember the details now, to find some piece of useful information, when the door in front of me slid open and a man walked through, unescorted. For a second I thought it was Tuck. Briefly, I hoped it was. The man wore a Mule Creek uniform and he had roughly the same rangy build, but he had no tattoos.

He stopped at the sight of me and we stared at each other. He was a little taller than I was and his hair was braided into tight rows along his scalp, something I'd never seen before.

"One of the neighbor boys," he said, "in my room. What fun." But his tone was more threatening than friendly.

"How do you know I'm from next door?" I said. I wasn't wearing a uniform.

He didn't answer. He just walked toward me and stopped about five feet away, leaning against the wall, relaxed and confident. Above his tight braids was a fuzz of loose hair like steam rising off his scalp. "Nothing personal," he said, "but I'm going to beat the shit out of you tonight."

I instinctively shifted my weight forward. I expected him to lunge, but he just continued standing there. Somewhere nearby, I heard the clang of metal against metal. And the music I'd imagined was still playing, the performance progressing inside me—the baritone telling me that the people who walked in darkness had seen a light, a great light.

"What are you waiting for?" I asked, even though I knew. And when the lights did cut out, I felt the man launching forward. I felt the churn of air a fraction of a second before impact. My hands closed around the fabric of his shirt, and I used his own momentum to roll him over and past me. I kicked him hard and then ran for the door. A memory of the room was still bright in my mind, still functional, but I struck a cold metal slab. The door was closed.

I heard commotion on the other side, the collision of bodies. Something had gone wrong. Our room hadn't opened. I felt for a knob, but there was none. And it was just as the man grabbed me and spun me around that I remembered the print reader. I didn't know if it was still in my pocket—but I heard something fall to the floor, or I thought I did.

The man was trying to use his weight to drive me down, so I kept moving, making myself a difficult target. Even with my hands bound, I managed to break his hold on my shirt. Blackness had sucked close and my breath was coming too fast. I no longer knew where I was. I no longer saw the room in my mind. The man clipped me a few times—they weren't direct blows but enough to show me how unsustainable this was. I was off-balance and slowing down. It was just a matter of time before I was overwhelmed. And then, one of us must have stepped on the print reader, because it activated—a sudden green glow in the dark, a reference point. I resisted the urge to reach for it, and I was rewarded by seeing the light lifted off the ground, held in his hand. That was all the information I needed.

I lunged at the man and kicked him hard in the groin. It was the kind of shot that he would've blocked if he'd been able to see it coming. A warbling shriek told me that he had not. The reader clattered to the ground. I almost kicked him again. I felt the strength inside me, the certainty that I had several long seconds to do what I wanted—freedom and access. But I managed to shut that impulse down.

I grabbed the reader, and when my hand closed around it,

the screen glowed in my palm. The last print—the doctor's thumbprint—was illuminated with a greenish light, a tiny hurricane seen from above. I heard the man groaning and then the scuffle of him moving on the floor. I ran my hands over the wall, following it until I found the doorframe, hoping to locate the familiar shape of a reader embedded there. I was trying to hurry without losing control. The roles were reversed—he could see me now, he had all the information.

I found what I was looking for. I pressed the doctor's thumbprint to the screen and the door opened. I was braced for the fight, ready for it—crouched low—but the hallway had emptied; the tumult was farther down. The inmates were being driven toward the room with the guards. I heard the sounds of their struggles: the growling, the cursing, the occasional higher-pitched cries of those in trouble. And then I was back in the hallways at La Pine and the smoke was overhead, a lowering ceiling, and my friends were alive, but they were also dead and they were following me and I knew where to go. I felt the building stepping out of my way, the hallway peeling back its walls. I held the thumbprint aloft. It made a star in the darkness.

"Follow me," I called. "We're supposed to go this way," I shouted. "This way." And though I couldn't see individuals, I sensed a shift in the atmosphere, a drawing closer, the instinctive moving toward the light. I felt as if the men were one man, as if they were all joined, and I sensed their pursuit as I ran. I stumbled over people on the ground. I careened off walls and slid into a still-locked door, the first of many that secured the passageway.

This is how they had corralled us, I realized. They'd sealed these doors sequentially, ensuring our one-way progress. Now I was blowing them open. And though I got faster, more practiced at unlocking them—at knowing, in the dark, exactly where the print reader would be—the men, the one man that was behind me, drew closer and closer, and the margin between us shrank away until I felt him almost on me, reaching, disturbing the air at the back of my neck. I opened one last door and found myself in a brightly lit room—the place where Davis had turned me over to the Mule Creek guards, a little lobby of sorts, a staging area.

Two uniformed guards were on their feet immediately. A third was frantically tapping at a wallscreen.

"I don't know," he was shouting and then: "Dear God."

One of the guards rushed me. He had a baton in his hand, and I thought that I'd have to fight him alone. But then all the men boiled through the doorway and I seemed to ride forward on their wave—it pushed me toward and through the outer door. We poured into the night, scattering into the strip of land that divided the two institutions. Immediately, the Mule Creek guardhouses clicked on their lights. A siren started to throb, but the sound was quickly cut short. No one wanted to acknowledge the escape. I was aware of the men around me. Some had stopped just outside the entrance, but most had kept moving, kept traveling. And I felt only exhilaration as I ran hard for the perimeter fence. I had rescued us from each other. I had pulled us from chaos into more chaos, but still—I hadn't left anyone behind. I hadn't left them there in the dark to die.

SIXTEEN

I slipped back onto campus—dodging through the two inactive fence posts, my hands still tied. I smelled the electricity in the air. It put a metallic taste in my mouth, and it tugged at the little hairs on the backs of my arms. I glanced over my shoulder and was surprised to see several Goodhouse boys crossing the boundary behind me. I hadn't been the only one. "Wait," a voice called. It was a student. "Wait!" But I kept going. I was headed east, toward the infirmary. I didn't know for sure that Dr. Cleveland was waiting there, but I assumed he'd be watching the results in his office. I picked up my pace. My lungs ached with the effort.

To the north, on the slope in front of Vargas, I saw numerous T-4s streaming down the pathways. Running lights outlined their domed roofs, and from a distance, the cluster of vehicles looked like the glowing spores of some dandelion head, drifting apart, dissipating in the wind. The sudden beauty of the school distracted me—the lights, the cool night air, the way I seemed to be floating inside myself, flying forward.

Without warning, a car pulled around a corner and stopped directly in front of me, bisecting my path. It was a sleek silver sedan with wide wheels and graceful curving fenders. I tried to reverse my course, but I couldn't. I stumbled and then collided with the car's hood. The driver's-side door popped open and there—there was Bethany.

"Oh my God," she said, "they tied your hands." I was heaving, unable to catch my breath. "Get in," she said. "Hurry."

I just stood there, saying nothing. The T-4s drifted closer. Someone nearby was shouting, not the authoritative rhythm of a proctor, but a more agitated staccato. It was almost painful to stop moving; there was some mechanism inside me that was still sprinting, still struggling.

"James," Bethany said, "get in."

I skirted the hood and opened the passenger door. The car lurched forward before I was fully inside. The motion sent me sliding across the leather seat.

"Are you okay?" she asked. "Are you hurt?"

I had no idea. I looked down at myself. Everything seemed intact.

"Is this your car?" I asked.

"No," she said. "It's Tanner's. I stole it. Well, not yet. We're still on campus, so I should say that I'm thinking of stealing it." She was wearing black pants with red polka dots on them and a matching tank top. It took me a moment to realize that these were girl's pajamas.

"You stole Tanner's car," I repeated. It occurred to me that maybe I'd passed out somewhere and that this was a vivid dream.

"Okay, focus," Bethany said. "What happened? Tell me relevant things." The engine was nearly silent and the headlights were turned off, but a screen on the dash displayed a clear picture of the road ahead. Below the screen, several components had been ripped out of the dashboard and were lying on the floor—black boxes with sprays of wires jutting from their backs.

"I don't know what's relevant anymore," I said. "Where are we going?"

"We're leaving," she said. We drove past the last building in the infirmary complex, and then we turned down a small access road that was marked STAFF ONLY. The path was edged with little solar lights, and I had the sense that Bethany was going way too fast. "How do you feel about Canada?" she asked.

"Sounds good," I said. I thought she was joking. "But you aren't wearing any shoes."

"We weren't supposed to leave tonight," she said. "I mean, you were in Confinement and so I was thinking Friday at the earliest." She shook her head. "Didn't I tell you to take it easy? To not get into trouble?"

"I don't think so," I said. "You didn't say that." The car bucked slightly as one wheel drifted off the path. I gripped the armrest.

"Is anything broken?" she continued. "I can't believe this is happening. I'm having a small crisis."

"You?" I said. "You're having a crisis."

"I didn't know what to do," she said. "I programmed everything so that you'd be alone and your door would remain closed, and then, at the last minute, Dad reassigned you. I think he knew I'd hacked his system."

"Wait," I said. "You programmed the door?"

"And he gave you a roommate," she said. "A real asshole from the looks of his record, and I wasn't sure if it was worse to lock you in or let you out, and I was totally panicking, and then suddenly you were outside, I mean, really outside." Her long hair was snarled in the back, as if she hadn't had time to brush it.

"You know about the Exclusion Zone," I said.

"Can you forgive me?" she asked. "I locked you in a room with a psychopath."

And I must have been in shock, because I almost laughed. "He wasn't so bad," I said.

We passed a restricted area, some warehouse-style build-ing encircled with concertina wire. A T-4 was coming toward us and Bethany slowed way down. I ducked low in the seat. "They can't see through the windshield," she said, and the other vehicle actually pulled off the road to let us pass. "And that," she said, "is why it pays to be the headmaster."

I didn't know where she thought we were going, but we must have been approaching the edge of campus. Our time was almost up. I stared at her, trying to memorize every de-tail. She wasn't wearing a bra. A panel of black lace ran along the edge of her pajama top. Silver hoop earrings tangled with her hair. She had the driver's seat scooted all the way for-ward, and despite this, she had to sit up straight to see out the windshield.

"Even though we won't make it to Canada," I said, "I think this was a great idea."

•

Bethany swung the car left and we pulled into a parking lot with a dozen T-4s in various states of disrepair. There were also a number of actual cars. Three of them looked beyond help—one was missing an engine, another lacked a front end. Be-hind the cars was a three-bay garage, but the bays were closed and the lights were out. We eased into a parking space and stopped. Bethany turned toward me.

"I looked into everything," she said, "everything you told me about, and well, it's bad news." She leaned forward to grab something off the floor and sat up with a small kitchen knife in one hand. It had a serrated blade and a wicked, taper-ing point. I must have looked surprised, because she said, "Here. I was pressed for time." She handed it to me. "Cut yourself free. I'll be right back."

I'd never held a real knife. I could see my reflection in the blade, just a blurry smear, but still, it was me—and this was an extension of my arm, some forbidden and ancient symbol of power. I felt arrested just having it in my hand. Before I could start cutting, though, Bethany had returned. She was carrying two gray backpacks. She tossed one onto the seat behind me.

"I've had those packed for a week," she said. "Okay, get in the back and lie on the floor." But her command only made me feel more confused. She stood beside the open door, shaking out a pair of green coveralls. "I'm going to pretend that I'm fixing Tanner's car," she said. "Working on some software, testing it out. There's a service exit just ahead. They might buy it."

"Have you worked on Tanner's car before?" I asked.

"No," she said.

I cut the wire binding my hands—funny how easy it was with the right tool, the right blade. "But they've let you take out other cars?"

"Once," she said. "Sort of."

"During a security breach?" I asked.

"Not exactly," she said.

She attempted to zip her coveralls, and the edge of her pajama top snagged in the metal teeth of the zipper. She yanked at the fabric, only jamming it further.

"And won't Tanner notice," I asked, "that his car is gone?"

"You mean his limited edition Maybach Excelsior Roadster?" she said. "Fully solar-powered? Only twenty-three in the United States?"

I looked at the console. I could see the marks where she'd hacked out whole sections of electronics.

"They actually aren't great vehicles." She gave up on the zipper, got in the front seat, and closed the door. The engine started as she touched the wheel. "Hard to repair," she said. "Lots of nonstandard parts. I wouldn't buy one myself."

"This isn't going to work," I said.

"Let's just say, it's not optimal."

"I have a chip," I said. "It's not going to work."

"I have a displacement program," she said. "It's already running. We just have to get past the gate. If we subdue the guards, we might have enough time."

"For what?" I asked. "And who's going to subdue the guards?"

"You know, I don't like to feel out of control," she said, her voice rising. "I'm more of a planner. I'm into schedules and itineraries—diagrams and lists." She paused. "Schematics."

"Listen to me," I said. I grabbed her arm and turned her to face me. She was trembling. Her hands had left sweaty prints on the leather steering wheel. "I don't know that you should do this."

"They're going to kill you," she said. "I'm not just being dramatic. I'm not exaggerating. Dad needs to push you until—how did he put it—*the organism exceeds its capacity for endurance.*"

As soon as she spoke these words, I knew they were true. I'd felt this outcome, felt it circling me, even as I'd been unable to name it. Still, it was jarring to hear it aloud. "Your lips are sort of turning blue," I said. "Maybe you should take one of your pills."

"Did you hear me?" she said, her voice rising. "Did you hear what I just said? My father is going to kill you and put slices of your brain in a refrigerated drawer."

"You don't have to convince me," I said. "I believe you."

"And do you want to know why? Because of me." She thumped her hand against her chest and I flinched. "It was me. It was my idea, the drug—all of it. Not the testing and the nastiness. But everything else."

"You need to calm down," I said. "It's going to be okay." I had no idea what she was talking about. I was just trying to reach her with the tone of my voice, with the slow steady pressure of my hands on her shoulders. "Really," I said, "you need to calm down."

"How?" she said. "And now you have to get in the back and lie on the floor. We can't stay here. We don't have any time. Oh fuck." She rubbed at her face as if trying to wake up. "It wasn't supposed to happen like this."

I heard an alarm bell ringing in the distance, its sound muffled and remote. And then we saw headlights approaching. A T-4 drove past, traveling in the direction of the guardhouse. It didn't stop. Tanner's car seemed just like another in a long row of vehicles.

Bethany leaned forward and I thought she was going to kiss me, but she just pressed her cheek to my own and took a long, shuddering breath. "If I drop dead," she whispered, "just know that I'm really, really sorry."

I didn't know what to say to this. So I got in the backseat and lay on the floor. She put the car in drive and pulled out of the parking lot, onto another access road. We were driving slowly now, at a casual pace. It felt as if the wool carpeting under my cheek was growing—it was a moss invading my mouth, my nose, and my throat.

"I'm going to make this right," Bethany whispered. "I'm going to take care of you." But I was thinking of the recent breakout—and how the guards had simply opened fire on the truck. They hadn't hesitated.

"When we're out in the real world," I said, "you can't treat me like a pet. It can't be like it was in here."

"No," she said. "You're right about that. Nothing's going to be the same."

PART FOUR

AMONG THE TRUE BELIEVERS

SEVENTEEN

Bethany drove slowly down the winding access road to the guardhouse. We didn't want to seem as if we were in a hurry. I lay on the floor, staring at the little window in the roof. The full moon flicked past overhead, and it appeared amber in color—a leaf in autumn—the product of some tint in the glass. The quiet in the car was disconcerting and deceptive. "How many men are usually at the gate?" I asked.

"I don't know," she said. "But I don't want to hurt anyone. Not more than we have to."

"You mean me," I said. "You don't want me to hurt anyone."

The light from the guardhouse spilled onto the floor and the car slowed down. I tried to wedge myself lower. I heard the trunk release as we stopped. The raised lid acted like a shield, blocking the glare, keeping the backseat dark. Bethany rolled down her window.

"Sir," the guard said, "we weren't expecting you." And then he must have realized that Tanner wasn't in the car. He clicked on his flashlight and I saw its beam skim over the backseat.

"Robert should have called this in," Bethany said. "I'm a resident here and I'm fixing his NAV system. I'm just going to do a test drive."

"Please step out of the vehicle," the guard said. "And present identification."

"Robert's a family friend," she said. "Can you call him? Tell him I'm here?"

The guard's handheld chimed, and a voice said, "Checkpoint 5, please respond."

"Five here," the guard said. "It's a negative. Just a resident." And then he tapped the side of the car. "Please step out."

"Is there some kind of problem?" Bethany asked—and she had just the right note of civilian entitlement. "You can call my dad, too. He's the Director of Student Medicine. Maybe you've heard of him? A. J. Cleveland?"

"Ma'am, we're on lockdown tonight," the guard said. "This exit is closed. Nobody's getting out."

"Not even me?" she said.

"I'm not going to ask again," he said. I heard the rigidity in his voice, the adherence to policy. He was summoning enough official force to compel her. What struck me in that instant was not that he would do so but how long it had taken him—how civilians were allowed to haggle over compliance, to discuss and withhold it.

The guard reached down to open Bethany's door, but I was out of the car and on top of him, almost without thinking about it. He tried to grab his weapon, but I slammed into him with enough force to drive him to the ground. It was almost too effective. He was older than I'd expected, older than the proctors in the school. He had grizzled hair and a thick waist.

"Face down," I said. "Hands apart." I was mimicking the tone I'd heard my whole life—that cadence of detached authority—and I found that, surprisingly, it was right there, accessible to me. "Who else is here?" I didn't see the T-4, the one that had passed us.

"No one," the man said. "It's just me." He tried to bring his hands together and I stepped on one of them, grinding my heel into the fingers, making him gasp. "Keep your hands apart." He would have some kind of panic button on his ID bracelet. All the staff did. He relaxed his fists and lay on his belly. He was looking past me, and then he raised his head off the ground, his expression full of disbelief. I turned and saw Bethany standing in the illumination of the guardhouse, holding her father's antique revolver.

"Jesus," the guard said.

Bethany's hands trembled, and the barrel of the gun swayed to such a degree that I was included in the threat. "Careful," I said.

"I have little kids at home," the guard said. "Think about what you're doing."

"Actually," Bethany said, "you need to think about what you're doing, because I'm more likely to act in an impulsive and fear-based way. So," she added, "no sudden movements. No loud noises."

She was beside me now. The gun wasn't cocked, but neither of them seemed to notice.

"Please," he said, "don't do this."

I stepped forward to remove his handheld and his weapons. I tossed them away. The handheld made a crackling noise as it bounced, and then a voice said, "Checkpoints are now at Code 20. I need everyone to key in."

"What does that mean?" I asked Bethany.

But she just passed me the revolver. "Watch him," she said.

I didn't like guns and I hated this weapon in particular, hated the weight of the metal, the smooth wooden stock. It was familiar—I had fired it before. I had cleaned its cylinder. I hefted it and clicked the hammer back with such ease and confidence that they both paused. "I'll just aim for the stomach," I said, "like we discussed."

"Right," Bethany said. "Good." But she flashed me a quizzical and cautionary look as she turned to unzip one of the backpacks. She withdrew a small tablet with a white screen.

"Hold out your arm," she said to the guard. I stepped closer and kept the gun only a few feet from him. I was worried that he might grab her, try to pull her in front of him. But up close I saw the sweat streaming down his face and the way his eyes darted back and forth between us. He was too scared. I felt a pang of sympathy for him. I felt it but didn't show it.

Bethany removed his ID bracelet and laid it on top of the tablet. The two devices lit up simultaneously. The tablet projected a small holographic image, a long column of streaming white text, and Bethany began to use her fingertips to manipulate the lines of data. I leaned toward her, still watching the guard closely.

"What are you doing?" I whispered.

"Why is everything different in theory than in practice?" she asked. She cursed softly and squinted down at the shifting letters and numbers.

"Checkpoint 5, key in," the handheld said. "Twenty seconds remaining." And then another voice came over the handheld, almost interrupting the last transmission. "Check 5, we good? I can't get a visual."

I looked around the guardhouse, searching for a camera, but couldn't locate it. In addition to the usual fencing, I saw that the exit had a physical barrier, a retractable arm—and some kind of electromagnetic field, like the one they used at the main gate. I could discern a slight shimmer in the air, some projected light, but I wasn't sure what would happen if we tried to pull through it.

The guard's ID bracelet—the one that lay on top of the

tablet—started to beep. "What's happening?" I asked. "What does that mean?"

"I tripped something," she said. Bethany was staring at the device, seemingly at a loss.

"How bad?" I asked.

She shook her head. "I'm not at my best under pressure," she said. "I really need a quiet workspace."

I glanced at the empty access road, and some instinct urged me to action, promised me that hesitation would bring failure. I grabbed the bracelet, threw it to the ground, and crushed it with my foot. The beeping stopped.

"Problem solved," I said.

"No," Bethany said, "that's worse."

"Stand up," I told the guard. "Hands in front of you." The man got to his feet, but he was looking around, expecting help. I advanced slightly, pushing Bethany out of the way, aiming the gun at the guard's head. "Get in the trunk," I said.

A voice issued from a speaker inside the guardhouse. "Check 5. Check 5."

"Get in the trunk," I repeated. The guard moved slowly. He was trying to delay.

"You'll regret this," he said to me.

"Only if I shoot you," I said. I was the proctor now. "And then," I added, "only if you die."

•

I thought Bethany was going to plow through the exit. From the way she was gripping the steering wheel and hitting the gas, I was prepared for impact, prepared for the electromagnetic barrier to disable the engine, lock up the car in some dramatic way, spin us around. I didn't expect to see the arm retract and the film of light pass harmlessly over the exterior. We shot through the gate and into the night, and then I actually turned in my seat to stare at the guardhouse behind us, at the school growing smaller. I thought of Owen and felt a pang of regret.

"How did we just drive out?" I asked.

"It's hubris," she said. "Well, Tanner's hubris, anyway. He never put restrictions on his car. Pride is a great weakness. Though I have to include myself in that category, and I find that a little galling. I don't know if this is going to work."

"It just worked," I said.

"We're like ten feet down the road," she said. "Hubris, James. Remember?"

She took a hand off the wheel and reached for me, her cold fingers digging into my arm. I realized I was still holding the gun. I placed it on the floor and slid it under the seat, not wanting to touch her and it at the same time. "That was awful," I said.

"I sweated through my shirt I was so scared. But don't worry, I took a lot of medicine." She glanced at me, nodding earnestly. "I'm at the max, but it's helping, okay? No need to worry."

"Right," I said. "I'm not going to worry." I was braced for a swarm of proctors or the actual police. The road was narrow, and all the vegetation had been removed. There were no buildings, no lights, and the darkness felt pregnant and oppressive. We said nothing for a full minute, just sat there listening to the tires hiss on pavement. I folded her hand in mine. The contact restored some measure of calm.

"How long before they notice the guard is gone?" I said.

"Yeah," she said, "that's a bit of a problem."

She was wearing a thin black cord around her neck, something I hadn't noticed until she pulled on it, lifting it up. At the end of the cord dangled a small metal disk. It was a stopwatch, or something like it. I could see the numbers accumulating, minutes and seconds. She glanced at its face, and then the car accelerated. The momentum pushed me farther into my seat.

"We've got an appointment," she said, "with a friend of mine. It's going to be tight, though. We should have an hour." She tilted her head from side to side as if doing some internal calculation. "Twenty minutes to get there, twenty to find him. Okay," she admitted, "maybe less than a hour."

"Before what?" I asked.

"The computers catch on," she said. "I've been running the displacement program for seventeen minutes now and I jammed the camera signals, too, so security won't know exactly what to look for, but still . . ." She trailed off. "The system knows it's being hacked and it's getting better at identifying non–source code. I've actually been able to see it learning about me, amassing algorithms—now it recognizes my keystrokes. I had to write this last program with just my pinkie." She held up her hand, her pinkie finger extended. "Can you believe that? It took forever."

But I was thinking, *Less than an hour.* That was how long I was going to remain free. I looked out the window. Manzanita trees with their thin, twisted branches flashed in and out of view. Thick clumps of sagebrush covered the ground. We were really off campus now. Our narrow road doubled in size, and Bethany accelerated to the point that I scrambled for my seat belt. I reached across her and buckled her in, too.

"The airbag will probably kill me," she said. "But that's sweet of you."

"Tell me what's going on," I said. "What is the drug your father's testing?"

"Let's just start over," she said. "I think that's the best way. Don't look back."

"I'm not starting over," I said.

She tugged at the zipper on her coveralls, and when it

didn't move, she shrugged out of the top, freeing one arm at a time. "I just don't think you're going to react well," she said. "And I have to say, I feel responsible. More than a little. It's not that I didn't believe you." She hesitated. "Maybe I didn't want to know."

"Just tell me," I said.

"I'll wait until we're in a public place," she said.

"I'm not going to freak out."

"You say that now," she said.

"I'm used to bad news," I said. "Trust me."

She took a deep breath. "The drug," she said, "limits fear. Essentially eradicates it."

I don't know what I was expecting, but it wasn't this. "That's not the drug they gave me," I said.

"It is," she said. "And I know you had a reaction, because Dad was overjoyed. I read his notes. And he couldn't wait to plug you back into his Exclusion Zone experiment. It's why he's full of school spirit these days."

"I don't remember being fearless," I said. "I mean, right now, I can barely look out the windshield without being terrified."

Bethany smiled. "That's just my driving," she said.

I remembered the first night I'd fought—I'd felt titanically strong, righteous, able. I hadn't dwelled much on what had happened after it was done. Other than my guilt over Tuck, there was no residual feeling, no dreams. That night had happened and then receded—unlike the fire, unlike La Pine.

"Are you freaking out?" she asked. "It's all my fault. I'm so sorry."

"It's not a big deal," I said, shaking my head. "I mean, in the scheme of things. Everybody knows they test drugs on us. I thought it was going to be worse."

"Not a big deal? Have you even been listening?" She turned to stare at me, and I had to point to remind her that she was driving.

"Don't kill us," I said.

"Do you know how much a drug like that could be worth? Think about it. A soldier who doesn't feel fear? Come on. Billions of dollars."

"But I *was* afraid," I said. "At least, I think I was."

"James," she said, trying to get my attention, "billions of dollars."

"I heard you," I said.

"It's not about one or two doses," she said. "It's about what happens over time. When you take it, you don't make long-term memories. That's why people don't feel the stress afterward. There's no trauma, because there's no deeper evaluation."

"That sounds pretty good," I said. But I remembered Harold, the way he'd been hunched over, his spine protruding like a snake underneath his skin. "What happens to the boys who don't come back?" I asked.

Bethany was silent for a moment.

"What do you think?" she said.

The lines of the highway slipped under the car, an irregular thread, one that seemed to pull us toward our destination. I leaned my forehead against the glass of the passenger's-side window. It felt cool against my skin.

"It can't remain a secret," I said. "Not after tonight." I remembered the stampede out of the Exclusion Zone, the students who'd followed me back through the fence onto campus. "The school will figure it out," I said.

She gave me an incredulous look. "You really think they don't know? I can tell you, Swann Industries is definitely not suffering an ethical dilemma." She shook her head. "Money," she said, "is the worst drug of all."

•

It was a beautiful, clear night, and we were somewhere rural, passing the occasional farmhouse and barn. A thick spray of stars dotted the sky. I hadn't seen anything like this since Oregon. There was a button on the armrest of the passenger door. I pushed it and was startled to see the glass of my window retract. A current of warm air filled the car.

Bethany was quiet for a long time. Finally she said, "I have something for you." She reached into the backpack, which was open on the seat beside her. "Here," she said. She withdrew a single piece of quickpaper, one embossed with the Goodhouse logo, and handed it to me. I looked down and saw my name and ID number. "It's a scan of your intake form," she said.

My grip on the paper tightened. I felt a bright spark of anticipation, something that was a little like the fear I reportedly could not feel. "What's in it?" I asked.

"It's you," Bethany said. "Well, some of it has been redacted."

I scrolled through the pages. It was a form that had been filled out when I'd arrived at La Pine. I'd been three years old, and there was a description of me at that age—quiet and serious. I read the notes. I'd had a toy car that I carried everywhere and would not relinquish. It said I liked drawing and puzzles, which amazed me, as I couldn't remember doing either. And then I felt a little jolt of surprise. "I'm already eighteen," I said. My birthday was printed at the top of the sheet. "As of last week."

At first Bethany didn't say anything. Then, after a long pause, she said, "Happy birthday."

The second page detailed the genetic legacy of both my parents and myself. The language was opaque, talking about RNA polymerase and provisional synthesis. The names of my father and mother had been covered with a black, highlighted box that said AUTHORIZATION REQUIRED. I touched the black lines, but they were the same texture as everything else. "The school said it didn't keep any family information," I said. "It's all supposed to be encrypted."

"Yeah, they say a lot of things. You'd be surprised at what Tanner has on his computer." Bethany smiled. "God," she said, "even his porn is ostentatious."

"We can find my parents," I said. I laid my hand on the quickpaper as if it were a holy relic. "Thank you."

Bethany was glowing with triumph. She reached over to me and I kissed the pad of her thumb and then tasted her palm, which was salty like the electrolyte drink her father had given me.

"It's strange how you just keep living and things keep happening," I said. I stared at the halo around the moon, at the white moths that appeared and disappeared in the headlights, little bits of floating paper. I let my hand hang out the window. The warm breeze exploded between my fingers. We drove past a broken-down house with cows standing on the porch. The rusted hulks of ancient cars briefly lined the roadway like a fence, and then it was open land. A rabbit's eyes flashed orange in the headlights.

"Who was your mother?" I asked.

Bethany shrugged. "Mom was one of those back-to-barter tent-city people grinding their own barley flour and weaving ponchos," she said. "She's dead now, of course. I don't really remember her. Dad met her when he was doing charity work up north." Bethany shrugged as if the term *charity work* was ridiculous. "It was some roving-doctor thing, physicians without borders. Dad was full of idealism back then, everything he accuses me of, really. He didn't want to marry her, and Mom wouldn't abort the baby even though it was defective. The baby is me, by the way."

"I got that," I said. Just then, without warning, Bethany turned the wheel and the car veered off onto a dirt road. Rocks rang like buckshot against the metal frame. A wave of dust rose around us and she rolled up the windows, though I could still smell dust coming through the ventilation system.

"Dad told her I had a hypoplastic left heart and she'd better just flush me. I read all their correspondence. He deleted everything, but he never could scrub a hard drive. They gave me a ventricular pump, then a heart transplant, and then one of those new hybrid synthetic hearts that were supposed to be better than the real thing. Dad made me get the surgery. He said I could go off my medications, but then it came out that the hybrids were defective."

I thought about the scar on her chest. They must have broken her ribs, I realized, to get inside. "Defective, how?" I asked.

"There's not really a pattern." She shrugged again. But her casual tone was a little too disinterested. "Some people have normal transplant rejection, others have some kind of necrosis in the tissues that spreads out. Very nasty. Most just have a heart attack."

"Most?" I said. "How many?"

"I'm supposed to avoid stressful situations," she said. "Though, honestly, having a hybrid heart *is* a stressful situation."

"But you don't feel sick, right? You don't have any symptoms?" I scooted closer and slid a hand onto her shoulder. I felt the tension there.

"Dad thinks he's God," she said. Her voice was suddenly thick with emotion. The tendons on her forearms stood out as she gripped the steering wheel. "And when you're a god, there are never any consequences. You can just do whatever you want."

She looked so despondent, I wanted to comfort her—to communicate some level of empathy. "It's not your fault," I said.

"Yes, it is," she said. "Dad hit on this formula and he's

been handing it out like candy, picking boys with different genetic profiles, pumping them full of it. Killing some of them. Cutting them open. He thinks he can save me, and now"—she took a deep breath—"there are billions of dollars."

She drove faster even as the road narrowed and its surface grew more heavily pitted. We rounded a tight corner, nearly missing the remains of a wooden fence that a previous traveler had punched through.

"Slow down," I said.

But she ignored me. "I know that Dad thinks he got tricked. He never wanted a kid, especially not one like me," she said. "He really loves me, you know, but the feeling of it drives him crazy. He resents it."

She suddenly pulled the car off the dirt road and into a field. I clutched at the armrest. We hit a pothole and my head grazed the ceiling as I bounced in my seat. A large tree loomed ahead of us, and I thought we were going to crash, but Bethany turned the wheel and we skidded to a stop a few feet from the trunk.

"And that," she said, "is how you park a car."

I let go of the armrest. My fingernails had left little impressions in the leather.

Bethany grabbed one of the backpacks, unzipped the top, and pulled out a handheld. It was the homemade one I'd seen the other night. She began to type a message. Inside the open pack I saw several plastic bags of pills—white powder-filled capsules. The image of a swan was screened onto the front of every bag.

"I take it these are not technically your property," I said.

She smiled. "I'm afraid," she said, "that Dad's secret is about to leak." She finished her message and tossed the handheld onto the floor.

"What are you doing?" I asked.

"The components are too distinctive," she said. "You ready? This is kind of a big deal. Leave the file too." She climbed out of the car and slammed the door shut.

I started to put the piece of quickpaper on the seat beside me, but at the last minute I folded it and tucked it into my pocket. I wasn't going to relinquish this document, not when my parents' names were here, inside that black box—assembled and whole, but not yet visible. And besides, I was no longer subject to proctors digging in my cuffs, pinching the seams of my shirts. I was a private citizen now, and I intended to act like one.

EIGHTEEN

As soon as we'd both stepped out of the car and closed the doors, the windows went opaque and the headlights blinked once. I looked around—at the night sky, at the quiet, moonlit hillside.

"Congratulations," Bethany said. "How do you feel?"

"I'm a wanted fugitive," I said, trying it on.

"It's an exciting development," she said. The empty arms of her coveralls hung limp at her sides, the zipper so snarled in her shirt that it puckered the fabric. Bethany grabbed one of the backpacks and pulled out a fistful of clothing. "Turn around, please," she said, and before I could ask why, she'd ripped her tank top in half and wiggled out of the coveralls, letting them drop to the ground. She wore only a pair of black underpants with a red bow on the front. Her breasts were small, the nipples a deep rose color. "You were supposed to turn around," she said. But she sounded more amused than angry. "A gentleman would have complied."

"You should've thought of that before you ripped your clothes off," I said. I took an involuntary step toward her, but she pulled a black dress over her head, tugging and adjusting it.

"I have a shirt for you," she said. "I think your pants are passable, although I'm a little disturbed to think you're wearing my father's clothes. I'm definitely going to need some therapy." She passed me a dark-colored shirt. I held it up. It was made of heavy fabric. It looked expensive. "Hurry," she said. I pulled off my old shirt and shrugged into the new one, buttoning it over the thick layer of gauze that was wound around my chest. "What's that?" she asked.

"A souvenir," I said.

Bethany ducked down to look at her reflection in one of the car's mirrors. She was applying makeup to her face, drawing black lines on her eyelids and painting a bright pink layer of lipstick on her lips. "You don't have to do that," I said.

"We need to look the part," she said. "Social norms allow for men to be a little slovenly, but never women. It's really irritating. You know, I had a toy as a little girl, a big vacuous blond head whose sole purpose was to be made up. I hated that thing." She was dusting her face with different powders, dropping the containers onto the ground when she was finished. "It sat on my dresser," she said. "Usually I was too weak to get out of bed and cover it, and when I finally did make the head into something I could bear to look at, Dad took me to get a psychiatric evaluation."

She straightened to face me. She looked much older now, and her features appeared sharp and unfriendly.

"Okay," she said. "You just got out of the military. I have your papers linked to your ID. I'm sorry, but you have that high and tight haircut. It's the only believable story. And you have to wear a hat." She passed me a baseball cap. It had a large N and Y intertwined on the front—orange lettering on a blue field. "Lots of guys wear these at night," she said, "so don't think it's weird."

The guard began to bang on the inside of the trunk. I could hear him screaming something, but it was muffled and unintelligible. A taillight shook. He was trying to kick it out.

"What's going to happen to him?" I asked.

She knocked on the side of the trunk. "It won't be long now," she called. "Hang in there." And to me she said, "Come on." She grabbed my hand and led me up the hill, hiking through the thin, dry grass. The stopwatch dangled and spun at the end of the black cord around her neck. Her palm was moist but her fingers were cold.

"Javier will let him go," she said. "After a while."

"Who's Javier?" I asked.

"He's our ticket to Canada," she said. "And I, for one, cannot wait to corrupt my American vowel sounds with a little Français. Did they teach you any other languages?"

"Why would they?"

She kept checking the stopwatch, glancing at it and walking a little faster. The muscles in my calves burned with the effort of our climb. I tugged on her hand, willing her to slow down. She was breathing too hard. "Stop for a minute," I said. But she kept climbing.

"I'm so sorry, James," she said. "For all of it. I wanted to use a delivery truck from the factory. That was my first choice, to get you out, put you in a crate of cupcakes. That would've been memorable, right?"

"We're in the middle of nowhere," I said. I gestured to the stars that dotted the sky overhead. They were bright, the way they had been in La Pine, up in the mountains. "We just ditched our car. How are we going to get my chip out? Have you thought about that? How are we going to eat? In a few hours it will be over a hundred degrees. Do we have water?"

"Just a little farther," she said.

"Because if we don't have a plan"—I reached to stop her, to make sure I had her full attention—"then maybe we should just stay here and you can take your clothes off again."

She smiled at me. "Boys," she said, "always have such thoughtful commentary." And then I looked over her shoulder and saw—stretched out in the valley below us—a tent city, a sprawling light-speckled grid that was so vast I couldn't clearly delineate its boundaries. Two giant nuclear cooling towers stood in the distance, blacker than the nighttime sky.

"Holy shit," I said.

"It's one of the more notorious ones, so we're in luck," she said. "If it were a weekend, we definitely wouldn't be able to get in."

We started down the side of the hill. At the entrance to the city there was a large metal gate surrounded by a crowd of people. A short guard tower—or at least that's what it looked like to me—aimed a large spotlight at the crowd below. The gate was wide enough to admit everybody at once, but it was closed and the people outside were being funneled through a building that was some kind of checkpoint. A large sign read EAST ENTRANCE. Inside the walls of the city I saw thousands of lights demarcating streets. The streets themselves were so populated—so densely packed—that they appeared, from a distance, to be a shifting kaleidoscope of movement.

We were on a path now, winding down a rocky slope, practically tripping over our feet as we hurried. It was easier than hiking up, but more precarious.

"I thought tent cities were for homeless people," I said.

"Who told you that?" she asked. In the distance a ribbon of highway curved across the countryside. A silent stream of cars filled the road—red taillights and pearlescent headlights, a beautiful artery. As I watched, a single car exited. It was headed in our direction, pulling into the enormous parking lot below us.

"If it was the police I think they would have their lights

going," Bethany said. "So that's reassuring." And then we had to stop talking, because we were approaching the edge of the lot and there were civilians nearby. Trash littered the ground, debris mixed in with the dirt—bottles and bits of paper and the thin, rattling skin of plastic bags. As we got closer to the crowd at the gate, we passed a few people squatting in the road, holding cardboard signs asking for assistance. Their clothes were ragged and uniformly dirty. One woman had a baby on her lap. Bethany tugged my arm.

"Stop staring," she whispered. We merged with the crowd outside the gate, joined the line that was waiting to pass through the checkpoint. I felt the heat of the spotlight as we stepped into it. A metal fence encircled the city. It had barbed wire at the top, looping curls of rusted spikes. In contrast, a pristine white tent with a red cross over the door had been erected between the city and the parking lot. It had a large sign that read DOCTORS AVAILABLE; another, smaller sign said, simply, POTABLE WATER.

I looked at the people in line with us. Some of them appeared to be regular civilians—the sorts I'd seen from afar—or like proctors out of uniform. But others seemed unusual to me—they had arms and necks covered with tattooed images and words. One woman had a series of metal bars inserted through her eyebrow. I saw one child, a boy of maybe ten or eleven, reach into a woman's purse without her noticing. I pulled Bethany's backpack in front of me. Music played somewhere inside the city, the percussive thump of a dance track. Every so often there was a large whooping noise as a crowd of people cheered some invisible feat. "How long have we been gone?" I asked.

She pulled the black cord over her head and passed the device to me. "You keep it," she said. "It's making me crazy." I glanced down. Thirty-seven minutes had elapsed.

"And how long do we have left?" I asked.

She just shook her head. "I don't know. But once we're inside, we'll have an advantage."

I divided the crowd in front of us into likely groupings of people. "We'll be here for seven minutes," I said. "Optimistically."

I felt as if the chip inside me were a pulsating beacon, some terrible thread tying me to the school, still pulling my heartbeat into the servers there, still holding me captive. I wrapped an arm around Bethany, bringing her closer. A man ahead of us had his arm around a woman, so I knew it was okay, that it wouldn't make us conspicuous, but still it felt bold, a secret in plain sight.

"Thanks," Bethany said. She was almost shivering. I tightened my grip. I had a fleeting moment of compassion for her father. He was right to worry. "Did I ever tell you about the Superman costume I made when I was a kid?" I said. I wanted to distract her. She smiled up at me, expectant. "My first headmaster was a huge comic-book fan, and sometimes he let us read the really ancient first editions on our wallscreens—you know, the versions where they don't swear and even the bad guys are wholesome. Anyhow, one day we got this idea."

"Who's we?" she asked.

"My friends," I said. It was an innocuous question, but still it conjured the past. "Anyway, we stole some linens from the school Dumpster. I think they were old bedsheets. We tried to dye them with berries and eggs. I'd read something about how antique paints were made out of egg. We actually sewed a shirt and cape, but they started to rot. The proctors thought we'd stashed a dead animal somewhere as a joke."

"James," she said seriously, "that is a very sad story."

"No, it's not," I said.

"But it makes me sad to think of you as a child," she said. I ignored this. "We took turns wearing the costume," I said. "It did stink, though. I guess that could be its super-power."

I checked the watch. We were almost at the front of the line. Bearded men in black T-shirts with the word SECURITY printed on the front were motioning people forward, telling them which screening station to report to, how much the entry fees were.

"I don't have any money," I said.

"The military," she said, "pays pretty well." And then she pressed something into my hand. It was a slim white plastic card. On one side was the seal of California, a woman in Roman dress, sitting before a harbor. A bear ambled at her feet. The other side bore the name James Mitchell Madison. I looked at Bethany, surprised. "It had gravitas," she said.

A guard directed us toward Screening Station 4. We walked down a hallway and stopped in front of a metal desk. A man sat behind it, and a small fan was clipped to the edge of the desktop. A silver ribbon was tied to the fan's metal face. It waved like a streamer in the breeze.

"ID," the man said. I gave him the white card. He had the same detached and efficient demeanor as a proctor. He scanned my card with a handheld, glanced at the screen and then at me. Then he did the same for Bethany. I felt so obviously wrong. I didn't know how to stand, how to be normal.

"Is this woman with you?" he asked. I nodded. "Say yes to confirm the voiceprint," the man intoned.

"Yes," I said.

"And what is your business here tonight?" he asked. He was clearly looking at me.

"I'm on leave for a few days," I said. And when that wasn't enough. "Don't want to waste them."

"Make sure you stay together at all times. Do not leave the visitors' areas for any reason. To do so means immediate expulsion without a refund. You will report to the East Exit at or before 10 a.m. Do you agree to a one-time fee of fifty dollars?"

"Yes," I said.

"All transactions inside city limits will be conducted in cash. Anyone who asks you to pay by another means is not authorized to make that request. Do you understand?"

I nodded, and Bethany nudged me. I was supposed to sign a small screen on the man's desk. I looked for a stylus and then used my fingertip, which left a green contrail on the black screen. I only just remembered to sign Madison instead of Good-house—in fact, my capital *M* started with a curved line. The man approved the signature, then printed two yellow badges, each of which had a barcode and a time stamp. I stuck the badge to the front of my shirt. "Next," the guard called. His attention had already shifted to the people behind us.

We took a few steps, moved through a metal turnstile— and then we stood on the hard-packed dirt of the city itself. We were inside.

•

I was unprepared for the noise, for the press of the crowds, for everything, really. All around me people were touching— couples walked with their arms draped across each other's shoulders or clasped around each other's waists. Many of the women wore very little clothing, short pants and shirts that ended just below their breasts. Some women had metal rings in their belly buttons, and one had actual jewels glued to her skin, a stripe up each leg. I saw no uniforms, no obvious displays of rank and status, at least not the kind I was used to seeing. Music threaded through the crowd. It spilled out of doorways. Everyone seemed to be talking at once, and for a moment I forgot myself, forgot the stopwatch, the pressure of time. The crowd was effervescent, shifting and tumbling like a turbulent river.

I realized that we were in some kind of open-air market. Vendors lined both sides of the walkway, standing in front of little stalls that displayed watches, sunglasses, kerosene stoves, jewelry, plastic shoes, musical instruments, packaged food. One vendor had hundreds of scarves hanging on a wooden rack. Each scarf had gold disks sewn along its edges. When a breeze lifted the fabric, the disks sparkled—they made a glittering wall. I must have stopped to stare, because Bethany pulled at my arm.

"Keep moving," she said. "If you stop too long, they'll try to sell you something."

I nodded, but I was disoriented. I kept bumping into people. Bright orange bicycle taxis sped through the crowd, pinging their bells. The sound was supposed to alert pedestrians, but the din was constant. Quickpaper banners hung on the sides of tents. They advertised everything imaginable—a female dancer whose skin was painted blue and silver, some kind of hot-pepper vodka, something called a Quaker Friends meeting. One giant-size banner hung across the street itself, with the words *East Market* spelled out in what appeared to be flowers and stems. Everyone and everything seemed to be moving and colliding.

The only point of stillness was a knot of conservatively dressed men and women. They were silent, holding up a series of printed paper signs. MODIFICATION IS A CRIME, they read. And: BLESSED AS YOU ARE BORN.

I tightened my grip on Bethany. These people had the disapproving look of a proctor on a bad day. "What's their problem?" I said.

"They go where the sinners are," she said. "They bus them in from Yreka and the valley. Just ignore them." But it was spooky how quiet they were, how calm and focused. It made me remember the day of the bus attack, the way the crowd had surrounded us, all united in one purpose. As we walked past, one of the citizens lifted his sign. "God bless," he called, and the other sign holders echoed this sentiment. "God bless," they said. "God bless."

I looked away. "So where's this Javier?"

"Other side of town." She waved to an empty pedicab and the driver stopped. "How much to West Market?" she asked.

I didn't hear the driver's answer, because I was staring at his forearm. It bore a single black tattoo—a thick zero with a lightning bolt through the middle like a slash.

"Never mind," I said, grabbing Bethany's arm. "We'll walk."

"James," she hissed, but I pulled her after me into the crowd.

"He's a scumbag," I said. "Did you see his tattoo?"

"We need a ride," she said. And then I saw another man with the same tattoo on his neck—the zero, the lightning bolt. The man was talking on a handheld, and the tattoo was above his shirt collar, nestled between colorful stars and some geometric patterns.

"What is this place?" I asked.

"There's a lot of different people here," she said. "Think of it as a watering hole in the desert."

"Animals eat one another at the watering hole," I said.

"Good point," she said. "Maybe don't think of it that way." She waved for another pedicab.

This driver was older. He looked somewhat dehydrated, all sinew and ropy muscle, but he had no tattoos. We climbed into the passenger compartment. It took a few minutes to get out of the thick of things, to break free of the crowd. We turned onto a quieter street lined with shops and restaurants. I was keeping track of every turn, picking out landmarks, looking over my shoulder so that the way back would be recognizable.

We passed a residential section, mostly canvas structures treated with some kind of solar paint. And then we neared an area marked QUARANTINE, a few blocks of tents cordoned off by yellow plastic tape. "Hold your breath," Bethany whispered. Several security guards stood at intervals, enforcing the boundary. She reached into her bag and pulled out one of the white powder-filled capsules and slipped it into her mouth. All our talk about her father and it hadn't occurred to me that the drug could actually work—that it was, on some level, a success.

•

West Market turned out to be an old warehouse that had been repurposed as some kind of club. Tables were set up outside, and they had flames in the middle, fire flickering within a brazier. There was an eerie red light inside the building itself. Through the windows I could see dark, shadowy outlines of backlit people. The pedicab dropped us off in front of another group of sign holders. THE WAGES OF SIN IS DEATH, one of the signs read. OBEY HIS LAW, read another. The men holding these signs were still and quiet until I made eye contact with one of them. "God bless," he said.

West Market looked a little shabbier, a little rougher. It was almost as crowded as East Market, but the clientele was less celebratory, more watchful. Bethany led me to an alley behind the club. A large rat sprinted along the passage ahead of us.

"Do you know where you're going?" I asked.

"Stop worrying," she said, her voice tense and a little breathless.

"Right," I said.

She stopped at an unmarked door. The surface was dented and pockmarked. "Okay," she said. "Let me do the talking. Just until we know for sure—" But she didn't get a chance to finish her sentence. The door opened, flying outward with a percussive boom, as if it had been kicked. We jumped back. A man in a crisp white shirt stepped through the opening. He was maybe fifty, his brown skin taut along his cheekbones. He had a cigarette clenched between his lips.

"This way," he growled. And as soon as we were inside, his face split into a wide smile. "Welcome," he said. "And my apologies," he added. "I should have sent an escort."

We stood in a reception area with a fireplace, a white velvet sofa, and a chandelier that was made out of tubes of light. It was the most beautiful room I'd ever seen, an intense contrast to the filth of the alley. There was a mural on the ceiling— painted faces and lush, tropical-looking foliage.

Bethany opened her mouth to speak, but the man cut her off. "Not yet," he said.

We followed him down a long hallway, past a secretary at a large desk, past a fish tank with darting neon-colored fish. The air smelled strongly of ginger and cinnamon. The hallway had motion sensors embedded in the walls, little red blinking eyes. I didn't see any cameras, but I recognized some of the architecture, the way the secretary's desk was elevated and projected slightly into the corridor, the way the reception room was sunken by a single step. It was the sort of layout I was familiar with—the preservation of a sight line, the main-tenance of security. I felt the building closing around me like a trap. I began to sweat.

The man took us into a room that had one of the plastic therapy tables that I recognized from the infirmary. A large sign on the wall read YOU WILL HAVE THREE WEEKS TO REPORT TO A DMV OR A POLICE STATION TO REGISTER ANY FACIAL MODI-FICATIONS. BY AGREEING TO OUR SERVICES YOU WAIVE YOUR RIGHT TO CLAIM ANY AND ALL DAMAGES. Someone had drawn a smiley face on the edge of the paper.

"I'm not modifying my face," I said.

Javier pressed his hand to a small wallscreen. A keypad appeared, and he typed in a numeric code. "Okay." He smiled. "Now we can talk."

"Did you find the payment?" Bethany asked.

"The Maybach," he said. "It's exquisite." He stepped toward me and held out his hand. In the other one he cradled the lit cigarette. "I am Javier," he said. "A pleasure." I shook his hand and said my name. "Yes, I know," he said. "We will be sorry to lose our littlest mastermind, but she says you're worth it."

I looked at Bethany, and she shrugged. "I did some work for these guys," she said.

"When?" I asked.

"Recently," she said. And for some reason this answer irritated me—it brought to mind just how much I didn't know, about her life, who she was, what she did.

"So, let's start by getting that chip out," Javier said. "And then we'll move on to the fun stuff." He walked over to the sink to wash his hands.

"What fun stuff?" I asked.

He began tugging on a pair of latex gloves and arranging a scalpel, scissors, and several other sharp-looking instruments on a lined tray. "In the interest of full disclosure, Bethany, now would be a good time," he said.

"James," she said, "I don't want you to freak out, but we have to do a small operation."

"That freaks me out," I said.

Bethany nodded. "I didn't tell you everything," she said, "because I didn't want to scare you." But she was the one who seemed frightened.

"Just take out my chip," I said.

Javier looked at Bethany. "Perhaps a little sedation is a good idea?" he asked.

"Don't touch me," I said to him. "If you touch me, I will literally kick your face in."

I backed toward the door, but the handle was locked. I eyed the keypad that was still visible on the little wallscreen. I remembered the code he'd entered, but I couldn't be sure what it would do.

"We can't just take out your chip," Bethany said. "I mean, we can, but the real problem is your eyes. The iris is very distinctive and they'll scan yours at the border."

I looked at the metal instruments on the tray—a hooked retractor, several wickedly sharp lancets, and a small pair of forceps. "So what happens?" I asked. "How do you alter an iris?"

They were both quiet for a moment. Maybe it was the word *modification*—because it implied retention of the original— but I'd just imagined an implant or an injection. I hadn't made the necessary leap.

Bethany crept forward. I leaned away from her, my weight shifting toward the exit. "I'm sorry," she said, "but we've got to take the old ones out."

NINETEEN

I pulled at the locked door handle—a fruitless gesture that I felt compelled to do nonetheless. "I need time to think about this," I said.

"You can have one minute," Javier said.

"I already sort of committed you," Bethany said. "I may have signed some paperwork on your behalf."

"No." I shook my head. "Things are different now. You can't just force me. You can't cut my eyes out."

"We don't need the whole eye," Javier said. "You keep the sclera."

"I'm keeping the whole thing," I said.

"If it helps," Javier said, "I had the procedure done myself. It doesn't hurt. Much. And our doctor is very good." He paused. "I mean, I'm the doctor, but I'm really good."

Bethany stepped closer, as if she were approaching a fractious animal. "You have to trust me," she said. "This is our best option. We'll get you to recovery, get going as quick as possible."

"Not if I'm blind," I said. I thought of the crowds outside, the thousands of strangers. "And what if you drop dead? What happens to me then?" I edged away from her, creeping closer to the keypad on the wall.

"I don't blame you for being mad," she said. Her expression was hopeful and apologetic.

"You think I don't recognize this setup?" I asked. "The locked door, the sterile room. I feel right-fucking-at-home." My surroundings began to take on a dreamlike quality; they seemed to be shrinking, warping, diminishing. The muscles in the back of my legs twitched. I felt like I was going to throw up. But Javier and Bethany took my sudden quiet for acquiescence. They saw a fire banked, resistance countered.

"It's going to be okay," she said. "I won't let anything bad happen to you."

"You can't promise that," I said.

"Let's start with the good news," Javier interjected. He pressed his hand to the wall. A large screen lit up. On it was a picture of myself, or rather, the person I'd been a year ago. The picture had been taken in Oregon. My cheeks were rosy, as if I'd just stepped in from the cold. I realized that this was my official ID photo, the one visible only to the proctors. I'd never actually seen it. "You can have any eye color you like," Javier said. "Brown or blue or gray." He flicked his hand over the screen and my eye color changed. "Anything but what you have."

Even as I'd aged—even as my bones had lengthened, as my musculature had built and broadened—my eyes had not changed. They were all I'd retained from my childhood. Their bright green color was unusual and I'd hoped that perhaps, in some possible future, my mother would see me and know me from my eyes alone.

"And now for the bad news," Javier was saying. "These implants are synthetic. The most common defects are an inability to focus, night blindness, light sensitivity. There is a one percent chance that the graft will be weak and you will see objects and colors, but they'll seem distorted and create a lot of noise your brain can't process. There is also an even smaller chance that one eye will graft well and the other will not. In that case, you may choose to have the damaged eye removed, but we recommend wearing a patch." He paused. "Cheaper," he said. "Much cheaper."

"Just take out my chip," I said.

"You leave as you are or as we make you," Javier said. "Those are your choices. We don't do partial work."

There was a knock on the door. It opened, and a man with a wide, bulbous nose stepped partway into the room. "Sir," he said. He nodded toward the hallway. Javier followed, sucking hard on his cigarette. They left the door slightly ajar, and the indistinct murmur of their voices hummed in the room.

"We can't go back," Bethany said. "I sold Tanner's car. You have to do this or we'll both be caught."

"I don't want anything grafted onto me," I said. "I don't want to be augmented, tinkered with, cut up, or fucked-up. I won't do it."

"You're not thinking straight," she said. "Take a moment to think. This is the only way."

"One percent," I said. "How do we know that's even the right statistic? Who is this guy?"

"He's famous."

"For what?" I asked. "He works out of an alley in a tent city."

"Trust me," she said.

But I couldn't feel her, not in the way I was accustomed to. She was just a face—her words were just sounds. I saw this clinic not as a passport to another life but as the resurgence of an old one. "My body is the only thing I own," I said. "There is nothing else. And even that's fifty-fifty at this point—I eat their food, I do their work, I take their drugs."

"James," she said, "you're with *me* now."

I shook my head. If something went wrong, all the blackness would pour in like smoke. I'd be trapped in memory, unable to wake. Her father would be there, waiting for me, with the building on fire. He would find me, after all. I ducked past her. I grabbed a scalpel off the tray.

She sucked in her breath. "No," she said. "You're making a mistake." Her face was crumpled slightly, a distressed, pinched-mouth expression that took me a moment to identify as grief. "Don't do this," she said. "Just talk to me."

"We're leaving," I said. "Come on."

"Don't," she said. "Just wait." She began to inch toward the door, and I felt her intention—she wanted to lock me in.

We both moved at the same time, but I was faster. I made it into the hallway and yanked the door closed before she could follow. I felt the slight reverberations of her pounding against it.

Javier stood alone, leaning against the wall. He gave me a cold look of appraisal. There were a number of thin white scars on the back of his hands, and the initials GHS were tattooed into the web between his thumb and forefinger. "If you leave," he said, "you can't come back."

And so I left.

The secretary stood up as I shot past her desk and crossed the lobby. I burst through the door into the alley, then rounded the corner and hurried into the open city, weaving in and out of the streets, unsure where I was going, quickly becoming lost in the crowd. It was dawn and the sky was just starting to pale in the east. A light rain had begun to fall, water drumming on the canvas tents. The air had filled with the mineral smell of dirt.

"Hey," somebody called. A man was following me. I picked up my pace. "Hey!" The man started to jog. "You there," he called. "Stop him!" People turned to stare. I gripped the warm metal handle of the scalpel. I had only a few seconds before it would be obvious that I was in flight—that something was wrong. I took a deep breath and made myself stop. I turned to let the man approach and tucked my hand, the one with the weapon, behind me. I resolved to kick him in the gut as soon as he was in range, but then I saw that he was smiling.

"You dropped your hat," he said. He jogged up to me, holding out my baseball cap. I touched my head as if to confirm that it was gone. "Like a bat out of hell," he said. "Boom! You took us by surprise. Where you coming from?"

I took the hat and tugged it on, pulling the brim low. I slipped the scalpel gingerly into my pocket. "Thanks," I said, and turned to leave.

"I don't know your story," he said, "but cities like this fly in the face of God." The man came up beside me. He had a sign tucked under his arm. I recognized the bold black print on the white field, but I couldn't read the words. He wore brown slacks and a white shirt that was styled like a proctor's—button breast pockets and a loop on the shoulder, almost like an epaulet. "They attract the worst kinds," he added.

"Yeah," I mumbled. He followed me through a cluster of food carts. Trash cans overflowed with wax paper and bits of food. There was vomit on the ground. People stood at little tables, eating and drinking.

"You look pristine," the man said. "No tattoos, no nothing."

"I was in the army," I said. "Is there a bathroom around here?"

The man nodded. "Right there." The bathroom was only a few feet from us, but it required a $2 cash payment. I had only the card.

"I guess I don't need to go," I said. "Anyway, thanks." I'd have to find somewhere else to remove my chip. I thought of the stopwatch and I walked faster, but my desire to get away from the man only intensified his curiosity. He continued walking beside me.

"What branch were you in?" he asked. "You don't look like army."

"Matter of opinion," I said.

"You don't talk like army, either," he said.

"Fuck off," I said. "How's that?"

"Is it drugs, brother?" he asked. "I know about that trouble."

I kept being jostled and elbowed, the sort of contact that was never unintentional at Goodhouse, that was always a harbinger of something worse. It set me on edge. And on top of that, the little bells that the pedicabs rang to announce themselves seemed to be chiming everywhere. I kept scanning the crowd for Bethany, hoping to see her familiar shape. I'd made a mistake. That was rapidly becoming clear. I'd been impulsive and irrational, and now that the crisis had passed, I was seeing my situation with more clarity. Javier's clinic was not the Exclusion Zone. It was not more of what I didn't want. If I'd stayed, it would have been my own choice. And now I was alone in a crowd, the thing I'd wanted to avoid. I felt ashamed, as if I'd fulfilled some genetic destiny, as if I'd succumbed to my own true nature even as I'd fought against it.

A pedicab almost collided with me, and I jumped out of the way.

"Somebody's trying to tell you something," the man said.

"What?" I said. I thought I'd glimpsed Bethany, or maybe it wasn't her, just another girl in a black dress.

"Not me," the man said, and he pointed to the heavens—at the pink, spreading dawn. "Him."

•

The man's name was Bob Hawkins, and he wanted to sit in a café and talk about God—about how the Devil was fighting to claim the planet, using his henchmen to destroy the righ-

teous. He offered to buy me breakfast from a cart, but I was
distracted. All I could think about was finding a quiet bathroom where I could be alone with the scalpel in my pocket. I
remembered the cluster of sign holders, and I asked him if his
companions had a building nearby, a gathering place. "It's
been too long since I've stood in a house of worship," I said.
And he must have thought I was going through some kind of
withdrawal; he kept staring at my hands, which trembled even
though I clasped them together

"You're a good kid," Bob Hawkins said. "I can see you're
from nice people." He clapped his hand against the stitches
on my back, sending a bolt of pain all the way to my knees.
"All you have to do is put your foot on the path," he said.
"God will do the rest."

"Amen," I said.

The church was a large white canvas tent at the edge of the
market. It had one big central room, and it was connected to
another, smaller tent by an open-air passageway. Two hefty
men with rosebuds tucked into the lapels of their jackets stood
at the entrance. They waved us through and nodded to my
companion.

Later, I would try to remember everything about the scene.
The symbols on the felt banners that hung like colorful pen-
nants along the walls, the faces of the faithful, and the woman
who stood at the lectern speaking in a singsong voice. But, at
the time, I was too consumed with my own purpose. I felt as
if I were drawing the school toward me. The chip was a hot,
glowing coal in my belly.

A spray of roses stood on the altar, a thick mat of crim-
son petals—blooms that seemed almost waxy in their perfection. My companion nudged me. Everyone around us got to
their feet to sing. Wind tugged at the taut canvas sides of the
tent, causing them to snap and vibrate. The air smelled of a

woodsy incense—pine pitch and myrrh. In Oregon I'd visited the logging camps, and I remembered that the whole forest had smelled like this—like the hearts of the trees had split open.

I excused myself to use the bathroom. I told Bob Hawkins I'd be right back, then I walked to the rear of the church and inched down the far aisle, feeling conspicuous, heading toward a little blue curtained door that had the word RESTROOM stenciled above it. The scalpel tapped my leg with each step, and I covered the blade with my hand so no one bumped it. "I know you are frustrated," the woman at the pulpit was saying. "I know you are hurting. But you are not alone. Not anymore. You need God, but he also needs you. There is a fight coming. You will be asked to commit everything. He will test you. He will have you feel his mercy, even as you are the instrument of his wrath."

I ducked behind the blue curtain and followed a passageway that opened into a larger room. Two portable toilets stood in the middle like green plastic towers. One was occupied. I stepped into the empty stall, and the stench reminded me of a boxer. I breathed through my mouth. The person in the toilet beside mine coughed, and the sound was depressingly loud. I would have to be totally silent.

I lifted the front of my shirt and tucked the hem in so it would stay up and away. I unwrapped the gauze that the doctor had used to cover the stitches on my back. I wound it around my arm, saving it, trying to keep it clean. The light in the restroom was very dim. I couldn't see the black dot on my skin, but I'd marked the site so many times that it had left a small raised scar on my stomach. I knew I had to cut deep to be sure I got the chip. I thought an inch should do it, roughly the depth of a finger joint.

I stuffed the whole roll of toilet tissue into my waistband

below the chip site, then leaned forward, my head pressed against the green plastic wall, my legs as far behind me as I could get them. I needed to keep blood off my pants, if I could. I withdrew the scalpel and tensed. I kept almost pressing the blade into my skin, thinking I was going to do it, but pain stilled my hand every time. I took a blob of sanitizer gel from the little canister affixed to the side of the toilet and smeared it over my belly and hands. I tried to imagine that it wasn't a body, that my stomach was just a piece of cardboard, but this made it even more difficult. Someone knocked on the stall door.

"Just a minute," I called back.

I was angry with myself for being squeamish. I tried calling myself a coward, but this only made it harder to cut. It wasn't until I thought of my belly as something beloved that I was able to press the knife in. When I imagined this work as delicate and gentle, then I was able to part the skin and the fat. I imagined my hand was like the soft fabric of the shirt, caressing, caretaking.

I was terrified of going too deep, of cutting into my intestines. I tried to stop when I felt the resistance of muscle and then angle the knife in a wide circle about an inch across. Blood soaked the toilet paper almost instantly. I imagined that the hole was already there, that I was simply finding the strength to empty it, but the pain was disorienting. It flowed through my back and into my arms. I removed a bloody mass of something and it was done, or I hoped it was. I tossed everything into the toilet. I stuffed the wound with gauze and wrapped it tight. Someone knocked again on the door. "A minute," I said.

I didn't have any place to wipe my hands, and the tissue at my waist was useless. I tried to use the sanitizer to wash away the rest of the blood, but it turned everything into a pink goo. There was a filter at the top of the toilet, some kind of air-purifying screen, and I reached up and used this to wipe off whatever I could. I was dizzy. I adjusted my shirt, stepped out of the stall, and almost lost my footing.

A long line of people waited for the restroom. One man pushed past me and slammed the door. The sound was like a gunshot. Another man in line had his eyes closed, head bowed in what appeared to be prayer. Two others were deep in murmured conversation. A black fog hovered at the edge of my vision. I stepped into the hallway. I had to get out of here. My body was liquid with pain. One of the heavy canvas walls of the tent undulated slightly. I pulled on the edge, to see how far it would lift. Only about an inch. I was going to have to walk out the front door.

I returned to the church and was dimly aware of two things. First, it was much more crowded. All the seats were taken and dozens of people were packed into the aisles. The early-morning service, it seemed, was standing room only. Second, a new voice was preaching. A man stood at the pulpit, his cadence rhythmic and hypnotic and somehow familiar.

"If you understand nothing else," the man said, "it's this one thing: Just as the dawn arrives, each morning, here on earth, so does God's call. It arrives each day. God calls you, each day, to battle." And here his voice deepened and slowed. "This is not a human war but a God-given one. And I should know." The crowd called out their encouragement. Some people were waving, palms outstretched. Most of my attention was on the act of walking—on the simulation of normal, uncomplicated movement.

"Excuse me," I said. I had to push past several church members. And then, perhaps because every face was riveted, I glanced at the pulpit. I saw a man in a tan sport coat with a red rosebud affixed to the lapel. It took me a moment to see beyond the clothes, beyond the context—to see the face that I recognized. I stopped and stared. It was Tim—Timothy Goodhouse, my supervisor at the factory. He stood at the lectern, transformed into a civilian, but the slight flattening of his vowel sounds, the way he leaned his head forward and looked up through his lashes, was immediately recognizable.

"Who is that?" I said to the woman next to me. She was tall, plump, and middle-aged. She had a metal stud in the side of her nose. Her long, graying hair cascaded down to the middle of her back.

"Quiet, brother," she said. She remained transfixed, staring over the crowd. Hanging from her neck was a gold chain with a charm—a Zero bisected by a lightning bolt. I saw the same symbol tattooed on the upturned wrist of the man beside me. Above it the word *purity*. I was close enough to see the little hairs on his arm and the weave in the fabric of his clothing. I momentarily touched my face to make sure it was blank of expression. The felt banners overhead—the lamb and the lion, the dove and the cross—had been subtly altered. The halo on the dove was slashed through; the lamb stood astride a bolt of lightning. This was a Zero church. There were hundreds of believers here. We were packed shoulder to shoulder.

"You are good people," Tim said. "You *want* to feed the hungry, minister to the sick, protect the weak. Compassion is a virtue. Right?" The crowd murmured, unsettled—some people saying yes. But Tim was shaking his head. He was holding up his hand, the one with the stump for a finger. "You are wrong," he said. "Compassion is the knife at your throat. And how do I know? Because I was not always guided by the Holy Spirit." He let his gaze travel slowly across the room. It was unreal to see him, to see him so altered—Tim, one of us. He seemed to be taller, more substantial, the feeling from the crowd buoying him, forming him in some way, infusing him with authority. He opened his arms wide, as if to encompass us all.

"The waters have turned to acid, the seas have risen, the heavens storm, the earth is fallow. And we know how the Devil operates. We can see the problem. God himself has called us to action. And yet—" Here he paused as if overcome. "And yet, how do we respond?" he asked. "We feed. We clothe. We educate. And I tell you, *good people*, that it does you credit. But your compassion is, absolutely, killing you."

That pine pitch smell was back—a bitter, musky smell. I'd seen the bodies at La Pine, some of them, anyway. I'd certainly smelled the flesh cooking along with the acrid stench of every burnt mattress and shoe and floorboard. I'd thought about the water inside us. That was the only part of the boys to escape. Spongy insides turned into vapor, a gas pulled out of the little window opening, sucked into a cloud, blown into the forest.

Someone handed me a white cylinder. I just stared at it. Another cylinder was being passed nearby and people were slipping paper money into an opening at the top. Tim was generating donations with his speech, revenue for the Zeros. I quickly passed the cylinder to my left. That's when I noticed how badly I was bleeding. The woman in front of me had a large purse slung over her shoulder, a printed cloth bag, and we were packed so tight that the bag was actually wicking blood from my wound. A spreading red circle ate through the pattern on the fabric—blood rich with the doctor's drug, blood that had once carried oxygen to my organs. Now it was merely a stain.

"Excuse me," I said, but the man beside me didn't move. I was just shifting my weight, preparing to force my way through the crowd when I glimpsed Montero—standing less than twenty feet away.

He stood near the altar. Thick, wavy hair framed his face. He, too, wore a suit with a rosebud in the lapel, but he looked uncomfortable in it, uneasy. He was part of a line of men that created a sort of human barrier between Tim and the crowd. And a few feet from Montero was the giant, with his thick neck, the black undulating tattoos staining the skin of his cheeks. My first thought was that they must have escaped after all. Tim must have known them, he must have helped them, gotten them a print. But that wasn't right. If they were fugitives, they wouldn't be here, out in the open, so bold, so unafraid.

"Let me," Tim said, "be a tool in your hand, a hammer brought down. We are fighting for the destiny of a planet. And you can step away. You can abdicate, claim it's too hard. You're free to do that." He paused. "Or you can acknowledge that it *is* a fight, that it has come to you, and that you didn't ask for it, but you will stand up with your God. You will link arms on this battlefield."

As his voice rose, the people around me began to shout their encouragement. An organ started playing and a hymn broke out, the lyrics projected in the air above Tim, tall white letters, the words *verse* and *chorus* blinking like a warning. I was cold with shock, and whenever Montero swept the crowd with his gaze, I bowed my head as if overcome by prayer.

I had to get out of there. I said, "Excuse me," again to the man beside me, but he didn't hear, or didn't want to. The crowd was packed too tight. Everyone's mouth was opening and closing, creating a river of noise. And then I realized that I was thinking about it all wrong. That I had been stupid to believe that Mule Creek inmates were wandering around the factory, sneaking over to our side, their absence going unnoticed and unreported.

Someone opened the door. That was the pattern of the

Goodhouse attacks. The Zeros appeared like a virus, multiplying and overwhelming, and always—someone opened the door. And that was when I knew what Montero was not. He was not an inmate, not a convict. He was not breaking out of the Ione campus. He was breaking in.

TWENTY

I had just turned and started toward the exit when a dozen civilian police officers poured through the entryway. All of them wore black helmets and body armor. They were faceless human shapes, cutting through the crowd with the confidence of training and the aggression of purpose. I saw them as if they were all connected—some tentacle unfurling, reaching. I was briefly certain that they were headed toward me, that I had been identified, and I felt again the magnitude of my error.

"Illegal search," someone yelled. "Illegal search!"

An officer told everyone to remain calm. "Stay in your seats," he said. "Stay where you are." But this had the opposite effect. The crowd surged in all directions as people pushed for the exits. It felt like we'd all taken a step closer together. My arms were actually pinned to my sides now, and I was struggling to free myself, pushing against the woman with the purse. Tim alone seemed composed. He remained at the altar, standing behind a shield of flowers.

"Welcome, brothers," he called. "This is a peaceful gathering."

"We need everyone to sit down," one of the officers said. Another one held something that looked like a gun with a large boxy nozzle. He swept it over the crowd, searching.

"We have nothing to hide," Tim said. "We are happy to comply."

One woman near the back of the church screamed, "Get your hands off me." She appeared to be struggling. "Don't touch me!"

"This is private property," someone else said. "Come back with a warrant."

The crowd was bearing me toward the hallway that led to the restrooms. I felt the hands of those behind me clutching my shirt, and I was actually holding on to other people, trying not to be pulled down. We were all fused in this moment, some unwieldy animal, and I promised myself that if I survived, I would never go back into a crowd—never willingly.

I had to push hard to get into the hallway. The lady with the purse was still in front of me, and we moved together into the room with the green towers. The far wall had a large panel of canvas that had been drawn to one side, revealing a wide gap. A mass of people shoved their way through it, out into the clear morning light. I could tell there were police nearby. I heard shouting. I felt the crowd resist as if they were one organism absorbing a blow. "Stay where you are," an officer called, and his voice was very close, alarmingly so. "Stay where you are."

Someone grabbed the woman I'd been following and threw her to the ground. I started to run. I glanced behind me and saw a thick line of police moving to cover the back entrance. The white sides of the tent rose above them like a glacier. I passed a narrow alleyway and saw more police advancing at a run. I didn't feel my wound now. Even my legs were numb. I accelerated, and it seemed to take no effort at all. The landscape of the tents sailed past as if the city itself were moving. I didn't know where I was, and most of the shops were closed anyway, some kind of metal webbing drawn down over their entrances.

Nothing was familiar, and this only added to my disorientation.

A pedicab shot past, overloaded with people. "This way, kid," someone called. "This way." I had no idea who'd spoken. I was running blindly. I felt like I couldn't get a full breath. At last I stumbled onto a road that I recognized. It was the one that cut through the residential tents, the road I'd taken with Bethany. Suddenly the path that I'd memorized snapped into place. I knew where I was.

I hid in the quarantine area. There were no sick people there, of course, only solar generators, canned food, and portable water-treatment kits. It made sense—located deep in the residential section and heavily guarded, it was a sham for the public. I embedded myself among the valuables. I crawled between cans of beans and cooking oil. If the contents shifted I'd be crushed, but there was no way I could get to Javier's tonight, and I was almost too exhausted to care. I located a few jugs of water and broke the seal on one of them. I drank deeply and then poured the rest of the contents over the wound in my belly. I hoped Bethany wasn't on the streets, wasn't running, wasn't risking herself. I willed her to be safe.

I must have fallen asleep, because I lost track of time. I awoke to find the tent blazingly hot, the metal tins around me burning like coils in some larger oven. I drank more of the water, but it did nothing to ease my thirst. I remember pulling the intake form out of my pocket, unfolding the quickpaper. I tried to read it, but I couldn't focus my eyes. I was squinting and straining even though the document was right in front of my face. The tent cooled down rapidly after sunset and I began to shiver, to alternate between hot and cold.

At one point I rolled over and saw Tim lying beside me. He was wearing a student's uniform, a man dressed like a child. "We have to tell somebody," I said. I started to shake him, to pull at his clothes, but he remained inert and peaceful. "Wake up," I said. "Tell them you made a mistake. Tell them." But his clothes started to come apart in my hands. He was melting into the cans, melting into me.

A few times I awoke and remembered to drink—to pour water over the wound, which was now excruciatingly tender and oozing a thick, blood-tinged pus. I wanted to see Owen again, wanted to tell him that our status was nothing, just a preoccupation, a distraction from this, from some deeper river of life. I felt always on the verge of getting up, always on the verge of finding the strength to crawl out, to walk back to Javier's. But soon the water jugs were empty and I was unable to replace them. I was entombed, and I realized for the first time that I might die here, that the poison of the infection might thicken my blood, devour my tissues; that it might fight me, and win.

•

"She didn't come for you," a man's voice said. "I'm a little surprised."

Dr. Cleveland, I thought. That's who it sounded like. I opened my eyes. I was sitting in the passenger seat of a vehicle I didn't recognize. A blanket had been tucked around me, but it was unusual, brown and coarse, and there were bits of plastic tape stuck to its surface.

I heard a rasping sound and turned to see Dr. Cleveland kneeling in the back of a cargo van, securing a stack of boxes to the floor, cinching down a strap. I felt nothing at the sight of him, not even surprise. "Well, we tried," he said. "Didn't we? That's all you can really ask of yourself."

My fever seemed to be gone, but it had consumed some essential spark of life. I had almost no strength. Through the windshield I saw a row of houses—wood-sided, gray-and-white-painted structures—and a laundry line where clothes shuddered and kicked in the wind.

"Don't worry, James," Dr. Cleveland said. He clapped me on the shoulder. The contact startled me—it filled me with a kinetic sort of despair, something that seemed to radiate out from his touch. He was real. This was real. "So," he said, stepping past me to sit sideways in the front seat, "after you allowed my daughter to drive at a high rate of speed, and after you led her into what is essentially a den of drug addicts and thieves, where did you leave her?"

I looked over at him, looked into his bright blue eyes. She had not been found. She had not turned up in a hospital somewhere, hadn't been caught on the streets—and this gave me hope. I had not failed completely. I could, at least, keep her secrets.

"I saw her collapse," I told him.

"Where?" he asked.

"In the crowd at the church," I said, improvising. "But then the police arrived and we got separated."

Dr. Cleveland leaned forward, and the tension in his face created a wrinkle on his forehead, a deep, vertical fold. "Did she look like she was in cardiac arrest?" he asked.

"She looked bad," I said. "Really bad."

Dr. Cleveland didn't react. After an uncomfortably long time he said, "I don't need a heart monitor to know you're lying, and instinctively I want to dismiss this youthful loyalty that you feel toward one another. I want to diminish it in some way, but I think"—and here he paused—"I think I have merely forgotten what it was like."

He opened the driver's-side door and walked around to my side of the vehicle. I pushed the lock button on the armrest, but it was his van and my door opened at his touch. Fresh air flooded the cab. It was heavy with some kind of sweet fragrance. "I want you to know," he said, "that I will find her. It's just a matter of time."

We were parked in a driveway. A high chain-link fence cut through the backyard, and beyond this fence, in the distance, I saw a field of parked cars—a quilt of color. "Where are we?" I asked.

"You don't recognize it?" He gestured for me to climb out. "I guess you've never seen it from this side."

"Proctors' Quarters," I said. And I felt hopeless, looking at the familiar landscape, at the orderly flower beds, at this approximation of a civilian residential street.

Dr. Cleveland grabbed and steadied me. I was wearing the same pants, but my shirt was gone. It had been replaced with a black sweatshirt. He tugged its hood over my head, and then he looped an arm under mine, supporting me as we walked toward the back door of a small wooden house. A neighbor was working in a raised garden bed. The doctor waved to her, and she stopped what she was doing, openly staring. "Nosy bitch," he said under his breath. I was having a hard time staying upright, and he all but dragged me up the back stairs and onto the porch. He opened the door and helped me inside to a little civilian kitchen.

Everything was white—the countertops, the cabinets, even the walls, which were covered with tiny white tiles with an opalescent sheen. I realized that this must be his home. Bethany's home, too. This is where she'd returned to every night, and I'd not even thought to imagine it.

Dr. Cleveland walked me over to the kitchen table and deposited me into a chair. The incision in my side ached. On the wall across from me were dozens of photographs of his daughter. A whole panel had been dedicated to her childhood. I even glimpsed the hated doll head in one of the pictures. It was sitting on a box, under a Christmas tree—a pink-skinned head with yellow hair. A ten-year-old Bethany stood beside it in a fuzzy bathrobe. Her feet were bare and her expression was very serious, almost adultlike in its intensity.

"How did you find me?" I asked.

"I took some precautions," Dr. Cleveland said. He set a plastic storage tub on the table and then began to pull the pictures off the wall, to stack them in the box.

"Another chip?" I asked.

"I sewed it into your back," he said. "I hope you're not offended. It did save your life."

With each picture he lifted off the wall, he left a place where the paint was a shade whiter, the opposite of a shadow, a memory of what had once been there. I was starting to feel a little better, a little stronger. I sat up in my chair, but the more awake I was, the more confused I became. "Why am I not in the dormitory?" I asked. "Or Protective Confinement?"

"Because you are still *at large*," he said.

But it was an unfamiliar term. "I'm where?" I asked.

"Kidnapping," the doctor said. "Theft. Not to mention a tracking chip found in the latrine of a Zero church. It's quite a story."

He leaned over and grabbed a quickpaper magazine off the kitchen countertop. He scrolled through something and then tossed it onto the table. I looked at the page. It featured an almost unrecognizable picture of me. I glared at the camera with a malevolent expression on my face, one hand raised. It had been captured from a video feed and was slightly out of focus. Below the headline, ENDANGERED, there was another title—GOODHOUSE STUDENT, 17, ABDUCTS MEDICALLY FRAGILE GIRL.

"You know, abducting a child carries twenty years in a federal prison," he said. He raised an eyebrow. "Something to think about."

"I'd feel right at home," I said.

He pulled the last of the pictures off the wall and tucked them into the sides of the box. "Are you ready to tell me where she is?" he said.

"I obviously don't know," I said, "or I wouldn't be here."

"You had a falling-out," he said. "But not immediately, I don't think."

He was too close to the truth. I stood up. I had to lean on the countertop to walk the length of the kitchen, and even then, I was shaking with the effort. From the window over the sink I saw the soybean field where I'd worked with Owen. The plants had yellowed slightly, but I didn't see any work details, which was unusual. "We had a falling-out," I said, "because I saw someone I recognized. A proctor from school."

"That would be Timothy," the doctor said. He lifted the flaps at the top of the box and snapped them closed. "He's a speaker-elect for the Holy Redeemer's Church of Purity."

His offhand tone surprised me even more than his certainty. "How did you know?" I said.

"I was following up on a tip." He smiled. "A rumor about inmates in the factory. And I would have been able to do much more, except for one little problem. Do you know what that was?"

"Your daughter," I said.

"No," he said. He put the magazine on top of the box. "My patient. Or should I say patients," he corrected. "They were found wandering around campus. And now I've had to offer my resignation."

I leaned more fully against the countertop. The idea that I was somehow responsible for this turn of events filled me with the kind of satisfaction that was hard to keep to myself. "Those rooms are illegal," I said. "Even for us. You can't do that."

"Quite illegal," he said.

"And they've shut you down, haven't they?" I felt strength building inside me, determination. "They've confiscated your research."

"Oh yes," he said. "An investigation is pending. They've cordoned off my office—the entire basement level, actually." But his eagerness to confirm his own downfall began to make me nervous. "And poor Robert," he said, "he was really hoping for an early retirement. But he's had to hold one press conference after another. I'm afraid that it just reflects so badly on him."

I walked to the kitchen door and looked through the glass panel at its top. It was almost fully dark now. Purple-and-white bunting spanned the front of Vargas. A Goodhouse flag hung from the old clock tower, draped like a pennant. Several civilian cars traversed the main road, and two proctors used glowing orange wands to direct traffic.

"How long was I in the tent?" I asked.

The curved white roof of the pavilion was just visible off to my left. I opened the kitchen door and heard the distant sound of singing, many voices in concert with each other. "What day is it?" I said.

But I already knew the answer. I was looking at a full parking lot. I was listening to the ceremony itself playing out in the distance. It was Founders' Day.

•

The doctor clicked on a wallscreen, and in my haste to pivot—to turn and see what he was doing—I must have lost my footing. I fell to the ground, legs slipping out from under me, hands clutching at the countertop, but not fast enough to get a grip. I lay on the floor, feeling the weight of my body. I'd been inert for so long, it had left me incredibly weak.

"You know," the doctor said, "half the people on the

planet can't remember a world before Goodhouse." He stood near the kitchen table, seemingly unaware of my difficulties. "Fifty years," he said, "is a long time." He was scrolling through dozens of security videos. Time stamps spooled across the bottom of the display, and I had an accelerating feeling of dread.

"What's happening?" I asked.

"Tanner thought an evening service would be more elegant, more dramatic." The doctor selected a video and expanded it to fit the screen. "Quite a nice event, really. Though I'm no longer invited."

The screen showed the interior of the pavilion—hundreds of stadium-style seats packed with people. It was easy to spot the students, that navy-colored stripe at the top of the auditorium—and then, below them, the civilians with their colorful clothing. Little star-shaped lights dangled overhead, all of them suspended at different heights, seeming to float, to obliterate any sense of a ceiling.

"My father used to tell me that every setback was just an opportunity in disguise," Dr. Cleveland said. He minimized the video, then selected another. A man wearing a blue sash across his suit stood at a podium. "At the time, I thought he was patronizing me—you know, the way adults tell children that everything will be okay when, clearly, it will not. But now I think maybe he was correct."

"You told Tanner," I said. "Right? You told him about Tim?"

But the doctor was distracted. "Told him?" He frowned at me. "James, you don't look well."

I'd managed to sit up, but I was leaning against the cabinets, unable to do much more.

"Maybe you'll feel better," Dr. Cleveland said, "if you tell me where Bethany is." He hefted the box he'd packed and then stood over me. "Give me the truth," he said, "and I'll take you with me. Out into the world, like a real citizen."

"And if I don't?"

On the screen behind the doctor, the man with the sash was smiling, lifting his hands, clapping and turning—he'd been giving an introduction of some kind.

"You once asked me if I was helping the Zeros. Well"—he shrugged—"it turns out, they're helping me."

"Helping you with what?" I said.

"There isn't going to be a scandal," he said. "There isn't going to be an investigation of my methodology. You know, cleanup is part of any experiment," he said. "You wash out your glassware. You incinerate your trash."

I shook my head, trying to understand him fully.

"You shouldn't have run out on me, James," he said. "You shouldn't have opened the door."

"I didn't," I said.

"I could have helped people," he said. "I could have saved lives." And here he actually looked pained. "But you forced my hand."

I heard a sound, a percussive boom that made the cabinets rattle, that seemed to shake the floor beneath me. The video screen turned white. The doctor did not react to this noise, did not flinch or look around. He just stared at me, gauging my expression.

"I hate to cut this short," he said, "but you need to make a choice. You can die here with your friends or you can tell me where my daughter is."

I couldn't pull myself up, but I used what strength I had to strike him, to kick at his leg. He merely grunted and took a step back. "I can't say I'm surprised," he said, "but it was worth a try." He balanced the box on his hip and spoke into a hand-held. "I need some cleanup at the house," he said.

"Copy that," a voice said. The words were faint, seemingly distant.

"Don't put your faith in the police," the doctor said. "They won't be here anytime soon." And then he turned to go.

"Bethany knows who you are," I said. I was reaching for a way to hurt him. "She knows you and rejects you."

The doctor gave me a weak smile. "But I will be there when she outgrows her adolescent infatuations and misconceptions. And you," he said, "will not."

•

I managed to get to my hands and knees. The image of the pavilion disappearing—that starlit auditorium, with its rows of students and administrators and civilians—filled me with terror. This terror gave me strength that only moments ago had been impossible. I crawled through the kitchen door. The doctor was already in his van, backing out of the driveway. I watched his red taillights disappear down the street. In the distance, an alarm throbbed, a computer-generated voice repeated a message that I couldn't quite make out.

Pushing for some reserve, I summoned the strength to walk into the backyard, to stumble over to the chain-link fence and look out at the campus. There was a tower of black smoke where the pavilion had been. I strained to see through it to find the familiar curving roofline. I hoped the building had been damaged and not obliterated. But I saw only smoke, a thick, shaking blanket in the floodlit sky.

I tried to scale the fence, to make hand- and footholds out of its little diamond-shaped openings. I slid repeatedly to the ground. I kept looking over my shoulder, afraid that someone would materialize just behind me, a Zero, a man in a red mask. It would be smarter to hide, to wait out the attack. But every student who was not participating in the ceremony would be locked in his room. They would be beating on the doors, terrified and trapped.

The barbed wire had been removed, and when I reached the top of the chain-link fence, I sat there straddling it, trying to catch my breath, certain that I would simply fall when I tried to descend. I glanced behind me and saw the neighbor woman standing on her porch, her handheld pressed to her ear. All of a sudden a series of explosions detonated near the heart of campus, far to the south. The sound was so deep and disorienting that I didn't immediately know I was falling. I slammed into the ground and lay there, unable to draw a breath, the wind knocked out of me. I tried to roll onto my side, but there was something wrong with my left arm. At first I thought I'd reinjured the elbow, but then I realized that the whole arm was useless and limp. The pain was so intense that I just sat there, heaving on an empty stomach, unable to focus.

The campus had gone completely dark. There were no backup lights, no sirens, and somehow this darkness created a terrible kind of intimacy. Voices floated over the soybean field, people screaming, people calling to each other. Everything seemed very close now. Several cars pulled out of the parking lot. They were small civilian vehicles, and as they sped toward the main gate, they were met with a burst of gunfire—little green tracers that arced through the air, coming from the guardhouse itself. At first the shots fell short of their targets, but then the lights seemed to adjust themselves, they lifted and lengthened their trajectory. The tracers swept through the line of cars, entering one windshield and then another. One of the cars flipped, and made an awful crunching sound as it spun through the field beside me. The others just swerved into each other, blocking the road. And still, people were leaving the parking lot and driving toward the exit, almost as if they didn't know what else to do.

A large tour bus tried to clear a path, tried to ram its way through the pileup, but now the tracers were coming from other locations, too—the parking lot itself, the field opposite my own—beautiful arcs of light, graceful as spirits. They found their mark and the bus crashed into the knot of vehicles, swerving, then nosing to a stop.

And then there were no more cars, no more attempts at an exit. I saw a group of masked men running down the main road. Without a word they broke into three groups and disappeared onto the campus. I was still leaning against the fence, sitting exactly where I'd fallen. It had been only a few minutes, but the amount of destruction was staggering. Someone in a nearby car began to moan, and in the distance, two thick columns of smoke rose into the sky, smudging the stars, bending slightly in the wind, until they had the look of some inverted rainbow, corrupted and colorless.

This was beyond anything I'd ever experienced, and only the thought of Owen could compel me to my feet. I clutched my injured arm to my chest and staggered forward. One of the wrecked cars had its headlights aimed at the field in front of me. I would have to go around the beam or step through it. To save time, I decided to cut closer to the main road.

I doubled over as I approached the wreckage, my eyes scanning the darkness, alert for any kind of movement. Every step sent a little spike of agony through my shoulder, and I struggled to keep my breathing quiet and my footsteps soft. One of the windshields ahead was smeared with a dark liquid and had what appeared to be a mat of hair pressed against the inside of the glass. I looked away.

I crept past the bus. The damaged engine chuffed slightly. A little tendril of smoke leaked from its hood. That's when I saw the word UTAH on the vehicle's license plate. There was a picture of a rock formation and then the words SALT LAKE

CITY underneath. I stopped. The dormitory that I'd helped to prepare, the one that was meant to house the choir, they were coming from Salt Lake City. Some piece of that alternative life had found me—it had rolled to a stop right here.

The door wasn't locked. It was a bifold, and it was loose, just pulled halfway across the entrance. I took a few steps inside, careful to stay below the windows and out of sight. The bus was partway in the field, its back end in the dirt, its front tires on the road. I thought it would be full of people, but I saw only one—a student lying prone in the aisle. There was blood on the floor underneath him and a trail of blood leading from the driver's seat. The boy wore a uniform like ours, only his was beige in color. I touched his shoulder. He didn't move.

I got behind the wheel and put the transmission in gear. I located the switch for the lights. It was in the same location as it had been in the camp trucks I'd driven in Oregon. As I gunned the engine and cut the headlights, the bus roared up onto the road with much more power than I expected. I'd never driven anything like this before, and with one arm I could barely steer. Warm blood soaked into my pants. It was his blood, that boy in the aisle, that boy who was the same size and shape as myself.

I tried to stay low in the seat, but this was almost impossible. I was headed toward Vargas, which appeared intact, though it looked like one of those ancient historical photos, something from its days of decline—black windows, with a full moon over its shoulder. And beyond Vargas, I saw the lights of Mule Creek, a bright wall in the distance. Two civilians tried to flag me down, arms waving over their heads, but I couldn't stop. I'd never make it otherwise. I cut the wheel hard to the right and pulled across the lawn at the back of the building. I'd wanted to take the main road. It would be much faster, but it was probably full of Zeros.

I chose an interior pathway, a concrete track that had been built for T-4s and pedestrians alone. The bus was so much bigger. The tires kept catching at funny angles, wrenching the steering wheel from my already tentative grip. At one point I found myself on a steep, narrow pathway between Schoolhouses 1 and 2. I rode the brakes hard and the vehicle shuddered. I scanned the path ahead, and was checking and double-checking every shadow when a group of three students bolted out of a doorway. They were only twenty feet from the bus, but none of them even looked at me—a fact that seemed incredible until I heard gunfire. They were being pursued. A Zero in a proctor's uniform and red balaclava appeared from out of the same doorway.

I acted instinctively. I accelerated and yanked the steering wheel in his direction. He tried to jump backward, to gain the safety of the stoop, but I hit him. I scraped the bus along the brick wall of the schoolhouse, momentarily losing control. I heard metal tearing, a shrieking sound like the warning of a hawk, and then I was free. A spike of adrenaline made me feel that I was glowing from the inside, like I was converting my flesh into some kind of nuclear substance—raw energy.

I swerved into the residential section of campus. The back windows of the bus exploded into a cloud of glass. Someone was shooting at me. I hunched lower in my seat. Several bullets struck the dashboard to my right. I passed a cluster of Level 1 and 2 dormitories that were on fire—the front doors locked, little hooks of flame curling out of the bedroom windows. It was all happening again, I thought; it had never stopped happening. The Zeros had stayed inside me, inside my dreams and hallucinations, and now they had found their way here, climbed out of my mind and into the night.

I turned a corner, clipping the side of the bus against a low concrete pillar. Then I saw Dormitory 35. It was intact—the whole row was intact—and I accelerated, meaning to ram the front of the bus into the side of the structure, to break it open, to bypass the door altogether. I managed to brake just in time, to bring the bus up short, almost at the staircase itself.

I couldn't ram the building. I had no way to communicate with the people inside. I would almost certainly injure my friends, perhaps kill them outright. I put the bus in park and climbed out, taking the keys with me. There was a foul smell in the air, a thick toxic fog, things burning that were never supposed to burn—solar paint, linoleum, rug fibers, drywall. Bodies littered the walkway nearby.

I ran up the front staircase and yanked uselessly on the door handle. "Owen," I called. I thought I heard muffled voices inside, heard the tap of a fist or a foot. "Can you hear me?" I turned to search for a rock, something I might use to beat at a window—that's when I saw a man's body pinned under the bus. It was the Zero, the one I'd struck earlier. He still wore his red balaclava and his proctor's uniform. His mask was askew. The eyeholes showed white skin in the place of eyes. The webbing that secured his Lewiston to his side had caught on a piece of twisted metal, and his limp body had been lifted slightly off the ground and dragged. A small rectangular screen glowed through the fabric of his pants.

In order to rip open his pocket, I had to crawl partway under the bus, something that would have been considerably easier with two arms. It took a full minute for me to free what turned out to be a handheld. On the screen was a timer—ten minutes falling away toward nine. It was running some kind of software, something the Zeros had created. I touched the screen. Nothing happened.

I groped for one of the man's hands and lifted it. Two of his fingers were gone. A length of bloody bone protruded from one of the stumps. I dropped the hand. I wiped my fingers on the ground, wanting to erase the contact.

The bus shifted overhead. I heard footsteps. Someone was

walking up the stairs. I pulled my legs out of sight, tucked myself completely underneath. "It's clear," a voice said. "We got him."

The men didn't linger. They were in a hurry to go—to get on with things. I stared at the spot where the boy lay prone above me. I reached again for the mangled hand of the proctor. This time I didn't hesitate. I cradled it in my own. One finger was completely intact, and the screen activated at the dead man's touch. I frantically scrolled through the handheld, hoping nobody could see its glow. I searched until I found the security settings, then scrolled down to the subheading *Residential*. I attempted to override the lockdown. I kept tapping *Unlock all*, but every time I did so, the handheld asked for additional authorization. It wanted a code—four letters or numbers. There were thousands of possible combinations. "Shit," I said. I typed in the word *pure*. Incorrect. I typed in the word *zero*. Also incorrect. My grip was getting rubbery—a warm glow filled my chest. I remembered this feeling. It was shock. My body was pulling blood out of my arms and legs, shutting down every nonessential function.

It was hopeless. I didn't know the code, and the smell of smoke was stronger now; either the wind had shifted or the fire was moving closer. And then I thought of something that Bethany had said the night she'd visited me in the infirmary. I used the light from the screen to illuminate the man's name tag, illuminate the sequence of four digits that were stamped in the lower right corner. It was his employee number, 4358. I typed it in. The handheld authorized.

I expected to get an immediate response. I expected to hear students kicking open doors, streaming out onto the pathways. But nothing happened. I realized that they didn't know, that everyone would stay exactly where they were unless they were told otherwise. I found the PA system under CAMPUS

UTILITIES. I selected the word *Broadcast*, and specified that it should be schoolwide. A little picture of a camera appeared. From under the bus I could see a subtle shift in the light outside as every screen on campus lit up. I was about to activate the camera, about to send a video of myself into every room, but I thought better of it. I needed the boys to follow me without question. I needed authority. Instead, I activated the audio portion only.

"This is Davis Goodhouse, your class leader," I said, imitating his voice, approximating his smooth and commanding tone. "Your dormitories are now open. Leave immediately. Make your way to the Exclusion Zone. You all know where that is. Do not stay in your rooms. You are not safe there." I closed the transmission. There was a pause, and then doors were opening everywhere. A ragged, discordant cheer rose, disembodied, from the campus, absorbing all other sound. But I had one more thing to do.

I turned on the lights.

Every one.

TWENTY-ONE

By the time I got into Dormitory 35, it was empty. "Hello?"
I called. I went from room to room. "Hello?" Owen's box of
painting supplies had been pulled out from under his bed and
left open. A half-eaten Swann Industries chocolate bar lay on
the floor. I hoped that meant that he'd been here, that he'd
escaped. I did a quick check, room to room, and then I headed
out. I'd been gone only a few days, but seeing all the familiar
items—the heaps of linens, the uniforms, the trunks—was disorienting. I'd done what I could. It had not been nearly enough,
but this life, my life as a student, had come to an abrupt and
total stop.

I'd intended to drive to the factory. I was closer to that exit,
and I knew there'd be a gate there, a place where the big trucks
loaded and unloaded their cargo. But once I returned to the
bus, I made a different plan. The boy I'd assumed was dead,
the boy whose blood had soaked into my pants, had rolled over
onto his back. He was alive—his chest rising and falling, his
lips moving slightly.

"Fuck," I said. I couldn't just leave him. I put the bus in
gear. The gunfire had stopped, and this gave me the courage
to steer into the heart of the campus. The first thing I noticed
was that things looked so much worse with the lights on,
with the damage in full color. Even with Dr. Cleveland's drug

inside me, I struggled not to see the details. I was sure that everything I witnessed tonight would be replayed, would be endlessly considered, minutely inspected, in dreams, in memory. I was afraid that I'd be invaded by these images, and so this time I was careful. I allowed myself to look only at the path ahead and nothing more.

I wanted to drop the boy at the infirmary, to leave him where he'd be found, where he'd receive some help. This would put me near the access road I'd taken with Bethany, near an exit, or close enough. But when I got to the infirmary, I didn't recognize it. The building had been completely destroyed. The two upper stories had cascaded into the basement. Part of the façade was intact, windows still in recognizable shapes, but these were just sections of walls, lying on their sides, their edges dissolving into piles of smoldering brick and debris. Still, wounded students had congregated nearby. They didn't know where else to go. Many had brought their injured friends. A few T-4s were abandoned at the site, parked haphazardly on the grass, but all the proctors were missing. At the arrival of the bus some boys fled in panic, but others surged forward, waving, expecting help.

It was then that I spotted Owen's abstract for the mural, that large oblong canvas full of children and well-meaning adults and one tiger. The painting appeared to be leaning against a stranded T-4. I angled the bus so that I passed within a few feet of it. And then I hit the brakes. The painting was propped on someone's lap, obscuring the face and torso of whoever was behind it.

I cut the engine. I slid out of the driver's seat and hobbled down the little staircase. Several boys tried to get onto the bus. "Back up," I shouted. "Stay back." Everyone complied, and I locked the doors behind me.

I ran over to the T-4 and pulled the canvas away. It was Owen. "Are you all right?" I asked. "Are you hurt?"

He smiled before he opened his eyes. The birthmark on his cheek seemed very prominent, a blotch of brown. "I recognize your voice," he said.

I felt a huge rush of relief. I'd found him. He had been spared. "Get up," I said. "We're leaving."

Owen didn't move, just gave me a dreamy, disconnected look. "I'm imagining you," he said, "as a civilian."

"Get up," I repeated. But something was wrong.

"You're dead, too," Owen said. "That's why we can see each other."

"What are you talking about?" I knelt beside him, looking for a wound. I found a small bullet hole in his forearm, but this injury wasn't really bleeding. It was just a hole. I pulled open his light blue work shirt, and there was blood everywhere, bright like paint.

"How did you do that?" Owen wondered. He was looking at the torn shirt. "You ripped off the buttons."

"You're going to be okay," I said. The fear in my voice was audible. I looked around for a nurse, for any trained adult, but I didn't see one. Only dozens of students, some of them terribly wounded, others just huddling together, waiting to be told what to do. Some of the younger children were openly crying, and one boy had his legs pinned under a pile of bricks. He was screaming—a wild, wailing sort of sound. "You're going to be fine," I said again. "You're going to be okay."

"I always thought you were paranoid," Owen said. "Just full of shit."

"I'm going to lay you down," I said. "Just lean into me." But with one arm I didn't have much control. I slid him sideways, and he groaned with pain. I pressed my hand against the wound on his chest.

"You're hurting me," he wheezed. "Stop. Get off."

"I have to do this," I said.

We sat for a moment, me trying to press without hurting

him, his expression growing slack. "Stay awake," I said. "Open your eyes."

He whispered something I couldn't understand. I leaned closer. He was mumbling about going back to the dormitory to get a painting. "Before they burn it," he said. "Come back with me." And then he arched his back slightly as if he were lying on something sharp and couldn't get comfortable.

"Everything's fine," I said. "Don't worry. We're all safe. The painting is safe." I squeezed his hand more tightly. I leaned in close and hummed the tune that he'd liked so much, the one we'd heard that night in the soybean field. I had no conversation now, nothing to say, nothing but these notes, reaching for whatever spark of consciousness still flickered inside him. I was whispering to what remained, offering this—a final benediction, a song without words.

Owen seemed to stop breathing, and then a moment later he took one more breath. I was smoothing his hair now, that clipped scrub brush. My hand passed over the birthmark on his face. "I'm here," I said. "I came back."

•

I thought this was the worst moment—that wrenching, unbelievable moment when the world tilts, when people you love are pulled behind the curtain of death. I thought I was enduring it right there, in the dirt beside the infirmary, with my hand on Owen's still-warm skin. But some things grow worse over time, more complex. That's how it is. You miss the dead, and then you live your life without them, and you realize slowly, painfully, incrementally, what it is that you've lost.

A helicopter passed overhead, with its rhythmic pulsation of rotors. More boys were arriving, walking around the bus, crowding the pathway. Bitter smoke suffused the air. I tried to get to my feet, but wasn't able to. Everything seemed remote.

I was on the other side of some invisible barrier. I was alone with Owen. We were alone.

It was Davis who recognized me. He squatted down so we were face to face. His angelic features—his serene expression— were in horrible contrast to the chaos around us. I remember he wore a gray T-shirt. It was torn across the shoulder, but he appeared otherwise unhurt. "James," he said. And I must have looked catatonic, because he touched my face, turning it slightly as if to confirm my identity. "You in there?"

"Did the boys get to the zone?" I asked. He dropped his hand. "How many made it?"

At first I thought he was angry, that he would strike me the way he usually did, holding his body still until he lashed out. But I had merely surprised him.

"That was your voice on the broadcast," he said. "No fucking way. That was you."

"How many made it?" I asked.

"A lot," he said. He glanced at Owen's body and then at me, at the blood on my shirt.

"It was Dr. Cleveland," I said. "He was one of them. No matter what they say officially. It was him."

"What do you mean?" Davis said. Smoke from the rubble made a black pillar in the sky. It was wide like a road, a passage into the heavens.

"When the experiment is done," I said, "you clean the glassware. You incinerate the trash."

Davis frowned and shook his head. "He wouldn't do this," he said. It didn't occur to me that he was in shock, too—that anything so human could happen to him, as well.

"I should have known," I said. "I should have stopped him." I was still holding Owen's hand. I was talking in fragments, unable to organize my thoughts, unable to think beyond the slack fingers clasped in my own, beyond the sense that I had to leave, that I couldn't leave, that I was trapped. Davis would never let me go.

But then I looked more closely at him. Davis was tugging at the torn edge of his shirt. His eyes had a wild, confused look. He was himself, but also someone new.

"Who else?" he asked. "Was there anyone else?"

"They were already here," I said. I thought of all the temporary proctors I'd seen at their orientation. "They've been here for weeks."

I struggled to stand, but I lost my balance. Davis reached out to me, and I flinched away. "Come on," he said. "I'm trying to help you." He pulled me to my feet, and I staggered from him, clutching my arm, colliding with the metal side of the bus. The key automatically unlocked the door and illuminated the interior. There was a terrible moment when I saw Davis contemplating this new piece of information.

"You drove through campus?" he said. "In that?"

"Let me go," I said.

Davis wanted to know how I made the announcement. I gave him the Zero's handheld. "It's all there, probably," I said. He wanted more explanation, but Owen lay dead on the side of the pathway and boys were stepping over him as if he were merely a pile of clothes. Another helicopter passed overhead, a silver sheriff's star painted on its belly. "I have to go," I said. "Just stay back."

But Davis was quick. One moment he appeared motionless and the next he was behind me. He reset my arm, lifted and rotated it so that the shoulder joint slipped back into the socket. The pain was electric at first, overriding all my senses, flooding every interior circuit. But then it subsided.

"Go on," Davis said. He stepped back as I sagged against the bus. "I didn't see you," he added.

I moved my hurt arm, wiggled my fingers. It was sore but functional. "No," I said.

He looked startled. "Just go," he said. "I'm letting you leave."

"It's too late for that." I unclipped the key from my belt loop and passed it to him. "You're going to drive me."

•

I rode in the dark luggage compartment, bracing myself against a wheel well. The thrum of the engine ricocheted off the metal sides, an endless, moaning growl. I had Owen's painting with me. I picked the staples from the wooden frame, using the stiff canvas to lever them out, tearing the fabric slightly until it came free. Then I threw the frame aside and rolled the canvas. Before we'd left, I'd tucked Owen's body more fully against the T-4, where no one would trample it. I'd tried to make a purposeful memory of my friend, to absorb the details this time—the slight chipping of his front tooth, the way one ear sat a little higher than the other.

Every time the bus slowed, I was sure that Davis was being stopped, that I was going to be found and arrested. I could also hear the others when he slowed—the boys whom he'd packed into the seats. They were students with broken bones and contusions. Many had left the dorm without shoes and had torn their feet as they ran. Davis was driving them to the Red Cross center outside the tent city. We'd agreed on this. At Ione there was too much chaos, too many critically injured. I knew all the boys onboard would receive better and faster care off campus.

In the following months I'd watch Davis become something of a folk hero. In the media he'd be hailed as a compassionate leader, an independent thinker. Because of him, hundreds of boys had found refuge in the Exclusion Zone. The Mule Creek guards in their towers had been able to protect them. I'd go on to watch dozens of interviews with Davis. I'd see him tell and retell his story—my story—and wonder at how he was able to be bashful but resolute, brave but personable. The Vice

President of the United States would eventually pin a National Service Medal to his chest. If anybody at Goodhouse suspected that Davis's story was untrue, they didn't want to say so. Nobody reprimanded him for leaving campus. The busload of students he'd driven to the Red Cross center became part of his legend.

But at the time, as I sat huddled in the dark luggage compartment of the bus, my legs aching as I used them to brace myself against the constant motion, it was all just a hunch, a gamble. Davis and I had agreed that I'd climb out when we were close to the tent city. I was waiting for a quick blast from the horn, that was our signal. And it seemed like I was waiting a long time. Just when I'd decided to lift the latch on the compartment door, I heard it—a single, sharp note. Davis didn't fully stop. I had to jump, and the landing was hard, the ground unyielding. The bus sped past me, generating a cloud of dust in its wake.

It took me a moment to orient myself. I was within sight of the east gate. I could just make out the crowd waiting at the entrance. In the distance, the two nuclear cooling towers darkened the horizon, their massive hourglass shapes like hefty tombstones. Sagebrush grew in fragrant clumps. Manzanita trees rose out of the dry earth with their smooth bark and clawlike canopies.

I wasn't a stranger to this land anymore. I got to my feet. For the first time in days, I knew exactly what would happen next. I knew that I would vault the fence and head to West Market. I knew I would knock on Javier's door and find it open. It felt predetermined, like I was being guided and protected, a notion that I've retained over the years. I'm not sure who I saw standing in the night, leading me forward. But I saw something—an indistinct shape—a person, a shadow. I had the impression that I was not alone. I began to run. I breathed in the smell of this once-foreign desert. I felt powerfully alive, in motion, connected. All the boys who had once called me a friend seemed to be walking with me, in lockstep. I felt that they were forming a bright shield around me—and that I belonged exactly where I stood.

EPILOGUE

In January I returned to La Pine. The school was boarded up, and everything familiar was blanketed in snow. I was a fugitive now. My newly grafted irises were overwhelmed by the bright light, and my brown eyes burned with a chemical ferocity. I'd brought flowers—a dozen purple and white asters. I'd clutched them close to me as I rode the bus north, riding it through Klamath Falls, past the old Saddle Dam, staring at my own reflection, ghostly and half-visible in the glass of the bus window.

It had been almost a year, exactly, since the fire at La Pine, and the first building I visited was the old dormitory. It had partially collapsed. I walked up and touched its siding. The paint had melted and cooled in sagging ripples. Little climbing vines had now threaded their way upward—thin brown stalks that would leaf after the thaw. Campus was unnervingly quiet—no bells for classes, no droning PA announcements, no proctors issuing directives. Western hemlock swayed and creaked in the breeze. A blue jay scolded somewhere in the forest. I put my hand on the front door of the dormitory. It was ajar, but I couldn't bring myself to push it open.

I walked over to the chapel instead. The building was tiny and antiquated-looking, with its green clapboard siding and

its yellow trim. It seemed dwarfed by the landscape that surrounded it, by the tall, swaying trees, by the swell of the Cascade Range in the near distance. A sudden gust of wind blew
clumps of wet snow from the treetops. I went inside, surprised
to find it unlocked.

Half the pews were gone, and the others were disordered.
The harpsichord was missing, as was the podium. Even the
cross over the altar had been removed. Mice skittered across
the wooden rafters overhead, and a sloppy bird's nest filled a
tiny alcove where a saint had once stood. I walked toward the
altar. I pulled off my gloves. *Here*, I thought, *I'll leave the asters
here*. But when I stepped forward, I saw that there were already
flowers on the riser—white lilies with vermillion streaks and
pink-spotted throats, a clutch of them, arranged in a porcelain
vase. They seemed fresh.

These were expensive flowers, more beautiful than anything I could afford. They smelled like summer. They were
bright and unblemished. My asters were dog-eared and hadn't
kept well over the journey. And, after a long hesitation, several
deep, cold breaths, I stuffed them into the open mouth of my
bag. I turned and walked out the front door.

"Are you ready?" Bethany asked. She was waiting for me in
the shadow of the church. We'd traveled here together, but I'd
wanted to see the campus alone. She wore a thick white parka
with a fur-lined hood. She glanced down at the flowers. "What
happened?"

"I think I crushed them on the bus," I said. "They're turning brown."

"Brown's a color, too," she said. "What's wrong with
brown?"

"Let's get out of here," I said, but there must have been a
slight catch to my voice—a rupture—because Bethany snagged
the pocket of my jacket and pulled me close against her. We

stood there, leaning into each other, two small figures against a vast landscape of winter.

"We'll keep them," she finally said. "We'll press one."

We'd been together for seven months now, waiting for Javier's procedures to heal, for my irises to graft and solidify, living in a safe house not far from Ione. It had been possibly the worst and best place to be as the federal manhunt had cast its net across the country, as the reward for my capture had doubled, then tripled. Last week we'd decided that I'd healed enough to go. Javier had injected an organic filler over my cheekbones, into my forehead and my chin. It had slightly altered the planes of my face, but the modifications were temporary. They were already melting away, already unreliable. With all the media coverage of the Ione attack, we'd been forced to change our plans. We couldn't risk the border now, couldn't cross the way we'd hoped. We'd have to go on foot.

We waited for a long time, standing there together in the ruins of La Pine. The cold crept through my boots, through my thermal socks, through the synthetic fabric of my coat. Our breath made clouds of condensation in the air. From where we stood, I could see the gap in the trees where the dormitory had once been, and I felt suddenly that I was exhaling smoke, that the vapor from the fire had somehow been trapped inside me—and here it was, finally expelled, finally dissipating.

Somewhere in the forest a branch snapped. We both started.

"Let's go," I said.

I grabbed Bethany's hand and we left, following a buried pathway—one that was invisible, except in my memory.

•

Now, years later, it's easy to order it all: Ione was just the third in a long string of incidents, the beginning of a broader struggle.

Goodhouse survived another four years, eleven months, and twenty-seven days. Many boys died before the last school shut its gates. But in those initial confusing weeks, when I was still hidden in a safe room beneath Javier's clinic, the story was only beginning to unfold.

Dr. Cleveland's neighbor was the first to publicly identify me. She had a picture of me on the fence, turning to look at her, my mouth open, my teeth bared like an animal's. There were conflicting reports about my level of involvement in the attack. I was considered a protégé of the vanished Dr. Anthony Josiah Cleveland, possibly an accomplice. My history at La Pine seemed to verify this story. How else could I have survived? And there was more evidence, too.

On campus, we were always on camera. Of course, we knew we were being filmed. But I never realized the full extent of it until I saw my life replayed across a dozen media channels. In this narrative, all my actions were the actions of a criminal: I was a thief; I was unruly and wild in a Disciplinary Committee hearing; I conspired in the factory with Zeros who stood, just off camera, in the shadows. I attacked two of the school's most exemplary students—Creighton Goodhouse and Davis Goodhouse—students who were leaders and mentors for the rest of the boys. The administration had tried its best: pairing me with a model roommate, disciplining me, sending me to confinement. But then, there it was—a video of me destroying the machinery at the factory, of me firing a gun, of me scaling a fence even as the infirmary exploded in the distance.

There was another story, however. One that passed through the Goodhouses, from campus to campus. As the only student to ever escape and remain free, as a boy who had kidnapped a girl and stolen an $800,000 sports car, who'd left his identification chip in a Zero latrine, I became something of a legend. In this version I was not a collaborator, not a cautionary tale.

Mine was a story that every student knew, a story of wrong-thinking made right.

I also watched an interview with the boy I'd thought was dead on the floor of the bus. He was a tenor who'd fallen sick on the night of the performance, who had at the last minute stayed behind in the visitors' quarters. He'd been shot in the stomach and yet he'd survived, his voice rich and precise. Three months after the attack the boy would sing at a tribute for Tanner, and for the others who had been inside the pavilion at the time of the explosion. I watched memorials for slain proctors. I met their children through the news programs. I heard their wives speak. I learned things I'd never have guessed otherwise—how constrained they'd felt by their jobs, how they had demerit quotas to fulfill, how they'd monitored each other to minimize friendships with students. We were having strangely parallel experiences. We were pieces of a larger machine, each performing our functions, together but alone, constantly seen but not understood.

Swann Industries issued a series of statements denouncing terrorism, renewing their commitment to working closely with law enforcement, and stressing their dedication to service and excellence. Four months after Founders' Day the company announced that it was excited to seek FDA approval on a new drug to treat battle fatigue and post-traumatic stress. It was already under government contract. Again and again I saw interviews with members of the Holy Redeemer's Church of Purity. They looked sincere as they condemned the Ione attack as the work of radicals. They were saddened, but ultimately unsurprised, to learn that Goodhouse boys had participated in the planning, motivated by the love of power, by the brutal joy of killing. They said it hardly mattered why. The boys were irredeemable. What more proof did we need?

•

Bethany and I took the bus north. It was almost midnight by the time we reached the outskirts of Porthill, Idaho. We didn't go into the city but got off the bus at Bass Lake, a small outpost two miles from the Canadian border. To the east of us, the Selkirk Mountain Range jutted into the clouds. To the west, the Kootenai River cut a deep ribbon through the land. On the American side, a military base had been built on the ruins of an old airport. Overhead, fighter jets banked steeply and filled the air with the roar of their engines. We hiked through the darkness, staying near the road but inside the treeline.

My mother still lived in Porthill. We had her address, but there was no safe way to contact her. I wanted to see the neighborhood, to see where I'd grown up, but getting that close was too risky. So this was our compromise—in the morning we'd go around the city, skirting the edges, close enough to see everything at a distance. Then we'd ascend Hall Mountain, get above the border patrols, and cross over on foot. The oxygen would be thin and the terrain rough. Even though Bethany still had a few of her pills, I was worried.

After an hour of walking we moved more deeply into the forest and found a flat patch of land with enough space for our tent.

"We can put it here," Bethany said. She was trying to catch her breath, leaning against the trunk of a large pine tree.

"Sit down," I said. I handed her a little tube that had three or four breaths of pure oxygen inside. She pushed it away.

"I'm fine," she said. "You're hovering."

I slipped the backpack off my shoulder. It took only seconds to pitch the tent. I programmed it for a snow setting and it launched several long cords into the ground. Within minutes we were inside. Bethany immediately lay down on the floor, too exhausted to move. She'd cut and lightened her hair, and it made her look older. It made her eyes bigger and her features sharper.

I unpacked our things. I checked the seal on our medical kit. I took off my jacket for the first time all day. Then I zipped together two sleeping bags that were made of such thin material that I felt constantly astonished they worked at all. I opened the tent flap and scooped snow into the mouth of a metal canteen that would melt and purify it.

"I like watching you work," Bethany said.

"You and every other civilian," I said. I pulled the tent flap closed. I spread out the sleeping bag and lay beside her. This was the part of the day I looked forward to most, the part where we felt the freest—inside our tent, our little bubble of nowhere in particular.

"Tomorrow," I said, "if we get caught—"

"They will shoot you," Bethany said. She pressed her body against mine. "On sight," she added.

"Only if they recognize me," I said.

"I will shoot you," she said, "if you do anything stupid."

I looked at her. "Shoot me with what?" I said.

"You won't see it coming," she said. "So you don't need to know."

I slipped my hand into the hood of her jacket, feeling the tendrils of her hair, which were stiff with frost. I thought, then, of that very first crime, of her barrette concealed in my pocket. "If something happens," I continued, "I want you to denounce me."

"James," Bethany murmured, "that's not even the right word."

"You know what I mean," I said. "You have to convince the police that I kidnapped you."

"But," she said, "it was the other way around."

Bethany tucked her cold fingers under the cuff of my sleeve.

The solar bulb in the roof had not fully charged. It flickered and dimmed, casting a diminishing light over us. I felt her body twitch with exhaustion, drifting on the margins of consciousness. When I thought of the places that were waiting for us if we were caught, I was most afraid for her.

"Do you think that we can get used to anything?" I said. "That there's no limit?"

I waited for her answer. But Bethany made a small, murmuring noise. The wind blew and the walls of the tent shook. She was already asleep.

ACKNOWLEDGMENTS

On June 2, 2011, the state of California shuttered the Preston Youth Correctional Facility—formerly the Preston School of Industry—a juvenile rehabilitation center located in Ione, California, roughly fifty miles outside of Sacramento. In its 117 years of operation, Preston helped rebuild—and destroy—many thousands of lives. *Goodhouse* owes a significant debt to the memoirs of the men who lived in Preston as wards of the state. Without Dwight Edgar Abbott's *I Cried, You Didn't Listen*, Ernest Booth's *Stealing through Life*, Edward Bunker's *Education of a Felon*, Ray D. Johnson's *Too Dangerous to Be At Large*, Ernie López's *To Alcatraz, Death Row, and Back,* and Bill Sands's *My Shadow Ran Fast,* I would not have been able to write this novel.

I would like to thank my agent, Jennifer Walsh, for believing in this project, and for offering invaluable feedback and enthusiasm.

Many thanks to everyone at FSG: Jeff Seroy, Katie Kurtzman, and my editors, Sean MacDonald, Emily Bell, and Courtney Hodell, who is a close and careful reader.

To everyone else at William Morris Endeavor—Laura Bonner, Kathleen Nishimoto, Maggie Shapiro, Ashley Fox—many thanks.

Thanks, also, to my parents, for their unflagging support

over the years—as I crept off to coffeehouses to eat muffins and give serious thought to the problems of imaginary people in invented situations.

And to my intrepid readers, Chelsey Johnson, Malena Watrous, Robin Romm, Erika Recordon, Xeni Fragakis, Donal Mosher, Ismet Prcic, Ruta and Joseph Toutonghi, and Mike Palmieri—and my teacher Ethan Canin, who offered help and advice when it was needed, thank you.

I especially want to thank Gill Dennis and Stephanie Allderdice, who gave me the gift of their time, as well as the benefit of their rich and fearsome imaginations. Without them, the book would not be what it is.

Thank you, Alex Hebler, for the hours and hours with Beatrix and Phineas.

And finally, I owe a very special debt of gratitude to my husband, the writer Pauls Toutonghi, without whom this project would never have been completed. Thank you for allowing this world to move into our house, invade our personal landscape, and become real after all.